ON THIS
FOUNDATION

Books by Lynn Austin

All She Ever Wanted
All Things New
Eve's Daughters
Hidden Places
Legacy of Mercy
Pilgrimage
A Proper Pursuit
Though Waters Roar
Until We Reach Home
Waves of Mercy
Where We Belong
While We're Far Apart
Wings of Refuge
A Woman's Place
Wonderland Creek

REFINER'S FIRE

Candle in the Darkness
Fire by Night
A Light to My Path

CHRONICLES OF THE KINGS

Gods & Kings
Song of Redemption
The Strength of His Hand
Faith of My Fathers
Among the Gods

THE RESTORATION CHRONICLES

Return to Me
Keepers of the Covenant
On This Foundation

www.lynnaustin.org

THE RESTORATION CHRONICLES • BOOK 3

ON THIS FOUNDATION

LYNN AUSTIN

BETHANYHOUSE
a division of Baker Publishing Group
Minneapolis, Minnesota

Published by Bethany House Publishers
11400 Hampshire Avenue South
Bloomington, Minnesota 55438
www.bethanyhouse.com

Bethany House Publishers is a division of
Baker Publishing Group, Grand Rapids, Michigan

Printed in the United States of America

Library of Congress Cataloging-in-Publication Data
Austin, Lynn N.
    On this foundation / Lynn Austin.
        pages ; cm. — (The restoration chronicles ; 3)
    Summary: "Inspired by the biblical account of Nehemiah, Jewish cupbearer to the King of Persia, this story tells of the many dangers in his return to Jerusalem and the great opposition his people faced in their efforts to rebuild the city wall"— Provided by publisher.
    ISBN 978-0-7642-1518-6 (cloth : alk. paper)
    ISBN 978-0-7642-0900-0 (pbk.)
    I. Title.
PS3551.U839O5 2015
813'.54—dc23   2015016137

Scripture taken from the HOLY BIBLE, NEW INTERNATIONAL VERSION®. Copyright © 1973, 1978, 1984 Biblica. Used by permission of Zondervan. All rights reserved.

Cover design by Jennifer Parker

Photography by Mike Habermann Photography, LLC

24   8 7 6 5

To my husband, Ken
and to my children:
Joshua, Vanessa, Benjamin, Maya, and Snir

So this is what the Sovereign LORD *says:*

"See, I lay a stone in Zion, a tested stone,

a precious cornerstone for a sure foundation;

the one who trusts will never be dismayed."

ISAIAH 28:16

The Citadel of Susa, Persia
The Fourteenth of Adar 473 BC

Mordecai knew what it was to wrestle with death and win. From his room in the citadel in Susa, he had listened to news of the battles all day, his messengers racing in and out like bees to a hive. The angel of death had hovered close from the time the sun set on the Twelfth of Adar, throughout the night, and all day on the Thirteenth. According to the last report Mordecai received as the pale, early spring sun finally set on this murderous day, his fellow Jews had slain five hundred of their enemies in Susa. He had prayed for the children of Abraham scattered among the 127 provinces of the Persian Empire and wondered how they had fared. In particular, he wondered about The Land Beyond the River, where his fellow Jews held such a precarious foothold in Jerusalem. Within the vast Persian Empire, the Jews' enemies outnumbered them and certainly outmanned them in terms of military experience. Mordecai's people were tradesmen and farmers and scholars, not soldiers. Even so, he knew they would fight hard for their families and their lives. And clearly, God had fought with them.

The night grew darker. He should snuff out the sputtering oil lamps and go home now that the Thirteenth of Adar—and the danger—had ended. But he was too weary from the strain of several sleepless nights to manage the walk and the stairs. Mordecai unstrapped the sword that he'd worn all day in the event that their enemies prevailed and laid it on the floor. He sat down on the window seat overlooking the moat and slumped back against the pillows. The open window was a dark void, the moon and stars hidden behind a gray blanket of clouds. He inhaled the crisp spring air and closed his eyes for a moment to rest.

A knock on his door startled him awake. Instinctively, Mordecai reached for his weapon. He unsheathed it but remained seated. "Who is it?"

"Just me, my lord." The door slowly opened, and one of the soldiers who had been stationed outside his door for the past day and a half appeared in the shadowy opening. "I'm sorry for disturbing you, my lord."

"You may come in." Mordecai's shoulders relaxed as he laid down his weapon. "What hour is it?"

"The third watch, my lord."

Mordecai rubbed his eyes. He had slept on the window seat longer than he'd intended. The night was more than half over.

"Your aide, Yaakov ben Hashub, has asked to speak with you. He says it's important."

At this hour of the night it must be. Apprehension helped Mordecai shake off his sleepiness and come fully awake. "Send him in." It was an indication of the extreme duress they were all under that even Yaakov, who had been Mordecai's right-hand man throughout this ordeal, needed permission to enter his chambers. Yaakov's pale face and dark-rimmed eyes revealed his exhaustion after this long, bloody day. Surprisingly, he herded three small boys into the room as he entered.

"Forgive me for disturbing you, my lord, but . . . but it seems the fighting hasn't ended after all."

Dread made Mordecai's skin crawl. "What do you mean? According to the king's edict, the fighting was supposed to end at sunset. The Thirteenth of Adar is over."

"The fighting isn't in the streets—it's here. In the citadel."

"What?"

"Several members of your personal staff and their families were attacked in their homes an hour ago."

Mordecai scrambled to his feet, his movements stiff. "No! That's impossible. We've had guards stationed everywhere."

"Yes, we did. But we sent the guards home too soon—all but the one outside your door. And we trusted the wrong people. Our enemies found breaches in our security and used them to attack your closest staff members." Yaakov's deep voice trembled with emotion. "Two men and their families were slaughtered before we could sound the alarm."

"And your home, your family . . . ?"

"The warning reached me before the assassins did. My family is safe."

"Which of my staff members were killed?" Mordecai asked, fearing the answer.

"Bani ben Zaccai and his family . . ."

"God of Abraham, have mercy," Mordecai whispered.

"And your scribe, Hacaliah, and his wife." Yaakov swallowed, battling his grief. "These are Hacaliah's three sons. They survived, but they saw . . ." He didn't finish.

Mordecai needed a moment to regain control. He scrubbed his hands down his face, pulling his beard. He wished he could awaken all over again and discover that this had only been a dream.

Yaakov cleared his throat. "This retaliation was personal, my lord. Against your administration. The assassins knew who to target, where they lived, how to circumvent security. They deliberately waited until after sunset, when we believed the fighting was over and returned home to get some sleep."

"These attackers were already waiting inside the citadel?"

"It appears so, my lord. All of the outside gates and doors have been under guard for days."

Mordecai moaned. "I'm responsible for this. How could I have been so shortsighted? We made so many meticulous plans to safeguard our people in all parts of the empire, and yet I failed my closest associates, right here in the citadel."

"None of us expected it, my lord. But we believe that all of the murderers have been captured or killed. The ones taken alive will talk before morning. We'll learn the extent of the conspiracy."

"It has to be Haman's sons and their allies, seeking revenge. I would stake my life on it."

Mordecai paced some more, battling exhaustion and rage as he tried to decide what to do. "I'll send word to Queen Esther and ask her to petition the king. The ten sons of Haman will all hang for this. In the meantime, we need an extra day to finish destroying our enemies. Esther must ask the king's permission to track them down and kill them today, too. We'll find them wherever they're hiding. This isn't finished."

He crossed to his worktable and scrabbled around in the dim lamplight, searching for a pen, for parchment. "Have someone summon Hathach, the queen's eunuch," he told Yaakov. "He'll need to deliver my message to Esther without delay. She'll have to take the initiative again as soon as possible and approach the king unbidden with this request."

"Wouldn't it be quicker to petition him yourself, my lord?"

"Perhaps. But Xerxes will be more inclined to act if he understands that his wife's life is threatened."

Mordecai was so caught up with fury and regret, so angry with himself for letting down his guard, that he forgot about the three small boys until he heard a shaky sob, a sniffle. He looked up. They still wore their nightclothes, their dark hair sleep-tousled. The youngest child rubbed his eyes, his face damp with tears. All three wore the same blank-eyed look of desolation and horror that he remembered seeing on his young cousin Esther's face the day she'd been orphaned, the day he had adopted her as his own. Mordecai hadn't been responsible for the deaths of Esther's parents, but he was responsible for these. The retaliation had been directed against him and his staff.

He closed his eyes and bowed his head as he carefully banked his roaring anger, letting the hot coals simmer for a moment so the warmth of compassion could replace it. When he was in control again, he lifted his head and stepped toward the children. He guessed the oldest to be around seven or eight years old, the younger boys four or five, young enough to still have their baby teeth. Mordecai crouched in front of them.

"What's your name?" he asked the oldest one.

"Nehemiah ben Hacaliah," he answered in a whisper. His eyes were dry, as if he was trying to be brave and not cry. His gaze met Mordecai's for only a moment before darting frantically around the room as if more assassins might leap from behind the curtains or the closed doors.

"And these are your brothers?"

He nodded. "Ephraim and Hanani." The last was an affectionate name, probably short for Hananiah. The youngest child's narrow chest shuddered with quiet sobs. Judging by his red-rimmed eyes, he'd been crying for some time. He looked up at Mordecai, his dark eyes brimming.

"I want my mama," he said.

Mordecai longed to hold the boy and comfort him, but the oldest brother, Nehemiah, appeared so wary that Mordecai feared he might attack anyone who tried to touch his siblings. Nehemiah grabbed Hanani's hand and pulled him closer to his side.

"Were these children there when it happened?" Mordecai asked his aide. "In the same house?" Yaakov nodded.

"We hid when the bad men came," Nehemiah said. "I told Ephraim and Hanani to be very quiet."

"I'm glad you did, son. That was a very wise thing to do. You're a brave young man."

"No, Abba was the bravest. He fought back."

Mordecai didn't know what to say. Was it better to let the boy talk and tell what he'd seen and heard, or would it be kinder to encourage him to forget this terrible nightmare? As if he ever could forget. Mordecai cleared the lump from his throat. "I'm so very sorry for what happened," he told the children. "Your father, Hacaliah, was a good man. He worked for me here in the citadel. I know I can never take his place, but I promise to take care of you from now on. You will lack nothing."

Except parents to love and nurture them. What a stupid thing to say. Mordecai searched for better words, words of comfort or hope, watching helplessly as Nehemiah's gaze continued to scan the room like a trapped bird desperate to escape. His slender body, braced to run, was so tense that Mordecai feared he would jump out of his skin if anyone tried to touch him, even to reassure him. The two younger children were the opposite, limp and boneless with fatigue and shock, as if they might collapse into a heap any moment. They needed sleep. Mordecai wondered if they would ever truly rest again.

"You're safe now. I won't let anything happen to you. And if there's anything you need—"

"We need a place to hide," Nehemiah said.

Mordecai waited a long moment before saying, "Yaakov and one of my guards will take you someplace safe, where you can get some rest and—"

"Will the bad men try to kill us, too?" Nehemiah asked. He continued his eerie scanning of the room—window, door, second window, then back again. Never resting.

"The men will never come back. I promise you that the enemies who did this will be found and executed. You have my word. Until then, the guards will watch over you. They'll stay with you for as long as you'd like."

"But Abba knew the men who came to our house. He opened the door to let them in, but they tricked him."

"You heard all of this?" Mordecai asked, and Nehemiah nodded. "Lord, have mercy . . ." he whispered beneath his breath.

He turned to Yaakov. "Take them to my home. See that they have something to eat and a place to sleep."

"Yes, my lord." Yaakov turned toward the door, motioning to the boys to follow him, but Nehemiah didn't move. His brothers didn't either. The two younger ones inched closer to him, clutching him tightly, clearly terrified. Mordecai didn't know what to do to calm them.

"Would you rather stay here with me? Have a look out the window and see how high up we are. And the soldiers outside my door won't let anyone inside."

Nehemiah nodded, eyeing Mordecai's sword, lying unsheathed on the window seat. He led his brothers in a tight huddle as he went to inspect the view.

"Very well," Mordecai decided. "The three of you may stay here, then. Yaakov, can you find one of my servants and ask him to bring some blankets and more cushions, and maybe something simple to eat? Then send a messenger to Hathach, Queen Esther's servant." Mordecai crossed to the window seat and closed the shutters. "Come," he said, patting the cushion. "You can lie down here and rest."

Nehemiah helped Hanani onto the seat and the two younger boys immediately lay down, curled into tight balls. Mordecai wasn't surprised when Nehemiah remained sitting upright on the bench, his eyes open and watchful. His dangling legs didn't even reach the floor.

Even with the shutters closed, the cold night air seeped into the room, so Mordecai removed his outer robe and covered the children with it. Alone while he waited for his servants, he allowed the dreadful news to fully sink in.

He had failed the men closest to him. Two of them had died because of his lack of foresight. So had their families. How naïve he had been to believe that his enemies would restrict their murderous revenge to a single day. How foolish to imagine that his people would be free from all threats after a mere night and day of fighting. Throughout their history, God's people had always had enemies who tried to wipe them from the face of the earth, as Haman had just attempted to do. Would the children of Abraham ever find peace and rest?

Mordecai sighed. No. There would be no rest until the promised Messiah finally came to set them free.

Part I

The Lord determined to tear down the

wall around the Daughter of Zion.

He stretched out a measuring line and did not

withhold his hand from destroying.

He made ramparts and walls lament;

together they wasted away.

Her gates have sunk into the ground;

their bars he has broken and destroyed.

LAMENTATIONS 2:8–9A

CHAPTER

1

SUSA, PERSIA
DECEMBER, TWENTY-EIGHT YEARS LATER

Nehemiah descended the winding staircase to the palace
kitchens, then paused in the arched doorway, savoring
the warmth from the blazing hearth fires and enormous ovens. The aroma of roasting meat and baking bread
greeted him. He enjoyed this part of his job, especially on early
winter days like this one when it was difficult to heat the cavern-
ous palace rooms upstairs. He watched the sweating, red-faced
cooks and scullery lads bustle around, chopping vegetables,
skinning a goat, and plucking waterfowl. These men would
probably prefer to work in a cooler room.

No one glanced up as Nehemiah entered the huge work area,
which was large enough to prepare food for the king and thousands of his guests. As the king's trusted cupbearer, Nehemiah
inspected the palace kitchens and storerooms daily, making
sure that nothing and no one who might pose a threat to King
Artaxerxes ever passed through the delivery doors and into the
kitchen and up the stone stairs to his dining room.

The narrow windows stood open, and Nehemiah heard the
rumble of wooden wheels outside and the heavy tread of oxen

as a delivery wagon approached. The shipment of wine he expected had arrived. He crossed the smoky work area to unlock the wide delivery doors, opening them to a blast of chilly air that rushed inside along with a swirl of dried leaves. A cart piled high with clay storage jars and cushioned with straw pulled to a halt outside. Nehemiah unsheathed his sword as he prepared to probe the straw for stowaways. "Good morning, Shaul," he said to the driver who had led the yoked team of oxen. The driver finished fastening the reins to a post and turned. It wasn't Shaul. It was a stranger. Nehemiah tensed.

"Who are you? What are you doing here?"

"I'm Shelah ben Hobiah. I'm making deliveries for Shaul today."

"Not without consulting me, you're not! Why wasn't I told? Who let you through the gate? Who's responsible for this?"

"I said it would be all right," a voice from behind Nehemiah said.

He spun around to face Joed, the palace clerk who kept track of deliveries and payments.

"Shelah is a friend and—"

Nehemiah still had his sword in his right hand, but he gripped the front of the clerk's tunic with his left one. He pulled Joed close until their faces were inches apart. "No one enters this citadel without my authorization, understand? No one! I want both of you *out*! And don't come back." He released Joed and pushed him outside through the open door.

"But . . . m-my lord . . ." Joed sputtered. "I-I've known Shelah since childhood. I can vouch for him and—"

"I don't doubt that you can. And King Xerxes also knew the man who entered his bedchamber and murdered him. One of his own courtiers." The familiar rage boiled up inside Nehemiah, and in an instant he was back in his bedroom the night his father opened the door to an acquaintance and forfeited his life. He gave the clerk another shove, propelling him backward and

20

causing him to stumble against one of the oxen. "King Xerxes' heir can't afford to trust anyone," Nehemiah said. "Every leek and lentil and wineskin will be carefully inspected by my staff and me before it enters this palace—along with every man who delivers it, cooks it, or serves it. It's the only way to keep our sovereign King Artaxerxes safe and secure."

"Please, my lord . . . I won't let it happen again—"

"You're right, Joed. You won't. Guards!" He shouted for the king's guards, watching from their posts inside the kitchen. "Escort these men all the way over the bridge and out of the citadel."

"And the shipment of wine, my lord?" one of the guards asked.

"Send it back. Tell them the next time there's a new delivery-man I need to be informed."

Nehemiah turned and went inside again, slamming and locking the door behind him. All activity in the kitchen had halted, as if the icy wind had frozen the men in their places. He saw two young cook's assistants exchange looks, as if they thought him an unreasonable tyrant. They hadn't worked in the kitchen very long, and even though Nehemiah and his staff of cupbearers and security personnel had thoroughly investigated these newcomers' backgrounds, they would always be suspect until they'd proven themselves. He walked toward the table where they had been plucking a brace of fowls, the feathers sticking to their hands and dusting the table like snowflakes. "You think my actions are extreme? That I'm being overly cautious?"

"No, my lord." Both young men shook their heads, but the look they had exchanged said otherwise.

"Listen, all of you," he said, addressing the entire kitchen staff. "In just a few months the king's official representatives will arrive from every satrapy and province in the empire, and the annual round of banquets will begin. The month-long event could easily turn into a security nightmare if we let down our guard. The Persian court has a history of intrigue and power struggles and assassinations. One tiny slip, such as accepting a shipment from an unknown deliveryman, and King Artaxerxes' life could be in danger." Indeed, as his cupbearer, Nehemiah would also forfeit his life.

He gazed at the cooks and assistants and scullery lads until satisfied by their submissive cowering that they understood the seriousness of today's breach. "Back to work, then. The king expects to be fed on time."

Nehemiah stayed at his post in the kitchen for the remainder of the morning, watching over the kitchen staff as they finished preparing the midday meal. When King Artaxerxes called for his food, Nehemiah ascended the winding stone stairs to the dining room along with the waiters who carried and served the lavish meal. He bore the king's flask of wine and golden drinking *rhyton* himself, his presence assuring Artaxerxes that every morsel of food, every drop of wine had been carefully inspected. If the king so desired, Nehemiah stood ready to taste each dish and sip from every flask before the king did.

After the meal, Nehemiah was on his way down to the kitchen again when one of the other cupbearers met him on the stairs. "There's a man at the Gate House asking to see you."

"Do you know who it is? Not that hapless clerk I fired this morning, begging for his job back, is it?"

"No, my lord. I've never seen him before. But judging by his clothing and appearance, he's a Jew."

Nehemiah wondered if his fellow cupbearer or any of the other security personnel he worked with knew that he was also a Jew. Probably not. Like them, Nehemiah wore the uniform of the palace staff.

"I'd better go and see who it is. Take over my duties until I get back." He strode through the palace corridors and across the open plateau to the Gate House, annoyed at the disruption. Whoever the visitor was, he would have to pass a security check before being allowed into the palace and citadel. Nehemiah swung open the door, prepared for an argument—and there stood his brother. Was he seeing things? He gave a cry of joy before swiftly crossing the room and sweeping him off the floor in a massive bear hug.

"Hanani! What in the world are you doing here? You're supposed to be in Jerusalem!"

Hanani gave a gasp of laughter. "Put me down, you crazy man! I can't breathe!"

Nehemiah set him down again, laughing as he held his brother at arm's length. "Let me look at you! I can't believe you're here! I didn't think we'd ever see each other again."

"Nor did I," Hanani said, wiping his eyes.

"How long has it been, my brother? Twelve years?"

"Nearly thirteen."

Nehemiah embraced him again, then said, "I should have gone to Jerusalem with you and Ephraim. As soon as you left, I regretted my decision and wished I had chosen differently." He remembered praying all night as he'd agonized over whether or not to join Rebbe Ezra's caravan and move to Judah with his brothers. At the time, he felt that he owed Mordecai a great debt.

"You look wonderful, Hanani!" he said. "The Promised Land must agree with you. I can't tell you how happy I am to see you! How is Ephraim?"

"He's well. Married with a baby on the way."

"And you? Are you married?"

A grin lit up Hanani's face. "Yes. My beautiful wife has given me a little son and a daughter. What about you, my brother?"

Nehemiah waved away the question. "Too busy to look for a wife. But tell me, why are you here? You haven't decided to return, have you?"

"No, not at all," Hanani said. "I'm an aide with the official delegation from Judah. I work as a scribe, like Abba did."

Nehemiah's smile faded at the mention of their father. For

the second time that day, he felt a stab of grief as he relived the night when their father opened the door to his assassin. "Do you remember Abba, Hanani? You were only four."

"Not very well. I remember that he was very tall with thick black hair—like you. And I remember his laughter, booming like thunder, and how he used to throw me up in the air and catch me."

They both fell silent for a moment. "So, why are you here?" Nehemiah asked again. "Your delegation is a few months early for the tribute ceremonies."

"We came to present our report to King Artaxerxes ahead of time and request a reduction in tribute. The drought in Judah has lasted for two growing seasons. Our people are suffering. And we're required to pay taxes to the provincial treasury, too."

"Is Governor Ezra with you?"

"No. He retired as Judah's governor a few years ago. The nobles and district leaders convinced him that he had accomplished his work as our leader and teacher. He's writing and studying now, using his vast knowledge to compile a history of our people. I understand it's something he has always wanted to do."

They had remained standing all this time, and now Nehemiah felt restless to be on the move again, unable to contain the nervous energy that fueled him and kept him working from before dawn until long after sunset. "Would you like to walk with me, Hanani? I'll show you the palace courtyards and the *apadna*, where the king holds banquets for several thousand people. They're quite impressive."

"Maybe tomorrow. I was hoping you would come with me to meet the others. There's so much to tell you."

"Now? I would love to hear about life in the Promised Land but . . ." Nehemiah glanced around for a moment, wondering if he could spare a few hours this afternoon. He scrolled through a mental list of his responsibilities before deciding. "Very well. I'll come with you. But I can't stay long."

Hanani led the way out through the King's Gate and across the bridge to the city. "I had forgotten how imposing the citadel of Susa is," Hanani said, glancing over his shoulder at the towering palace. "Some of the others who've never been here before were awestruck by the sheer size of everything. They said they feel like ants beside all these soaring buildings."

"That's exactly the king's intention," Nehemiah said. "Such grandeur is a fitting backdrop for the throne of the Persian Empire."

"Yes, but does the king understand the true cost? His taxes are crippling us. Many of the people in his empire are destitute, including our fellow Jews in Judah."

"Truly? I had no idea." Nehemiah wondered if living here in Susa all his life had blinded him to the empire's problems. If he had returned to Jerusalem with his brothers, would he also view such Persian opulence with different eyes?

"So, what's your job now, in such a splendid palace?" Hanani asked, breaking into his thoughts as they walked.

"I'm King Artaxerxes' cupbearer."

"Really!" Hanani halted in the middle of the crowded street, causing several pedestrians to bump into them.

"Yes, really. It's my duty to ensure the safety of his food and wine. But the job involves much more than that. The king's cupbearers are responsible for many other aspects of security in the citadel besides the food. As you can imagine, Artaxerxes is extremely concerned about safety after what happened to his father." He paused, then added, "Of all people, you and I can understand that. Right, Hanani?"

"Of course. And I'm very proud of my big brother. Tell me," Hanani said as he continued walking through the busy streets, "how did you rise in prominence to such an important job? When I left, you were working as a government aide."

"King Artaxerxes assigned court security to Mordecai when he learned that, years ago, he had uncovered a plot against the king's father and was honored for it. He asked Mordecai to find and employ trustworthy court attendants to handle security in the citadel. I didn't want the job at first. I couldn't see how I could serve the Almighty One as a cupbearer. But Mordecai convinced me that God needed men of prayer and faith in all occupations, that a cupbearer held a position of even greater trust than a palace guard. And he was right."

They reached the Jewish section in the lower city of Susa, breathless from the vigorous walk, and went inside the house of assembly. A fire blazed in the brazier, and Nehemiah removed his outer robe in the overheated room. "I'd like you to meet my brother Nehemiah," Hanani told his delegation from Jerusalem. He introduced each man to Nehemiah before adding, "He now serves in an even more important position in the palace than he did when I left—he's cupbearer to the king."

Everyone seemed pleased at the news, but Nehemiah quickly set them straight. "Unfortunately for your delegation, my work as the king's cupbearer isn't going to be of much help to you. If I were an aide, I might have been able to make sure your petition reached the throne room. But while I have very close access to King Artaxerxes and enjoy his utmost trust, I am not allowed to speak in his presence unless he bids me to. However, I will be happy to contribute any insights into the Persian court that might be helpful to you."

"That would be much appreciated."

"Maybe it would help if I had a clearer picture of the situation in Judah," Nehemiah directed. "For starters, tell me about Jerusalem."

The room fell silent, as if he had asked about a tragic death. Indeed, the leader of the delegation gave a heavy sigh before speaking, his face somber. "Our fellow Jews who survived the exile and are back in the province are in great trouble and disgrace."

His words and the grave tone with which he spoke shocked

Nehemiah. He let them sink in for a moment before leaning forward in his seat. "Go on."

"When I look at this magnificent city of Susa with its towering walls and pillars, the stunning citadel perched on the hill, they reflect the splendor of the king who reigns here. Our reigning King is the Almighty One, yet His city is a pitiful reflection of His power and glory. The walls of Jerusalem are broken down, and its gates have been burned with fire."

"Wait," Nehemiah said, leaning closer still. "Are you saying there are no walls at all around the city? That the people are defenseless against their enemies?"

"That's right. When the Babylonians burned the city, not only did the gates burn, but the heat of the flames caused the limestone building blocks to crumble. The Babylonian army demolished all our fortifications."

"And even though the eastern approach to the city has always been protected by a steep slope," another man added, "all the supporting terraces have disintegrated, first from the fire, then from rain and weather."

"Some men in our community attempted to rebuild the walls a number of years ago," the leader continued. "But the enemy nations around us were able to get an edict from the Persian king, forcing us to stop. They even made us destroy what we had begun to build."

"That's outrageous!" Nehemiah's anger flared like oil on hot coals. "What about the Holy One's temple? Surely that's protected and secure?"

"No, the temple is also unprotected. And without walls, the Levite guards have their hands full safeguarding the temple treasury. We can't trust the governor in Samaria or his provincial guards to protect us, even if he agreed to send them. We're hated by all of our surrounding neighbors—the Samaritans and Edomites, the Ammonites and Arabs. They would like nothing better than to see us all in our graves."

"There's no way to fortify the city?" Nehemiah asked.

"If we attempted to do it without King Artaxerxes' permission, it would be interpreted as an act of rebellion. And where would we get the funds? As it is, we're here because we can't afford to pay the taxes he has imposed. Rebuilding the walls would be an impossible undertaking."

Nehemiah shook his head, unable to grasp what he was hearing. "So you're telling me that the city and the temple mount are both completely vulnerable? Our enemies could come in and kill our people and destroy Jerusalem and the Almighty One's temple all over again?"

"Completely vulnerable," the leader confirmed. "And because of it, the number of robberies and vicious attacks has been escalating after two years of drought. Our enemies strike at night, looking for food and grain because of the famine. No one feels safe."

"A young friend of mine named Yitzhak ben Rephaiah was killed several months ago," Hanani added, "when his home in Jerusalem was robbed. Yitzhak was about to be married and had just built a new home for his bride. The thieves killed him and emptied his storehouse. In fact, he lived very close to Ephraim and his family. It could have been him."

Nehemiah felt a powerful anger building inside him as the picture of the city's helplessness grew clearer. Security was his livelihood, his passion. He was beginning to understand what their leader had meant when he'd said their people were in great trouble and disgrace. But what could he do? "I need to return to my responsibilities in the citadel. We'll talk again," he promised as he left them.

The leader's words continued to echo in Nehemiah's mind throughout the afternoon and evening, long after he returned to his spare living quarters in the citadel for the night. *"Great trouble and disgrace."* The report appalled him, not only for the sake of the people who were being robbed and killed by their enemies, but for the Almighty One's sake. Nehemiah unbuckled his sword and removed his uniform. His bed had been prepared for him, but he wasn't ready to sleep. He opened the shuttered window and looked out at the vast sprinkle of stars above the roof of the palace.

Just as the magnificent city of Susa brought glory and honor to the Persian king, so, too, should the city and temple of the one true God bring glory and honor to Him. The lack of city walls and gates meant shame and disgrace. The heathens could easily destroy Jerusalem again as they had 140 years ago. Even worse, this vulnerability sent a message to their enemies that the Holy One was unable—or unwilling—to protect His people.

Nehemiah closed the window and paced the floor. Then, knowing that his work would begin before dawn and that he needed to sleep, he snuffed out his lamp and sank onto his bed. Somehow, seeing Hanani again and being reminded twice today of their father's tragic death made him feel like a child—helpless, vulnerable. He had saved himself and his brothers on that long-ago night by hiding in a hollow corner between the wall and the huge wooden chest his father had propped at an angle in the room. Nehemiah and his two brothers had often hidden in that space when playing games. And although all of Nehemiah's instincts urged him to find a way to protect his brothers once again—to protect all of his people in Jerusalem—he had no way to do it.

"Our fellow Jews who survived the exile and are back in the province are in great trouble and disgrace."

Alone, in his room, Nehemiah didn't try to stop his tears.

Chapter 2

JERUSALEM
EARLY FEBRUARY

Today Chana found it hard to believe the words that the Levite temple musicians were singing: *"Delight yourself in the Lord, and he will give you the desires of your heart."* That promise wasn't always true. The desire of Chana's heart had been to marry Yitzhak ben Rephaiah and live in the home he had built for her. But Yitzhak was dead, and God could never grant her heart's desire. She shivered as a gust of wintry wind swept across the temple courtyard. It dragged gray storm clouds with it, and she felt the first sprinkles of rain. They needed rain. In fact, her nation was praying for the winter rains to pour from the heavens in steady sheets, soaking the cracked earth and bringing it back to life. But as quickly as the spitting raindrops started, they stopped again, proving as worthless as the song's promise.

The evening sacrifice at the temple was nearly over. Chana looked forward to returning home again and warming her wind-burned cheeks, rubbing life back into her icy toes and fingers. She watched the priest remove a coal from the altar fire and carry it into the sanctuary. He would use it to light the incense on the golden altar that stood before God's throne room. As the fragrant aroma ascended to heaven, the priest would offer prayers for her people. It was the moment for Chana to offer her prayers, too—but for what? Hadn't she prayed for nearly a year for her heart to heal so she could feel something besides endless grief? She glanced at her younger sisters, Yudit and Sarah, standing beside her with their heads bowed. Yudit's lips moved as she silently prayed. Chana wondered what she prayed for. Was it for her?

Another blast of wind rocked Chana, plastering her long robe to her legs. She had covered her wavy black hair with a shawl in case it rained, and she reached up to grab it before the wind whisked it away. At last the sacrifice ended. She huddled close to her sisters as they waited for their father to rejoin them. "I love that song that the choir just sang, don't you, Chana?" Yudit asked through chattering teeth.

Chana nodded, guilt-stricken for having pouted the entire time instead of participating in worship. She knew the folly of being angry with the Almighty One. Bitterness was a poison that had the power to destroy her. But on cold, gray days like this one, when the clouds hung over Jerusalem's mountaintops like a smothering blanket, her grief threatened to smother her, as well. After Yitzhak died, she continued coming to the temple to worship God, clinging to a slender thread of faith. Some days, especially during the annual festivals, the bond that connected her to the Almighty One seemed as thick and strong as an anchor rope. But most days the thread seemed gossamer thin, a spider's tendril. No matter how she felt, Chana remained determined to hold on to the Holy One and not let go, even when it seemed He had let go of her.

Minutes passed as she watched the departing worshipers leave the temple courtyards. At last, Abba bustled up to them, his plump cheeks as round and red as pomegranates. "There you are, my beauties! What a lovely sight you are on such a dreary day."

Sarah stood on her toes to kiss him, then linked her arm through his. "We knew you'd be cold, so we made soup to help you warm up. And we baked bread, too. I hope it's still warm." Sarah was Chana's youngest sister, with hair as dark and glossy as a raven's wing. Thick lashes rimmed her wide, brown eyes, giving her the innocent look of a child much younger than her seventeen years. She and Chana resembled each other the most.

"Wonderful!" Abba said. "I do believe I can smell it from here."

"No, you can't, Abba," Sarah said, laughing.

They crossed the open courtyard toward the western side of the temple mount, and as another gust slammed into her, Chana feared they would all be blown off the mountaintop in the wind. She wrapped her arm around Yudit's waist, huddling close as they walked. Yudit was nineteen and the independent sister, the one who didn't care if her curly brown hair frizzed around her face like a lion's mane or her fingernails were ragged and broken from moving stones and digging in the dusty earth to plant rosemary and sagebushes in front of their house. Not that herbs or anything else could grow without rain.

They reached the steep steps leading down to the city, and Chana released her sister to grip the handholds as she descended. Halfway down, Abba paused to catch his breath. "You girls feed me too well," he said, patting his bulging middle. "Let me catch my breath." It puffed like smoke in the cold air as he spoke.

They rested for a moment, then continued downhill toward their house, built near the ruins of the city's western wall. Chana hoped the coals on the hearth had kept their house warm while they'd been gone. She longed to run ahead to escape the biting wind, but her gregarious father couldn't help stopping to greet people along the way. As ruler of the half-district of Jerusalem, he always took time to listen to people's concerns and to share their joys. He knew who was ill, which families didn't have quite enough to eat, and who the latest robbery victims were. The bad news always grieved him. But Abba also loved sharing people's joy. He savored every morsel of happy news in Jerusalem from betrothals to births to bar mitzvahs. Yitzhak's father, Rephaiah, who was ruler over the other half-district of Jerusalem, worked closely with Abba.

"Once we're married, we'll reign over Jerusalem as king and queen," Yitzhak used to tease. "Our sons will be little princes."

And now he was gone.

"I'm going to run ahead," Chana told Yudit, "and make sure the soup is still warm." Abba had stopped to talk to Uzziel, one of the goldsmiths, and Chana didn't want to get into a conversation with Uzziel's wife, who always gripped Chana's arm with viselike fingers, holding her captive as she recited a list of eligible men, including her youngest son. On any other day, Chana was happy to perform her social duties for her father, but not today. She hurried down the Street of the Bakers to her home near the Tower of the Ovens, named before the destruction of Jerusalem and the exile. No bakers lived on the street anymore, and the ovens and tower lay in ruins.

Thankfully, the main room of their house was still warm and so was the soup. Chana lit two lamps, spread a cloth on the table, and placed cushions and pillows on the stools and chairs so they could sit down to eat as soon as Abba and her sisters arrived. All three of them were laughing about something as they blew in through the door, as if pushed inside by the wind. "Close the door!" Chana chided. "You're letting all the warm air out."

"You don't have to shout," Sarah said.

She hadn't meant to. Chana helped her father remove his cloak and hung it on a peg for him. But instead of sitting down, Abba remained standing. He turned to Chana, cupping her face in his icy hands, and kissed her forehead.

"Listen, my angel. It will soon be a year since Yitzhak was taken from us. Even if you had been married to him, a year is enough time to mourn. He wouldn't want you to grieve any longer. How he would hate to see you so sad!" He caressed her cheek with his thumb.

"And when Mama died, didn't you grieve?" she asked, her throat tight. "Don't you still miss her?"

"Such foolish questions you ask," he said, lowering his hands. "Of course I do. Of course I understand your grief. A thousand times a day I am reminded of your mother. You have her soft, brown eyes, Chana. And her generous heart. But you're only twenty-three years old, my angel. Your whole life waits for you. Didn't the Almighty One say it wasn't good for man to live alone?"

"Then why haven't you remarried, Abba?"

"That's different. I enjoyed the gift of marriage for more than twenty years. And besides, who says I won't marry again?"

"Have you met someone, Abba?" Sarah asked. She had been making such a racket, clattering the dishes and tableware, that Chana was surprised she had overheard their conversation.

"No, my little cherub, I haven't met anyone."

"Promise us you won't marry a Samaritan or an Edomite," Yudit said. She was taking the bread from the warming shelf above the hearth, wrapping it in a cloth so it would stay warm and moist.

"Never!" he said with a frown. "No need to worry about that! Not only does the Almighty One forbid mixed marriages, but Gentile women lack spirit. It's probably beaten out of them by their fathers. I like a woman who isn't afraid to speak her mind, like your mother—and like her three beautiful daughters," he added with a smile. Chana tried to brush past him and end this uncomfortable conversation, but he stopped her.

"Listen, my angel. I'm not bringing up this subject to cause you more pain but because it just so happens that I know someone who would like to be introduced to you."

"Oh, Abba, no! Please—"

"Just hear me out. He serves as a member of the council with me and is the ruler of the district of Beth Hakkerem, about an hour's walk west of Jerusalem."

"'House of the Vineyard?'" Sarah asked, translating the district's name. "Are there any vineyards left in Judah after two years of drought?"

"Your friend must be pretty old if he's a district ruler," Chana said. "I don't want to marry an old man."

"He's only thirty-seven. I already asked."

"Abba, that's fourteen years older than me."

"Yitzhak was ten years older than you," Yudit said. Chana rolled her eyes at her.

Abba was relentless. "He's a nobleman. And the fact that he has risen to such an important position on the council at such a young age should tell you how brilliant he is."

"Well, I can see that you're already an admirer of his, Abba."

"I am. He has offered some very wise advice during some of our council meetings, and I've never heard him raise his voice or lose his temper—like several other members I could name."

"Who, Abba? Who?" Yudit asked, always alert for juicy gossip.

"Never mind, my cherub. I shouldn't have said that." He turned back to Chana. "He's a landowner with extensive vineyards. And quite wealthy. Some of his wealth is inherited, but most of it he earned by his own hard work and shrewd business skills. You would have a lovely home and servants to wait on you and—"

"And if he's such a good catch, why isn't he married?" Chana asked. "Let me guess—he's ugly as a toad."

"No, I bet he's as short and bristly as a sack of straw," Sarah said.

"I think he must be tall and spindly like a palm tree," Yudit added, not to be outdone. It was a game the three of them played since childhood, watching people passing by and comparing them to objects or animals.

Abba ignored them, still praising his friend. "Well, he was married, but now he is a widower, so he's well acquainted with grief. He has two sons—around age sixteen or seventeen, I think."

"Abba, they're nearly grown. They'd never accept me as their mother."

Abba exhaled and took Chana's hands in his. "Well, my dear . . . now that I've heard all your objections and excuses, you should know that I've invited my friend to visit this evening. You girls can decide for yourselves if he's a toad, a sack of straw, or a palm tree."

"Not for dinner!" Chana said.

"No, just for a glass of wine before he heads home."

"Abba—"

"And he's bringing the wine. It's from his vineyards. He has been bragging to me for ages about how wonderful his wine is—and I have been bragging to him about my three beautiful daughters. We decided it was time to put the truth of our claims to the test."

Chana broke free from Abba, shaking her head. She strode to the hearth to fetch the soup. His clumsy attempts at matchmaking annoyed her but didn't surprise her. In fact, it was Abba who had convinced her to consider Yitzhak for a husband. He had sung Yitzhak's praises for months before she finally agreed to meet him. And they had fallen in love. But it would take a miracle for it to happen a second time. Chana wished she could invent an excuse to avoid meeting their guest tonight, but her fierce love for her father would never allow her to disappoint him. Abba was a good man, a righteous man, down to the very marrow of his bones. Yet regardless of what this noble winemaker looked like, how wealthy or wise he was, Chana already knew he could never measure up to Yitzhak. It wasn't only her grief, she decided, that kept her from enjoying life again. It was the anger that refused to ease or go away.

Anger at Yitzhak's murderers and at her own helplessness. If only his killers had been caught and brought to justice and punished, maybe then the rage that burned in her soul would finally die out.

"Chana, darling," Abba said, interrupting her thoughts. "I don't ask much of you, but please erase that unattractive frown and put on a welcoming smile before my friend arrives."

"I'm sorry, Abba." She tried to smile for him, but she knew it looked forced, like a grimace.

"You're under no obligation to marry the man or even to like him. But he is a colleague of mine, and I've invited him to our home."

Her father had followed her to the hearth, and she pulled him into an embrace. "Of course, Abba. I'll be charming and welcoming. The perfect hostess. I'll even make some date cakes to enjoy with his wine."

"That's my girl!"

"You haven't told us his name," Yudit said. She and Sarah had taken their places around the table and she patted the cushion on her father's chair, inviting him to sit down.

"His name is Malkijah ben Recab."

"That's a mouthful," Chana blurted. "What do his friends call him?"

Abba smiled. "They call him Malkijah ben Recab."

Chana's first glimpse of Malkijah ben Recab that evening revealed that they had all been wrong about his looks. He was neither a toad, nor a sack of straw, nor a palm tree. He was as tall as the doorframe, neither fat nor thin, but sturdily built. He arrived with the promised wine, wearing a pleasant smile and a robe that had been woven from the very finest wool. He proved to be quite charming, too. He listened attentively as Abba introduced his three daughters, then said, "I know when I'm defeated, Shallum. Your three daughters are much lovelier than my finest wines. I admit defeat. Here is your prize." He handed Abba the wineskins.

"Well, now!" Abba crowed. "Didn't I tell you? But come in, Malkijah, come in. I have been waiting with great anticipation to taste your wine."

His appearance was pleasant—no one would call him handsome—but Chana would never be swayed by such shallow considerations as good looks. He wore his dark hair and beard trimmed short, and his broad face and nose looked slightly flattened, as if he had run into a wall as a child. But his ebony eyes looked kind, and his manner as they enjoyed the wine and the conversation was calm and peaceful, as if nothing ever rattled him. She thought of several outrageous things she could say to test his unflappability but kept them to herself for her father's sake.

As the evening progressed, Malkijah praised the date cakes Chana had made, complimented Abba on his beautiful home, and managed to find something charming and graceful to say to Chana and each of her sisters. By the time he thanked everyone for a lovely evening and prepared to leave, she couldn't find a single fault with him. Was he an excellent actor, or was he always this nice?

Chana stood near the door as Malkijah said good-bye, and he paused to look into her eyes for a long, unnerving moment. "I hope we'll have the opportunity to meet again, Chana," he said. Then he smiled, showing his perfect teeth, and left.

"There, that wasn't so bad, was it?" Abba asked.

"Of course not. He was very pleasant and charming. . . . But I'm just not ready to court anyone yet. Please understand, Abba."

He rested his hands on her shoulders. "Don't let grief become a way of life, my little Chana. Don't let it define your days and quench your spirit. From the time you were a little girl, you were always so happy, wearing flowers in your hair or a bright scarf or pretty sash. And you used to carry joy around with you like a basket of diamonds sparkling in the sunlight. Now you carry ashes. You were my happy little bird, singing so sweetly, but now you've allowed your grief to lock you up in a cage. I only wish I knew how to open the door and set my little bird free again."

Tears filled Chana's eyes as her father pulled her into his arms. "I wish I did, too, Abba," she mumbled into his wide chest. "I wish I did, too."

CHAPTER
3

THE DISTRICT OF BETH HAKKEREM
MARCH

Nava set her sloshing water jug in the dusty path and sank down to rest alongside it, the weeds scratchy against her bare legs. Was this her tenth trip from the well to her father's vineyard or the eleventh? She had lost count. Either way, her arms and back muscles ached, her blistered feet felt tired and sore. She needed to rest and tie her raggedy sandals back on. She needed a new pair—these were her brother's outgrown ones—but her family couldn't afford new shoes.

Everywhere Nava looked, toward the distant hillsides, the pastures, or the grain fields, the vegetation was dry and brittle. Lifeless. The color of dust. The leaves on the pomegranate and fig trees outside her house looked faded and brown. Neither the early rains nor the later rains had come, and the dry season would begin next month.

With her sandal refastened, Nava stood and lifted her water jug, balancing it on her head. She saw Mama walking toward her with an empty jug, on her way back to the well. "Are we nearly done?" Nava asked as they passed each other. Mama shook her head and kept walking. Abba had asked them to haul water, pouring it on each vine in hopes of coaxing a crop of grapes from his vineyard. With luck, they would harvest enough for her family to use and have extra to sell. Nava was already tired of hauling water. But when she finished watering the vineyard, she and Mama still needed to water the kitchen garden and the meager crop of vegetables they'd planted—onions, garlic, beans, lentils—enough to sustain her family in the coming year. After that, Nava would draw water for the little flock of goats that provided her family with milk and cheese.

She reached the terraced vineyard at last, and her father paused from tending one of the spindly plants to point out the next vine that needed water. "Is this the last row?" she asked him.

"The upper terrace still needs watering."

Nava lowered the jug and carefully poured out the contents, making sure every precious drop went into the thirsty ground and down to the roots of the plant. It would be six more months before the grape harvest, six more months of watering. She straightened again, stretching her back.

In the enclosure below, one of her goats began bleating, setting off a chorus of hoarse cries. "They're thirsty, too," she told her father. "I'd better take care of them before I water the vegetables." Her father simply nodded as if too weary to reply. Discouragement had withered him along with his plants. She'd heard him telling Mama last night that the barley plants were all stunted and shriveled from the drought and the harvest would be small.

"I needed that crop in order to pay back what I owe," he'd said. "Now I don't know what I'm going to do." It had been impossible to water an entire barley field. Nava hated to add to his worries, but her goats were almost out of grain, their bins all but empty. And the field where they usually grazed had dried up long ago. Parched and brittle, the grass had been chewed down to the roots.

"There's barely any grain left for the goats, Abba," she said, wincing as she told him. "Should I take them up into the hills tomorrow to graze?"

"There's no grass up there, either. I already asked the others. The grazing lands are as dead and dry as the rest of the countryside."

"We can't let the goats starve."

"No. That would be cruel."

She waited before asking, "Well, what are we going to do, then?" Nava held her breath, hoping he wouldn't decide to slaughter them before what little flesh still clinging to their ribs was gone, too. Farming families like hers couldn't afford to be sentimental about their animals, but Nava had raised her little herd of milking goats since they were kids.

"We may have to sell them," Abba finally replied.

She swallowed her tears. It was better than slaughtering them, she supposed. "But then we won't have any milk or yogurt or cheese."

"I know. And if I had any other choice . . . But I had to mortgage our land and borrow money to pay the king's taxes and feed our family, and there's no other way to pay back what I owe." He gestured to the barley field a stone's throw away where Nava's two brothers worked. "There's not even enough barley growing out there for our family to eat, let alone to sell and pay my debts. And Malkijah ben Recab is coming today to collect what I owe him."

"What does it mean to mortgage your land? It still belongs to us, doesn't it?"

"Not if I don't pay my debt. It will belong to Malkijah."

Nava walked the few steps to where Abba stood and wrapped her arms around him, hugging him tightly before letting go. She loved his familiar scent of earth and sweat and fresh air. Neither of them spoke as he hugged her in return. Then she lifted her jug again and set off for the well.

From the sloping rise of the terraced vineyard, Abba's fields of wheat and barley stretched out below Nava. She saw Mama in the distance, returning from the well, balancing a full jug on her head. A small grove of ancient olive trees stood behind their fieldstone house and animal pens. Most of the trees had been planted by Abba's ancestors before the exile. Nava loved this beautiful, pitiful patch of farmland and knew Abba loved it even more. He had moved here to the Promised Land from Babylon to fulfill his dream of working his ancestral land, harvesting olives and grapes to make oil and wine from his own trees and vines. He had left everything behind to make the journey with Rebbe Ezra's caravan thirteen years ago when Nava was only three years old, arriving to find a pile of rubble where their ancestors' home once stood. Weeds and thistles overran all the fields. The vines and olive trees had needed pruning so badly that they no longer bore fruit. Nava's parents and two older brothers had worked hard to restore their land—and now? Now her father's dream had dried up and blown away like dust when, for the second year in a row, the winter rains had failed to come.

Nava made several more trips to the well and was pouring water on the last of the grapevines when she heard a distant shout. She looked up and even from far away, she recognized the tall, lanky figure striding up the footpath that led from his family's fields to hers. Her heart beat faster at the sight of their neighbor's son, Dan, as if she had just run all the way up the hill to meet him. She dribbled a little of the precious water on her hands and used it to splash the dust and sweat from her face.

Dan was two years older than Nava and had been her best friend for as long as she could remember. Their families had traveled in the caravan together from Babylon, sharing all the joys and sorrows of the journey and their new life in the Promised Land. But Nava had never been concerned about her appearance until a year ago when her friendship with Dan had warmed into something much more. On a trip to Jerusalem with their families for Passover, Nava and Dan had talked as they walked all the way there and back together—and everything had changed. They would be married one day, Dan promised. He would ask Abba for her hand as soon as he could afford to support her. But for now, neither family could afford the dowry or the bride price. Dan's father, Yonah, was as poor as Abba and couldn't afford another mouth to feed if his only son married.

Nava smiled as she watched Dan approach, walking with a spring in his step and carrying a sack slung over his shoulder. His beaming face seemed brighter than the sun. "What did you bring?" she called out to him.

"You'll see!" he shouted back. His grin broadened.

Nava quickly emptied her water jug and hurried down the stepped slope to meet him, jumping over the low stone walls of the supporting terraces. Her tattered, broken sandals slowed her down, so she slipped them off and carried them the rest of the way, even though the dry, stony soil bit into her feet. They were both laughing and out of breath when they finally met up. Dan held up the bulging sack. "I brought a present for my beautiful little Nava."

"For me? What is it?" It could have been filled with stones and Nava still would have loved him for bringing it. But he opened the sack with a flourish, and she looked inside to see a limp mound of brown and tan feathers. "Are those quails?" she asked in surprise and delight.

"Three of them. For you and your family."

"What about your family? We could all share them."

"Don't worry, I caught enough for my family, too. I chased a whole flock of them right into my net."

She wanted to hug him but modesty forbade it until they were married. "These are wonderful, Dan. I can't believe it! It must have taken so much time and hard work to catch them."

"And patience. But I'm learning to be a patient man. I'm

going to marry you someday, Nava, and in the meantime, I can't have you starving to death, can I?"

"You're wonderful!"

He slung the bag over his shoulder again, and they walked along the footpath together toward Nava's house. "Mama and I will pluck the feathers and gut the birds and cook them for dinner tonight." Quails didn't have much meat on their tiny frames, but added to soup or stew they would stretch to make a satisfying meal for her family. And the broth would be delicious. They were almost to the house when they saw a man approaching from the opposite direction, riding sidesaddle on a donkey. Only a wealthy man could afford to ride such a fine, well-fed beast. Abba had seen him, too, and he left his work to walk down the hill from the vineyard to meet him. It pained Nava to see her father walk with his head bowed and his shoulders slumped, as if carrying a heavy load on his back. The stranger must be the man who was coming to collect Abba's debt—a debt he couldn't repay. The joy Nava had felt a moment ago when Dan had shown her his present vanished.

"Oh no," she moaned.

"The vulture is circling," Dan said under his breath. "And I'm sure he'll visit my father next."

"Do you know him?"

"Unfortunately, yes. Malkijah ben Recab holds the mortgage on my father's farm." They headed down the hill, reaching the stranger the same time Nava's father did.

"Good afternoon, my lord," Abba said in greeting.

Malkijah ben Recab slid from the donkey's back before replying. "Good afternoon. It's very warm for springtime, isn't it?" He wore a robe of fine, white linen with a scarlet band around the hem and neck and sleeves. The turban on his dark head of hair was also of the finest linen.

"Yes, my lord. Yes, it's very warm." Abba barely looked up, staring down at his dust-covered feet. He cleared his throat.

"I'm sorry, my lord, but I can't pay back what I owe you today. It looks as though my barley crop will fail from lack of rain. I'll give you everything I do harvest when the time comes, but I already know it won't be enough to cover the debt."

Nava ached for him. She was sorry now for complaining about hauling water. Malkijah stepped closer, his dark brows knit in a frown, and for a horrible moment Nava feared he would confront her father, demand what was due him. But he shook his head sadly as he rested his hand on Abba's shoulder. "I understand, my friend. Everyone in this district is suffering. We've prayed and prayed for rain, haven't we? But the Holy One must have His reasons for not answering us."

Abba finally dared to meet his gaze. "Perhaps when I harvest my grapes I can repay you."

"Yes . . . perhaps." Malkijah appraised the terraced hillside as if assessing the vines with the eyes of an expert. "Because of the extreme circumstances, I normally would be willing to wait until the grape harvest—but I have to pay the king's tribute, as well as my provincial taxes. And my crops have also suffered from the drought."

Abba scratched his beard. "I have a small flock of goats. Would you take them to help repay my debt?" he asked.

Nava covered her mouth as tears sprang to her eyes. Dan moved closer and rested his hand on the small of her back. He knew how much she loved her little flock. If she looked at him, she would burst into tears.

"Don't you need your goats for milk?" Malkijah asked. "I don't want your family to starve."

"I have nothing else to give you, my lord. Besides, we have no grain left to feed them. The goats will die if you don't take them."

"In that case, of course I'll take them. I'll send one of my sons or my manager over for them tomorrow morning."

"Thank you, my lord," Abba said. "I'm very grateful to you."

There was nothing more any of them could say. Malkijah looked around for a way to boost himself onto his donkey again and led his animal over to a large stone. He bid them all good day after he'd mounted, then rode up the footpath to Dan's farm.

"My father can't pay him back, either," Dan said. "Our land is mortgaged to him, too."

Abba heaved a tired sigh. "At least Malkijah ben Recab is being kind and understanding about it."

"I don't like him," Dan said. "He says he cares about us, but he certainly doesn't show it. He doesn't help any of us. He just keeps taking more and more, raising our debts higher and higher."

"He has to pay taxes, too," Abba said.

"Have you seen where he lives?" Dan asked. "I have. And I don't feel a bit sorry for him. But I am sorry for my father and for you and for all of the other farmers in our district who are suffering. He took Nava's goats, just like that," he said, snapping his fingers.

"What else could he do?" Nava asked, trying to soothe him. She had rarely seen Dan this angry.

"What else?" he repeated. "He could have offered to give you some grain to feed your flock so you'd still have milk and cheese to eat. He owns a huge flock of his own. But, no. When he took your goats, he took the food right out of your mouth!"

There was nothing Nava could say in reply. Even Abba silently watched the figure on the donkey grow smaller and smaller as he climbed the rise to Dan's farm. "I need to go home," Dan said. "I need to be there when our noble 'rescuer' talks to my father." He handed the sack with the quails to Nava. She had forgotten all about them.

"Thank you again for the birds, Dan. It was so kind of you."

He gave a short, mirthless laugh. "I don't want your family to starve," he said, mimicking Malkijah. "But unlike him, I decided to do something about it." He turned and strode away. Abba turned away as well and trudged up the rise to his vineyard.

Nava lifted her jug for the trip back to the well. Why didn't God answer their prayers?

THE CITADEL OF SUSA
APRIL

Nehemiah's workday was nearly over, and the sun hung low in the sky when he was called to the citadel's Gate House. Once again, it surprised him to see his brother Hanani. "I've come to tell you good-bye," Hanani said. "We're leaving tomorrow morning, early."

Nehemiah's heart squeezed. He hadn't realized how lonely he'd been before Hanani had arrived or how much he'd missed both of his brothers. The time spent with Hanani these past four months had been an unexpected and welcome gift. "Why are you leaving?" Nehemiah asked. "Your petition still hasn't reached the king."

"It looks like it never will. The king's advisors have made it clear that we must pay every cent of the taxes we owe, regardless of the drought back home in Judah."

"That's too bad." His brother would leave tomorrow; they would likely never see each other again. "Listen," Nehemiah said, "stay here at the palace and dine with me tonight so we'll have one last chance to visit before you go."

"I would like that," Hanani said.

"I'm done working for today. Come with me, and I'll show you around." Nehemiah led the way out of the Gate House and across the open area to the royal palace. Soaring walls and crenelated watchtowers loomed above them as they entered the citadel. "Do you remember coming to Mordecai's quarters when we were children?" he asked.

"Not very well. It was nighttime, wasn't it? And even if I did remember, I'm sure everything has changed."

"True. Security increased tenfold after the king's father was murdered. They made sure the royal palace was constructed with walls within walls. It's impregnable." He led Hanani through some of the vast public spaces—the large outer court-yard, the smaller central courtyard, then the inner courtyard. "The king's throne room and living quarters are isolated from these public spaces," he explained. "Access is very limited." Nehemiah showed his brother the largest courtyard of all, the huge, open-air terrace called the apadna, covering more than 108,000 square feet. Six rows with six pillars in each row held up the soaring roof, each pillar more than sixty-five feet tall and topped with twin pairs of carved bulls.

"What in the world is this space used for?" Hanani asked.

"Formal ceremonies and state banquets. At the New Year Festival, representatives from every province come to greet the king and deliver their annual taxes. He sits on that raised platform."

"Well, if the king's goal is to make his subjects feel small and insignificant, I'd say he achieved it with this space!"

The tour ended in Nehemiah's private quarters, where they ate dinner and sipped wine and talked until late into the night. Hanani agreed to stay overnight so he wouldn't have to walk back to the Jewish section of Susa in the dark. The awareness that they would never have this chance to talk again made their time together bittersweet.

Nehemiah didn't sleep well and awakened before dawn. He rose as quietly as he could and went to the window that overlooked the steep valley on the south side of the royal citadel. Spring had arrived, and he could open the shutters to let in the mild air. For weeks he had fasted and prayed as he'd grieved over the situation in the Promised Land, and last night's dinner with his brother was the first full meal he'd eaten since Hanani came to Susa. Jerusalem's lack of safety or protection, and the resulting blight and disgrace on God's reputation, had caused Nehemiah to mourn as if a loved one had died. Now he closed his eyes in prayer.

"O Lord, God of heaven, the great and awesome God, who keeps His covenant of love with those who love Him and obey His commands, let your ear be attentive and your eyes open to hear the prayer your servant is praying before you day and night for your servants, the people of Israel. I confess the sins we have committed against you, including myself and my father's house. We have acted wickedly toward you. We have not obeyed the commands, decrees, and laws you gave your servant Moses. . . ."

Nehemiah paused and opened his eyes, aware that even though everything he'd just confessed was true, he had no way to make atonement for himself or for his family. The Almighty One would be justified in ignoring his prayer. But Nehemiah also knew that the God of his fathers was a compassionate and gracious God, forgiving wickedness, rebellion, and sin. He closed his eyes again and continued.

"Remember the instruction you gave your servant Moses, saying, 'If you are unfaithful, I will scatter you among the nations, but if you return to me and obey my commands, then even if your exiled people are at the farthest horizon, I will gather them from there and bring them to the place I have chosen as a dwelling for my Name. . . .'"

He paused again. The faint rim of pink light on the eastern horizon appeared hazy through his tears. The sun would rise soon, and Hanani would go home to his wife and little ones, where they would be in danger from their enemies, just as Nehemiah's parents had been. Jerusalem needed walls and ramparts and gates like the ones here in Susa. If only he could find a way to make Jerusalem—and his brothers—safe and secure. God had redeemed His people from exile, just as He had redeemed them from Egypt by His powerful hand. Yet the restoration seemed incomplete if they remained in danger. He closed his eyes again and continued to pray.

"They are your servants and your people, whom you redeemed by your great strength and your mighty hand. O Lord, let your ear be attentive to the prayer of this, your servant, and to the prayer of your servants who delight in revering your name—"

He turned when he heard a sound behind him. His brother stood in the doorway, already dressed. "Nehemiah, what's wrong?" he asked. Nehemiah hadn't had time to wipe the tears from his eyes. He scrubbed both hands down his face as he turned toward the window again.

"Remember the night Mama and Abba died?"

"Of course. How could I ever forget?" Hanani came to the window to stand beside him. "I also remember that you never cried, Nehemiah. Not even once. And I couldn't stop crying."

"You were so young. Much too young to see the things we saw and hear what we were forced to hear."

"Is that why you're upset? Did celebrating *Purim* two weeks ago remind you of that night?"

"Only indirectly. . . . Listen, you know I've always felt responsible for protecting you and Ephraim—"

"You saved our lives. I don't know how you thought to hide so quickly. Or how you knew to make sure we stayed quiet." Nehemiah remembered how Hanani had struggled in his arms as he'd held his hand tightly over his mouth. He would never forget the smell of wood from the chest they'd hidden behind, the damp odor of the plastered wall as they'd huddled in the corner. Nehemiah brushed away another tear, impatient with himself.

"All this time, I've been imagining that you and Ephraim were safe and happy in Jerusalem. That I'd finished my job and—"

"Nehemiah, we're grown men with families of our own. You don't need to take care of us anymore."

He shook his head, unable to shake off the weight of responsibility he felt for them. "Ever since you told me about the conditions in Judah and how your friend Yitzhak was murdered in his home, I haven't been able to get Jerusalem out of my mind. I've been fasting and praying about the situation, asking the Almighty One what I can do, how I can help."

"In that case, I'm sorry I told you. I'm sorry for upsetting you, especially since there isn't anything you can do."

"There has to be. I earn a living by keeping the king and his household safe. I know everything there is to know about security."

"Nehemiah, you have a wonderful career here. Find a nice wife. Have children."

"I would probably go insane worrying about their safety. . . . No, now that I know what the situation is like in Jerusalem, I can no longer look at all the splendor here in Susa without seeing it differently and grieving. I can't get over the fact that nearly thirty years after Purim, our people are still being murdered by our enemies in the middle of the night. I believe we both feel the same way about that."

Hanani rested his hand on his shoulder. "I can see that time hasn't healed those wounds. Listen, my brother—"

"Most of all, Hanani," he said, raising his voice to drown out his brother's attempts to comfort him. "Most of all, Jerusalem is God's city. His dwelling place. It shouldn't be a shame and a disgrace to Him. You've seen the splendor of this Persian king's house. Shouldn't the heavenly King's dwelling place evoke awe and respect, not ridicule? Our enemies should tremble at the thought of robbing or murdering His people. The restoration of our land, promised by all the prophets, isn't complete if we still live in fear."

"You're right, you're right. But there's nothing you or I can do about it."

"What if there is? What if the Holy One *does* want me to do something about it? Maybe God made me the Persian king's cupbearer for a reason."

"You mean, the same way He made Esther the queen?"

"I stand in King Artaxerxes' presence every time I serve his wine."

"But do you dare risk your life and petition him unbidden, like she did?"

"No. I'm not a courtier. I'd never be allowed to present a formal petition. Look how unsuccessful your delegation was in presenting yours. I'm not allowed to speak a word in the king's presence unless spoken to. But if the Almighty One were to make a way for me . . ."

"I see what you mean. In that case, I'll pray that He will provide a way."

The sky grew lighter outside, the stars faded. Nehemiah heard the familiar morning sounds as the king's household began to stir. "I need to go," Hanani said. "The other men in my caravan plan to eat a quick breakfast and leave as soon as it's light."

"I'll walk there with you." Nehemiah led the way out of the citadel, through the King's Gate and over the bridge to the lower city, ignoring the people and carts and pack animals he passed along the way. Hanani's caravan was loaded and ready to leave. All too soon, it was time for him and his brother to part. "I think it's harder to see you go now than it was the last time," Nehemiah said. They embraced, then he stood and watched until the last camel was out of sight.

Throughout the morning, Nehemiah battled tears of anger and frustration and loss as he performed his security duties in the kitchen and inner rooms of the palace. Hanani was right; the palace's vast spaces and towering pillars did make him feel dwarfed. He was powerless, an insignificant man, unable to change a thing in Jerusalem a thousand miles away. Was it really the Almighty One who had put this burden for Jerusalem on his heart? Could he really dare to ask the king for permission to rebuild Jerusalem's walls? If so, then God would have to give him the courage to speak . . . and give King Artaxerxes a heart that would listen.

JERUSALEM
MAY

Chana glanced in the small bronze mirror, then handed it to her sister. She was ready to go. The reflection she'd seen was of a young woman whose dark eyes looked tired and sad. But what difference did it make? The yearly festivities for Shavuot, the Feast of Weeks, weren't going to be very festive this year. "I don't understand why we're even bothering to celebrate," she had told her father earlier. "Everyone is saying there isn't much grain to harvest because of the drought."

"We keep the feast because God's Torah commands us to," he had replied. "In the words of God's prophet, 'Though the olive crop fails and the fields produce no food . . . yet I will rejoice in the Lord, I will be joyful in God my Savior.' And so we will go up to the temple and rejoice. Grain or no grain, the Almighty One is still our God. We must have faith that He knows what's best for us."

So Chana had crowded into the tiny bedroom she shared with her sisters, bumping elbows and stepping over one another as they'd bathed and changed into their finest robes. Now she was ready. She was about to open the door and go out to the courtyard to wait with their father when Yudit stopped her. "Chana, please help me do something to tame this horrible mass of hair!"

"Why? It looks beautiful that way—like a lion's mane."

"I don't want to look like a lion. I want my curls to behave so I'll look pretty."

Chana was taken aback. This was new. Her nineteen-year-old sister had never bothered to tame her unruly hair before, in spite of Chana's pleas to let her comb it. "Since when did you start worrying about your hair? Or caring if you look pretty?"

"She wants to look nice in case she sees Alon ben Harim," Sarah said, passing the mirror to Yudit.

"Sarah! Hush!" A blush like ripening grapes spread across Yudit's cheeks as she gave Sarah a swat. "You weren't supposed to tell!"

"Oh, stop fussing. Chana won't say anything, will you, Chana. Besides, she's not blind. She's certain to see you and Alon staring at each other with eyes like baby calves." Sarah struck a lovesick pose, imitating a lover in a swoon. Yudit swatted her again.

Chana shook her head at their foolishness. "I won't tell your secret, Yudit. I think it's nice that you and Alon have noticed each other. Come here, and I'll see what I can do with your hair." Yudit dragged a low stool across the room and sank down on it. Chana gently pulled the wooden comb through her curls to try to tame them. "I think it's wonderful that my carefree, independent middle sister has fallen for someone. And I'm not surprised. It is springtime, after all. The time when 'Flowers appear on the earth and the season of singing has come.'"

"Are you girls nearly ready?" their father called from outside their closed door. "We don't want to be late." Chana detected a note of exasperation in his voice.

"Yes, Abba. Another moment," Yudit called back. A year ago, Abba would have gone on ahead of them and let them walk up the hill to the temple mount alone. Now he and the other fathers and husbands no longer allowed women to walk alone in Jerusalem, especially at night.

Sarah flopped down cross-legged on the rug to watch. "What about you, Chana? Have you decided if you're going to let Abba's friend court you? You know, that nice man who brought us the wine?"

"His name is Malkijah ben Recab," Yudit mocked in a deep voice. "He likes to be called Malkijah ben Recab."

"I haven't decided anything," Chana replied, tugging on a snarled curl.

"Well, I liked him," Sarah said. "He was very charming and kind. He said we were all lovely, remember?"

"She's right," Yudit said. "Even you have to admit he was charming, Chana. . . . Ouch!" She grimaced as Chana combed another tangled lock.

"The two of you seem much more interested in him than I am," Chana said. "Maybe one of you should court him."

"We can't," Sarah said. "Yudit and I can't get married until you do."

For the third time, Yudit gave her youngest sister a swat. "Will you just be *quiet*?"

"Well, it's true, isn't it? Abba said it's a tradition that the oldest sister must marry first."

The stuffy little room suddenly felt very warm to Chana. Was she preventing her sisters from getting married? Mercifully, Abba called to them once again before the conversation could continue. "Girls . . . ? I don't believe it's possible to be any more beautiful than you already are."

Sarah leaped up and went out to appease him, and a moment later Chana finished making Yudit's corona of hair behave. But she couldn't stop thinking about her sister's words. By taking so long to get over Yitzhak's death, she might be standing in Yudit's way if she and Alon did fall in love.

Chana took Abba's arm as they hurried from the house and made the uphill climb to the temple, letting her sisters walk ahead of them. "Abba," she asked when she was sure they were out of earshot, "is it really true that the oldest sister must marry before the younger ones do?"

"Well . . . that is the way things usually work," he said with a sigh. "But it's not written in the Torah as an unbreakable law. More of a tradition, you might say."

"So, I'm standing in the way of Yudit getting married?"

He stopped, already puffing from the effort. "You know how free-spirited Yudit is. She'll find a way to do as she pleases. But what worries me more, my angel, is that if you wait too long, your choice of eligible men will begin to dwindle."

"Because I'll be considered too old?"

"You need to come to a decision, Chana. Do you want to get married and have children, or are you content to remain single and never be a mother?"

She pondered Abba's question as they started walking again. Just this morning as she and Yudit had shopped in the marketplace she had paused to watch a young mother with her toddler. The boy wobbled on unsteady legs as if the earth kept shifting, but his delight in everything he saw had made Chana smile. "Look . . . look!" he said, stopping every few steps to point his chubby finger at something new. A year ago, Chana had anticipated having Yitzhak's child, picturing a tiny boy with Yitzhak's curly hair, his laughing eyes. And as she'd watched the toddler this morning, Chana had longed for a baby of her own to hold in her arms.

"Yes, I do want to get married," she told her father.

"The sad truth is that men your age want to marry younger women, like Yudit and Sarah, who can bear them many children. I fear you'll soon be left with very old men—widowers or men no one else wanted."

"You're trying to scare me, aren't you? You want me to court your friend Malkijah from the council."

"I'll be honest, my angel. I do wish you would give Malkijah a chance. He is still very interested in you. What would it hurt to take time to get to know him? That's all I ask. If you find he's not to your liking, I won't force you to marry him."

Sarah was right—Malkijah had been charming and pleasant. And not bad-looking, even with his crooked nose. "I guess it wouldn't hurt to try," she said.

"That's my girl! I'll invite him to visit again. Perhaps for Sabbath dinner this time? In fact, how about this Sabbath?"

Chana wanted to say no, that Abba was moving too fast. But she remembered how Yudit had preened in front of the mirror, longing to look pretty for Alon ben Harim, and she relented. "Fine. This Sabbath. For dinner."

The following Friday morning, Sarah and Yudit dove into the dinner preparations with Chana as if the two of them were the ones who needed to impress Malkijah ben Recab. Sarah set the table with their finest cloth, Yudit arranged their best dishes, and the three of them planned a menu of soup and fresh vegetables and roasted fish. There was much discussion about what each one should wear and how they should fix their hair, and Sarah was especially critical of Chana's hair. "Don't pull it back so tightly away from your face. It makes you look old and sad."

I am old and sad, she wanted to say. *Malkijah may as well know the truth.* "How should I wear it, then?" she asked instead. Her sister took over, pulling a few tendrils free to curl around her face. Chana didn't even bother to look in the mirror at the result.

Malkijah arrived just before sunset with wine for Abba and a present for each of the sisters. "Just a little something for going to all the bother of cooking for me," he said. Chana's present was a beautifully woven basket of fresh figs; Yudit's a lovely pottery jar filled with honey; for Sarah, a plate of sweet pastries made from dates; and for Abba, a sample of some of his best wines. Chana wondered if her father would feel obligated to Malkijah after so much kindness. Would she be unable to refuse a marriage proposal?

They sat down to eat the leisurely dinner in the courtyard beneath a starry sky. Malkijah was an attentive dinner guest, never letting the conversation falter and making sure that everyone seated around the table had a chance to speak and to be heard. When the dinner ended hours later, he led Chana outside the courtyard gate and stood beside her as they gazed up at the star-studded sky together. Her home was built close to the wall that had once encircled Jerusalem, but they could easily peer over the stubby remnant of it and see the rubble of demolished homes on the western hill. "I often wonder what that section of the city looked like before it was destroyed," she said. "It always looks so eerie in the moonlight, the haunt of jackals." *And thieves and criminals*, she added to herself. Evil men like the ones who had murdered Yitzhak.

"I want you to know how sorry I am about what happened to Yitzhak," Malkijah said, as if reading her thoughts. "He was a fine man. I didn't know him as well as I would have liked, but I never heard a bad word spoken about him, and that says a lot. You must miss him very much."

"Yes . . . I do." Chana blinked away unwanted tears.

"I won't talk about him if it's too painful, but I know from experience that sometimes it helps to talk about the loved ones we've lost. If everyone tiptoes around, afraid to mention their names, it can sometimes seem like they never existed or like they no longer matter. But of course they do."

Chana nodded, respecting him for his insight. "You're right. That's very true. And sometimes it does seem as if everyone is afraid to talk about him. . . . I understand that you lost your wife, as well."

"Yes. Rebecca died of a fever more than five years ago." Chana thought she heard a catch in his voice.

"I'm so sorry," she said.

61

"Ours was a love match, not an arranged marriage. She was my best friend, my companion. I understand that you loved Yitzhak the same way."

"Yes. But we never had a chance to marry."

"I wonder sometimes if we only experience that kind of love once in a lifetime. Or if the Holy One can surprise us and bless us with a loving companion a second time. I don't know. But I do know that I miss sharing my thoughts and disappointments with my wife. I miss seeing her warm smile at the end of the day and holding her in my arms at night. The reason I decided to marry again is because I don't think I'll ever find the happiness I once felt unless I do. And because Rebecca would want me to remarry and be happy."

Chana couldn't reply, moved by his touching words. She knew in her heart that Yitzhak also would want her to be happy.

"I've had inquiries from plenty of hopeful fathers," Malkijah continued. "And I've met many of their daughters. But I'm a wealthy man, and to be honest, it's difficult to tell if they're seeing me as a real person or as a wealthy husband with servants and a lavish home. I'm sure you must wonder the same thing since you're such a lovely woman. I'm sure I'm not the only suitor who has approached your father."

Was it true? Had other suitors asked Abba about her?

"Anyway," Malkijah said with a sigh, "as much as I hate to leave, it's late, and I must head home now. Thank you for such a wonderful evening, Chana. I enjoyed every minute and every bite of food."

"You're returning to Beth Hakkerem now? In the dark?"

"No," he said, laughing. "The trip takes nearly an hour in daylight when my donkey can see where she's going. She'd never manage all those stony hills in the dark. Besides, it really isn't safe to be out at night. I have a home here in Jerusalem. I use it during the holidays or when the council meetings last until very late."

"Thank you for coming tonight, Malkijah. I know we all enjoyed having you."

He acknowledged her words with a slight bow and said, "Let me step inside for a moment and say good night to your father and sisters." She followed him back to the courtyard, where her sisters had cleared the table and stacked the dishes. Abba still sat in his place at the head of the table, sipping the last of his wine, but he looked up at them as they walked inside together, a hopeful smile spreading across his face.

"Shallum, my friend, thank you for a most enjoyable evening," Malkijah said. "Next time you must all come to my home in Beth Hakkerem and share a meal with my sons and me. I'll show you my vineyards and winery."

"Your vineyards?" Chana asked. "What about the drought? Hasn't it affected your crops?"

"Of course. Everyone is feeling the effects. We must continue to pray for rain."

"We would be very happy to come," Abba said, rising from his seat to clap Malkijah on the shoulder. "Thank you, my friend."

"Excellent. I will talk to my servants and make the arrangements, then send you the details."

When he was gone, everyone turned to Chana, waiting for her reaction to the evening and their guest. She didn't know what to say, unwilling to raise everyone's hopes—especially her own. "He's very nice," she finally said. "I'm glad we invited him. I'm glad we'll see him again."

She was in bed, almost asleep when Yudit whispered, "Chana? Are you awake?"

"Yes . . . What is it?"

"I don't want you to feel obligated to marry Malkijah—especially for my sake. I just wish . . . I wish you were yourself again, you know? . . . That you were happy again. Abba and Sarah and I . . . we just want you to be the way you used to be before . . ."

"Before Yitzhak died? You can say his name, Yudit." She recalled what Malkijah had said about people being afraid to mention lost loved ones, and how sometimes we need to talk about them. He truly did understand. "I'm sorry for being so sad, Yudit. But each day gets a little better. I'm happier today than I was yesterday or the day before. And I believe I'll be a little happier tomorrow." She hoped it was true.

"That's good. I'm glad. . . . Good night. "

"Good night, Yudit."

CHAPTER

6

THE CITADEL OF SUSA
MAY

Nearly a month had passed since Nehemiah said good-bye to his brother, but the weight of sorrow he felt over Hanani's description of ruined Jerusalem never lifted. On a warm spring morning when the king called for wine, Nehemiah carried it up to the throne room himself, passing through the familiar succession of hallways and inner chambers and security doors. King Artaxerxes sat on his throne with his queen beside him, conducting state business and listening to petitions from a seemingly endless parade of courtiers. As Nehemiah poured out the king's wine and placed it in his hand, his thoughts were on Jerusalem, and he silently asked God to show him what he could do.

"Are you ill, Nehemiah?"

He looked up, startled from his thoughts. King Artaxerxes was speaking to him. Nehemiah's heart sped up. "No, Your Majesty. I'm not ill." He had never been sad in the king's presence before. It went against all the rules for a servant to allow his emotions to show. In fact, Nehemiah had warned all of his staff members that no matter how serious their personal problems were, they must keep their feelings to themselves and display a cheerful disposition in the king's presence. A servant's duty was to be positive and encouraging. But today Nehemiah's heavy heart prevented him from keeping up the façade.

"Then why does your face look so sad when you are not ill?" the king asked. Nehemiah's heart slammed harder against his ribs. The queen, seated beside Artaxerxes, also looked concerned. Nehemiah knew from Esther's story that a Persian queen could be very influential. But having the king's attention was so surprising, so unexpected, that he couldn't seem to find his voice.

"This can be nothing but sadness of heart," Artaxerxes said.

Nehemiah nodded. Should he tell the king that his brother had recently returned to Jerusalem? That he would never see him again? It would be the truth. But what if this was a God-given opportunity to intercede for Jerusalem? Nehemiah sent up a quick, silent prayer. *O Lord, give your servant success today by granting me favor in the presence of this man.* Then he cleared the knot of fear from his throat.

"Your Majesty is very perceptive," he replied. "It is sadness of heart."

"Go on . . ."

Nehemiah's legs felt limp. Might the king interpret his unhappiness as disloyalty? After all, a discontented servant had murdered Artaxerxes' father. Nehemiah's mouth felt as if he'd swallowed sand as he said, "May the king live forever! Why should my face not look sad when the city where my fathers are buried lies in ruins, and its gates have been destroyed by fire?"

He was careful not to name Jerusalem. And he didn't know where the idea to mention his ancestors' graves had come from, but he knew the Persians had a deep respect for ancestral burial grounds. The king frowned slightly, gazing intently at Nehemiah as if really seeing him for the first time—as a man and not simply a servant who worked in the background. Nehemiah tried to read his thoughts but couldn't. He waited, weak-kneed, recalling the words of Solomon's proverb: *"A king's wrath is a messenger of death."*

The throne room fell silent, the mumbling chatter of the courtiers stilled as if a gong had rung. How dare a mere cup-bearer speak his mind or reveal his feelings? Nehemiah could hear birds chirping outside the palace windows and the rustling of the wind. He felt as if he hung suspended over an abyss as he waited for King Artaxerxes' reply. Would he plunge to his death or be hauled back to safety? *O Lord, grant me favor in the presence of this man*, he prayed again. His fate wasn't in this king's hands but in his heavenly King's.

"What is it you want?" Artaxerxes finally asked.

Nehemiah breathed another silent prayer and replied, "If it pleases the king and if your servant has found favor in his sight, let him send me to the city in Judah where my fathers are buried so I can rebuild it."

Artaxerxes took a sip from his golden rhyton of wine before replying. Nehemiah thought he knew the king's moods and idiosyncrasies well after spending so much time in his presence and watching him respond to hundreds of petitions and requests. He didn't think the puzzled frown on his face was a look of anger, but of curiosity. Even so, Nehemiah couldn't seem to breathe.

"How long will your journey take, and when will you get back?" the king finally asked.

"You mean . . . it pleases the king to send me?" Nehemiah asked.

"Yes. It pleases me. You've served me faithfully all these years, and you have my complete trust. I know the servants you choose to replace you will also serve me well until you return."

Nehemiah's breath came out in a rush of relief. It was a

miracle! The Almighty One had answered his prayer. The king's unexpected praise fueled Nehemiah's courage, and he quickly set a time period for his mission. But then his mind raced ahead to the dangers he would face and the precautions he would need to take to ensure success. Judah's adversaries might try to prevent him from arriving safely. And Hanani had explained how their enemies had halted construction on the city once before. "If it pleases the king," he said, "may I have letters to the governors of The Land Beyond the River, so they will provide me with safe conduct until I arrive in Judah?"

"You may."

It still didn't seem like enough. Nehemiah remembered Jerusalem's history and how the northern approach to the city where the temple stood was vulnerable to enemy attacks. He would need to build a fortified citadel on that side. And he would need to rebuild all of Jerusalem's gates. "May I also have a letter to Asaph, the keeper of the king's forest," he added, "so he will give me timber to make beams for the gates of the citadel near the temple, and for the city wall, and for the residence I will occupy?"

"Your requests are granted," Artaxerxes replied. "In fact, I've decided to appoint you governor of Judah during your time there."

Governor? It was more than Nehemiah could have dared to ask for. He bowed his head. "Thank you, Your Majesty."

"I'll assign an army officer and cavalry to accompany you. . . . And, Nehemiah—good luck." The king nodded to his administrator to take over. Nehemiah followed the official from the throne room, feeling light-headed with joy and astonishment. Had Moses felt this way when the waters of the Red Sea miraculously parted for him? The gracious hand of the Almighty One had done this! He had answered Nehemiah's prayers.

◆ ◆ ◆

Nehemiah worked steadily in the weeks that followed, making all the arrangements for his journey: a caravan to transport the supplies he would need; the official letters of authorization with the king's seal; the military escort; and the details of the long trip itself with regular stops along the way. The distance from the Persian capital to the Promised Land was about one thousand miles, and he calculated that if they averaged twenty miles a day, the journey would take fifty-five days. After adding an additional eight days for resting every Sabbath, he concluded that it would take him sixty-three days to reach Jerusalem. But even as he planned and prepared, Nehemiah continued to wonder what he would find when he arrived. Were any sections of the wall salvageable, or would he have to begin with new foundations? Where would he find building stones and tools and workers? He knew he would have to build quickly, before Judah's enemies had a chance to sabotage his efforts or send a negative report to Susa and try to halt construction. Once the king sealed his decree it couldn't be rescinded, of course, but a king could issue a second order to cancel the first one's effect—as King Xerxes had done to halt the slaughter on the Thirteenth of Adar. Or what if a new king came to power before Nehemiah had a chance to finish Jerusalem's wall? Persian monarchs had a long, bloody history of power struggles and intrigues.

In spite of all these worries, Nehemiah could barely contain his excitement. The Almighty One had faithfully answered Nehemiah's prayer and granted him much more than he had dared to imagine. He longed to share the good news with someone, but who? There was no one. And besides, the fewer people who knew about his mission the better. It would be disastrous if news of it reached Judah before he did.

Late one night when Nehemiah lay in bed too excited to sleep, a new thought occurred to him. After all these years, after a childhood that had ended much too quickly and sorrowfully, might he finally find meaning in the loss of his parents on that long-ago night? Was it possible that the Almighty One had used the pain he had suffered to shape him into the man he'd become—and that the pain had prepared him for this very purpose?

For the first time, Nehemiah could think of his parents and accept consolation for their loss.

CHAPTER

7

DISTRICT OF BETH HAKKEREM
JUNE

The sun hadn't risen yet above the surrounding hills as Nava stood with her parents and two brothers in their wheat field, surveying their crop. The stalks looked dry and spindly, the kernels small compared to other years. Nava remembered wheat crops so thick she could barely push her way between the stalks, their ripe heads drooping beneath their weight. But this drought-stunted crop would be very small in comparison. Abba broke off one of the ripened ears and tasted it, chewing slowly. Nava couldn't bear the suspense. "Is it good, Abba? Is the wheat ready to harvest?"

He nodded. "It's ready." But the expression on his weather-wrinkled face betrayed his worry and disappointment. The whole family had risen early to avoid the summer heat and were waiting to begin. As soon as Abba pronounced the crop ready, he and Nava's brothers began making their way across the field with their sickles, cutting the ripened stalks and laying them on the ground. Nava and her mother followed behind, tying the stalks in bundles with pieces of straw. Bending over in the field all day was backbreaking work, but practice had taught Nava how to quickly tie the sheaves without scratching her hands on the brittle stalks. She was thankful that Abba had a crop to harvest, even if it was a meager one. Maybe he and Dan's father would reap enough grain to repay what they owed the man, with enough left over to feed their families in the coming months. Enough left over so she and Dan could be married.

The scorching sun rose quickly in the cloudless sky and before long, sweat dampened Nava's clothing and face. Her family was making good progress, the harvested sheaves were drying in the June sunshine—then she looked up and spotted two figures approaching on donkeys. One of them was the wealthy man in the snow-white turban and linen tunic trimmed with bands of scarlet, the man with the slightly crooked nose who had come three months ago. The other was his son, who had come the following day to take away her herd of goats. Nava dreaded the sight of them. Abba also spotted the men and for a moment he seemed to sway on his feet. "Sit and rest while I talk to them," he said, wiping his brow with his forearm. Nava watched him walk across the field to meet the men, carrying a sheaf of wheat for them to sample.

She sat down on the stubbly ground with the others for the first time all morning and took her turn sipping from the water jug. Her stomach rumbled with hunger. They had shared a meager breakfast just before dawn but it hadn't been enough to silence the ache in her gut. Her mother and older brothers must be hungry, too.

At first she watched from a distance as the man sampled the kernels and Abba gestured to the section of field they'd already harvested. Would it be enough to repay him? Nava stood up, unable to wait a moment longer. "I'll go see if they would like a drink or some water for their donkeys."

She hurried across the field to fetch the water jar and quickly filled it at the well, then poured it into the trough for the animals. She offered a cup to the strangers but they both declined.

The son hadn't bothered to dismount, and she could tell by the expression on Abba's face that the discussion wasn't going well. He looked exasperated, his cheeks flushed with emotion, his voice hoarse with it. "It's the best we could do in this drought," he said.

"I know, my friend. But what you need to understand is that I own the mortgage on your vineyard and fields. You borrowed money using them as collateral."

"And now I can repay you with this crop."

"I'm very sorry, but your wheat harvest won't be enough to repay your debts because two-thirds of the crop already belongs to me. The loan was an advance against your future crop. The third that belongs to you will help pay back a portion of the second loan I gave you when you borrowed money for food. But not all of it."

"I gave you my herd of goats in repayment."

"Yes, you did. But the debt still isn't paid in full. I'm sorry."

Nava's hand shook as she tried to pour more water into the trough, splashing it on her bare feet. It wasn't fair! After all their hard work, it still wasn't enough for this greedy man? She wanted to shout at him in outrage.

"Please forgive me if I failed to explain all of this to you when you asked me for the loans," the man continued. "And again when you mortgaged your land. Perhaps I wasn't very clear."

"You explained it, but . . . but I hoped this harvest would square things between us, and I would get my wheat field back."

"I'm sorry, but I can already see that this crop won't be enough. If only your barley crop hadn't failed, then you may have been closer to repaying what you owe me. But for whatever reason, the Holy One has withheld rain for a second year."

"You say only a third of this wheat is mine?"

"Unfortunately, yes."

"But I'll never get my land back unless I repay you. And if I give you my third to repay the loan, I'll have nothing left to eat.

I'll be forced to borrow even more money from you or watch my family starve. I can already see that my olives and grapes aren't going to amount to much this year."

"I'm not demanding repayment, my friend. I understand that the drought isn't your fault and that you're working as hard as you can. I'm more than willing to extend your credit for as long as necessary. Perhaps the crops will do better next year."

Abba ran his fingers through his sweaty hair and shook his head. "Even with rain, this cycle of debt will go on forever if you keep taking two-thirds of my crops year after year. There's no way out of this. I'll never get my land back. The debt will keep adding up if I have nothing left to give you in payment." He waved away the cup of water Nava offered him, saying, "Not now."

Nava ached for him as he battled his emotions. She longed to set down the jug and the cup and cling tightly to him, but she feared he would be unable to control his tears if she did. "I don't know what else to do," Abba said. They stood in the road for a long moment, the summer sun beating down on them, the donkeys swishing flies with their tails.

"Listen, my friend," the man said softly. "There is another way out of this dilemma that some of your fellow farmers have chosen to take. But I'm afraid it's a costly decision."

"What could possibly be more costly than losing my land or watching my family starve?"

The man exhaled. "I would be willing to make sure your family has enough to eat without adding another loan to your account . . . but your daughter would have to work for me and become my bondservant."

The proposal was so unexpected, so horrible, that Nava felt the panic of not being able to breathe. *A bondservant?*

"No!" Abba shouted. "No! Never! Take me as your slave, not her. No!"

"If I took you, then who would work this land and bring in

next year's crop? Don't you see? The land technically belongs to me until the mortgage is paid, so you're already working for me."

"Take one of my sons, then. Not my little girl. She's too young."

"How will you bring in a good crop without your sons? For all of our sakes, your sons need to stay and help you work the land. Your daughter will be well cared for, I promise you. She'll be part of a staff of servants whose families are in the same position as yours and can't repay their debts. The truth is, I don't need another servant, but I'm making this offer as a kindness to you and your family."

Nava could no longer hold back her tears. She loved her family and longed to do whatever she could to help them, but leave home and go to work for this man? Become his bondservant? It was unimaginable. And what about marrying Dan?

Abba wrapped his arm around Nava's shoulder. "How is it a kindness to make my little girl your slave?" he asked.

"Believe me, I've been searching for a way to help families like yours in my district. I've talked it over with the priests and other leaders in Jerusalem, and they've assured me that this is the provision prescribed by the Torah in cases like this. It's not my idea. It's in God's law."

"And how long will Nava have to be your bondservant?"

"The term of service given in the Torah is six years—"

"*Six years!*"

"And no longer. After that she goes free, even if you haven't paid off your debt."

Nava covered her mouth to keep from crying out. Six years as this man's slave? Six years until she and Dan could be married? It was more than one-third of the lifetime she'd already lived. It seemed like forever.

"And even if I agreed to this, my land would still be mortgaged to you?" Abba asked.

"Yes. Unless you choose to sell your land to me to pay off all of your debts."

"Don't do it, Abba," Nava said, unable to remain quiet. "You can't sell your land."

"If I did, we would all starve for sure," he said.

The nobleman spread his hands, backing away a few steps. "Listen, I understand how overwhelming this must be. You don't need to decide right now. Talk it over with your family. And talk to some of your neighbors who are facing the same difficult choices. I'll come back tomorrow." He mounted his donkey and left with his son, returning the way they had come.

Abba didn't watch him go. He trudged back to the field and picked up his sickle to return to his labors without saying another word. Nava could see that his heart was no longer in his work. Only a small portion of this crop was his? It didn't seem fair.

"What happened? What did he say?" Mama asked him.

Abba simply shook his head. "We'll talk about it later."

Nava had the rest of the morning to think about their situation while she worked. As her shock gradually began to wear off, she was unable to control her tears at the thought of being enslaved for six long years. But what other choice did her family have?

By noon the sun was unbearable, and they stopped working to sit in the shade of the pomegranate tree and eat a small meal. In a halting voice, Abba explained to everyone what the man had told him. Mama covered her face and wept. Nava's brothers vented their anger with loud protests. Abba seemed heartbroken.

"I think we should accept the man's offer," Nava said, trying to sound brave. "When he comes back tomorrow, tell him I'll work for him."

"Nava, no!"

"It's okay, Abba. I want to help you and Mama. And this way, you'll get to keep your land. I don't want that horrible, greedy man to have it. It's yours. It belonged to our ancestors."

"I know, but there must be some other way."

Nava knew that there wasn't. They all returned to the field later that afternoon and worked until sunset. Then Abba walked up the path to talk to Dan's father. He wouldn't let Nava come with him, and the evening seemed endless until he finally returned. She heard him open and close the gate as she and Mama were laying out the sleeping mats, getting ready for bed. Nava was afraid to ask him what he and Dan's father had talked about, but Mama wasn't. "What are our neighbors going to do? What did you decide?"

Abba shook his head. Nava saw him swallowing, struggling for control as he replied. "We have no choice," he said hoarsely. "If Nava is willing to go—" He swallowed again, turning to her. "If you're willing to do this for us . . ."

She went to him, holding him tightly. The knot of grief and sorrow in her chest felt as if it might swell and burst and shatter her heart. She would be a bondservant for the next six years. Somehow she managed to choke out the words, "Of course I'm willing, Abba." He gave her a crushing hug, then freed himself from her grip, kissing her forehead before fleeing outside into the darkness. Her mother sat with her face covered, weeping. Nava crouched beside her and wrapped her arms around her as they wept together.

The rest of the night seemed like a bad dream. This was the last time she would sleep in this house, this bed. The last time she would get up in the morning and watch the sun rise over this beautiful, hilly patch of land where she had always lived. How could she bear saying good-bye to Dan? To be separated from him? Would she be allowed to visit him or her family in the years ahead?

She didn't sleep. She finally ran out of tears as dawn approached and her eyes burned from weeping, her head ached. As her room grew lighter, she heard a soft, familiar whistle outside her window.

Dan.

She quickly dressed and tiptoed outside to meet him. They had always been very careful to remain modest in their relationship and refrain from showing their affection until they were married, but Dan suddenly pulled Nava into his arms, hugging her tightly. She savored the moment, loving the feeling of his strong, protective arms surrounding her. She never wanted him to let go. "Let's run away," he whispered. "I can't bear the thought of you going away!"

As much as Nava longed to be with him, she knew they couldn't run away. "I need to help my family, Dan. Abba will lose his land if I don't do this. My family will starve."

His arms tightened around her for a moment longer, then he pulled away. "Nava, there's something that rich man didn't tell you or your father. I walked into Jerusalem last night and talked to the priests myself—"

"Dan, you shouldn't have! It's too dangerous to walk alone at night!"

"Just listen. According to the Torah, Malkijah could give you to one of his sons for a wife."

"But I'm already promised to you."

"He won't care. Malkijah ben Recab takes whatever he wants, and no one can stop him. Besides, it's legal according to the law. The priest told me that as long as he takes care of you as a daughter-in-law and not as a servant, he's within his rights. He could marry you himself, for that matter."

"No. It's too horrible to even think about."

"You would be rich, Nava, with beautiful clothes to wear and servants to wait on you."

"But I love you. I want to marry you, no matter how rich or poor we are. Marrying anybody else is . . . is . . . I could never do it!"

Dan pulled her into his arms again. "I'll wait for you. And if I can't marry you, then I won't get married at all."

"Will we at least get to visit each other during that time?"

"The priests said that it's up to your master. He owns you. He gets to decide." Dan hugged her tenderly, then bent to kiss her for the very first time. "That kiss seals you as mine," he said when their lips parted. Tears filled his eyes and trailed down his cheeks. "Don't forget me, Nava."

"Dan, wait—" But he turned away from her, and she watched him sprint across the fields toward home as if he couldn't bear to look back. Nava sank down on the ground and quietly wept, her sorrow and grief unbearable. As the stars faded and the sky grew light in the east, she heard her family stirring inside the house. Nava stood and wiped her eyes. If her parents saw her crying it would make it even harder for them to watch her go. She needed to be brave for their sakes.

She couldn't eat breakfast, her stomach sick with fear. Before her family had a chance to return to the wheat field with their sickles, Malkijah's son arrived. "My father wants to know if you've made a decision," he said. Once again, he didn't bother to dismount. He would take Nava away just as he'd taken her herd of goats.

"My daughter has agreed to become your bondservant," Abba said, his voice hoarse. "But if I had any other choice—" He began to weep and couldn't finish. Nava had never seen her father cry. She went to him, hugging him tightly.

"It's all right, Abba. Everything will be fine." She hugged her mother, too, and then picked up the sack with her meager belongings. Her sandals had come apart again, so she would have to walk barefooted until they were fixed. When she looked up at Malkijah's son to tell him she was ready, she saw him appraising her from head to toe and remembered what Dan had said. Her stomach churned with dread. Her new masters had the right to take her for a wife. She lifted her chin, unwilling to let her family see her fear, and followed the donkey as it returned the way it had come. She had never been separated from them before, not even for a single night, and couldn't imagine living apart from them. Or from Dan.

Why wasn't the Almighty One helping them? Why didn't He answer their prayers for rain? They were His people, this was His land. Abba had left Babylon so they could all live here and worship Him in Jerusalem. Why was God making them suffer this way?

The summer day was already growing hot. The dirt road felt warm beneath Nava's bare feet as she followed the plodding donkey. She didn't dare look back.

CHAPTER

8

SAMARIA, CAPITAL CITY OF THE LAND
BEYOND THE RIVER

Nehemiah stood in Governor Sanballat's throne room, enduring the preliminary formalities and official introductions. He'd witnessed this process countless times in King Artaxerxes' throne room and understood the necessity of the ritual, but it still tried his patience. Like boys playing in the streets, sizing each other up, the assembled men would choose allies, assess their enemies.

"Governor Sanballat. Thank you for arranging this meeting," Nehemiah said when it was his turn to speak. He made sure to address the Samaritan governor as an equal and not let his posture or expression convey submission. "And thank you for your gracious hospitality, hosting us here in your palace." He used the word *palace* in an effort to flatter the governor, but it couldn't begin to compare to the Persian palaces where he'd served as cupbearer. This room was a shabby copy of a Persian assembly hall, paneled with cedar and warmed with tapestries and carpets. But the furnishings looked worn and threadbare, as if used by Persian royalty for a dozen years, then discarded. The overall look reminded Nehemiah of an aging noblewoman struggling to keep up appearances after falling on hard times. From the moment he entered Sanballat's palace, Nehemiah had been assessing it from a security standpoint, and he was surprised to find that it failed every test. A determined enemy could find dozens of ways to breach its defenses and assassinate the governor.

Nehemiah turned to the other gathered leaders, showing respect but not deference. "And it was good of all of you to come on such short notice. As the new governor of the province of Judah, I believe it's important for me to meet my fellow leaders." He had longed to go directly to Jerusalem to survey the city's defenses, but his experience with politics and protocol had taught him that he needed to pay an official visit to the other provincial leaders first, establishing his credentials as Judah's new governor, claiming his rightful authority. A few days before reaching Damascus, he'd sent messengers ahead to Samaria to announce his arrival and arrange this meeting with Judah's neighbors. Now he took careful note of each of these men—the rulers of the Ammonites, Edomites, Ashdodites, Samaritans, and Arab tribes. Except for the Samaritans, who had been transplanted to the Promised Land by the conquering Assyrians more than two hundred years ago, these neighbors were his peoples' historic enemies. Nehemiah had no reason to believe that their enmity had changed. Today's meeting tested everyone's willpower and strength.

"I bring greetings to each of you from King Artaxerxes' court," he continued, "along with the king's sincere desire that we work together for the good of his empire and for the people we govern." Nehemiah had listened to his peers' long introductions knowing that these men were in a position to either help or hinder his work. Sanballat, leader of the Samaritans on Judah's northern border, presided over the gathering while the others deferred to him. The oldest of the gathered leaders, he struck Nehemiah as a seasoned politician, wily and duplicitous, determined to surrender none of his power as the leader of the province known as The Land Beyond the River. A large, beardless, heavyset man, he sat on his throne with his hands resting on his protruding belly. Sanballat's elaborate robes, decorated with purple fringe and gold braid, looked much too hot to wear on a summer day and necessitated a team of servants with palm branches to keep him cool.

"So, you're the new governor of Judah?" Sanballat said when the preliminaries ended. Nehemiah detected a tone of ridicule in his voice.

"Yes, I've been appointed by the Persian emperor Artaxerxes. Here are the letters he sent to announce my appointment." He passed around the emperor's decree, watching the other leaders' reactions. Tobiah the Ammonite governed the territory east of Judah across the Jordan River and was Judah's closest neighbor. He passed the letter on after only a cursory glance. Tobiah was a popular Jewish name, meaning "the Lord is good," and he appeared to be Jewish with his traditional beard, head covering, and fringed robe. Nehemiah wondered how he had become the leader of Israel's long-standing enemies the Ammonites, descendants of Abraham's nephew, Lot. Tobiah was quiet and self-contained and hard to read. Nothing stood out about him, neither height nor weight nor facial features nor clothing, as if he wanted to blend in with the crowd and not draw attention to himself.

Geshem, ruler of the Arab tribes beyond Judah's southern border, took even less notice of Nehemiah's letter, passing it to his aide to study. The ruler of an Arab confederacy that stretched from Egypt to Arabia to southern Judah, Geshem enjoyed favored status under the Persian king and had visited his court on a yearly basis. Nehemiah remembered the bearded, dark-skinned chieftain in his flowing white robes and *keffiah*, and hoped Geshem wouldn't recognize him as a former cupbearer.

The Edomite leader, whose territory also bordered Judah

to the south, seemed to take his cue from Geshem. Only the leader of Ashdod, to the west of Judah, showed any interest in examining the decree. These men were seasoned politicians, and Nehemiah was not. But his years of service at the emperor's side had taught him a great deal, even if he had simply served the king's wine. Foremost in Nehemiah's mind was the fact that his appointment had ultimately come from the Almighty One. That alone gave him the courage to stand up to these men. The hand of the Lord God was upon him.

"What I find odd," Sanballat said, twisting one of his glittering rings, "is that we've heard no complaints from the Persian authorities about the way I've governed the Judean territories since your last governor retired. Therefore, what's the true reason why you've been sent?"

Nehemiah remained unruffled, anticipating this question. "I can't pretend to read the emperor's mind. Nevertheless, as his letter states, I will assume leadership of the province from now on. And in case there's any question of the letter's authenticity, my authority is clearly visible in the official Persian military escort that accompanied me."

Sanballat smiled coldly. "No one has questioned your credentials. You needn't be so apologetic."

"I don't recall apologizing."

"I believe I speak for the others as well as myself," Sanballat continued, "when I question why King Artaxerxes has suddenly decided that a governor is necessary at all. Judah is such a tiny, insignificant territory of little economic importance."

Nehemiah knew the Samaritan was baiting him, trying to diminish his authority by degrading his nation. He'd witnessed this maneuver among the Persian courtiers on occasion, and knew he must control his temper. "Since you regard Judah as such an insignificant territory, I'm happy to relieve you of the burden of governing it."

Sanballat ignored Nehemiah's comment and went on. "Perhaps there is simmering political or religious unrest in Judah that I was unaware of. You're a Jew, and I'm obviously not. Have you been sent to cool tempers? Eliminate agitators?"

"You would know much more about any simmering unrest than I would. I haven't even seen Jerusalem yet, nor have I met with the Jewish council leaders and priests."

Tobiah the Ammonite abruptly took over the interrogation. "Like you, I also have a Jewish ancestry. When the Babylonian army carried your forefathers into exile, mine were spared their punishment and were allowed to remain behind on our land. As the Almighty One helped my family grow and prosper and spread across the province, we came to the aid of the beleaguered Ammonites, who looked to us for leadership and direction. While you were in exile, I have enjoyed a good relationship with the Ammonite people, living and worshiping together, forming marriage and business partnerships."

Nehemiah struggled not to react to Tobiah's condescending tone or the implication that his ancestors were more deserving than Nehemiah's. Whatever else Tobiah believed, he was not a follower of the Torah if he had intermarried with Ammonites.

"We both know," Tobiah continued, "that the Judeans have a long history of rebellion against political authority. The fanatics among them claim homage only to the Holy One and will accept no king but a descendant of King David. They await a Messiah to free them from bondage to the Gentile nations. Perhaps you've come to fulfill that role, Governor Nehemiah?"

Again, Nehemiah was careful not to react to the inflammatory question. "If I'm the promised Messiah, I haven't been made aware of it. The letters of authority I carry with me are stamped with the Persian emperor's seal, not the Holy One's." He was tired of this game and eager to complete the journey to Jerusalem, sixty miles away. But he dared show no sign of weakness or weariness.

Geshem the Arab took up the questioning next, beginning

with a meandering lecture about trade routes and tariff agreements, making it clear that he enjoyed a monopoly on the spice trade. Tired as he was from the journey, Nehemiah found the speech difficult to follow. Was Geshem threatening him or asking for a bribe? Either way, Nehemiah didn't dare react. Clearly, Geshem had no intention of relinquishing the control he held over these lucrative trade routes, especially to a newly arrived Jew.

"Once I've met with my district leaders," Nehemiah said when Geshem's speech was finally finished, "you will be welcome to make an official state visit to discuss trade agreements. But I won't promise that the old agreements will remain unchanged. As governor it's my duty to make decisions that are in the best interests of my people, even if they conflict with the policies of the past." Geshem didn't reply, but his displeasure was evident in his simmering gaze before he angled his face to the side and lifted his keffiah to hide his expression.

"I'm curious, Nehemiah," Sanballat said, taking control again, "what, exactly, was your previous leadership role in Susa? What experience are you bringing to our region?"

Nehemiah formed his answer carefully to avoid a lie. "I have personally served the Persian emperor in his royal citadel in Susa for the past decade. Mine was a position of the very highest trust. King Artaxerxes is a wise and astute leader, and he never would have appointed me as Judah's governor if he didn't think I had the experience or capability to lead my people."

Sanballat gave a mocking laugh that made his stomach jiggle. "Listen, Nehemiah, I think you'll find life in Judah quite different from what you're accustomed to in Susa—in the royal citadel, no less! You'll have much to learn about how we do things out here beyond the river. But there's no need for you to begin your term as governor in complete ignorance. My aides are very experienced and quite willing to teach you how things are done in your new little territory. Why not stay here for a few days and let them brief you?"

It required all of Nehemiah's willpower not to react to Sanballat's condescending attitude or the smirk on his face. "Thank you, but there's no need. As you've said, my little territory is small and insignificant. I'm sure I'll be able to learn everything I need to know very quickly."

"As you wish," he said with a shrug. "But at least stay and enjoy our hospitality for a few days. I believe you'll find the amenities much cruder in Jerusalem than here in Samaria. And especially compared to life in Susa."

"Please don't think me rude or ungrateful. I will be happy to return to Samaria and accept your offer of hospitality at a later date. But for now, you must understand that I have traveled more than a thousand miles. I am very eager to reach my destination before I rest."

"Another time, then?"

"Certainly. Another time."

⋄⟫ ⟪⋄

Tobiah watched Judah's new governor walk out the door and wondered if all his hard work and political ambitions had just walked out the door with him. Without warning and appearing out of nowhere, this upstart newcomer threatened to undo all of Tobiah's careful political maneuvering, toppling the network of business and social relationships he had nurtured in Jerusalem all these years. The muscles in Tobiah's hands ached from bunching them into fists. His head throbbed from clenching his jaw, but he wouldn't reveal his distress to Sanballat or anyone else. The Samaritan governor would ask what was wrong, and Tobiah didn't want to reveal his long-held plans to annex Judah and Jerusalem to his own Ammonite province.

Tobiah was standing in the courtyard outside Sanballat's throne room after the meeting, waiting for his servants to finish their preparations for the journey home, when one of Sanballat's servants approached. "The governor would like to meet with you in his private chambers." The servant spoke softly so none of the other provincial leaders could overhear him.

"Now?" Tobiah asked.

"Yes, my lord. Follow me, please."

Tobiah wished he had more time to recover his balance after meeting Nehemiah, but refusing this request would raise too many questions. He followed the servant to Sanballat's private quarters, where he found the Samaritan and Geshem the Arab already waiting. The room had cushioned seats and a table with flasks of water and wine and bowls of grapes and dates. But neither of the men were sitting down or eating. Tobiah had worked closely with these powerful men for several years and could see that they were as disturbed by this new Jewish leader as he was. "What did you think of Judah's new governor?" he asked the other two.

Sanballat twisted one of the heavy rings he wore on his fingers, exposing his unease. "I found Nehemiah a very difficult man to read. No sign of vain pride or temper, even when provoked. I think he'll be hard to intimidate."

"And possibly even harder to bribe," Geshem added. The Arab chief paced near the window, his long robe trailing across the worn carpet, his keffiah shadowing his dark face.

"Everyone has a weak point," Sanballat said, pulling his ring off and shoving it on again. "We simply don't know Nehemiah's weaknesses, yet. We'll give him a measure of control, let him think he's in charge—"

"It isn't a question of *giving* him control," Tobiah said. "You saw the decree he carried. It's from the emperor himself. Nehemiah *is* in control of Judah—and he knows it!"

"I find it very disturbing that someone has come to promote the welfare of the Jews," Geshem said. "They're so much easier to handle when they're leaderless and beaten down."

"Yes, I'm upset about that, too," Sanballat agreed. "We've

worked hard to keep them submissive. I don't like the fact that they now have an advocate. And a savvy one, from all appearances."

"Not only is he an advocate for the Jews," Geshem added, "he claims to have worked closely with the Persian emperor himself. I've been to Susa; I don't recall ever meeting this man."

"Didn't you find it odd that he was so young?" Tobiah asked. "Or that he had the bearing and build of a soldier instead of a diplomat?"

"I want to know what he's up to," Sanballat said. "I think he's dangerous."

"The entire situation is dangerous," Tobiah agreed. "We've maintained a nice balance of power here since their last governor retired. We've kept the Jews in their places, living in a state of fear—and profited nicely at the same time."

"As governor of The Land Beyond the River," Sanballat said, "I still hold a great deal of power. And I will not allow that to change. Nehemiah will learn to submit to my authority or suffer for it."

"*Your* authority?" Tobiah's hold over his temper began to slip. "What about the emperor's decree? It was sealed with his ring. Nehemiah is the governor of Judah from now on, not you." And not Tobiah, either, or his son Jehohanan, whom he'd been grooming to rule with him. If anyone should suddenly appear on the scene as the Jewish savior and sit in the governor's residence in Jerusalem, Tobiah thought it should be him. He had the experience, the political and religious connections.

Sanballat sat down and lifted a cluster of grapes from the plate, popping them into his mouth one by one with a show of nonchalance. "It doesn't matter. There's little Nehemiah can do to change the Jews' situation. He'll soon learn the value of cooperating with me—and the pain of not cooperating. Nevertheless, until he does, we can't take our eyes off him for a moment."

"What's your plan for keeping an eye on his activities?"

Geshem asked. The Arab leader's furrowed brows and hawk-like nose made him look fierce, combative. Tobiah knew the value of keeping him as an ally.

"I have eyes and ears in Jerusalem," Sanballat said. "The high priest's grandson is married to my daughter. Rest assured that I'm monitoring all of the activities of the religious leaders."

"And my son Jehohanan lives in Jerusalem," Tobiah added. "His father-in-law, a man named Meshullam, is on the ruling council. They keep me informed about everything that happens in the council meetings. Believe me, some of the local leaders will be as concerned as we are that an outsider is taking charge."

"What's more," Sanballat added, pouring wine from the flask into a cup, "my hometown of Beth Horon is only a few miles north of Jerusalem along one of the main roads into the city. I have eyes and ears there, too. Come, gentlemen. Let's sit and enjoy a toast to our continued prosperity. We'll either win this newcomer Nehemiah to our side or make sure that everything he attempts to do ends in failure."

Tobiah refused the offered cup, knowing it would only seethe in his stomach. "I want to know the real reason he was appointed. Judah's last governor, Ezra, was primarily a religious leader, and he created havoc and confusion among my people with all his bans on intermarriage."

"Mine, as well," Sanballat said. "But this time the king's decree said nothing about religious reforms."

"So why send a political leader? And why now?" Tobiah asked.

"That's the big question." Sanballat took a sip of wine and set down the cup. "But if Nehemiah worked as closely with King Artaxerxes as he claims he did, in a position of highest trust, I can't help wondering why he was sent to such a remote, backward territory. It doesn't make sense."

Long after the private meeting ended and Tobiah returned to his home across the Jordan River, he continued to worry about Nehemiah's true agenda. When he could no longer calm his fears, he called his two closest aides into his chambers and confided in them. "Go to Jerusalem, to my son Jehohanan, and tell him I need to know exactly why Nehemiah is here. What is he up to? Why has he come? Follow the man day and night, and don't come back until you have answers."

CHAPTER

9

THE DISTRICT OF BETH HAKKEREM

T hat's my father's house up ahead."

Nava looked up from the dusty road and saw her new master's son pointing to a cluster of stately stone buildings perched on the hilltop in front of them. He hadn't spoken a word to her on the journey, nor had he stopped or slowed the donkey's plodding pace to allow her to rest. But Nava halted now in the middle of the road to stare at the home that would be hers for the next six years. A high stone wall encircled the house and barns. Terraced vineyards, guarded by watchtowers, covered the hillsides. Dozens of laborers harvested wheat in the field on the opposite side of the road, and Nava wondered if she would be sent to work alongside them. She saw an olive grove, vegetable gardens, orchards, and pastures, and shivered at the sight of so much land. Why did Malkijah need Abba's farm or his wheat crop if he already owned all of this?

Her master's son hadn't stopped, and Nava had to hurry to catch up with him again. She was breathless from the climb by the time they arrived at one of the entrances into the walled compound. A servant rushed forward to help the master's son dismount, then led the donkey away. "Come on. This way," Malkijah's son said, gesturing impatiently. Nava followed him through a maze of structures and courtyards completely enclosed by the stone walls. There were pens for the animals, living areas for her new masters and their workers, open areas where servants performed a variety of tasks, barns filled with hay, and storehouses full of clay containers. She glimpsed a winepress and an olive press. Nava hurried to keep up as her young master led her through a large kitchen courtyard with ovens and cooking hearths and then into an outdoor dining room with a trellised roof, covered with flowering vines. Could a king's palace be any grander than this? She gazed around in wonder and nearly ran into the son's back when he halted suddenly. Her new master, Malkijah ben Recab, came out to stand beneath the trellis in his impeccable white robe, his arms folded across his chest.

"Here's your new bondservant, Father," his son said.

"Thank you, Aaron." Malkijah appraised Nava as Aaron disappeared into the house behind him. Her mouth felt dry as she stood beneath his scrutiny. "Tell me your name," he finally said.

"Nava."

"You're very young."

"I'm nearly seventeen, my lord." She couldn't help trembling and was distressed to hear that it showed in her voice.

"I'm guessing you don't have much experience working in a house as large and lavish as this one."

She stared at him, too shocked to reply. Was he shaming her because her family was poor? Because she had arrived barefooted and in rags? She wanted to shout at him, tell him how happy her home was. How there was laughter and love inside her family's humble walls, that those things were worth millions compared to gold and other luxuries. But then he smiled, a crooked smile that twisted only half of his mouth. She was surprised to see kindness in his eyes. "You don't need to be afraid, Nava. I'm only trying to determine the best job for you to do here. What kind of work do you enjoy?"

She drew a deep breath and exhaled to calm herself. "I used to take care of Abba's goats, but you own them now. I used to milk them every day and make yogurt and cheese."

He smiled again. "Then that's what you'll do here. Penina is in charge of my kitchen, and Shimon tends my goats. You will be under their authority, and you'll need to do whatever work they require of you. Understand?"

"Yes, my lord."

"Good. Go through that gate right over there, and you'll find Penina in the kitchen courtyard. Tell her I said to show you to your quarters."

"Yes, my lord."

Nava crossed the courtyard on shaky legs. Her heart sped up as she neared the gate and heard a woman shouting on the other side of the wall. "You let the fire get too hot, you fool! Didn't I warn you to be careful adding wood? Now you've burned the master's bread, wasted his food! This will be your portion to eat tonight and tomorrow and the next day, burned or not!"

Nava slipped through the gate and into an enormous kitchen courtyard, twice the size of her entire house. Servants washed and chopped vegetables at wooden tables, sorted lentils and beans. One servant ground grain into flour with a hand mill, another kneaded dough. The heat from the hearth fire and clay oven pressed against Nava from across the yard, and she smelled the burnt bread. Presiding over the bustle was the shouting woman, who must be Penina. From the volume of her voice, Nava had expected to see a much larger woman, but Penina was short and thin and birdlike. She reminded Nava of the little wheatears that nested in Abba's fruit trees. Penina finished her tirade by giving the hapless servant boy a cuff on the ear that made him wince.

Nava was afraid to move, afraid to speak. She closed the

gate behind her and took a few steps inside, waiting for Penina to turn around and notice her. "Who are you?" Penina asked when she finally did.

"My name is Nava. I just arrived today. My master sent me to see you."

"Not *another* one!" She clucked her tongue, shaking her head. "Sent you to do what? I hope you know how to work hard, because I don't have time to teach you."

Nava could barely swallow around the lump in her throat. "Master Malkijah said I should help tend the goats. I know how to milk them and make cheese and yogurt from their milk. And he said I should help you with your work when I'm finished." To Nava's dismay, her eyes suddenly filled with tears. She feared Penina would shout at her for weeping, but instead, the little woman's demeanor softened as she looked Nava over, taking in her raggedy robe and bare feet.

"First time away from home, is it?" Nava could only nod as her tears spilled down her dusty face. "If you work hard and do as you're told, you'll get along just fine. . . . Rachel!" She shouted at a pretty, dark-haired woman chopping onions.

The woman laid down her knife and scurried over. "Here I am."

"Show Nava where to put her things. She can sleep next to you. Then take her to the goat pen to meet Shimon." Nava started to follow Rachel. "Wait!" Penina called. "Where are your shoes?"

"In here," she said, holding up her bag. "The strap keeps breaking. I could fix them if I had a bit of leather."

"When the stable boy comes with the straw for your pallet, tell him what you need. All right, everyone!" she said, clapping her hands. "Stop standing around! You can gawk at our new servant after your work is done."

Rachel led Nava to a low, narrow stone building with a rough-beamed ceiling and dirt floor. Inside, piles of straw pallets lay neatly stacked near the walls and the floor looked newly swept. "We share this room with the other women servants," Rachel said. She pointed to a wall of built-in shelves filled with neatly folded blankets. "Find an empty space and put your blanket in it."

"I didn't bring a blanket. I didn't know . . ."

"Well, put your other things in it, then."

Nava hurried across the room and stuffed the bag she had carried from home into one of the openings, then turned back to Rachel.

The woman smiled. "Poor little thing. You look like a scared lamb. Don't worry, you'll be fine. Penina shouts a lot, but you don't have to be afraid of her."

"Have you worked here very long?"

"About two years."

"I'm working to help my father pay back his debts."

Rachel nodded. "My husband owes money, too. Our children were too young to be bondservants—our son was three when I left and our daughter was five. So . . . here I am."

"Who's taking care of them?"

"My husband's mother." For a moment, tears glistened in Rachel's eyes. Then she regained control. "It's not so bad here," she said with an unconvincing smile. "At least we have plenty to eat and a warm fire when the weather gets cold. Come on, I'll show you the goat pen."

It was a very large enclosure with a manger of fresh hay for the animals and a trough of water. Nava spotted her own goats mixed in with all the others, and it was like seeing old friends in a crowd of strangers. "Come here . . ." she said, calling and whistling to them. "Come here and let me see you." One goat recognized her voice and ran to the side of the fence where Nava stood. The animal's stubbly fur tickled her cheek as she reached through the slats to hug her. "Look at you," she murmured. "Look how fat you've grown! They must be feeding you very well."

"Hey! Get away from those goats!"

The man who hobbled over, shaking his shepherd's crook at Nava, was white-haired and crippled with age. She remembered that his name was Shimon and quickly explained who she was.

"My new master said I should help you take care of them," she finished. "This one and some of the others used to be mine."

"Well . . . I suppose I could use some help." His voice resembled a growl. "Just remember that I'm in charge of them, not you. Don't do anything without asking."

"I'll remember."

"They've already been milked this morning. And fed. The boy delivered the milk to Penina."

"Should I come back later when it's time to milk them again?"

"You do that." He shuffled away.

"Shimon seems very old for a bondservant," Nava whispered to Rachel as they walked back to the kitchen area.

"Didn't you see the ring in his ear? That means he's here for life. Some masters kick out their elderly servants when they're too old to work. But our master finds ways for them to still be useful. He would never turn Shimon away and let him starve."

Nava followed Rachel through the gate and back into the kitchen courtyard, where the work continued nonstop. Rachel returned to her chopping board and Nava was about to ask Penina if she should make cheese with the goats' milk when the little woman turned to her and asked, "Can you sew?" Nava nodded. "That cloth sack over there is for your pallet. A stable boy is coming with some straw to stuff it. I'll give you another job when you're finished with it."

Mercifully, Nava's first day passed swiftly. Between sewing her pallet, making cheese, and milking dozens of goats with Shimon, she didn't have time to think about her family or Dan until she lay down on her new pallet that night. That's when the aching loneliness clutched her chest, shaking her like a helpless animal in the teeth of a predator. She rolled over to face Rachel on the pallet beside hers and saw in the moonlight streaming through the open window that she was still awake. "Rachel? Do we ever get a day off to go home and visit our families?" she whispered.

"Master always gives us the Sabbath day off. Penina has kitchen workers like me prepare twice as much food on the eve of Shabbat so there will be enough to eat. You'll probably still have to tend Master's flock in the morning, but the rest of the day will be yours."

"I'll be able to go home?"

"No . . . no, that's not possible." Rachel's sigh seemed to fill the room and settle over Nava like fog. "Most of us live more than a Sabbath day's walk away. Besides, our master says the roads are much too dangerous to travel alone."

"You mean . . . you haven't seen your husband or children in two years? Don't you miss them?"

Rachel's eyes glistened with tears in the moonlight. "More than I can say. But maybe it's better for my little ones if they forget me. They cried so hard when I had to say good-bye. And they're too young to understand why I would have to keep leaving them again and again."

Nava thought she might die if she couldn't see the people she loved for six years. She felt a cry of grief rising in her chest, and she rolled over onto her stomach to muffle it, burying her face in her new pallet. The stiff straw, poking through the rough cloth, scratched her skin like tiny claws.

Chapter
10

JERUSALEM
JULY

Three days after leaving Sanballat's palace in Samaria, Nehemiah stood overlooking his destination for the first time. Jerusalem, city of his ancestors, lay below him. His breath caught at the wonder of it—and also at the desolation of it. Piles of rubble and burnt stones lay scattered everywhere. The entire western hill looked like a ghost town with vacant buildings and barren, windswept streets. The temple on the hill above the city was a huge disappointment. Plain and unadorned, it had none of the splendor and magnificence of the pagan temples he'd seen in Susa.

Below it, the tiny portion of the city that had been rebuilt lay vulnerable and unprotected, the clay roofs baking beneath the summer sky. A few ragged remnants of the city wall stood intact, but they were insignificant beside the toppled portions and gaping breaches where gates had once stood. The sight reminded him of an old man's mouth with too many missing and decaying teeth. What was he doing here? What could one man possibly hope to accomplish?

As Nehemiah continued to stare at the depressing sight, the

captain of the Persian guards came to stand beside him. "The sun will set soon, my lord. We should prepare our camp."

"Of course, of course," Nehemiah said, struggling to recover. He pointed to the valley that lay west of the inhabited section. "We'll camp down there in that central valley. I understand there's a reservoir or a spring of some sort on the southwestern side of the city."

"Very well." The captain started to leave, then turned back when Nehemiah didn't move. "Aren't you coming, my lord?"

He shook his head. "My brothers live here in the city. I want to see them first."

"My men and I will accompany you there." The Persian was about to signal to the others when Nehemiah stopped him.

"There's no need. Set up camp without me."

"I cannot do that, my lord. You are the king's appointed governor, and it's my duty to protect you at all times."

Nehemiah understood the captain's concern. Hadn't it been his job to protect King Artaxerxes at all times? "You were duty-bound to protect me only as far as Jerusalem. And you've done that. Splendidly. You and your men are now free to return to Susa after you've rested and replenished your supplies."

"Where are the local soldiers who will take over our duties?"

Nehemiah faced the stark truth for the first time, and his stomach turned at the memory of his parents' helplessness. "There aren't any."

The captain rested his hand on the hilt of his sword as if preparing to draw it. "At the meeting in Samaria, each regional leader had his own militia. Where is yours? Who will now be responsible for your safety?"

Nehemiah started to say "No one," then changed his mind. "My safety is in the Almighty One's hands from now on."

"That seems foolhardy, my lord . . . if I may say so." The captain met Nehemiah's gaze for a long moment. This wasn't the first time they had locked horns. Accustomed to swift travel, the Persian captain neither understood nor agreed with Nehemiah's decision to rest for a full day every Sabbath. Nehemiah had stood his ground—the first test of his leadership—knowing that if he remained faithful to the Almighty One and His laws by keeping the Sabbath day holy, God would help him accomplish his goal of rebuilding Jerusalem's walls. A goal that seemed nearly impossible now as he gazed at the city in the fading daylight.

"Perhaps I am being foolhardy, Captain. But as you've just pointed out, I am the governor of this province, and so the decision is mine to make. You and your men will set up camp without me, and I'll join you later. I don't want to upset the citizens of Jerusalem by marching into town with a troop of Persian soldiers." Nehemiah placed his horse's reins in the captain's hand and strode off toward the city without looking back, following the dusty road toward one of the gaping holes where a gate once stood. He didn't get far before discovering that he and his caravan of soldiers had already attracted attention. A small delegation of men stood in the gateway, waiting for him.

"Have you come in peace?" their leader asked. The man kneaded his pudgy hands, as if squeezing water from them.

"Yes. Yes, of course I come in peace." Nehemiah spread his hands to show that he was unarmed. "My name is Nehemiah ben Hacaliah, and I'm a son of Abraham, like you. I'm looking for my brothers, Ephraim and Hananiah. Can you tell me where they live?" He decided not to reveal his role as their new governor yet, hoping for one undisturbed night with his family before making the announcement.

"Of course. I know the two sons of Hacaliah very well," the leader said. "Welcome to our city. I'm Shallum ben Hallohesh, ruler of the half-district of Jerusalem." He attempted a welcoming grin, but it looked unconvincing. As soon as it faded, the worry lines fell back into place on his face. "And the soldiers, my lord? They've come in peace, as well?"

"They're merely an escort. Don't worry, they'll be returning to Susa very soon. Now, if you could direct me . . . ?" He smiled at the knot of men and added, "I was hoping to surprise my brothers. They don't know I'm coming."

"I'll take you," one of the younger men offered. "My name is Jehohanan ben Tobiah. Follow me." They left the others with their unasked questions and entered the city. Nehemiah glanced over his shoulder as they started down the sloping streets of the city of David and saw the men still huddled together, watching him. "Some of us were hoping the soldiers would stay," the young man told Nehemiah as they walked. "Our city has become very unsafe. In fact, our entire district of Judah is unsafe. Your Persian soldiers could help stop the violence."

"I'm sorry, but they aren't mine to command. Nor are they authorized to remain here."

"That's too bad." The man didn't speak again, and a few minutes later they halted near the bottom of the hill in the lower part of the city. Nehemiah's guide gestured to a modest stone house. "This is it."

"Thank you very much." He waited until the man turned around and begin trudging back up the hill. By now the sun had set behind the western hills, but the sky remained bright with warm summer light. Nehemiah peered over the gate into his brother's courtyard and saw Hanani and his family seated outside on cushions around a low table. They were about to eat, and Hanani gently hushed his two children, who were talking at the same time, competing for his attention. Nehemiah was reluctant to disturb the cozy scene as he watched his brother recite the blessing over the bread, reminded of his own childhood with his two brothers. Before Nehemiah had a chance to interrupt, Hanani looked up and saw him. He bolted to his feet, startling his family and nearly toppling the table.

"Am I seeing things? Nehemiah?" He rushed to the gate,

LYNN AUSTIN

yanking it open with clumsy hands, and pulled Nehemiah into a bear hug. "I can't believe it! Is it really you?"

"Yes, of course it's me!" he said, laughing.

"But . . . how? What in the world are you doing here?"

"I missed you after you left. I decided to pay you a visit."

"You're a crazy man! Wait until Ephraim sees you! He won't believe it!" Hanani ran to the low wall that separated his courtyard from the next one shouting, "Ephraim, get over here! Come see who's here! You won't believe your eyes!"

A moment later, Nehemiah's middle brother appeared at the gate to his house next door. "What's all this shouting? We're trying to eat our dinner in peace and—" He froze when he saw Nehemiah. "I must be dreaming!" He stared in astonishment for a long moment before racing forward to hug him as Hanani had done. He made no effort to hold back his tears as Nehemiah crushed him in an embrace, lifting him off the ground. "This is a miracle! A miracle!" Ephraim breathed. "I thought I'd never see you again!"

"I know. Me too. Let me look at you, Ephraim." He held him at arm's length for a moment. "You've barely changed since I saw you last."

"Neither have you." Ephraim beckoned to his wife who stood near the gate. A small boy clung to her leg, staring at them wide-eyed. "Come meet my brother Nehemiah—he's your uncle—all the way from Susa, the capital of Persia! This is my wife and son." Hanani's wife and children were also on their feet waiting to be introduced.

"I can tell you're all brothers," Ephraim's wife said. "You resemble each other."

"Except that Nehemiah's built like a stone wall and we're . . . well, we're just a pair of lazy scribes," Ephraim said, laughing.

"Have you eaten?" Hanani's wife asked. "Come sit down and join us. We've just begun."

He let himself be escorted into the courtyard and was given

something to drink while the two women bustled around preparing a place for him to sit and combining their two meals into one.

"What are you doing here?" Hanani asked again. "I'm thrilled to see you, but how in the world did you get here? And what about your career in the palace?"

"God's hand was upon me, Hanani, and He answered our prayers. He made a way for me to speak my request to King Artaxerxes—"

"And you still have your head?"

"Yes," he said, laughing. "He let me keep my head. I told him how the city of our ancestors lay in ruins with their tombs disgraced, and he granted me a leave of absence to come here."

"Praise God!" Hanani murmured.

"I don't understand. Our ancestors' tombs . . . ?" Ephraim asked. "Do we even know where they are? And what do you intend to do with these tombs once you find them?"

Nehemiah couldn't help grinning. "Well . . . that's not the only thing I came here to do. The emperor appointed me Governor of Judah."

"What! That's unbelievable!"

"You're joking, right?" Ephraim added.

"I'm not joking. I've already met with our neighboring provincial leaders in Samaria, including Governor Sanballat, and showed them my official commission as Judah's governor, sealed by the emperor himself."

"Did you hear that, Ephraim? Our big brother is the new governor!"

"Very impressive! Maybe we should get him a throne to sit on instead of an ordinary cushion." The three of them laughed, and for a moment it was as if they were boys again, before the tragedy that had changed their lives had ever happened. By now the women had the table ready and everyone sat down. Nehemiah's mouth watered in anticipation as they passed around the food and filled their plates.

"How did you get here?" Ephraim asked. "How long did it take? You didn't travel all this way by yourself, did you?"

"The emperor assigned a detachment of Persian soldiers to escort me and—"

"Soldiers! Are you joking?"

Nehemiah shook his head as he scooped up a mouthful of lentils with his bread. "We had a good trip with no problems along the way, so it only took us two months. We traveled much faster than you did thirteen years ago because we weren't transporting women and children and household goods."

"Or several tons of gold and silver," Hanani added. "Remember that, Ephraim?" He nodded, his mouth full of food.

"But I noticed," Nehemiah continued, "that the farther we traveled from the Persian capital, the poorer everything looked. And once we reached The Land Beyond the River . . . well, it was like entering a different world."

"We haven't had a decent rain in two years," Ephraim said.

"I believe it. The dust swirled around us in huge clouds with every step we took. The fields and trees were blanketed with it. And I saw evidence of the crippling taxes Hanani told me about." He didn't want to think about it, but as Judah's governor, it would be his responsibility to deal with these issues, to help his people survive the drought and recover financially. He swallowed another bite of the spicy lentils. "Mmm, this is delicious. It's the first real meal I've eaten in two months."

"Have some more," Hanani's wife said, passing the bowl.

They talked and laughed as Nehemiah devoured the food, and it was as if he'd never been separated from his brothers. Each had married a sweet, pretty wife—both of them excellent cooks—and he found he envied his brothers' happy, domesticated lives. He watched Hanani caress his son, who had crawled onto his lap after dinner, and he thought of their father, a bear of a man, who had been as gentle as a lamb with Nehemiah and his brothers. But as night fell and the first lamps were lit,

Nehemiah grew restless, every little sound in the distant darkness putting him on edge. Nothing stood between his brothers' homes and the murky valley and rubble-strewn hills beyond. A determined thief or murderer could creep up on them in the shadows and enter their homes with no trouble at all.

Hanani saw him gazing out at the hills to the west after they'd eaten. "So what do you think of Jerusalem?" he asked.

"To tell you the truth, I had to look away after my first glimpse of it. With so much rubble spread across that western hill it was hard to tell if the city was being rebuilt or torn down."

"Hanani and I were disappointed, too, when we first arrived here with Rebbe Ezra. I guess we're used to it now and don't even notice the desolation anymore."

"That's the *Mishneh* out there," Hanani said, pointing. "The city's 'second quarter.' They say it was originally built during King Hezekiah's time when the Assyrians attacked the northern tribes. Jerusalem tripled in size back then because of all the refugees."

"No one lives there now," Hanani said. "There aren't enough of us to populate it. Jerusalem is a city of homes and buildings in the middle of ruins. The new construction hasn't caught up with all the destruction yet."

"Besides, it's too dangerous to live out there," Ephraim added. "It's become a hideout for vagrants and thieves. Make sure you don't travel alone after dark without your escort of soldiers."

"My escort won't be staying very long. They're returning to Susa without me after they've rested and gathered supplies." He saw his brothers exchange glances and remembered how his young guide had also wished that the soldiers would stay. He pictured the huge gaps he'd seen in Jerusalem's walls, and for the second time that evening, he battled a rising tide of hopelessness. Nehemiah trusted his brothers, but he decided not to reveal his plan yet to rebuild those walls. Not until he'd had a chance to survey the project himself.

"Stay here tonight," Ephraim said when Nehemiah was ready to leave. "Don't go out there alone."

Nehemiah started to argue, then realized that if he did leave, his brothers would insist on accompanying him. Unwilling to put them in danger, he spent his first night in Jerusalem at his brother Ephraim's house.

The next morning the three of them walked up the hill together to worship in God's holy temple for the first time. Their mentor, Mordecai, had made sure Nehemiah and his brothers had studied the Torah, so he was very familiar with all the sacrifices and offerings and their significance. His studies had created a picture in his mind of what Solomon's Temple must have looked like in all its glory, and this second temple paled in comparison to what he'd imagined. The Babylonians had demolished the walls that surrounded and protected it, stealing all the gold and bronze that once adorned it. Yet this was still the one place on earth where God had chosen to meet with His people.

Nehemiah's studies hadn't prepared him for the emotions he experienced as he watched the lamb being slain, knowing that it had died for his sins, knowing that when the pillar of smoke ascended to heaven, those sins were forgiven. His joy was indescribable. As the congregation bowed in prayer, Nehemiah's prayer also ascended to heaven. *Lord, you've given me this task of restoring Jerusalem's walls, and your gracious hand has been with me. Help me in the days and weeks ahead. I can't do this without you.*

On his second day in Jerusalem, Nehemiah visited Ezra. He found the white-haired rebbe behind his worktable in the temple's archives, nearly buried beneath piles of scrolls and clay tablets. Ezra looked up from his writing as Nehemiah introduced himself and greeted him with a smile and a warm welcome. "That explains the Persian soldiers down in the valley," Ezra said. "I was hoping we weren't going to be conquered a second time before I had a chance to finish writing my chronicles. Please, have a seat—if you can find one, that is—and tell me what brings you here."

Nehemiah cleared a stack of parchment from a chair and sat down, holding his papers on his lap. He showed Ezra the decree from King Artaxerxes with his appointment as governor. "I know you served as Judah's governor in the past, Rebbe Ezra, so I came to ask if you had any advice for me."

Ezra leaned back in his seat, studying him for a moment. "I was essentially a spiritual leader," he finally said, "entrusted with the task of religious reform. Not an easy job after more than one hundred years in exile. Babylon had invaded our people's hearts and minds in ways that are much more insidious than the invasion of our land. I'm still not certain how much lasting progress I've made."

"My commission is a political one, not a religious one," Nehemiah said. Once again, he decided not to mention his real mission until after he'd surveyed the walls and had drawn up a plan.

"Judah needs a strong, decisive leader," Ezra said. "But be prepared for opposition."

"From Judah's enemies?"

"Certainly from them. But also from some of the powerful landowners and noblemen among us who will see you as an outsider, infringing on their right to govern the land and the city."

Nehemiah was taken aback. "I wasn't expecting resistance from our own people."

"You'll get some, I'm sure. But once you've convinced them that you're in charge, most of them will work with you."

He would need all of them to work with him; he couldn't possibly accomplish such a huge task alone. "I stopped in Samaria on my way here and presented the king's decree with my commission to Governor Sanballat, Tobiah the Ammonite, Geshem the Arab leader, and a few of the other neighboring rulers."

"A smart move on your part. But don't trust our Gentile neighbors, not even for a second. Ever since this little patch of earth became a Jewish homeland again, they've been conspiring to accomplish what the Assyrians and the Babylonians and Haman the Agagite failed to do—which is to make sure every last Jew is buried in his grave. I recommend that you hold on to the Almighty One's words to Joshua when he became the leader of our people: 'Be strong and courageous—'"

"'Do not be terrified; do not be discouraged,'" Nehemiah finished, "'for the Lord your God will be with you wherever you go.'"

"Exactly. God also told Joshua not to make treaties with the Gentiles and not to intermarry with them. That's still very good advice."

"Thank you, Rebbe. I'm grateful for your counsel. And I would be even more grateful for your prayers." A sense of urgency made Nehemiah sit forward in his seat as he pictured Jerusalem's crumbling walls. "So tell me, what's the best way to win the support of the Jewish leaders and nobles?"

"Don't cater to them," Ezra said, shaking his head. "Take a stand. Lead them. The civic leaders and the religious leaders each have their own special interests, and they don't always agree with each other. If you try to walk a careful line between them, keeping them both placated, you'll never accomplish anything. Neither side was happy when I announced my mission to enforce Torah law, but I ignored all of them and did the work God gave me to do. Make your decisions and stick to them."

"That's good to know." Nehemiah wouldn't ask for their support in rebuilding the walls, he would expect it. Demand it. And if they refused, he would do it without their help.

"Be careful whom you trust," Ezra added. "Eliashib the high priest is the head of the religious leaders, but he has close ties with Governor Sanballat by marriage. Some of our civic leaders also have close connections with the Gentile nations around us."

"Do you think these men will act as spies, keeping an eye on me and reporting back?"

"No doubt they will."

Nehemiah sat back in his chair again. "That's sobering."

"Now let me ask you a question, if I may. Why you, Nehemiah ben Hacaliah? Why were you chosen to lead us?"

"I wondered the same thing when I saw Jerusalem for the first time yesterday. I was living in Susa, serving as King Artaxerxes' cupbearer, when my brother Hanani came with the Judean delegation. He told me about the situation here in the city, and ever since then, I couldn't get Jerusalem out of my mind. I began fasting and praying, asking God what I could do, and He made a way for me to present my request to the king. Artaxerxes granted me a leave of absence and gave me a commission as governor. And here I am."

"Do you feel called by the Holy One for this task?"

Nehemiah took a moment to reply. "Yes. Very much so."

"Good. Then don't let anyone or anything discourage you or keep you from your mission. When the Almighty One gives us a job to do, we can expect two things: both strength and wisdom from God and opposition from His enemies. Be strong and very courageous. You'll be in my prayers."

"Thank you, Rebbe. That means a great deal to me." The strain Nehemiah had felt since arriving in Jerusalem lifted for just a moment, knowing he had Ezra's support.

"Now," Ezra said, rising from his chair. "I would be very pleased if you would share dinner with my family and me this evening."

The invitation surprised Nehemiah. His responsibilities back in Susa had made it difficult for him to socialize. "I would be honored to come."

"Excellent. I'll tell my wife, Devorah, to expect a guest."

THE DISTRICT OF BETH HAKKEREM

Every day Nava's master, Malkijah, walked through the grounds of his estate, surveying his storehouses and flocks, vineyards and orchards, making sure that the work was being done exactly the way he wanted. He was firm with his servants but not cruel, and so far, Nava could find no fault with the way he treated her and the others. But he kept all of his servants on edge as they tried to perform their daily tasks to his high standards. This morning when Nava looked up from her work, she saw that he had brought his two sons, Aaron and Josef, on his inspection tour. When they stopped beside the pen where she and Shimon prepared to milk the goats, the sight of all three of her masters watching her made her as skittish as a sparrow. Shimon hobbled over to greet the men as Nava led the first goat to the stool to be milked.

"I see you still haven't taken the flock out to the grazing lands, Shimon," she heard Malkijah say.

"Not enough water or food for them out there. We'd risk losing the weaker ones."

"But since they aren't foraging, that means they're eating more feed than usual for this time of year."

"That's true, my lord."

Nava paused to hear what her master would say next, dreading what it might be. "Select my best milk goats, Shimon, and cull the rest."

"Of course, my lord."

She closed her eyes as sorrow tightened her throat. Her goats were among the weakest. Raised under harsher conditions than her master's, they didn't produce as much milk. Even the small joy these "friends" from home had given her might soon be lost.

She opened her eyes again, determined not to cry, and did her job quickly, coaxing out the last drops of milk. Then she waded into the herd to capture another goat and tethered it beside the low stool. Nava risked a glance at her masters as she sat down and saw Malkijah calling to the boy who helped clean the pens. He was ten years old and newly arrived from another desperate family who couldn't repay their debts. The boy hurried over, standing mute with dread before his masters.

"You're supposed to say, 'Here I am,'" Aaron told him.

"He's new here, Aaron," Malkijah soothed. "Give him time to learn."

"Well, that's why I'm teaching him," Aaron said. "From now on, boy, when your master calls, you must drop what you're doing and run to stand before him and say, 'Here I am.'"

The boy's voice shook as he stammered, "H-here I am." Nava understood his fear, and she ached for him.

"You missed the corners," Malkijah said, his voice kind, not harsh. He pointed to an area the boy had supposedly shoveled clean. "That isn't good enough. Do it over again, please."

"Y-yes, my lord." The boy nearly tripped over his own feet as he hurried to fetch the shovel. Nava rose to catch another goat, and she reached out to touch the boy's shoulder as he passed, trying her best to give him a reassuring smile.

"Shimon, that animal over there with the brown spots . . .

is she limping?" Malkijah asked. It was one of Nava's goats. How had her master seen the slight limp from clear across the enclosure?

"One of the bigger goats pushed her against the fence," Shimon replied. "I'm keeping my eye on her."

"Good. You may return to your work."

Shimon led another animal to his milking stool beside Nava's and sank down on it with a grunt. He had told her that his joints gave him pain each time he sat down or stood up. "What's taking so long, girlie?" he said in his customary growl. The old man's gruffness meant nothing. By the end of her first week of work, Nava had discovered Shimon's gentle nature beneath the gruff façade. "You have a nice way with the animals, girlie," he had told her, and they had been friends ever since.

"I wish our masters wouldn't watch us," she whispered.

"Just ignore them and do your work."

She bent to her task, resting her forehead against the goat's side.

Across the pen, one of her master's sons asked a question that Nava couldn't hear. But she heard Malkijah's response: "I worked hard for what I have. That's why I want my sons to learn every aspect of running this estate firsthand. The two most important things to watch out for are laziness and waste. They not only will ruin us, but they are insults to the Holy One, who has helped us prosper."

There was no doubt at all that Master Malkijah's estate was prosperous, his wealth unimaginable. His clothing came from the finest wool, the softest linen, dyed with the most expensive colors. He enjoyed plentiful food, and his servants ate well, too. But as Nava had already noticed, he reserved his harshest criticism for servants who were lazy or wasteful.

"I'll be working in my vineyard for the rest of the day," he told his sons.

"Do we have to come with you?" Josef asked. "It's too hot out there."

Nava knew what it was like to work beneath the blazing summer sun, yet she had always been willing to help her father.

"No, I want you to work with Shimon in the animal pens today. I want you to become familiar with everything he does and with the animals in his care. There is a great deal he can teach you."

"Yes, Father."

"We promise."

Nava's mouth went dry at the thought of being watched as she worked alongside Shimon all day. A few minutes later, Malkijah left for his vineyard, leaving his sons behind. Nava heard them laughing as they whispered together. They were up to something. The moment their father was out of sight, they turned their backs on the goat pen and walked away. "Don't you dare tell our father," Aaron called over his shoulder to Shimon as he sauntered toward the house, "or you'll be sorry."

Their disobedience stunned Nava. She thought of Dan and of her own two brothers. They would never dream of doing such a thing or being so disrespectful to their father. She and Shimon finished the milking, and as she carried the wooden buckets of fresh goats' milk to Penina in the kitchen, she heard laughter coming from Malkijah's wine cellar. Aaron and Josef emerged from inside the cavelike interior, each with a skin of stolen wine. Nava tried to look away and pretend she hadn't seen them but she was too late.

"Hey! Goat girl," Josef called. "You didn't see us, understand?"

"Yes, my lord."

"He's right," Aaron agreed. "You saw that worthless goat herder, Shimon, stealing our father's wine, didn't you."

As soon as they disappeared, Nava hurried into the kitchen courtyard with the milk buckets and told Penina what she had seen.

"Do exactly what they said and stay out of it," Penina said. "Our master will believe his sons before he'll ever believe you."

Rachel, who had been working alongside Penina, huddled close to Nava, keeping her voice low. "And the sons will take revenge if you tell on them. I've seen it happen before."

"But Shimon will be wrongly accused."

"It won't be the first time one of us was," Penina said. "Stay out of it." She moved away toward the hearth.

But Nava stayed right beside her, still carrying the milk. "Wouldn't our master want to know that his sons are liars and thieves? What kind of men will they become?"

"He has spoiled them ever since their mother died, and he's blind to their faults. I'm warning you to stay out of it. Go do your job now, and take care of the milk. Keep your mouth shut and your head down."

When Nava returned to the goat pen late that afternoon at milking time, Aaron and Josef stood leaning against the wall of the enclosure as if they had worked with the animals the entire day. She heard their father praising them for their hard work when he arrived home, and they all went inside together for the evening meal. The outward perfection of her master's estate had been deceiving—like a fresh fig that looked juicy and succulent on the outside but crawled with worms when cut open.

The next day Aaron was already waiting outside the goat pen when Nava arrived for the morning milking. He watched as she did her chores, then showed up again for the evening milking. He did the same the next day and the next until she realized that he wasn't overseeing the animals, he was watching her. At first she thought it was because she had seen him stealing the wine, and he wanted to send her a message. And maybe that was the reason in the beginning. But the look she saw in his eyes as he followed her every move wasn't a threatening look. Her master's son stared at her the way a glutton surveys a banquet of food. Nava knew exactly what Aaron wanted, and her growing panic made her so upset she couldn't eat.

When Aaron reappeared on the fourth morning as Nava sat

down on the milking stool, her hands trembled so badly she couldn't squeeze out any milk. The goat seemed to sense her nervousness and backed away, nearly upsetting the wooden bucket. "It's all right," she said, stroking the animal's flank. "There's nothing to be afraid of." She knotted her hands into fists to try to control their shaking, but the milk still wouldn't come when she tried again. Shimon led over the next goat and caught her glancing up at Master Aaron.

"Him again, eh?" He tethered his goat to the post and shuffled over to where Aaron stood. "Do you need something, Master Aaron?"

"No. I just enjoy watching your pretty little goat princess."

A surge of fear made Nava pull the teat too hard. The goat bleated and kicked, upsetting the bucket and spilling the milk. Nava quickly righted it then leaned her head against the goat's side, trying not to cry. She would be in trouble for certain. There was nothing Master Malkijah hated more than wastefulness. "Don't worry about it, girlie," Shimon soothed as he sat down again. "That goat gets ornery sometimes." He swatted the animal's hindquarters, sending her out into the pen with the others.

Later, after the milking was done and Aaron was gone, Nava went to Shimon, who was holding one of her goats, gently examining her sore foot. "I'm sorry about spilling the milk this morning, but Master Aaron makes me nervous when he watches me like that."

"Just ignore him."

Penina had warned her to keep quiet about what she'd seen, but Shimon had cared for her like a second father, and Nava couldn't hold her secret any longer. "Shimon . . . there's something you should know. I saw our master's sons stealing some of his wine. They told me to keep quiet about it, and I did. But . . . but they said if Malkijah noticed it was missing, they would accuse you of stealing it."

Shimon gave his usual growl of disgust. "I've known Aaron

since the day he was born. His father spoiled him too much after his mother died."

"I don't want you to get into trouble. What should I do?"

"Nothing any of us can do."

"Is there a way to make him stop watching me?"

"He'll lose interest before long and go on to something else."

But Aaron stood in the kitchen courtyard a short time later when Nava brought in the buckets of fresh milk. He sat down on a stool to watch Nava make cheese. Penina had complimented her on her goat cheese and had put her in charge of the daily task.

"Why don't you explain to me what you're doing, princess?" Aaron said. "After all, my father wants me to learn all about his estate."

She had no choice but to obey. "I'm making cheese from the milk, my lord." Did he hear the tremor in her voice or see it in her hands? "These bowls are different batches in different stages. I check them every day to see if they're ready for the next step."

He dragged his stool a little closer. "What's your name, princess?"

She dreaded telling him. Her name meant *beautiful*. "It's Nava, my lord."

He laughed and the ugly sound of it sent a shiver through her. "Tell me what you're doing now, beautiful Nava."

"This is the milk from this morning. I'll add the culture that will make it curdle, then leave it until tomorrow." Her cheeks burned beneath his scrutiny as she worked. "This second bowl is from yesterday," she said after covering the first one with a cloth. She used a knife to test the curd that had formed and said, "It's ready. Now I have to drain off the whey." She found a clay bowl with holes pierced through it and lined it with a thin cloth, then placed another bowl beneath it to catch the whey. She transferred the curdled milk into the colander with a spoon, not trusting her shaking hands to pour it without spilling. She stood very still when she finished, waiting for her pounding heart to slow down.

"Now what, beautiful?" he asked.

"I'll leave it until tomorrow to finish draining. Penina uses the whey." She fetched a third batch in another colander from yesterday and felt it with her fingers to see how much moisture remained. "This is ready. The cheese just needs salt, maybe some fresh herbs, and it's finished." She took a small pinch of salt from the bag and mixed it in. Then she formed it into a ball and wrapped it in fresh grape leaves. She was so engrossed in her work that she managed to stop thinking about Aaron for a moment. When he suddenly leaped up from his stool, he startled her. Without a word, he crossed to Penina working beside the hearth and pulled the little woman aside to speak with her.

Nava couldn't hear what he said, but judging by the way he gestured in her direction, she guessed it had something to do with her. Penina stared unhappily at her feet, nodding in agreement. Nava's skin prickled with a thousand needles. She busied herself with cleaning up, her hands clumsy as she washed the buckets and bowls and put everything away. She must have done something wrong. When she allowed herself to look up again, Aaron was gone. She was so relieved she had to sit down on a stool until her legs regained their strength.

At last she drew a calming breath and carried the finished ball of cheese to Penina, who was stirring a pot on the hearth. "This goat cheese is ready, Penina. Shall I season it with herbs today or leave it plain?" The little woman turned and studied her for so long that Nava was afraid she would have to sit down again.

"W-what is it? Did I do something wrong? Is Master Aaron angry because I spilled the milk this morning?"

"No, little one. You didn't do anything wrong. Your only fault is that you're much too pretty." Nava's heart hammered painfully as she waited for Penina to finish. "It seems you've captured our young master's attention, and he wants you taken out of the goat pen and the kitchen." Nava covered her mouth to hold back a cry. "You're going to work in the house from now on, serving our masters their meals."

"I-I can't do it . . . I don't know how. I would drop something or spill food on someone and—"

"Listen. It's a step up for you. Serving is a much better job than working in the smelly goat pen."

The courtyard blurred as tears filled Nava's eyes. "But I love working with my goats. I don't want to—"

"It doesn't matter what you want," Penina said harshly. She yanked the cheese from Nava's hand and turned her back on her, walking away. Nava followed, pleading with her.

"But our master asked me on the first day what I was good at doing, and I told him I was a goat keeper. Please, can't you speak with him and tell him I don't know anything about serving meals?"

"That's not how it works. You don't speak a word to our master unless he speaks to you."

"But I—"

Penina whirled to face her again. "When he gives you a job to do, you do it—whether you like it or not."

"But the way Master Aaron watches me . . . I'm so scared! There are dark corners and back hallways inside the house— and fewer people to see what's happening. What if he comes after me and . . . and . . ." She swallowed, unable to say the words out loud. "Would everyone look the other way like they always do and be too afraid to defend me? You said Master Malkijah would never believe my story. He would believe his son's lies."

The little woman stared at her for so long that Nava couldn't tell if she was going to pull her into her arms or yell at her some more. She did neither. "I know what you're afraid of," she finally said. "And I won't lie to you and tell you not to worry." Nava covered her mouth again as a sob escaped. "But you're a bondservant. You must do whatever your master says. And you must obey his sons, too."

"Penina . . . please . . ."

"Take off your apron and go. The housekeeper's name is Ruth. She'll see that you're bathed and cleaned up, and she'll teach you what you need to know." Nava didn't move, rooted to the spot by fear, powerless to change what was happening. "At least you won't smell like the goats anymore. And you'll finally have a pair of shoes that aren't falling apart." Nava still couldn't move. "Don't just stand there, girl, go on!"

"I-I need to tell Shimon—"

"I'll tell him. Get going."

But Nava saw Penina wipe her eyes as she turned away.

JERUSALEM

The summer afternoon was too hot to do anything, even nap. Chana's clothing clung uncomfortably to her skin as she sat in the shade in her courtyard, trying to stitch the hem of her cloak. She could barely grip the needle in her slippery fingers, and pushing it through the coarse cloth quickly became frustrating. At last she gave up and flung the project aside. Nothing seemed to move in the motionless air. Even the birds and insects were silent. So when the hurried slap of sandals against the cobblestone street broke the stillness, she sat up to listen. The sound halted outside her house, and a moment later her father burst through the courtyard gate, leaving it to swing wide open behind him. Sweat dampened his brow and ran down his flushed, overheated face. Chana sprang to her feet.

"Abba, what's wrong?"

He grinned. "Nothing, my angel. Yudit! Sarah! Come, come! I have a very important job for you to do!" Chana's sisters tumbled outside, awakened from their nap, but Abba was speaking so rapidly that Chana couldn't make sense of what he was saying. Something about preparing food for a splendid banquet. Had the heat gotten to him? She grabbed his arm to halt his wild gesturing. "Slow down, Abba, and tell us again: Who's coming to dinner?"

"The governor of Judah!"

"Governor Sanballat? Surely not!"

"No, no. Our own governor."

"I thought Governor Ezra retired," Sarah said. She and Yudit had hurried outside without putting on their sandals and Yudit had to dance from foot to foot on the hot paving stones.

"No, no, no. Not Ezra. We have a *new* governor, Nehemiah ben Hacaliah."

Yudit squinted at their father in the bright sunlight, her flowing mane of hair still tousled from her nap. "Since when?"

"He arrived two nights ago, all the way from Susa. Rebbe Ezra introduced him to our council members this morning and presented us with his official commission as governor. It was sealed by King Artaxerxes himself. We must prepare a banquet immediately to welcome him to our home."

"I think the sun has addled your brain, Abba," Chana said. She led him to the bench in the shade where she had been sitting. "You can't possibly expect us to cook a meal for such an important man."

"Especially in this heat," Sarah added.

"Besides, what makes you think he would even come to our humble home?" Yudit said. She had brought Abba a cup of water and stood fanning his face to cool him while he swallowed a gulp.

"Because it's already settled, my angels. He has agreed to dine with us tonight." All three of them began protesting at once.

"Tonight!"

"On such short notice?"

"What will we fix?"

"We'll never be ready in time!"

"Rephaiah will be coming, as well," Abba added after another sip of water. "And also the three men who have volunteered to serve as the new governor's aides, since he doesn't seem to have brought an entourage with him. I told them all to come after sundown."

Chana stifled a groan at the mention of Yitzhak's father, Rephaiah. This was getting worse and worse. She always found it difficult to be near him and be reminded of the beloved man they had both lost. Chana quickly tallied nine people to cook for, five guests plus her family. "Well, don't expect much of a banquet, Abba, since you're only giving us four hours to prepare it."

"I have every confidence in the three of you," he beamed. "You are your mother's daughters—may she rest in peace. Now I must get back." He downed the rest of his water and stood.

"Don't run up the hill in this heat," Yudit warned, but he merely waved his hand and hurried away as quickly as he had come. There was no way around it. They were left with the challenge of producing a meal on this sweltering day in only a few hours.

"Come on, we'd better see what we've got in the storeroom," Chana said, leading the way.

"Mama would have scolded Abba for an entire month if he'd done this while she was alive," Yudit said, grumbling as she lifted lids from storage baskets and clay jars to see what was inside.

"But she still would have cooked a feast," Sarah said, "so we'd better get started. For Abba's sake."

"At least there's a nice supply of wine from Malkijah," Chana said, pulling out what remained of his gift. There was no time to slaughter a lamb or goat, let alone roast it, so they did the best they could, preparing a variety of savory dishes and salads and sweets. Chana set the table for nine people and had only moments to wash her face and change her clothes before Abba and their guests arrived.

Her first impression of their new governor was that he was a very good-looking man but arrogant. He met her gaze for only a moment as Abba introduced each of his daughters to him, then lifted his chin and looked away without responding, his attention distracted by one of his aides. The four other men talked amongst themselves as they crowded inside the courtyard, but she noticed the governor scanning the walls and doorways and gates as if restless to escape. In fact, he studied the space so carefully that Chana expected to hear a dismissive summary of its inadequacies. She fought the urge to remind him that he wasn't in Susa anymore. He could hardly expect to dine in splendor. Even after they sat down at the table to eat, and Abba said the blessing over the wine, the governor remained attentive to every sound that came from beyond the circle of lamplight, as if expecting someone to jump out of hiding. What was he so afraid of?

But his worst fault in Chana's opinion was that he talked business with the other men the entire evening, peppering Abba and Rephaiah with endless questions. He made no effort at all to include her and her sisters in the conversation the way Malkijah had. She was not only bored by the man but furious at his lack of grace in complimenting his hostesses for the meal. Or even thanking them! The governor lacked charm and courtesy and could have been eating sawdust for all the attention he gave to the food.

Chana was staring at the sky above the courtyard later, watching the full moon rise, waiting for the boring evening to end, when the governor began asking what security measures were in place to ensure the safety of Jerusalem's citizens. Chana's chest tightened. She was afraid of what would come next. "Tragically, no measures have been taken," Rephaiah said. "My son Yitzhak was killed by a gang of intruders when they invaded his home in the night. He and Shallum's daughter, Chana, were about to be wed." He gestured to her, seated beside Abba.

"Yes, my brother told me about that," Nehemiah said. He barely glanced at Chana before returning his attention to Rephaiah. "I'm so sorry for the loss of your son. My condolences."

Chana waited for a word of sympathy for her loss, but it never came. She barely suppressed a huff of disgust as the men continued talking as if she wasn't even there.

"Guards are ineffective. The city is too spread out," Abba said.

"And there have been other robberies and assaults since the murder, but we've been unable to catch the culprits."

"Or prevent them from striking again."

Chana could no longer remain quiet. "Tell me, Governor Nehemiah. What do you plan to do about the violence?"

He glanced at her, as if surprised she was still there and that she knew how to speak. His forehead creased in a frown. "Your question is premature. I arrived only three days ago." He turned to Chana's father again. "I understand that the residence Governor Ezra used is unoccupied."

"Yes. It has been ever since he and his family moved out. Of course you'll want to live there."

"Would you like us to hire a staff of servants for you?" one of the aides asked.

"Yes, if you would."

Servants! Official residences! How could Nehemiah talk about such trivial things in nearly the same breath as Yitzhak's murder? Chana knew she was being rude, but she rose from the table without a word and went inside the house. She had to feel her way around her room without a lamp, but she located her bed and sank down on it, kicking off her sandals. The heat in the stuffy darkness made it difficult to breathe, and sweat glued her clothing to her body in a matter of minutes. But anything was preferable to sitting with Judah's arrogant new governor a moment longer. She listened to the distant mumble of conversation, hoping her sisters wouldn't follow her to ask what was wrong. But their manners were better than hers, and they remained at the table, enduring the boring conversation and their guest's staid gloominess.

She had begun to doze, exhausted after cooking the huge meal, when she awoke to Abba's boisterous voice. He was bidding his guests good night at last. Chana stayed where she was. Why bother being polite when the new governor had acted so rudely?

"Are you all right, Chana?" Yudit asked when she and Sarah finally came to bed.

"What happened to you?"

"Abba was afraid you were sick." Yudit carried an oil lamp to the niche beside Chana's bed, then sat down beside her.

"Tell Abba I'm fine," she said, yawning. "I decided I'd had enough of our new governor for one night."

"Did it make you sad when they talked about Yitzhak?" Sarah asked.

"No, it made me furious!" Chana sat up. "He never offered a single word of condolence to me, only to Yitzhak's father. When I asked him a question, he wouldn't even condescend to answer it, as if it was beneath him to talk to someone as unimportant as me. As if I was stupid for asking."

"That's still no excuse to get up and leave," Sarah said. "Just because our guest was rude, it doesn't mean you should be rude in return."

"I left because it was clear that my presence wasn't necessary, nor would my absence be noticed."

"You didn't even come back to say good night. And he's the governor."

"I don't care if he's the emperor! He barely acknowledged our presence, he didn't speak a word to us or even bother to remember our names, and he never offered a word of thanks or praise for the meal we worked so hard to prepare."

"He certainly was different from Malkijah ben Recab, wasn't he?" Yudit asked. She stood and pulled her robe off over her head. "Remember how charming he was when he came for dinner?"

Chana remembered. The contrast between the two men couldn't be greater. And Malkijah's sympathy and his understanding of her grief had touched her. "Well, at least we won't see Governor Nehemiah again after tonight," she said. "Once he moves into his own residence with his staff of servants, I'm sure he won't lower himself to dine in our humble house again. Or repay our invitation."

"Did you notice the way he kept looking all around while we ate?" Yudit asked. "As if someone might be crouching in the shadows, waiting to attack him? He never stopped. Does he even close his eyes at night?"

"I noticed," Chana said. "He struck me as a man who has so many enemies he can never relax. And as arrogant as he was, it's little wonder he has enemies."

"Even when he did manage a faint smile," Yudit said, "his eyes looked sad. And wary."

"You two should stop gossiping about him," Sarah said. She stood with her hands on her hips the way Mama used to do when she scolded them. "Not only is gossip wrong, but you should show a little respect for our new governor."

"It isn't gossip if it's true," Chana said.

Yudit giggled. "Abba is going to be mad when he finds out you weren't really sick, Chana—that you were just being rude."

She sighed. Abba rarely got angry, and he always forgave quickly. But knowing that he would be disappointed in her made Chana regret leaving the table. "Let's blow out the lamp and go to sleep. It's been a long day. All that work getting ready and not a smidgen of thanks or acknowledgment."

They lay in the dark for a long moment before Sarah said, "You have to admit that he was handsome, though."

"A handsome exterior without warmth or grace is like a gold ring in a pig's snout."

"Chana! You're terrible!" Sarah said.

"Oh, go to sleep."

CHAPTER

13

JERUSALEM

Nehemiah had been in Jerusalem for three days and still hadn't inspected the ruined walls or come up with a plan for rebuilding them. Nor had he told a soul why he had come all this way and what he intended to do. Tonight, as he'd dined with Jerusalem's two district rulers, he'd been reminded again of the young bridegroom's murder. When Shallum's daughter asked what he planned to do about it, her question stabbed his conscience like a knife. Guilt for failing to come up with a response plunged the knife deeper. He felt a measure of relief when the woman finally left the table and didn't return.

Now, standing in the street beneath a universe of stars, Nehemiah recognized the true source of his irritation with Shallum's daughter: Like him, she had also lost someone she loved, someone who'd been helpless and unarmed when attacked in the night. Nehemiah had looked away from her, recognizing her anger and grief. They were as familiar as his face in the mirror. He longed to assure her that he would rebuild the walls of Jerusalem if he had to lift every stone into place with his own two hands, but he couldn't reply to her question just yet. He couldn't reveal what God had put on his heart to do, because he didn't know who to trust. Rebbe Ezra warned of enemy spies among his own leaders.

The full moon rose as they'd dined, and it lit up the night as he and his three young aides, Jehohanan, Rehum, and Levi, left Shallum's house. In fact, the sky was nearly as bright as in the hours just before dawn, making it easy to walk down the Street of the Bakers to his brother's house. Nehemiah halted abruptly. Why not inspect the walls right now, tonight, while the city slept? The full moon certainly made it light enough to see his way. "Do any of you know where I could borrow a mule or a donkey?" he asked the men accompanying him.

"Of course, Governor," Jehohanan replied. "I'll make sure you have one first thing tomorrow."

"I need the mule now. There's something I need to do tonight. Out there." He pointed beyond the ragged stump of wall. He wouldn't wait until morning. He would survey the ruins now, when no one was watching. He would have liked to take his brothers along, knowing he could trust them. But after being reminded of the dangers tonight, he made up his mind not to involve them. He had come to Jerusalem to protect them and their families.

His aides didn't respond, perhaps wondering if they'd misunderstood. It occurred to Nehemiah that the men might be afraid. "You don't need to come with me," he told them. "All I need is a mount."

"My father-in-law, Meshullam, owns a mule," Jehohanan finally said. "He lives near the Horse Gate, on the Hill of Ophel. It's not far from here."

"Excellent. I would be grateful if he would let me borrow the animal." Nehemiah's anticipation grew as they climbed the Hill of Ophel and arrived at the house, just below the temple mount. Jehohanan managed to awaken the sleeping family without causing too much alarm, and the mule, which had been tethered inside the courtyard of the home to discourage thieves, was quickly prepared for Nehemiah to ride. The animal had a long, broad back, sturdy legs, and withers as high as Nehemiah's chin. He stroked its elegant muzzle, understanding why its owner would hide such a fine mount.

"You don't need to accompany me," he repeated as his aides led the mule outside and helped him climb onto its back.

"Where are you going, my lord?" Rehum asked.

He decided he would have to trust them. "I want to take a closer look at Jerusalem's walls. Or what's left of them, that is. I plan to ride in a circuit around the outside of the city." Surprisingly, none of them questioned him further and all three volunteered to come.

"The Valley Gate is the easiest one to ride through, my lord, if you want to begin there," Jehohanan said.

"Very well." They left the city through the shadowy hole where the Valley Gate once stood, and Nehemiah guessed by examining the ruins that it had once been a wide, casemate gate with chambers for the guards and probably a lookout tower on top. They passed through it in single file, the wide roadway blocked by huge, fallen stones, and emerged outside the city in the central valley that ran along the western side of the Jerusalem ridge.

Ahead, on the hill to the west of the city, lay the section his brother called the Mishneh, demolished by the Babylonian army and never rebuilt. Nehemiah could see that the huge area had once been enclosed by walls, forming a semicircle around the now-ruined houses, and that it had been joined to the walls that surrounded the City of David. There would be no point in rebuilding the Mishneh's walls since no one lived there. Too bad, since double walls provided a formidable defense, a double barrier of protection on Jerusalem's vulnerable western side.

Nehemiah gazed up at the full moon as his mule plodded forward. No walls would ever be strong enough to save his people without the Holy One on their side. Even if Nehemiah did everything in his power to ensure his people's physical safety, his efforts would be worthless unless they remained faithful to God. Repentance and restoration must go hand in hand.

Outside the gate, Nehemiah decided to direct his mount along the wall toward the south, moving slowly enough for the three men to follow him. He passed a long stretch of ruined wall, sloping downhill, that had no openings for gates. Insects whirred in the dusty night, then fell silent at the sound of footsteps. The dry air made the hairs on Nehemiah's arms stand on end. He saw trampled earth and the remains of campfires in the place where his Persian escort had camped before returning to Susa. "What is the reservoir in this valley called?" he asked.

"The King's Pool, my lord. It's at the very southern tip of the city. You can probably get a better glimpse of it in a minute."

Nehemiah saw the enormity of the task ahead of him. Not only were the collapsed walls ineffective, but the jumble of toppled stones formed a massive blockade, making it impossible for him to get near the base of the walls on his mule. It would require a great deal of effort for a building crew to wade through the boulders. And it would be a very dangerous place to work once they began shifting the fallen blocks. Yet a determined enemy could scramble right over the debris and enter the city.

Nehemiah rode on toward the bottom of the slope, where the waters of the King's Pool sparkled like stars in the moonlight. He halted again when he reached another gaping hole, marking the place where a gate once stood. The rubble covered an immense area, and he saw that the wall surrounding the Mishneh once joined the walls of David's city here.

"That was called the Dung Gate," one of the men told him. His voice sounded unnaturally loud as it broke the vast stillness of the night.

"And is that the Hinnom Valley, down there?" Nehemiah asked.

"Yes, my lord."

The place where people sacrificed their children to Molech. No wonder the Almighty One allowed this city to be destroyed. Nehemiah spurred the mule forward.

He had wanted to see if the walls could be repaired and reinforced or if they were so badly demolished that he would need to start over. Now, as he took a closer look, it encouraged him to see that the foundations were in good shape in most places. He would be able to build on top of them. Some sections would need only to be shored up and reinforced. Other sections, which stood at half their original height, could possibly be repaired. But in many places the wall was so broken down that the mule could have stepped right over it if the path hadn't been strewn with crumbled blocks of burnt stone. He would need to completely rebuild those sections from the ground up. And he would need to replace all of the gates. Not one of them remained, the timbers burned by fire in the great destruction of Jerusalem.

Nehemiah rounded the southernmost tip of the city and moved up the Gihon Valley toward the Fountain Gate. The dark outline of the ridge known as the Mount of Olives stood across the valley to the east. But he didn't get far, his way blocked by so much debris that his mount didn't have enough room to get through. The animal balked, refusing to clamber over the tumbled piles of stones. Nehemiah dismounted and continued on foot, climbing over the debris to examine the wall, aware of the danger of vipers and scorpions hidden in the crevices. Halfway up the valley he halted, too exhausted to proceed any further, and gazed at the long stretch of fallen wall in the moonlight. "Why so much rubble?" he wondered aloud.

"There used to be supporting terraces on this eastern side because of the steepness of the slope," Jehohanan replied. "But the terraces collapsed in the fire."

"And storms and rain and time did the rest of the damage, I suppose." The crumbled terraces had avalanched down the slope, cutting off Nehemiah's route. It would be even more challenging to reclaim the boulders and rebuild here than on the city's western side. From the top of the temple mount, Nehemiah had seen the steep cliffs on this eastern side of the ridge. Along with the deep Gihon Valley, they once formed a natural defense against the enemy. But no longer. His enemies could scale the cliffs by climbing up the slope of fallen rocks.

He returned to where they had tethered the mule, and his men helped him into the saddle. Nehemiah tugged the reins to turn the mule around. "Let's retrace our steps," he told the men. When they reached the Valley Gate once again, Nehemiah rode past it toward the north, ascending the slope toward the temple mount. He counted at least four more gates in this section of the city below the temple, the place where the main roads from the Mediterranean Coast, Samaria, and Damascus all converged. He identified the location of the gates by the gaps in the ruined walls and the remains of crumbled towers. Once again, he had to halt when the path became too littered with rubble for the mule to proceed. The fact that he could see the temple's rooftop in the moonlight made him angry. The fortifications around Jerusalem should include fortified walls around the holy temple.

Finally, Nehemiah turned back and re-entered Jerusalem through the Valley Gate. It had taken several hours to complete their journey and his men looked weary. They helped him slide off the mule, and he walked with them to return it to its owner. Afterward, they stood together in the moonlit street outside Ephraim's house.

"I haven't told any of the priests or nobles or officials what I came here to do," he said. "And I'm counting on the three of you to keep this confidential until I announce it. . . . But I intend to rebuild Jerusalem's walls." He saw surprise and disbelief, and maybe even doubt on their faces.

"It will be a monumental task, my lord," Jehohanan said. "It will take years—"

"No, it won't. It can't take years. We don't have years to spare. We need to rebuild quickly before our enemies try to stop us."

"Do you really think it can be done?" Jehohanan asked.

"Yes. And it will be done—God helping us. Good night, gentlemen."

Nehemiah lay in bed later that night, trying to sleep, and the enormity of the task did seem overwhelming. Every time he closed his eyes he envisioned avalanches of tumbling stones, stones that weighed so much a man couldn't lift them, stones that could shift and pin a man beneath their impossible weight. In spite of the assurances he'd given his aides, his midnight survey had discouraged him.

But Nehemiah's anger outweighed his discouragement. Anger at seeing Jerusalem in such a state. Anger that the ruins disgraced God's reputation, making Him seem powerless to defend His people. Yes, the task seemed impossible. But Nehemiah served a God of the impossible.

He climbed out of bed again and stood at the window that faced the temple mount. It wasn't visible from here, even in the moonlight, but Nehemiah closed his eyes and lifted his hands in prayer.

"Lord, you made a way for me to approach the king with my petition. You gave me favor in his sight. Help me now, I pray. Help me rebuild this wall and make your city and your people and your holy temple safe from our enemies. May Jerusalem's wall stand as a monument to your immeasurable grace."

CHAPTER

14

JERUSALEM

Chana dreaded changing into her good linen robe. The fabric would be scratchy, and her skin already itched with sweat. At least she didn't have to light a fire and cook a meal tonight. The sun was finally setting after a day that had been oppressively hot, and the evening promised little relief. They would need to hurry on their journey to Malkijah's estate in Beth Hakkerem, making the most of the fading daylight before darkness fell and travel became dangerous. Thankfully, Malkijah would provide a cart and animals and several trusted servants for the journey. After dinner, Chana and her family would spend the night as his guests.

She turned to her sisters, who looked boneless from the heat, lounging in the scant shade of their courtyard roof. "I feel like I'm melting," Yudit said.

"Well, come on. It's time to get washed and change our clothes. Malkijah's servants will be here soon, and so will Abba. We need to be ready to go. Have you decided what you're going to pack?" Neither of her sisters moved. They exchanged glances as if sharing a secret. "What are you waiting for? Come on, we need to get dressed."

"We're not coming with you, Chana," Yudit said. "We're staying home."

Chana thought it was a joke. "No, you're not. We already accepted Malkijah's invitation. He's expecting us."

"Actually, he's only expecting you and Abba to come."

Chana walked to where they sat and stood over them, looking down at them, waiting for them to start laughing at the surprise on her face. But neither sister smiled. "If this is your idea of a joke, it isn't funny. We don't have time to fool around like this."

"It's true, Chana," Yudit said. "Sarah and I are staying home so Malkijah won't have to be attentive to so many people. You'll have more time to get to know him."

"Don't be ridiculous. You can't stay home all alone."

"We won't be alone. Abba made arrangements for us. This was his idea."

"Just go and have a nice time," Sarah added.

Chana felt knocked off balance. "Why didn't you tell me sooner?" But she already knew the answer. She never would have agreed to go alone and be the focus of Malkijah's attention if they had told her. It was too much like courting, and she still wasn't sure that she wanted to court Malkijah or anyone else. Now it was too late to back out. She needed to take her own advice and hurry to get ready. She fought the urge to stomp her foot like a child. "I'm furious with both of you," she said as she strode into her room.

Her first trip to Beth Hakkerem was not getting off to a very good start. She yanked off her clothes and tossed them onto the floor. Splashed water on her face. Wiggled into her itchy linen robe. Dragged a comb through her hair. It wasn't until she saw her angry face reflected in the mirror that she pulled herself together. Grief over Yitzhak's death was one thing; self-pity was an entirely different emotion, an ugly emotion. And she was dangerously close to drowning in it. She pulled her head above its dangerous waters just in time, drawing a deep breath and releasing it in a sigh as she heard Abba arrive home. A few minutes later, Malkijah's servants arrived.

Several times on the nearly hour-long journey, Chana had been about to scold her father and let him know just how angry she was for pushing her into this dinner in the first place, then arranging for her to have Malkijah's undivided attention. But in the end, she remained silent. Abba loved her. He wanted only what was best for her, and he truly believed that Malkijah might be her last chance at happiness. They reached his home just as the light began to fade in the western sky, and what she could see of the estate in the twilight looked magnificent. Neatly terraced vineyards covered the surrounding hills. From the top of the rise where his huge stone house perched, she could see rolling farmland and distant valleys. Malkijah greeted them at the gate and took them on a quick tour of his winery. He showed them his barns and storehouses and animals, and the beautiful guest rooms where she and her father would spend the night. The pride he took in everything he owned was written all over his face, and Chana thought he'd never looked quite so handsome.

"I hope you will relax and enjoy yourselves this evening," he said. "My servants have prepared a feast for you."

It was indeed a feast. They dined in a lovely outdoor courtyard beneath a vine-covered trellis, and the air seemed cooler in the hilly district of Beth Hakkerem than it had in Chana's stuffy house in Jerusalem. Malkijah's two sons, Aaron and Josef, joined them for dinner, and Chana was relieved to see that they were older than she'd imagined—perhaps sixteen and seventeen. She needn't worry about trying to mother them if she did decide to marry Malkijah. They were well past the age of needing a mother.

Malkijah's home was the loveliest she'd ever visited; the meal, the most extravagant she'd ever eaten. Food fit for a king. Yet even as she sat at Malkijah's table, waited on by his attentive servants, eating his delicacies, she determined not to let his wealth dazzle her. The promise of great riches seemed empty without love. A thought occurred to her as she took in her luxurious surroundings, and she spoke it out loud. "It's hard to believe that such wealth still exists when the drought has gone on for so long."

"Chana's right. How do you manage it?" Abba asked.

"I'm fortunate to have enough manpower to keep my vineyards and gardens watered. There are several springs on my property and a small pond I can draw from."

"You're also fortunate," Chana said, "to have watchtowers in your vineyards and a wall surrounding your home. And servants to stand guard." Malkijah and his sons wouldn't be murdered in the night as they tried to defend their property the way Yitzhak had been.

"I recognize the need for vigilance," he said. "There are Gentile settlements all around us. I'd never forgive myself if one of my sons or my servants was injured on my estate. Their safety is very important to me."

The conversation over dinner covered a variety of topics, including the Torah. Malkijah's knowledge of the Law impressed Chana. The entire evening was so enjoyable she couldn't help comparing it and her charming host to the boring evening she'd recently spent with the ill-mannered governor. The only hint Chana saw that Malkijah's estate might be less than perfect was in the sadness she saw on the face of one of his servant girls. She was young, perhaps her sister Sarah's age, with a lithe, graceful figure beneath her shapeless dress. Chana recognized sorrow in the girl's eyes, grief and depression in the slump of her shoulders. She moved in and out of the dining area with her head lowered, her chin pressed to her chest as she waited on the table. Then Chana noticed something else. Malkijah's older son, Aaron, followed the girl's every move, watching her the way a predator eyes his prey. The girl seemed very aware of his gaze, and along with the sadness, Chana also saw fear. Something wasn't right.

As the meal neared an end, a servant bent to whisper something in Malkijah's ear. "I'm sorry," he said as he rose to his feet. "Will you please excuse me for a moment? I need to attend to this. I'll be right back."

"Of course," Abba replied, and he continued his conversation with Malkijah's younger son. Chana rose quietly from the table and followed the pretty servant girl as she left the room with a tray of dishes. "Excuse me," she called as they neared the kitchen courtyard. "May I have a word with you, please?"

The girl turned, her fear unmistakable. "Do you mean me?"

"Yes. What's your name?"

"Nava. Did I do something wrong?" The tray of dishes trembled visibly in her hands.

"No, not at all. Listen, Nava. Perhaps it's none of my business but you seem very unhappy. Can you tell me what's wrong?"

"Nothing's wrong." She stared down at her feet, her reply unconvincing.

"Are you being mistreated in this household?"

"No, ma'am. I-I haven't served at my master's table for very long, so it's still new to me . . . I didn't want to make a mistake in front of his guests."

That might explain the girl's fear, but not her grief. Chana decided to probe deeper. "I'm going to be honest with you, and I hope you'll respect me for that and be honest with me in return. My father hopes to arrange a marriage between me and your master. Malkijah seems very charming and his home is beautiful and well-run, but sometimes looks can be deceiving. I don't want to make a mistake and marry into a household that's unhappy or abusive."

"It's not abusive, miss." Nava still didn't look up. Chana waited, wondering if the girl would say more. Her patience was rewarded when Nava finally met her gaze and said, "I'm in love with a man from back home named Dan. We want to be married, but now we have to wait because I was sold as a bondservant to pay my father's debts." A tear slipped past her lashes and rolled down her cheek, but she couldn't brush it away with the heavy tray in her hands. She bent her head to wipe it against her shoulder. "I miss him. And I miss my home and my family."

"I'm so sorry," Chana said. "I heard that some of our people were being enslaved because of the drought, but . . ." She didn't finish. To see evidence of their poverty in this young girl tore at her heart.

"It isn't my master's fault," Nava said quickly. "If he hadn't been kind enough to make me his bondservant, our family would have starved."

"You were sold as a servant so they could eat?"

"Yes. At least now they'll have enough food until the drought ends."

"Sold for how long, Nava?"

"Six years. Or until Abba's debts are repaid." She bit her lip, struggling for control. "But my father owes my master a lot of money, and the crops have all failed, and I don't see how he will ever pay him back. Abba works so hard, and he loves his land so much—but it doesn't even belong to him anymore. It's mortgaged to my master."

"How long have you lived here as a bondservant?"

"A little more than a month."

Chana couldn't imagine being separated from her family for six years, but she did understand the pain Nava felt at not being able to marry the man she loved. "Thank you for your honesty," she said. Chana was about to return to the table when she remembered the way Aaron had watched the girl, and how frightened she had looked. "Are you afraid of Malkijah's son Aaron?" she asked.

Nava hesitated a very long time before finally replying. "Sometimes . . . when Master Aaron watches me . . . yes, I am afraid. I don't want to marry him. But the Torah says that my master or one of his sons has a right to take me for his wife."

"Are you certain the Torah would force you to marry someone you didn't love?"

Nava nodded. "I'm certain. Dan already asked the priests about it. But I'd rather be poor and marry Dan than stay here for the rest of my life, even if my master is rich."

Chana saw the girl's dilemma. She longed to help her but didn't know how. Maybe if she married Malkijah she might be able to intervene, but not now, not tonight. "I can understand why you would be frightened and sad. But so far, no one has harmed you, have they? And your master has been good to you?"

"My master is firm. And he likes everything a certain way. His way. But he has never been unkind."

"That's good to know. Thank you." Again, she was about to return to the dining room when Nava spoke, her voice tinged with fear.

"Miss, wait! Please don't tell anyone that I complained to you, please! I'm very grateful to my master for helping our family. It isn't his fault that I'm his bondservant, but . . ."

"But what, Nava?"

"I don't understand why the Almighty One would let this happen. Why doesn't He answer our prayers and give us rain so Abba's land can prosper again? None of this would have happened and I wouldn't be here if God had answered our prayers. And it would be so easy for Him to send rain, wouldn't it? Doesn't the Almighty One control the rain? But . . . but I don't pray to Him anymore. Why bother, since all my prayers go unanswered?"

In her lowest moments, Chana often felt the same bitterness toward God that Nava did. Yitzhak had been alive when they'd found him. He had lingered for two days, and Chana had prayed and pleaded with God to spare his life. But God hadn't heard or cared. Yitzhak had died. "I'm so sorry for what you've had to go through, Nava. I wish I could promise you that God will answer your prayers and change your situation. But I also know what it's like when the Almighty One doesn't seem to hear or care. Thank you for your honesty. And for trusting me enough to confide in me." Chana started to leave, but Nava stopped her again.

"Miss, wait. If you do marry my master . . . is there any way you can help me and Dan? Or my father?"

"I don't know. Right now I'm not ready to marry anyone, including your master." But Nava had raised a good question. How much influence would she have in this household, with a man who was firm and liked everything his way? Chana would need to find out.

"There you are, Chana." She heard Malkijah's voice behind her and turned. "We were wondering what happened to you. . . . You aren't pestering my guest, are you?" he asked Nava.

"No, my lord."

"Then I'm sure you must have work to do. Go."

"Yes, my lord." Nava bowed her head as she scurried into the kitchen carrying the heavy tray.

"It's my fault, Malkijah, not hers. I had a question, and I didn't want to bother you with it."

"It's no bother at all. Ask me anything you'd like."

"It's nothing. . . . Nava was very kind and helpful." Embarrassment made Chana's cheeks grow warm. She scrambled to change the subject. "Look, isn't the moon beautiful?"

"It is. Come, I want to show you the view from my rooftop." His hand rested on the small of her back as he guided her up the stone steps and showed her the breathtaking view. Gentle hills rolled away in all directions, and Chana could see the narrow ribbon of road they had traveled on from Jerusalem, winding between the hills. The silver-gray leaves of Malkijah's olive trees rustled softly in the breeze below them. It was the first time Chana had been completely alone with him, and his charisma was undeniable. He seemed to be pulling her toward himself like a fisherman hauling in his catch; she didn't know why she instinctively struggled to free herself from his net.

"It's magnificent up here, Malkijah. Thank you so much for such an enjoyable evening. You have a beautiful home, and everything is so well run."

"But . . . ?"

"What do you mean?"

"I still hear a note of hesitation in your voice. You don't seem convinced that you would be happy here with me." She didn't reply as her heart pounded harder. "I sense you holding back, Chana. Is it something I've said or done?"

"No, you've been wonderful and charming and generous and—"

"Am I wasting my time by pursuing our relationship?"

She couldn't look at him. "I honestly don't know."

"Tell me what my next step should be?"

She searched her heart for a reply before looking up at him. "You told me that you wanted to marry again because you didn't think you would ever find happiness unless you did. But to tell you the truth, I'm afraid to let myself fall in love again. I'm afraid I'll be opening my heart to all the pain and sorrow I felt when Yitzhak died. I don't think I could endure that again."

He covered her hand with his as it rested on the wall. "But wasn't there joy, too? Didn't Yitzhak bring you happiness?"

"Yes, of course."

"When you close the door against pain, you're cutting yourself off from the possibility of joy, too."

"I suppose that's true."

"Tell me, Chana, are you happy?"

She remembered how she had recognized the servant girl's sadness because it was so much like her own. "No . . . I'm not really happy."

"Would you like to be?"

Yes. She was so tired of the blanket of grief that pressed down on her, smothering her, making her temper short and stealing her joy day after day, draining her tears. Yes. She would like very much to be happy again. But she didn't think it was possible without Yitzhak.

"Believe me, I understand why you're afraid to love again," Malkijah continued. "But would you be willing to settle for contentment? For companionship? I believe we could find both of those things with each other because our stories are so similar. We understand each other's loss in a way that few other people can. And we both understand that our loved ones will always own a huge part of our heart."

She wanted to ask if he also felt bewildered and abandoned, resentful toward the Almighty One for taking the person he loved—but she didn't. He was waiting for her reply. "Yes," she finally said. "Yes, I believe I could find contentment here with you." It was the truth.

Malkijah smiled. "And what would the next step be? For you and me?"

Chana felt a rising panic as he drew his net toward the shore, even if Malkijah did show enormous kindness and understanding. "Maybe we should spend a little more time together to get to know each other."

He lifted her hand and placed it between both of his, giving it a gentle squeeze before releasing it again. "Good. I will be patient, and give you a little more time." He smiled his crooked smile and led her down the stairs and into the house.

CHAPTER
15

THE DISTRICT OF BETH HAKKEREM

The noise of a commotion jolted Nava awake. Running footsteps. Voices. Was someone shouting her name? She listened in the darkness, her heart racing.

"Nava! Nava, help me!"

It sounded like Dan's voice. She sat up and looked around, wondering if she'd been dreaming. But Rachel and some of the other women were also awake. One of them got up and lit a lamp.

"Nava, where are you?" the distant voice shouted.

It *was* Dan!

Nava leaped up from her pallet in a panic and struggled into her clothes. The steamy summer night made it difficult to get dressed, and her tunic became hopelessly twisted as fear pounded through her. Several minutes passed before she could get straightened out, and she ran outside in her bare feet, unwilling to waste more time. The shouts came from the center of the compound, near the kitchen. Other servants had awakened, too, and hurried there with her. Someone had lit a torch. And there was Dan in the middle of her master's courtyard, shouting and struggling to free himself as two burly men gripped his arms, trying to drag him away.

"Dan! I'm here!" Nava shouted. She tried to weave between the gathering spectators, desperate to reach him. But someone grabbed her from behind, yanking her to a stop, holding her back.

"Stay here, girlie. Stay out of it." Shimon, her friend from the goat pen.

"Let me go! That's Dan! They're hurting him!" But he wouldn't release her, in spite of her pleas. "I have to help him, Shimon. Please!"

"Stay here and wait for our master. He'll straighten this out."

At last Malkijah arrived, still fastening his robe, his sandals untied and flapping as he walked. Nava had never seen him look so angry. "What's all this noise? What's going on? You're disturbing my guests."

"We caught a thief breaking into your estate, my lord."

"I'm not a thief! I told you I was just—" Dan cried out in pain as one of the men holding him twisted his arm, cutting off his words.

"The evidence says otherwise, my lord. He scaled the wall to get inside, and we caught him sneaking around your compound."

"I came to see Nava. She'll tell you I'm not a thief. She knows me."

"Who's Nava? Who is he talking about?" Malkijah asked. Nava started to reply but Shimon cupped his calloused hand over her mouth, muffling her words.

"Hush, girlie!" She struggled against him but couldn't break free. Master Aaron had also awakened and stood outside with everyone else. He pointed to Nava from across the courtyard.

"That's Nava. She's your serving girl, Father." Everyone turned to her as Shimon finally took his hand off her mouth.

"Dan is my friend, from home," she said. "I've known him all my life, and he isn't a thief."

"Maybe they're working together, my lord," one of the men holding Dan said. "Maybe she's giving him information from the inside."

"I haven't stolen anything and neither has Nava," Dan shouted. Again, the man twisted Dan's arm behind his back. Dan grimaced in pain, speaking through gritted teeth, "I just came to see if Nava was all right."

"Please, tell them, Rachel," Nava begged. Her friend from the kitchen stood beside her. "Tell them I was asleep right next to you. We woke up at the same time, remember? I'm not a thief." But Rachel shrank back, too terrified to say a word. Would no one speak up to defend her and Dan?

"You had no right to climb over my wall," Malkijah said. "Or sneak around my home in the dark. You're trespassing."

"I was trying to find Nava so I could talk to her. I didn't know there would be a wall or that the entrance would be locked. I work with my father on our land all day, so I couldn't get here until after dark. It took longer than I expected, and everyone was asleep."

Nava thought of the danger Dan had faced in order to see her, walking all the way from home at night, and she loved him more than she'd ever thought possible. Suddenly one of the spectators standing off to the side moved into the circle of torchlight. Nava recognized the woman she'd talked to earlier tonight, the one who said she might marry the master. "Malkijah, wait," she said. "May I say something?"

Nava felt sick. What if the woman told her master how unhappy she was?

"Of course, Chana," Malkijah said. "I'm so sorry about all this unpleasantness. And I'm sorry we woke you up. This must be frightening for you after what happened to your fiancé."

"I wasn't frightened," she said with a wave of dismissal. "Listen, I spoke with Nava earlier tonight, and she told me she had a boyfriend back home, so I know that much is true. Maybe he really was coming to see her."

Aaron got his father's attention before he could reply. "Didn't you say you noticed that some wine was missing the other day, Father?"

"Dan didn't take it!" Nava tried to shout. "You know who—!" Shimon pressed his hand over her mouth again.

"Be quiet," he growled. "You'll be in much worse trouble if you go accusing Master Aaron."

Again, the woman named Chana spoke. "It seems to me it would be easy to prove the truth of this young man's claims. Did the guards find any stolen wine on him when they caught him? Or any with Nava, for that matter?"

"Well, did you?" Malkijah asked the men who were holding Dan's arms.

"No, my lord. We didn't find anything."

"Go search the girl's things," Malkijah ordered. He turned to Chana as two of his servants hurried off, and his voice sounded gentle as he spoke to her. "Some wine has disappeared from my storeroom. I was afraid it might be the work of thieves, so I asked my guards to be especially alert."

"We have a right to protect our property," Aaron said. He glared at Dan with his chin raised, his arms folded across his chest. Nava had feared Aaron before tonight, but at this moment she hated him.

"What if he's telling the truth?" Chana asked. "What if he isn't a thief?"

"He still had no right to break into our home," Aaron said before his father could reply. "He should be punished for trespassing."

"I just wanted to see Nava. That's the truth, and I'll swear to it!" Dan said. Nava could tell by the way he breathed that he was in pain. The men were hurting him.

"Can you blame a young man for wanting to see the girl he loves, Malkijah?" Chana asked. "I hope you'll show him mercy."

Malkijah turned to Dan again, his forehead knotted in an angry frown. "Is Nava your wife? Are you betrothed?"

"We're too poor to marry—"

"Then you have no right to be with her, especially in the middle of the night. Even if you aren't a thief, your own testimony accuses you of wrongdoing."

"But I love her—"

"She belongs to us now," Aaron said, taking a step toward Dan. "Forget about her."

"What do you mean she belongs to you?" Chana asked.

"It's what the Torah says," Aaron replied. "She's our bond-servant."

"Go back to bed, my dear. Please." Malkijah rested his hand on Chana's back, trying to guide her inside the house. "We'll talk about it in the morning."

"I know what the Torah says," Dan shouted. "That's why I needed to make sure Nava was all right."

The men returned from searching Nava's room before Malkijah could respond. "We found nothing, my lord."

"You can't convict someone without evidence," Chana said. "There should be two witnesses. Please, for my sake, let the young man go free."

Nava held her breath as Malkijah took a long moment to decide. "Get off my property," he finally told Dan. "And don't ever come near my home again. If you do, you will be punished." The two men dragged Dan to the gate and shoved him through it, slamming and barring it behind him. "Now everyone go back inside and get some sleep," Malkijah said.

Shimon turned Nava around and pushed her toward her dormitory. "Wait, wait. I want to explain to our master—"

"You heard him, girlie. Back to bed." She tried to resist, but Shimon was very strong for an old man. He left her at the door where Penina stood waiting. Inside, the room where Nava and the other women slept looked ransacked.

"Why won't anyone listen to me, Penina? Why won't they let me explain?"

"You don't explain anything to the master unless he asks. Not a single word—understand?"

"Why is it so wrong to tell the truth? I know who really stole the wine and—"

Penina grabbed her shoulders and gave her a little shake. "You came very close to destroying your family's lives tonight, do you realize that? And for what? I told you, our master will never believe anything bad about his sons."

"But the woman, our master's guest, she would believe me."

"Maybe. Maybe not. Are you willing to take that chance?" Nava started to reply but Penina interrupted. "You want to talk about the truth? Here's the truth, so you'd better listen: If our master tosses you out, your family will have no way to live. What will they do then? Your father will lose his land and they'll starve, that's what will happen. And it will be your fault—yours and that foolish boy who broke in here to see you."

Nava knew Penina was right.

"Go to bed and forget about him. That part of your life is over."

Impossible. Nava could never forget Dan. She helped the other women straighten up and arrange the beds, then laid down on her own. Dan had risked his life to come—and now he could never come back. Nava may never see him again, and she didn't know how she could bear it. She finally understood why Rachel didn't go home to see her husband and children. Seeing Dan tonight made the pain of their separation even worse.

The bitterness she felt toward her masters encircled her heart like a poisonous vine. Nava had tried to weed it out, but tonight it had grown bigger, stronger, watered by her tears.

JERUSALEM

Nehemiah smoothed the parchment scroll on the table in front of him, placing clay weights in each corner so it would lie flat. He and his aides had drawn this map of Jerusalem the day after they'd inspected the walls. "Now that I've surveyed the work, I need you to arrange a meeting for me with the Jewish leaders and nobles," he told them, smoothing the wrinkles beneath his palm. "I want to explain my plan to them as soon as possible. The work must begin immediately. We can't waste any time."

"I'll summon them right away, Governor," Jehohanan said. The young aide had proven to be the most competent of the three, the most eager to please. He tried to anticipate Nehemiah's needs and was careful to ask for details. "Would you like them to assemble here in the governor's residence?"

His residence. Nehemiah still felt uncomfortable living here. A smaller space would have been sufficient for him, like the room assigned to him as the king's cupbearer. In fact, all Nehemiah needed was a bedroom and this work space where he and his three aides met. But the servants hired to cook for him and wait on him also needed rooms, he supposed.

They had quickly set up living and sleeping quarters for him here and had shown him a list of provisions allocated to him as governor—oxen, sheep, poultry, wine. "I don't need all that food," he had told them. "I refuse to be distracted by housekeeping details. Keep everything simple and basic." His priority had been to compose this map of the city's walls and gates, then divide the work into smaller, more manageable segments.

"I assume the council chamber down the hall is the customary meeting place?" he asked Jehohanan.

"It is. We should arrange the conference for three days from now if you want all the district leaders to come. It will take a day to deliver the message, another day for them to travel here."

"They may be busy working their land, my lord," Levi said.

Nehemiah looked up at Levi and frowned. "I was told there has been a prolonged drought. That there isn't much to harvest."

"That's true, my lord, but some of the wealthier landowners weren't as badly affected as the small farmers."

"What should we tell the nobles if they ask the purpose of the meeting?" Jehohanan asked.

"Tell them they'll find out when they get here. I know our enemies will learn what we're doing sooner or later—I'd rather it was later."

"We'll deliver your message right away, my lord."

The three men were partway through the door when Nehemiah stopped them. "Wait! The priests should also attend the meeting. Inform the high priest for me, and tell him to make sure as many Levites and priests as possible attend. I'm sure they'll want to join in the work, especially when they learn that I plan to repair and fortify the walls of the temple citadel, too."

"But if you invite the priests and Levites, my lord, your council chamber will be too small to hold everyone."

Levi was right. Nehemiah had seen the long, narrow room where the council met. "Is there another place that's large enough, Levi?"

"There's the square where the Water Gate used to be. Will that work?"

Nehemiah thought for a moment, trying to recall what the square looked like. The area was large and open, but the rubble that had been shoved aside to create the space still lay in huge heaps all around it. "Too depressing," he decided. "Looking at mountains of stones from the ruined Water Gate will make our task seem overwhelming."

"If I may say so, my lord, the task already does seem overwhelming." The young aide, whose name was Rehum, still hadn't caught Nehemiah's vision. Nehemiah would have replaced him, but there was no one else.

"You may say that it seems overwhelming when you're talking to me, Rehum, but be careful not to say it to anyone else. That kind of negative thinking will doom us before we start."

"I'm sorry, Governor."

"Now, what about the outer court of the temple? Is there enough room to meet there?"

"Plenty, my lord. Thousands of people gather there during Passover."

Thousands of people. Nehemiah had seen them flocking to the temple a few days ago on the Ninth of Ab, the anniversary of the temple's destruction. Their desire to seek God's forgiveness had moved him deeply. "The people! Excellent idea!" he said, resisting the urge to shout. "We'll extend the invitation to them, as well. We won't obligate them to come, but if they would like to hear my announcement, they'll be welcome."

"What would be the point of inviting the people?" Jehohanan asked.

"The lack of security in this city has them living in fear. I want them to get as excited about rebuilding the walls as I am.

153

That way, even if the leaders balk at the idea, perhaps the people will join in the work without them."

"We could easily arrange for the meeting to take place in the outer courtyard of the temple," Levi said. "After one of the daily sacrifices."

"Excellent. God helped us do the impossible sixty years ago and rebuild His temple, didn't He? We can point to the finished building as an example of what we can do with the Almighty One on our side."

"That's a lot of people to inform, my lord—leaders, nobles, priests, lay people . . ."

"Then you'd better get started."

Three days later, Nehemiah's stomach fluttered as he surveyed the huge crowd gathering in the outer court of the temple after the morning sacrifice. They didn't know him. He wasn't a proven leader. Would they listen to him? Could he convince them to undertake this project? He had watched King Artaxerxes in action over the past few years and knew that people eagerly followed a compelling leader. One who was decisive. Inspiring. Charismatic. Nehemiah was none of those things. *But the hand of the Lord my God is upon me.*

He had instructed the nobles and officials and district leaders to assemble in the front, below his platform, to ensure they didn't miss a word. He also wanted to judge their reaction to his announcement. He recognized a few of the ones he had met—Shallum and Rephaiah from the district of Jerusalem. Malkijah, the leader of a wine-growing district west of Jerusalem. He saw that Eliashib the high priest had come. And Rebbe Ezra. The rebbe didn't know what Nehemiah planned, but surely he would throw his support behind this project.

Nehemiah gazed up at the cloudless sky, the summer sun already bleaching the color from it. He had fasted and prayed in preparation for this announcement, and the aroma of the morning sacrifice, pungent in the motionless air, intensified his hunger. He wiped beads of sweat from his brow, waiting until all but a few stragglers had assembled in front of him, then held up his hand for silence. He would begin his speech without elaborate greetings or a lengthy preamble.

"You see the trouble we are in: Jerusalem lies in ruins, and its gates have been burned with fire. The Almighty One's city, the place He has chosen to meet with His people, lies in disgrace, neglected and defenseless. Our enemies can point to its destruction as a visible sign of the Almighty One's judgment. And that's exactly what these ruined walls symbolize. In fact, on the ninth day of this very month, more than 120 years ago, the enemy destroyed God's holy temple because of our sin. We just held a fast to commemorate that tragic day.

"But now God has brought us back to our land. He has forgiven our sins. Restored us. The city of Jerusalem should serve as a testimony to His goodness and grace, not His judgment." Nehemiah paused dramatically, aware that he had their full attention. "Come, let us rebuild the wall of Jerusalem, and we will no longer be in disgrace. Let us rebuild it so the nations will know that our God is with us."

A murmur of excited voices swept through the crowd. He waited until it died away. "I know beyond a doubt that the gracious hand of my God is upon me, and that He will help us accomplish this task. He already answered my prayers and provided an opportunity for me to speak to the Persian emperor about this city. And God gave me favor in the king's sight so he would grant my petition. King Artaxerxes even provided letters of authorization to show to the governors of our neighboring provinces who might try to stop us. He gave me another letter for Asaph, keeper of the king's forest, who will provide timber for the beams and gates. All of these things testify to the fact that the Holy One is with us, answering our prayers, working on our behalf. There is nothing to stop us from rebuilding the wall."

Again, a wave of excitement rippled through his audience,

the voices louder this time. But some of the leaders seemed unconvinced. He gestured to the high priest, standing in front of him. "Did you have a question, Eliashib?"

"Rebuilding the temple was a huge undertaking that took several years. How many years do you expect it to take to complete the wall?"

"I expect to finish in a matter of months, not years. I have a plan—"

"Come now, Governor," a council member named Meshullam interrupted. "You can't possibly gather everything you need in a matter of months—laborers, tools, supplies, equipment, scaffolding. Surely it will take at least a year, if not more, to rebuild a wall that's several miles long."

"We don't have a year. Our enemies have tried repeatedly to stop our building efforts in the past, and we can't allow that to happen again."

"Even unopposed, the task will be impossible to accomplish in a few months," Meshullam said.

"My plan is to divide the work into smaller projects and appoint a leader to be in charge of each gate or section. He will assess his assigned work and decide what needs to be done. I've already finished a preliminary inspection, and the wall's foundations look sound, especially the portions where the wall was built on bedrock. Some parts of the wall will have to be completely constructed from the foundation up. Other sections will need to be repaired, but are otherwise sound. And I saw several places that are going to need to be fortified and reinforced to make them strong again. The gates must all be built from scratch, of course. The leader in charge of each section will be responsible for finding his own volunteers and equipment and supplies. And he'll be responsible for supervising the work. The skilled architects and engineers and builders among us will serve as advisors."

"Our enemies will surely try to stop us," the district leader of Mizpah shouted out. "They have in the past."

"True. That's why we must work quickly so it doesn't happen again. Listen, the most important thing—and the key to our success—is that we must work together. We all need to understand the importance of this project, the urgency. And we need to work as one man to get it done. The Almighty One has provided an open door. We need to walk through it in faith, trusting Him for our success."

"What you're asking of us is unprecedented," Rephaiah, one of Jerusalem's district rulers, said.

"You're wrong. There is a precedent—the construction of God's Tabernacle. Moses called for freewill offerings from all the people in order to build it. No one was taxed or compelled to give. And all of the people, young and old, men and women, rich and poor, brought what they had and offered it to God. Some could give only a little—wood or yarn or spices. Others were able to contribute costly things—gold, silver, and precious stones to create the high priest's breastplate. But no matter how great or small, everything the people gave was added together to accomplish the task. In fact, so many contributions piled up that Moses had to tell the people to stop. The tabernacle was quickly completed according to God's plan. And to His glory. Jerusalem's wall will be completed, as well."

Nehemiah sensed his audience's growing excitement. The people would support him, he was certain of it. But there was one more thing they needed to know. "Jerusalem's wall is real, but it's also symbolic," he said. "In a way, we destroyed the wall ourselves by relying on idols instead of on God. We destroyed it by desecrating His Sabbaths. By ignoring the laws He gave us, laws that teach us how to live. These ruins are a picture of what we did to our relationship with the Almighty One—we demolished it. Now it's time to rebuild what our sins have destroyed. It's time to repair the foundations of our faith and renew our covenant with God. To restore His laws and precepts, and live by them. Rebuilding this physical wall won't do us any good unless we also rebuild our lives with the Almighty One at the center."

He paused to wipe a runner of sweat trickling down his face. "God sees us as one people—the children of Abraham. He sent us into exile together, and He also brought us out together. Let's forget our past grudges and the differences that divide us—rich and poor, nobles and farmers, priests and people—and work together as one, as His chosen people. This good work of rebuilding the wall is what I came here from Susa to do. And it will get done, so help me God. Are you with me?"

A great cheer went up. "Let's start today!" someone shouted.

"Yes!"

"Let's do it!"

Nehemiah waited until the shouting died away. He couldn't help smiling. "I hoped you would say that."

"How do we begin?" Shallum, one of Jerusalem's district leaders, asked.

Nehemiah signaled to his aides to hold up the map. "I've drawn up this map of the city. The next step is for leaders and volunteers to come forward and each claim a section to repair—next to your house or your workplace or wherever you choose. Then gather your teams together so we can begin the work as soon as possible."

Nehemiah stepped down from the platform to the excited buzz of voices. He felt as if he could sprout wings and fly—and longed to run to a section of ruined wall and start piling building blocks on top of each other right now.

"Nehemiah!" someone called. He turned and saw his two brothers weaving through the crowd to join him, grinning broadly. "Why didn't you tell us what you were planning?" Ephraim asked, thumping his back.

"I thought I would surprise you."

"So, this is what you *really* came here to do," Hanani said. "Rebuild Jerusalem."

"Yes, and we're going to accomplish it together." He felt fearless, invincible. Convinced beyond a doubt that God was with him. For the first time he could ever remember, such inexpressible joy filled him that he wanted to dance. "Come work for me, you two. Move your families into my residence. Be my right-hand men."

Hanani laughed. "We're scribes, not builders."

"That doesn't matter. I need men of faith, most of all. Men who won't lose heart. They assigned three aides to assist me, but I'm not entirely pleased with them."

"I'm with you," Ephraim said. "All the way."

"Me too." Hanani encircled Nehemiah's shoulder and gave it a quick squeeze.

The wall was still in ruins, the job was immense. And for a moment, Nehemiah wondered if he truly did have the skills he would need to do this. He had seen firsthand the enormity of the task he faced: removing tons of rubble and rebuilding miles of crumbled walls, not to mention organizing thousands of unskilled men into a competent labor force. And he would have to accomplish it all before his enemies had a chance to stop him. But in spite of his doubts and fears, Nehemiah knew that the Almighty One was with him. And he had never imagined that he could feel so happy.

Part II

Your people will rebuild the ancient ruins

and will raise up the age-old foundations;

you will be called Repairer of Broken Walls,

Restorer of Streets with Dwellings.

ISAIAH 58:12

JERUSALEM

Chana pulled a fist-sized lump of dough from the bowl and absently rolled it in her hands to form a ball. All morning, she'd been unable to stop thinking about the governor's speech and his determination to rebuild Jerusalem's wall. If only he had come a year sooner, his wall might have saved Yitzhak's life. She would be a married woman by now, perhaps holding a child in her arms. The excitement she'd felt the morning Nehemiah explained his plan still sent shivers through her. The community would work together as one people. Every man in Jerusalem had volunteered to help, and she longed to join in this great work.

As she patted the dough between her palms to flatten it, she suddenly stopped, her task forgotten as an idea began to form. She chased the idea down different paths in her mind, asking "What if?" and "Why not?" And the seed of the idea slowly grew into a conviction of what she must do.

"Chana!" One of her sisters threw a pistachio at her from across the courtyard, barely missing her head. "Your bread is burning!"

She dropped the unbaked dough into the bowl and quickly yanked the burning flatbread from the stone griddle. Too late. The scorched bottom was as black as night.

"What's wrong with you this morning?" Yudit asked. "You're sitting here, but your mind may as well be in Susa."

"I've been thinking about something," Chana said.

"Getting engaged to Malkijah?"

"No. Not that." Although she could easily imagine herself living in his beautiful home, enjoying the luxury of servants, being free from the need to bake bread on steamy summer days like this one. She retrieved the new round of flattened dough and laid it on the hot stone, determined to watch it this time. "I'll tell you what my idea is, but you have to promise you won't laugh. And you can't tell Abba about it until I'm ready to tell him. Promise?"

"This sounds intriguing," Yudit said. She and Sarah left their work and hurried over to where Chana crouched beside the hearth. "We promise."

"I've been thinking about the speech our new governor gave the other day, and about his plan to rebuild the wall."

"That was so inspiring, wasn't it?" Sarah said. "I never heard such a fine speech in my life."

"It was," Chana admitted. "I wasn't expecting to be impressed by Governor Nehemiah, but I have to admit that I was. He acted so cold the night he came to dinner, but his speech was very impassioned and inspiring. I think he galvanized our people like no other leader has since Moses."

"Every man in Jerusalem is ready to sign up to help," Yudit said.

"So what's your idea?" Sarah asked.

"I'm going to ask Abba to let me help him rebuild his section of the wall."

"What!" Yudit looked at her as if she were crazy. Sarah's mouth fell open in surprise.

"Abba is overseeing the section between the Tower of the Ovens and the Valley Gate, and it's up to him to recruit volunteers. I'm going to volunteer."

"You've come up with some crazy ideas," Yudit said, "but building a wall? That's outrageous, even for you."

"Why? I think it makes perfect sense. All the young men in the city signed up to help their fathers, but Abba doesn't have any sons to help him. I want to show my support and do my part."

"You mean, actually work?" Yudit asked. "Lifting stones . . . and building a wall?"

"Yes. That's exactly what I mean. Listen, when Governor Nehemiah gave the example of the tabernacle, he said that everyone contributed—men and women, young people and old. Why shouldn't women take part in this project, too?"

"Maybe you're right," Yudit said. "I think it would be wonderful to work together as one people the way the governor described it."

"Then I want to help, too," Sarah said. "But I don't think Abba will ever let us do it."

Chana sighed as she turned the round of bread over to bake on the other side. "That's what worries me, too. But I'm going to tell him that there's a precedent for it in the Torah. We'll be just like Zelophehad's daughters."

"Like who?"

"I'll explain it later. Abba will be here any minute, and I don't want him to overhear us. I'll tell him my idea after we eat, when he's sure to be in a good mood. You have to keep quiet until then."

Their father arrived home from the evening sacrifice a few minutes later, and Yudit rushed to greet him with a cup of cold water. Sarah offered a basin of water to rinse his feet. They gave him extra portions at dinner and filled his wine cup a second time. Chana's sisters treated him so royally that she worried he would become suspicious. At last he pushed away his plate and leaned back in his chair with a look of contentment. "You girls seem especially happy tonight," he said. "Even you, Chana."

"I am, Abba."

She was about to begin the speech she had planned when he said, "Good. Then may I discuss something with you?"

She was thrown off balance for a moment, but replied, "Certainly, Abba."

"Would you two girls give us a moment alone, please?" he asked Yudit and Sarah. They went into the house, but Chana knew they would listen to every word.

"Malkijah asked me about a betrothal today. He wants to sign a *ketubah*. What do you say, my angel?"

"I . . . I need a little more time."

"Chana. He has been very patient with you, but it isn't fair to ask him to wait any longer. If you aren't interested, then it's time to set him free so he can look elsewhere for a wife."

Abba was right. She had no reason to delay any longer. She admired Malkijah and believed she could be content with him. She would be useful in his household. The night she'd visited his estate, she'd seen that he needed a wife, someone to speak on behalf of his servants and remind him to show mercy. And leaving Jerusalem would mean leaving the painful reminders of the past. Maybe she would find healing in the beautiful hills of Beth Hakkerem. Maybe even joy. Maybe the Almighty One would bless her with a child someday.

"I will agree to a betrothal, Abba—"

"Wonderful! That's wonderful news, my angel! You won't be sorry."

"But not yet. There's something I need to do first, and I'm afraid Malkijah won't allow it once we're betrothed."

"What is it?"

"I want to help you rebuild the wall."

"Help me? What do you mean?"

"I heard the governor's speech, Abba. He's right, our city is in disgrace. I want to help you repair your section of the wall. I want to rebuild right alongside you. Yudit and Sarah do, too."

Abba laughed, but it was a nervous laugh, without mirth. "Is this a joke, my angel?"

"No. All the other leaders have sons to work beside them, and we want to work with you."

"Be sensible, Chana. How can I allow such a thing? I'm a leader—"

"All the more reason to let us do it. You'll set an example. How can men refuse to work when the leader of the half-district of Jerusalem has three daughters who are doing their part? It will put them all to shame."

"I fear that I am the one who will be put to shame—along with the three of you. Rebuilding the wall is a man's job. It most certainly isn't something for women to do."

"What about the daughters of Zelophehad? Remember the story? Zelophehad didn't have any sons, so Moses agreed that his daughters could inherit his portion of land. We're like sons to you, and we want to have a share in what all the people are doing."

"I don't think it's the same thing, Chana."

Desperation made her reveal her deepest motive. "Listen, if I could just do this one thing—pile stones into a wall and build a fortress to keep out murderers like the men who killed Yitzhak, maybe I'll be able to heal from his death. Then I'll be ready to accept Malkijah's proposal."

"Are you bribing me, my angel?"

She managed a small smile. "If that's what it takes."

"And what will happen when Malkijah sees the woman he hopes to marry working on the wall like a common laborer? Have you thought of that? He will be outraged. I wouldn't blame him if he changes his mind about you."

"Then maybe it's better that he learns what I'm like now, before we're betrothed. Better that he knows I have my own mind, and that I'm not afraid to speak it. If he's outraged that I want to support my father and rebuild my city, then I don't want to marry him."

"I'll have to think about this."

The door to the house opened and Yudit and Sarah poured

out like water spilled from a jar, unable to keep quiet a moment longer. "Please let us do this, Abba, please," Yudit said.

"You want to build the wall, too, Yudit? Truly? What will Alon think? I thought you were interested in him?"

"I don't care what he thinks. Or what anyone else thinks."

"I also want to help," Sarah said.

"Sarah? My little cherub? . . . Did your sisters talk you into this?"

"Not at all. I think it's exciting. I'll finally get to do something besides cook and do boring housework all day. It'll be fun to be part of something this big."

Abba took both of Chana's hands in his. "How are you going to lift heavy stones with these delicate hands? How can I bear to see your fingers smashed and scraped and bruised?"

"There must be plenty of other tasks we can do besides lift stones. The important thing is that we'll be there, alongside you and the other workers, doing our part."

"Please don't say no," Yudit said. "Please let us do it."

"Yes, please, Abba," Sarah echoed.

Chana could see his indecision. He released her hands and squeezed the bridge of his nose between his fingers. "This isn't fair," he said. "You know I can't say no to my girls."

"Then don't. Say yes, instead."

"Everyone in the province of Judah is helping," Yudit said.

"Every man, maybe. I daresay my daughters will be the only women."

"You should be very proud of us for that," Chana said.

Abba gave a tired groan. "I must be crazy for saying this, but . . . I'll try to find something for you to do. But only—"

"Thank you, Abba!" They fell all over him, hugging him, kissing his cheeks.

"But only on a trial basis," he said, trying in vain to fend them off. "Maybe you can bring lunch or water for my workers . . ."

"Maybe move a few small stones?" Chana asked.

"We'll see."

Chana laughed and kissed him again. For the first time in a very long time, she felt truly happy.

"Now, what about Malkijah?" he asked when they finally finished hugging him. "Can I give him an answer about your betrothal? Are you ready for me to arrange a ketubah?"

"I-I guess you and Malkijah can arrange a ketubah. As long as our engagement isn't official until after we help rebuild the wall." But Chana couldn't help but feel a tiny shiver of misgiving at the finality of the decision.

CHAPTER

18

SAMARIA

Tobiah had a lot of time to ponder what his next move should be as he left his Ammonite capital early in the morning for the long journey to Samaria on horseback. His new enemy, Nehemiah, had proven to be more dangerous than Tobiah had ever imagined. In a single act of political genius, Judah's new governor had proposed to rebuild Jerusalem's wall, igniting flames of patriotism and religious fervor and uniting his deeply divided population.

The long drought made fording the Jordan River easier than usual, and as Tobiah crossed into Judean territory, his anger burned as hot as the summer sun. This territory should be his, not Nehemiah's. He had invested years of hard work currying favor among the Judean leaders and priests, laboring to help solve Judah's many economic and security problems. His goal was to forge an alliance between Judah and Ammon, with himself as the leader. But he was no longer the savior they'd been waiting for—Nehemiah was.

Tobiah knew he needed help in ridding the province of this new threat. His allies, Sanballat and Geshem, must have heard the news by now that Nehemiah was fortifying Jerusalem. If not, Tobiah needed to warn them. Afterward, on the way home, Tobiah would make a secret visit to Jerusalem to speak with the powerful noblemen he knew on the council and among the priests. Surely not everyone in Judah welcomed their new governor and his ambitions with open arms.

The heat had nearly exhausted Tobiah and his small retinue of men by the time they reached Sanballat's hilltop palace in Samaria. But Tobiah didn't waste any time before conferring with his allies. "Why the urgent message to meet with Geshem and me?" Sanballat asked after his servants had closed the door on their private meeting. "I assume this must be very serious to summon us to a second visit so soon after the first?" The Samaritan leader's face looked flushed and overheated in spite of the servants who continually fanned him with palm branches. Tobiah wondered if his news would give the heavy man a fit of apoplexy.

"It is serious. I sent two of my men to visit my son in Jerusalem with orders to follow Judah's new governor. Jehohanan even managed to be appointed as one of Nehemiah's aides. They found out what his agenda is and why he came to Jerusalem." Tobiah paused, waiting to see if they already knew. It appeared they didn't. Tobiah's robe clung to his sweaty back as he sat forward in his seat. "Nehemiah has drawn up plans to rebuild Jerusalem's wall. He has the full support of the people. The work will begin immediately."

"He's fortifying the city?" Geshem asked. "Why?"

"Don't be naïve," Sanballat said. "Why does any leader build walls and citadels? He wants freedom. Power. Self-sufficiency."

"The letters Nehemiah showed us from Susa didn't say anything about building a fortress, did they?" Tobiah asked. He wished now that he had studied the letters more carefully instead of trying to show his disrespect by ignoring them. "But since that's what he's doing, he's obviously going behind King Artaxerxes' back."

"I agree," Sanballat said. "The Persian king couldn't have known what Nehemiah intended, or he never would have allowed it. A fortified city is the first step toward rebellion, a necessity for an independent nation. We need to send a message to King Artaxerxes immediately."

"What else did your informants tell you?" Geshem asked. His anger was clear in his dark frown, his incessant pacing. He had risen from his chair at Tobiah's news, as if already imagining how an independent province of Judah would threaten his trade monopoly.

"It seems Nehemiah gave a speech at the temple in front of all the leaders and priests and people," Tobiah continued. "According to my son, he mesmerized them and rallied them into action. There was a stampede to volunteer for his massive building project. Everyone is getting involved."

"Their enthusiasm won't survive this heat," Sanballat said. He looked uncomfortable in the ridiculous, ornate robe he insisted on wearing even on the hottest days. But in spite of the Samaritan leader's words, Tobiah could tell that he was worried. Both men were. "When this summer heat wave breaks, the rains will begin," Sanballat continued. "The work will have to stop during the rainy season. After that, it will be time for the people to return to their homes to plow and plant their crops. The enthusiasm of the masses won't last after that. It rarely does last for very long."

Tobiah shook his head, wishing he could believe Sanballat's confident prediction. His allies hadn't heard the firsthand report about this compelling new leader, as Tobiah had. "Nehemiah is proving to be a very inspiring leader," Tobiah told them. "He has everyone in Judah convinced that the wall can be rebuilt in a matter of months. They're cheering him on, offering their full support."

"Months?" Geshem gave a derisive laugh. "Impossible. I've been to Jerusalem. I've seen the destruction. There isn't a single gate that's still intact."

"Geshem is right," Sanballat said. "Besides, how can Nehemiah afford the supplies he needs?"

"He claims to have a letter from King Artaxerxes addressed to the keeper of the king's forest, granting him permission to cut all the timber he wants."

Geshem huffed in anger. "Nehemiah forgot to mention that little detail when he met with us."

"Where will he get a workforce of experienced builders?" Sanballat asked. "Most of the Judeans are farmers and shepherds."

"He asked all the people to volunteer as the workforce."

"Amateurs? What do they know about constructing a city wall? It will topple over in the first strong wind."

"I think you're missing the point," Tobiah said. "It doesn't matter *how* he plans to rebuild the wall. What's alarming is that he was in Jerusalem for what . . . barely a week? And he already managed to gain the full support of the masses. He somehow inspired them to forget their differences and work together on a common project. An enormous, impossible project. That's a clear display of leadership genius. From there it's not a huge leap to imagine him starting a rebellion, convincing the people that he's the promised Messiah."

"Except for one thing," Sanballat said. "He hasn't solved their economic problems. How does he plan to pay for all the costs involved in rebuilding his wall? The people can't afford higher taxes, so his only recourse will be to suspend tribute payments, either to our provincial treasuries or to Persia. Or both."

"Withholding tribute would definitely constitute a rebellion," Tobiah said. He suddenly realized that because of the close ties he had fostered between his own nation and Judah, his political power and governorship also would be in jeopardy if the Persian king responded with force. He closed his eyes as he caught a glimpse of his own small empire toppling. Nehemiah had to be stopped.

"I think we need to pay a state visit to Jerusalem," Sanballat said.

"And do what?" Tobiah said miserably, slumping back in his seat. "Do you have a plan?"

"The people have known me as their governor ever since Ezra retired. They don't know this newcomer yet. Nehemiah hasn't proven himself, in spite of his rallying speech. We have to convince the people to rethink this building project. We'll show them the foolishness of the idea and also of their leader."

"So we'll tell them the idea is preposterous and that it risks Persian retaliation?" Geshem asked. "Will they care?" He looked skeptical.

"We'll sow a few seeds of doubt and discouragement and wait for them to grow," Sanballat said. "The common people have enough problems without this upstart governor asking them to do even more. We'll help them see that such an immense task can't possibly be accomplished without a great deal of manpower and money. The people will never agree to another increase in taxes. If we ridicule their leader, the people will see him for the fool that he is."

"In the meantime," Geshem said, "we need to send a delegation to Susa and tell King Artaxerxes what Nehemiah is doing."

Sanballat winced. "That could be risky. What if Nehemiah really does have the king's permission? I think we'd better wait and ask to see Nehemiah's papers again. Find out if he really is authorized to rebuild the wall."

"I've been thinking as I've listened to you talk," Tobiah said. "Maybe there's something else we can do to bring a swift end to Nehemiah's popularity. He currently has the support of the common people, but this drought has impoverished thousands of them. The divide between the rich and the poor gets wider and deeper every day as more and more farmers are forced to mortgage their property and go into debt. It wouldn't take much to start a riot, poor against rich. And the division and hatred would certainly halt Nehemiah's building project."

"Won't that backfire on us?" Geshem asked. "Aren't we among the wealthy ones?"

"That doesn't matter," Tobiah said. "As long as the unrest puts Nehemiah's popularity in jeopardy. Unless he's a seasoned leader, and I'm guessing that he isn't, he won't be able to solve the problem and get his project back on track. He'll never be able to appease both the rich and the poor. And he's powerless to end the drought—or the enormous taxes the Persians impose."

"Can you light the right fires to start the unrest, Tobiah?" Sanballat asked. "Do you have the right connections in Judah?"

"Yes, in fact, I do." He smiled, pleased that Sanballat was dependent on him, for once. The Samaritan leader would be in Tobiah's debt when this was over. "Yes, I know exactly which fires to stoke. And my son is in the perfect position to stoke them."

"Good. Then we're counting on you to do it. In the meantime, I believe it's time for the three of us to pay Nehemiah a state visit."

CHAPTER
19

THE DISTRICT OF BETH HAKKEREM

The evening meal had been an elaborate, multi-course affair. Nava was weary from a long day of work, serving her master and his distinguished guests. As she had moved in and out of the outdoor dining room carrying platters and trays of food from the kitchen, she had overheard snatches of their conversation, enough to learn that the men had come from Jerusalem and that they and Master Malkijah were planning a building project. From the sound of things, it would be an enormous undertaking.

At last Malkijah and his guests left the table and moved to the upper terrace to enjoy the cool breeze and sip wine beneath the stars. Nava grabbed a tray and hurried out to clear the table, hoping to finally go to bed. She nearly halted and ran back to the kitchen when she saw that Master Aaron hadn't left the table with the others. He remained in his seat, sprawled comfortably on the cushions, and now he watched her every move. She didn't dare retreat. Nava quickly piled as many dishes as she could safely carry onto her tray and lifted it up, planning to return to the kitchen and remain there until he left.

"Nava," he said before she could safely escape. "Put down that tray and come here."

Her heart pounded painfully when she glanced around and saw that they were alone. She had to obey. The plates rattled as she set the tray on the table with shaking hands. She walked around to stand in front of him as she'd been instructed to do.

"Here I am." Where were the other servers who were supposed to help her? Ever since she'd been assigned to work with the household staff, Nava had been careful never to work by herself, especially when Aaron was nearby. And now she was alone with him.

"Look at me, Nava." She lifted her eyes from the floor to his face. He had drunk a great deal of wine at dinner and his eyes looked bleary, his words sounded slurred. "Why don't you like me?" he asked.

"I . . . I don't understand. . . . You are my master. . . . I work for your father—"

"You know exactly what I mean," he snarled, making the hairs on Nava's arms prickle. Her heart pounded harder. "I've seen you go out of your way to avoid me, and I want to know why."

She could barely breathe. She stared at the floor again, trying to think. "Servants like me are supposed to stay in the background and—"

"You're lying! You know how I can tell? You're looking at your feet again and I told you to look at me." She lifted her chin. "That's better. Now, don't you find me handsome, Nava my beauty? Your name suits you well, by the way. Very well. I could eat you up, like a luscious bowl of fruit."

Fear brought tears to her eyes. She let them roll down her face without wiping them. "I'm in love with the man who climbed the wall to see me that one night. His name is Dan. We're going to be married when my service here is finished and—"

Aaron's harsh laughter cut off her words. "You belong to us for the next six years, Nava. You'd be a fool to believe your hot-blooded young man will wait that long. I know I wouldn't. In fact, I don't want to wait another night." He pulled himself to his feet, his eyes slowly scanning her from head to toe. Nava's skin crawled as she took a step back. Her tears fell faster. He could do whatever he wanted and she couldn't stop him.

"Please, my lord . . . I-I answered your question. . . . May I finish my work now?"

"I asked you if you found me handsome and you didn't answer me."

What could she say? She didn't dare tell him that his deviousness made him repulsive to her, no matter what he looked like on the outside. If only the ground would open up and swallow her. Just as her knees began to go weak, she heard the housekeeper's voice behind her.

"What's taking you so long, Nava? This table should be all cleared by now and—oh. I'm sorry, Master Aaron. I didn't know you were still here. Do you need something, my lord?"

"I need Nava." He spoke so softly that only she heard him.

"Pardon me, my lord?" the housekeeper asked. Nava took advantage of the interruption to grab the tray of dishes and flee to the kitchen. When the housekeeper, whose name was Ruth, joined her a moment later, Nava sat crouched on the floor beside the worktable, sobbing, her knees unable to hold her a moment longer. "What's wrong with you?" Ruth asked. "What happened in there?"

"Nothing happened . . . but . . . but—"

"Then why aren't you working?" The housekeeper was a sturdy, large-boned woman with a round face and coarse black hair, streaked with gray. She often carried a switch with her and Nava had seen her use it on servants who were lazy or idle. But Nava feared Aaron more than she feared Ruth.

"Master Aaron keeps watching me and trying to get me alone with him, and . . . and I'm terrified of him, Ruth. I know what he wants and . . . and I'm so scared!"

"You foolish girl. Stop crying. Stand up." She grabbed Nava's arm and pulled her to her feet. "Don't you know that he has a right to take any bondservant he wants for his wife?"

"Yes, I know. That's why I'm so afraid!"

"If he wants you, that's a good thing. You would be mistress of this household. That's nothing to snivel and cry about."

"But I don't love him. I love someone else and I don't want—"

"Wake up, Nava. You're a bondservant—a *female* bondservant. The bottom of the heap. Nobody cares what you want or don't want. If I had a chance to marry the master and be mistress of this household, believe me, I would take it."

"But he won't marry me, Ruth. I've seen what Master Aaron is like. I've heard the lies he tells. Once he has his way with me, he'll deny that it ever happened. Nobody will believe me. And none of the other servants will stand up for me or tell Master Malkijah the truth."

Ruth turned away and began taking the dishes off the tray, piling them near the basin of water to be washed. Nava waited for her to say something, but it was as if Nava had never spoken. "Please help me, Ruth. I-I don't know what to do."

"You might be right about young Aaron. Everyone knows what he's like." She picked up a plate and swished it in the water to wash it, then handed it to Nava to dry. "But even if he does have his way and refuses to do the honorable thing, it could mean your freedom. Don't you want to go home to your family? Six years is a long time."

"Not for that price." Her tears began falling again at the thought of having to tell Dan she was no longer a virgin. "I'm in love with a man from back home."

"That fool who broke in here and woke everyone up?"

"Yes. And he may not want to marry me if . . ."

Ruth sighed and dropped more dishes into the water with a splash. "That's too bad, but there's nothing I can do about it."

She gestured to the pile she had already washed. "Start drying. I'd like to get to bed before dawn."

"Can't you please make sure I'm never alone with him? Make sure there's always someone else working with me? And that I don't have to walk back to my room alone at night? Please, Ruth."

She sighed again. "I'll try. It's all I can promise you."

"Thank you." Nava felt only slightly relieved.

"You're a strange one, Nava. Most girls who are as pretty as you would use their beauty to their advantage. They wouldn't resist our handsome young master's attention, but use it to help them get ahead. I admire you for not acting foolishly. And I wish you luck. You'll need it."

"Why do you say that?"

"Because if Aaron is anything like our master, he'll get what he wants, one way or another. Master Malkijah always does."

Nava barely slept, waking with nightmares that left her trembling and in tears. She was still struggling to recover the next morning when her master called all of his servants together in his central courtyard. Even the guards and farm laborers and shepherds had been ordered to come, as well as the kitchen and household staffs. They crowded into the estate's inner courtyard near the goat pens.

"I have an announcement to make," Malkijah began. "Judah's new governor, Nehemiah ben Hacaliah, has drawn up plans to rebuild the wall around Jerusalem. He's asking every able-bodied man in the province to volunteer to join him so the work can be completed quickly."

Nava had traveled to Jerusalem with her family for Passover and the other feasts and seen the miles and miles of crumbled wall surrounding the city. How could they rebuild that jumbled pile of burnt stones and rubble—and do it quickly? It seemed to her that the task would take years to complete. Wouldn't it be dangerous to try to shift such huge piles of stones? She wondered if Dan had volunteered. And if her father and brothers would also help.

"I'll be overseeing the repairs to the Dung Gate at the south-ern tip of the city," Malkijah told them. "That means clear-ing away the rubble, restoring the surrounding stonework and supports, rebuilding the gatehouse and tower, and setting the doors and bolts and bars of the finished gate in place. All but the most essential laborers among you, such as a handful of guards and enough men to care for the animals, will move with me to Jerusalem to help me rebuild the gate. I'll also need to take additional kitchen and household staff with me to serve the needs of those workers. Penina and Ruth—I'll leave it up to you to decide who stays here and who you can spare."

Nava heard whispering as everyone glanced around, wondering who would stay or go. As one of the newest servants, she would likely be left behind, stuck with the jobs that no one else wanted.

"I'll be traveling back home for Shabbat each week," Malkijah said, raising his voice above the murmuring. "While I'm away, my sons Aaron and Josef will oversee my estate."

His words sent a shiver of horror through Nava. She would have no protection at all with Master Malkijah and most of the servants away. She had to make sure she was among the workers who went to Jerusalem.

The moment her master dismissed everyone to their duties, Nava ran to plead with the housekeeper. Everyone else was trying to talk with her as well, some begging to stay, others pleading to be among those who went to Jerusalem. Nava had to wait until the very last servant had spoken her wishes, and she saw that Ruth was losing patience with this disruption to her well-ordered routine. The housekeeper headed toward the kitchen when the last servant had spoken with her and Nava hurried to jog along behind her.

"Not you, too," Ruth said when she saw Nava. "What do you want?"

"Ruth, please! I can't stay here in Beth Hakkerem with Master Aaron in charge. You know what will happen."

"The master and his guests are waiting for their breakfast. Grab that platter and put it on the table before the food gets stone-cold."

Nava lifted the platter and followed Ruth into the dining area. Malkijah and his guests were already seated but she was relieved to see that Aaron wasn't there. She set the platter in the middle where they could all reach it, then continued to beg in a soft, urgent voice as she and Ruth returned to the kitchen for more food.

"Please help me. Please make sure I'm assigned to go to Jerusalem."

"The master will want more experienced workers than you with him in Jerusalem. He may be entertaining other noblemen, or even the governor."

"Please, Ruth! I'll do anything you say but please, please don't make me stay here with Master Aaron. Please!"

"That's enough, Nava!"

She wondered if she had gone too far and made Ruth angry. But a moment later the housekeeper mumbled, "I'll see what I can do."

Nava wished she still believed in prayer. She would pray to be far, far away from Beth Hakkerem, far away from the danger. But why bother? The Almighty One never seemed to answer her prayers.

CHAPTER

20

JERUSALEM

The sun was just beginning to lighten the sky behind the Mount of Olives as Nehemiah walked with his brothers from the governor's residence to the open plaza near the Valley Gate. Today he would organize his section leaders so they could start rebuilding the wall. He was so eager to begin that his brothers had trouble keeping up with him, their footsteps crunching on the quiet streets of the slumbering city as they hurried down the sloping road behind him.

"Did they make you get up this early in the morning when you lived in Susa?" his brother Hanani asked, yawning loudly.

"Even the sun has sense enough not to rise this early," Ephraim added. "Why don't you?"

"We need to make the best use of the available daylight," Nehemiah replied. "I asked my section leaders to meet here before the morning sacrifice so we can finish in time to go up to the temple. If we start building right after that, we can get a lot done before the heat saps everyone's strength." He slowed his steps to their pace, aware that he was asking a lot of them. His brothers and their families had moved into the governor's residence with him so they would be available to work closely with him. The stars had still been out this morning when Nehemiah had awakened them. They had grabbed a quick bite to eat, gathered their things, and started walking, but his brothers' eyes still drooped with sleep.

"Are the maps and lists all ready?" he asked them.

"Yes, my lord and master," Hanani said with mock seriousness.

"Sorry," Nehemiah said. "I got used to ordering people around in Susa."

"You're certainly very good at it," Ephraim muttered.

"I had to be. The emperor's life depended on it. And now the security of Jerusalem does."

"Well, just don't run ahead of the Almighty One," Ephraim said, "and decide to crown yourself king."

By the time they reached the Valley Gate, about halfway down the western wall of the city, the sun had inched higher above the ridge, quickly warming the morning. People had begun to stir in the nearby houses, and he smelled the aroma of cooking fires and heard the grating of hand mills as women ground flour to make bread. Mounds of rubble lay piled all around the area inside the Valley Gate, but he refused to let it discourage him. Soon all these stones would be gone, God willing, and the elaborate gatehouse would be rebuilt.

"I've decided to set up our project headquarters in this open area," he told his brothers. "It's not very spacious, but it will be a convenient place to oversee the work since the site is easily reached from most sections of the wall."

"That's very fair of you, Nehemiah," Hanani said with a humorless laugh. "That way, *everyone* will have to walk uphill to confer with you—those working near the very bottom of the ridge will have to climb up here to talk to you, and those working near the temple will have to climb uphill again *after* they talk to you."

"It's for my convenience, not theirs," Nehemiah said. "So I can move quickly to wherever I'm needed."

"And you are quick, I must say," Ephraim said. He was still trying to catch his breath after their brisk walk.

One by one the other leaders began to arrive, moving between the houses like shadows in the early dawn light. His three aides, Rehum, Jehohanan, and Levi, were among the first to join him. Of the three, only Jehohanan looked awake and alert. Nehemiah again wished he could have investigated these three men thoroughly before taking them into his confidence as he would have done in Susa, but there hadn't been time. Instead, he'd been forced to rely on the judgment of the officials who'd recommended them. But he knew without a doubt that he could trust his brothers and was glad they'd agreed to be his right-hand men.

Rays of sunlight streaked the sky above the Mount of Olives as the last of the leaders arrived. Time to begin. "This is an exciting day for all of us," Nehemiah said. "Each of you has volunteered to oversee a section of the wall or to rebuild one of the ten gates. For those of you who require lumber, you'll need to talk to my brother." Ephraim lifted his hand so everyone would know who he was. "He's in charge of procuring timber from the king's forest a few miles south of Jerusalem. But he's going to need wagons and teams of oxen and mules to haul it here, so if any of you can spare your wagons or teams, please let Ephraim know. I hope by now that you've had a chance to survey your assigned section and have begun to gather your workers," Nehemiah continued.

"People from my district came forward to volunteer in great numbers," someone shouted.

"Mine too."

"Good." He paused as Hanani handed him the map. "This morning I want to go over this map of the sections and their leaders so you can see who will be working alongside you and so I can learn who you are. I'll start at the north side of the city near the temple mount and proceed around the wall to the west. The first leader is Eliashib, the high priest, who will oversee the restoration of the temple's citadel."

"My fellow priests and I have committed to rebuilding the section of wall from the Sheep Gate to the western corner," Eliashib said, "including the Tower of the Hundred and the Tower of Hananel."

"Excellent. I know that's asking a lot of you and your men. The Babylonians completely destroyed the citadel and its gates when they broke through to invade the city, so it will be a huge task to rebuild it. We'll need fortified towers and a reinforced wall because that section is still the most vulnerable. We all know that our enemies typically attack from that direction. And you've also volunteered to repair the Sheep Gate and reset its doors, I see?"

"Yes, Governor. The sheep used for the daily temple sacrifices come through that gate, so I intend to consecrate it for holy use. My grandfather, Jeshua ben Jozadak, arrived with the first group of exiles who returned with Zerubbabel, and he would have been overjoyed to see these gates and fortifications rebuilt."

"Didn't your grandfather help rebuild the temple?"

"Yes. And served as its first high priest."

Nehemiah continued reading from his list, calling each section leader's name and then memorizing each face. He was thankful for his training as a cupbearer, which had taught him to remember names and faces. The king's life had depended on his ability to recognize every palace worker on sight so he could spot intruders. When he read the name Meshullam, son of Berekiah, it seemed familiar to him. Nehemiah tried to recall why.

"I'm Meshullam. And along with repairing a section on the western wall, I will also make repairs opposite my living quarters on the eastern wall."

"Very good." Nehemiah recognized him now. He had borrowed Meshullam's mule the night he'd inspected the walls. "And I see that the men of Tekoa are listed next . . . but I don't have a name for the person in charge of that section."

"We haven't chosen one yet, Governor," a volunteer replied. "Our nobles shirked their duty and refused to put their shoulders to the work. They disdain manual labor."

"Where is Tekoa?"

"Six miles south of Bethlehem and eleven miles from Jerusalem. We're ashamed of our noblemen, my lord, but very proud to be the hometown of the prophet Amos. And we've also volunteered to do double duty and repair another section on the opposite side of the city, near the wall of Ophel."

"May the Almighty One reward your labor. You're to be commended for your enthusiasm in spite of your leaders' bad example." As Nehemiah continued reading the names, he was surprised to see that the leaders of Gibeon and Mizpah had volunteered to make repairs. Both towns were under the authority of Governor Sanballat, and Mizpah was an important Samaritan administrative center. Nehemiah resisted the impulse to question the two leaders and ask where their loyalties truly lay. Instead, he made a mental note to watch them closely. Continuing around the perimeter of the city, he came to another name he already knew. "Rephaiah, ruler of the half-district of Jerusalem, will repair the next section."

"Yes. Gladly," Rephaiah said. "If the wall had been built a year ago, my son Yitzhak might still be alive."

Nehemiah quickly moved on, but not before recalling the grief-filled eyes of Yitzhak's young bride-to-be. He had dined with her at the home of her father, Shallum, ruler of the other half-district of Jerusalem. Did the woman now understand why he hadn't answered her question that night? He read the names of four more men who were each repairing a section along the western wall and saw that her father, Shallum, had volunteered to make repairs between the Tower of the Ovens and the Valley Gate. "Hanun and the residents of Zanoah will rebuild the Valley Gate, right behind us," Nehemiah continued. "That will be a huge job, Hanun. An important job. And I see you've also volunteered to rebuild the wall all the way to the Dung Gate. That's an extraordinary length. Have you had a chance to look over the work?"

"Yes, Governor. The original wall was built on a steep, rock scarp that is still intact. We'll only need to add three or four feet of wall to its height."

"Even so, thank you for your willingness to tackle a huge job. . . . That takes us as far as the Dung Gate. A very big task considering that it's one of Jerusalem's main gates at the junction of the Hinnom and Kidron Valleys. I see that Malkijah ben Recab, ruler of the district of Beth Hakkerem, will be rebuilding that gate."

"Yes, Governor Nehemiah. I'm Malkijah. We met the other day."

"I remember." Malkijah had struck Nehemiah as a very personable man, extremely astute—and obviously very wealthy, judging by his clothing and his staff of servants and the fine wine he had given Nehemiah as a welcoming gift.

"I have already consulted your engineers," Malkijah said, smiling his crooked grin. "And they've instructed me on the best way to proceed and the type of gate I should construct. I'll be working closely with them."

"Very good. Your gate and the next section all the way to the Fountain Gate are extremely critical to the southern defense of Jerusalem. The Pool of Siloam is within this section, too. Have you decided what to do about it, yet?"

"Yes. King Hezekiah constructed the Pool of Siloam so it would be accessible to the new settlers in the Mishneh, but since the Mishneh is no longer populated, I plan to close off outside access to the pool by building a wall on that western side."

"Excellent. Thank you. Now we come to the long stretch of wall on Jerusalem's eastern side, above the Kidron Valley. I've had a chance to examine it with our engineers, and we've concluded that the central section of the old wall was too badly destroyed and there is too much rubble from the supporting structures to rebuild it. The supports were constructed over a period of many years—and we don't have years. Instead, we'll build a new wall higher up on the slope and make the steep cliff and rubble field part of our defenses. That means the city will be smaller than before the Babylonian destruction, and a few of the houses that already have been rebuilt will end up outside the new wall."

He took a moment to mop the sweat from his face as the section leaders talked among themselves. The sun had reached the rim of the ridge and shone directly into his eyes as he faced the gathered men. "Because of the great difficulty the cliff presents, and the fact that we'll be building a new wall from scratch, I've divided the eastern wall beyond the Fountain Gate into much smaller sections." He consulted his list again and read off the names of each leader as far as the House of Heroes. "What is the House of Heroes, by the way?" he asked.

"Tradition says that it dates back to the time of King David and served as a barracks and an armory for his legendary Mighty Men. But the remains of it will now be outside the wall you propose to build."

"I see. That's unfortunate, but right now we don't have much use for an armory or a barracks." Nehemiah continued reading, putting a face with each name. He was encouraged to see that a good number of priests and temple servants had volunteered to rebuild sections of the wall adjacent to their residences. Even tradesmen such as the goldsmiths and the merchants' guild were taking part in his project. "I believe that covers everyone," he said when he reached the Sheep Gate on the north side once again. "Thank you."

Nehemiah could tell by the sun's height that the morning sacrifice would begin soon, but there was one more thing he wanted to say. "I know it's time to dismiss you so we can make our way up to the temple, but before I do, I want to emphasize how important it will be to work closely with the men making repairs on either side of you. Each section of the wall must join tightly together with the ones on either side," he said, lacing his fingers together to demonstrate. "And of course the walls must fuse seamlessly into the gates. A vertical seam will weaken the wall, just as strife and contention and jealousy weakens our community. Gentlemen, we must work together as one man for the good of all God's chosen people."

Nehemiah felt euphoric as he turned to his brothers and his three aides for the uphill walk to the temple. Then he froze when he saw a look of concern on Ephraim's face. "What's wrong? Did I forget something?"

"You'd better read this. It arrived this morning from Samaria. One of your servants brought it here while you were speaking." Judging from Ephraim's expression, it wasn't good news.

"Tell me what it says. Did you read it?"

Ephraim nodded. "Governor Sanballat will arrive for an official state visit in two days, along with Tobiah the Ammonite leader and Geshem the Arab."

"Well." Nehemiah exhaled. "That certainly didn't take long. The Samaritan governor has obviously heard about our building project. I wonder if we have a spy among us. . . . In any event, let's go," he said as he started walking uphill with the others toward the temple. "We're going to need the Almighty One's help now more than ever."

"How shall I instruct your servants to prepare for their visit?" Ephraim asked.

"Tell them to do the bare minimum. I can't afford the time or the expense of entertaining these men. If they're going to barge in uninvited when I have work to do, then they can hardly expect royal treatment."

"Won't they be insulted?" Hanani asked.

"I really don't care. Our work on the wall is much more important. We're off to a good start in spite of this latest distraction. Every section of wall and every gate has a capable overseer. Some men may have bitten off too big of a piece, and a few, like the nobles of Tekoa, have disappointed me by not volunteering at all, but I believe this work will be accomplished quickly. I'm very pleased."

"Do you think Governor Sanballat and the others will try to stop us from rebuilding the wall?" Hanani asked.

"No doubt. But they won't succeed. Rebuilding Jerusalem's wall is God's work, and from now on, those who try to halt its progress are opposing the Almighty One. They will become His enemies as well as ours."

Jerusalem

Nava stopped every few yards as she climbed the stairs to the temple mount, taking time to scan all the faces for a familiar one. She had attended the morning sacrifice every day for the past week and recognized many of the same people, such as the old woman with the tattered head scarf who wept when she prayed; the group of young Torah students who followed their rebbe like a string of chicks behind a hen; and the new governor, Nehemiah, who never missed a day of worship. But Nava was losing hope of ever finding Dan or her father and brothers among the crowd of worshipers.

Thanks to her master's housekeeper, Nava had moved to Jerusalem to work in Malkijah's city house. The city's population had swelled in size, as it did during the annual pilgrimage festivals, with hundreds of men from every corner of the province flocking to rebuild Jerusalem's wall. The sounds and sights of construction were everywhere, and the noise even drifted into her master's kitchen where Nava worked during the day. From sunup until sundown, the activity on the wall halted only during the daily sacrifices and on the Sabbath.

Nava felt certain that Dan would volunteer to help. Maybe

Abba and her brothers had, too. Her master supervised repairs to the Dung Gate using volunteers from his district of Beth Hakkerem, but she doubted that Dan or Abba would work for him. So where were they working?

She paused to catch her breath and look around when she reached the top of the stairs. The early morning air already felt warm. Then she hurried over to a group of young laborers who were standing together, talking. "Excuse me," she said. "Where are you from?"

"Beth Zur," one of them told her.

"Have any of you seen a young man named Dan ben Yonah from Beth Hakkerem?" The men shook their heads and Nava moved on. The people she had questioned this past week had come from all over the province of Judah, and she had met workers from places like Mizpah and Tekoa and Gibeon. Whenever her master's cook needed spices or fresh fish or something else from the marketplace, Nava had offered to go, taking a different route each time, hoping to run into Dan. Instead of eating breakfast, she spent the time every morning at the temple, searching for her family and for Dan and his family, desperate to let them know she was here and could visit with them once in a while.

Nava continued searching the crowd as the priests sacrificed the lamb and laid it on the altar. Sometimes the Levite choir sang, but even they had volunteered to repair sections of the wall. She watched another priest take a glowing coal from the altar using special tongs and a fire pan, then carry it into the sanctuary where only they were allowed to go. This was the time when she was supposed to pray, while the fragrant aroma of the burning incense ascended to heaven. Nava still wasn't convinced that the Almighty One listened to her prayers, but with nothing to lose, she closed her eyes and whispered the words that she prayed every morning. *Please help me find Dan and my family.*

When the service ended, she hurried toward the stairs with all of the other worshipers, scanning the faces in the crowd once again. None of her master's other servants came to the morning sacrifice, and she didn't dare to be gone for very long. With fewer servants and many laborers to feed, Nava worked harder here than she had in Beth Hakkerem. Malkijah's house was small but still opulent, with beautifully paneled walls and exquisite rugs on the floors. Along with feeding his workers every day, he also liked to entertain important people whenever he could. Sometimes those multi-course meals lasted well into the night.

Nava was halfway across the courtyard when she suddenly glimpsed Dan's face in the crowd. Was she seeing things? After hoping and searching for so many days, had she only imagined it? She wove between the other worshipers who were moving much too slowly, craning her neck to see. It was Dan! He stood near the top of the steps leading down from the temple mount, and if he had continued walking down the stairs she would have missed him. But he had halted, stepping aside for some reason, and he turned his head in her direction.

"Dan!" Nava shouted. It was a miracle! But with the court-yard jammed with people, he didn't hear or see her. He wasn't expecting to see her. She elbowed her way through the flowing stream, calling his name, ignoring the stern looks and loud shushing from people all around her. "Dan! Dan, wait!"

He looked up when he heard his name, then froze when he saw Nava. He didn't move, didn't run to her as she'd expected him to, and for a horrible moment she wondered if he had found someone else. Maybe he'd decided not to wait six long years for her, like Master Aaron predicted. But when she reached him, she saw the love brimming in his eyes as he whispered her name, and she knew that none of what she'd imagined was true. Dan loved her. "Nava . . . is it really you?"

"Yes! I thought I'd never find you," she said, panting to catch her breath.

"And I thought I'd never see you again." His voice choked and it was a moment before he could speak. She could tell that he wanted to hold her and kiss her the way he had on the morning she'd left home. And she longed to fling herself into his arms, too, but she didn't dare, especially in the temple courtyard, surrounded by so many people. "Are you all right, Nava? That's all I wanted to know that night I came to Beth Hakkerem to see you. Are they treating you well?"

Nava hesitated, unsure whether or not to tell him about Aaron. There was nothing Dan could do about her master's son, and she knew he would only worry. "Yes. I'm treated well."

"Have that man's sons touched you? I don't see how they could resist a beautiful woman like you, but—"

"His sons are in Beth Hakkerem, and I'm working here in Jerusalem. There's nothing to worry about."

His shoulders sagged with relief. "If they ever lay their filthy hands on you, I'll murder them. It's as simple as that."

"You don't need to worry, Dan." She rested her hand on his arm to soothe him and again the urge to hold him tightly and feel his arms surrounding her was so powerful that she quickly pulled her hand away.

"Where are you going? Can we walk together?" Dan asked.

"I have to return to Master Malkijah's house. It's here in the city on the Hill of Ophel." They started down the stairs, and when the crowd crushed them close together, Nava reveled in the warmth of his bare arm against hers.

"I'll be working here while Malkijah helps rebuild the wall. Did you come to Jerusalem to work on the wall, too?"

"Yes. They called for volunteers, and since there's not much to do on Abba's farm because of this drought, I decided to come."

"Are you working at the Dung Gate with the other men from Beth Hakkerem?"

"No, I refuse to have anything to do with your master. I'm

195

helping on the eastern side of the city with the new wall that they're building on top of the ridge."

"That's wonderful! Maybe we'll get to see each other more often. I'm allowed to come here to the sacrifice every morning." They reached the bottom of the stairs, and Nava pointed to the left. "Malkijah lives down this street near the governor's house. Walk with me and I'll show you."

Dan reached for her hand now that the crowd had thinned. His grip felt warm and calloused and wonderfully familiar. "I don't know which is worse, Nava, not seeing you at all or being with you and not being able to hold you in my arms."

"I know. I feel the same way." She squeezed his hand. "I'm so glad I found you."

"Listen, the reason I came to the temple today was to pray. I haven't been to any of the sacrifices since coming to work in the city, but today I came to pray for our future. There may be a tiny sliver of hope for us."

"I could use some hope."

"There's an undercurrent of unrest that may work in our favor. The governor's aide, a man named Jehohanan who is very high up in the new governor's administration, came to our worksite the other day. He's been visiting other sites, too, and talking to all the poor families like ours. He says we would have a chance of being heard by Governor Nehemiah if we staged a protest at the temple. Jehohanan is on our side, Nava, and he's against all the wealthy landowners who are holding our mortgages and taking us as bondservants. He's helping us meet together after work and get organized so we can confront the governor as a group. Jehohanan says if we refuse to work on the wall unless the governor helps us, he'll have to do something about greedy men like Malkijah."

"Dan, please don't do anything to get in trouble. What if Jehohanan is wrong about the governor being sympathetic?"

"Rich men like your master need to be stopped. Our two

families aren't the only ones who are suffering. The same thing is happening all over the province, with other rich landowners taking farms and crops and enslaving children."

"Shh! Someone will hear you." They were close to her master's house, and she pulled him to a halt, lowering her voice. "I know how poor our people are. Most of the women I work with are bondservants for the same reason that I am. My friend Rachel had to leave her husband and two small children behind, and she can't even visit them. But what good can come from a protest?"

"We'll get the governor's attention if we all stop building the wall. Besides, we can't possibly make the situation any worse than it already is, can we? Maybe the governor really will listen to us and do something about it."

"Please be careful, Dan. Malkijah is a very powerful man. You already made him angry once before when you broke into his house. I don't think he'll be as forgiving the next time."

"I don't care. I hate him. And I'm not afraid of him."

"I need to go. Malkijah's house is the last one on this street, so you'd better turn back. You can't take a chance that anyone will see you or recognize you."

"Can we meet again tomorrow in the same place? Before the sacrifice?"

"Yes. I'll be there. But, Dan, promise me that you'll be careful."

"I will. I love you, Nava."

"I love you, too." She pulled her hand free from his and ran the rest of the way home, knowing that if she was near him one moment longer, she wouldn't be able to resist the urge to throw herself into his arms and cover his beloved face with kisses.

CHAPTER
22

JERUSALEM

Chana finished packing the bread she had just baked into one of the carrying baskets and covered it with a clean cloth. "Are you ready to go?" she asked her sisters.

"I think so," Yudit said. "We can always run back home if we forgot something."

Chana's nerves twitched with excitement. Today she would finally start rebuilding Jerusalem's wall. She had barely been able to sit still beside the hearth all morning, waiting for each round of flatbread to slowly turn brown on the stone griddle. She and her sisters had been giddy with anticipation as they'd prepared this midday meal for Abba and his workers. Chana hoped he hadn't changed his mind about allowing them to stay and work afterward.

"That's everything," Sarah said. She lifted one of the water jars they had filled at the spring this morning and balanced it on her head. "Lead the way, Chana."

"Do you think the workers will appreciate how hard it was for us to cook all this food and bake bread on such a blistering day?" Yudit asked. "The paving stones are almost as hot as the hearthstones."

"I'm sure the workers already know how hot it is," Sarah said. "It must be terrible to work out there without any shade, moving all those heavy stones."

"We'll find out how hard it is soon enough," Chana said. "The two of you can leave after we deliver the food if you want to, but I'm planning to stay and work this afternoon."

"I'm staying, too," Yudit said. "Unless Abba goes back on his promise."

"He wouldn't dare!"

Chana's arms ached as she walked down the Street of the Bakers from their house carrying the heavy load. A few minutes later she passed the governor's headquarters near the Valley Gate, where a knot of men stood around a worktable, conferring beneath a roof made of rushes. Even before she left the city through the gate, she could hear shouts and grunts and the clang of tools in the distance, the in-and-out whooshing sound of a saw, like breathing, as someone cut wood. The road led immediately downhill into the steep valley from the gate, and Chana and her sisters had to turn around to see their assigned section. It began to the left of the gate and continued north all the way up the hill to the Tower of Ovens. The jagged remnants of the wall weren't even half their original height, and a jumbled blanket of fallen stones littered the slope below it. But what stopped Chana in her tracks were the laborers. They had removed their tunics in the broiling heat to work in nothing but their under breeches. Their bare chests glistened with sweat. She whirled around to face the other way at the same time that her sisters did.

"Maybe we shouldn't be here," Sarah said. "Those men are . . . indecent!"

Chana wondered if her cheeks were as red as Sarah's. "No, come on," she said, turning around again. "We've all seen a man's bare chest before, haven't we?"

"Not that many at once!" Yudit said. She had turned around again, too, and she stared at them, wide-eyed.

"Just find Abba, and don't look at the men," Chana said. "And quit staring, Yudit! It's always indecent to stare at people no matter how many clothes they have on."

"Or off," Sarah said.

Abba called for a lunch break when he saw Chana and her sisters coming, and the men quickly gathered around, grateful for the food and water. They sat down on the ground in a circle and passed around the basket of bread, putting the bowls of cooked lentils, spiced chickpeas, chopped cucumber salad, and roasted eggplant in the middle where everyone could use their bread to scoop into them. While they ate, Chana explored the site, unable to sit still. The long stretch of wall was difficult to get close to because of the steepness of the slope and the scree of toppled stones. She could see where some of the men had labored all morning to clear an area directly in front of the wall, and judging by the orderly piles of rocks, other workers had sorted stones according to size. Nearby was a pile of logs and the saws the men were using to cut them. She hoped the laborers would eat quickly and return to work so she could join them.

"Thank you for the food, my angels," Abba said when the men finished and the baskets and bowls lay empty on the ground. He placed one hand on Chana's back and the other on Yudit's and tried to gently herd them back toward the gate. "You deserve a long nap this afternoon after all that cooking."

Chana wiggled away from his guiding hand. "I have no intention of resting, Abba. I'm staying here to work."

"So am I," Yudit said.

"You promised we could, remember? Now give us jobs to do."

"I . . . but . . . you . . ." He was so flustered that Chana wanted to laugh. He was ruler of the half-district of Jerusalem, yet he couldn't speak. She would have felt sorry for him under any other circumstances, but she was not backing down.

"A promise is a promise."

"How did I ever let you talk me into this?" he asked, tugging his beard.

"It doesn't matter, Abba. But you gave us your word. Tell us what everyone is doing, and we'll see what we can do to help."

"Well . . . as soon as we finish clearing some of those blocks away from the wall, we'll erect the scaffolding. They're cutting the wood for it over there. As you can see, we're fighting the slope of the hill, so both the stones and the scaffolding could easily shift. It's dangerous work, which is why I wish you would go home and—"

"We won't stand where it's dangerous," Chana said. "What else needs to be done?"

He hesitated, then said, "We need to build a crane and anchor it in place, then outfit it with ropes to hoist the larger blocks to the top of the wall. Again, it's very dangerous work because if one of the ropes should happen to break—"

"You can't discourage us, Abba. What are all those tools for?"

She could see he was losing patience, but, being Abba, he answered just the same. "We use the levers to pry up the blocks so we can fasten ropes around them and lift them with the crane. The barrows are for moving the lighter stones. The chisels and cutting tools are used to smooth off the rough, broken edges so the stones will fit together better."

"And how will they actually build the wall? They can't just pile up all these rocks, can they?" Chana hoped that if she kept her father talking, he would get used to having her and her sisters here.

"No, there is a system to it. We set the largest stones in place first, width-wise, then wedge the smaller ones in between along with mortar until it's a solid layer. We'll make plumb lines and level lines from those cords and clay weights over there. Each course of stones must be straight vertically and level horizontally in order for the wall to stand. If it isn't, the wall will topple."

"It sounds important to get that right," Chana said.

"It's very important. We're fortunate that the foundations are solid in our section. We won't have to dig trenches for new foundations like they do on the northeast corner."

Abba had called it "our" section. Chana smiled to herself. He was softening. She had been looking around while he talked to see which task she and Yudit and Sarah could handle, and she decided that the simplest job would be to sort stones, picking up the ones they could easily lift and piling them to one side. She retied her scarf around her hair so it hung down her back like a horse's tail, and as soon as Abba was distracted by a question from one of the workers, she made her way up the hill through the debris to where the men sorted rocks. She knew better than to ask Abba's permission. Why give him a chance to stop her? Yudit and Sarah hurried up the hill to join her.

"Be careful, my angels!" he said when he discovered what they were doing.

"This isn't hard at all, Abba," she called down to him as she threw another rock onto the pile she was making.

"We're stronger than you think, Abba," Yudit told him.

"You girls better watch out for snakes," one of the workers warned as Chana bent to lift another stone. She dropped it in surprise, barely missing her foot. But she wouldn't let a snake or the other workers discourage her. "Thanks for the warning," she said, smiling at the man.

Everything about the work should have made Chana run home—the intense heat, her aching back from bending all afternoon, the way the rough stones scraped and cut her hands. The worker had been right about snakes, and she shrieked when she spotted one slithering between the stones near her feet. Yet Chana felt happier than she had in a long time and knew that working on Jerusalem's wall was having a healing effect. She was fighting back against Yitzhak's murderers. They would never sneak inside the city again. No other woman would have to suffer the senseless grief that she had suffered.

"Hey, Chana!"

She looked up to see why Yudit had called to her. Her sister's hair looked like a glowing halo around her beaming face. "What, Yudit?"

"You're singing again!"

It was true, Chana realized. She had begun to sing as she worked.

CHAPTER
23

JERUSALEM

Nehemiah was standing deep in the foundation trench that his workers had dug on the northeastern corner of the wall when the messenger arrived. "We spotted the provincial governors and their entourage," the man said, panting. "They're about a mile north of here on the Damascus Road."

Nehemiah stifled a groan. He would have to lay aside his work for this official state visit. His brothers, his aides, and all the men on his council would have to stop working, too. Many of those councilmen supervised a wall section or a gate, and Nehemiah hated to take them away from their work, but he must follow protocol. "Is their delegation a large one?" he asked.

"It appears to be. They brought soldiers with them."

"Very well." He brushed dirt from his hands and reached up to Hanani, who stood on top, for help climbing out of the trench. "Tell my staff to go to the Yeshana Gate and get ready to greet them," he told the messenger. "I'll be there shortly." He turned back to the men digging the foundation trench and said, "You need to make it deeper. The ground has shrunk because of the drought. When the rains finally do come, the earth will swell and cause the foundations to shift. Expansion and shrinkage are facts of life in our climate, so our foundations must be deep."

"Yes, my lord."

He saw Hanani eying his dusty, sweat-soaked tunic. "Shall I have someone bring you a clean robe, *Governor*?" he asked with a grin.

"I suppose I should change. Thanks." He looked at the bustle of work all around him, the jumble of scaffolding and ropes and tools, and hated to leave. The sounds of progress—shouting workers and pounding chisels—were like music to his ears.

"You know it's going to be impossible to disguise what we're doing," Hanani said.

"I wouldn't hide it even if I could."

His brother left to help the messenger alert the council members and district leaders that the delegation was about to arrive. Nehemiah quickly doused his face and hands with water and put on his clean robe, which arrived just in time for him to stand at the gate and welcome the procession. Sanballat led the way, of course, overdressed in the oppressive summer heat in heavy, ornate clothing. Sweat ran down his round face, which was as red as his robe. It took two horses to pull him and his chariot, while Tobiah the Ammonite and Geshem the Arab rode on horseback. A gaggle of their underlings and aides swarmed around them, raising clouds of dust on the parched road. Sanballat had also brought an escort of mounted cavalry and foot soldiers, which Nehemiah recognized as an attempt to intimidate him. He remained unfazed.

"Welcome," he said, forcing a smile. "I hoped your first visit could wait until we weren't quite so busy. As you can see, we are in the middle of a major building project."

"What is this you are doing?" Sanballat asked, gesturing to the scaffolding that framed the Yeshana Gate. He was playing dumb. It was obvious to anyone with eyes what they were doing, even though work at the gate had halted to allow the delegation to pass through without the risk of falling rocks and debris.

"The walls of Jerusalem are in need of repairs," Nehemiah replied. He could play dumb, as well. "I decided that the months between the end of summer and the beginning of the winter rains were a good time to get the work done. Please follow me, if you will. I have prepared my assembly hall for your visit. My councilmen and district leaders will join us shortly."

"I think I'd like to see some of your work, first."

Nehemiah had anticipated this request and was ready with a reply. "You can get a glimpse of the work right here at the Yeshana Gate. But I'm afraid it would be impossible to take your delegation any place else. We're still in the very early stages of construction, and a great deal of rubble litters most of the sites. The Yeshana Gate is an exception because it's been in use all these years. This way, please."

Sanballat didn't move. "You're rebuilding the wall around Jerusalem." It was statement, not a question.

"Yes. We are."

Sanballat laughed out loud. He turned around in his chariot to face his associates and the Samaritan army that had accompanied him. "Did you hear that? What do these feeble Jews think they're doing? Will they restore the wall? Will they offer sacrifices for divine help? Will they finish in a day? Can they bring the stones back to life from those heaps of rubble—burned as they are?"

"Just look at what they are building!" Tobiah added with a mocking laugh. "If even a fox climbed up on it, he would break down their wall of stones!"

Nehemiah signaled to his aides and continued walking so his guests would have no choice except to follow. But all the way to his residence, he silently prayed to the Almighty One. *Hear us, O our God, for we are despised. Turn their insults back on their own heads. Give them over as plunder in a land of captiv-*

ity. Do not cover up their guilt or blot out their sins from your sight, for they have thrown insults in the face of the builders.

It seemed to take forever for the three leaders to refresh themselves and settle into their places in the council chamber, longer still to plow through all of the formal introductions and welcomes. Nehemiah could barely control his impatience and would have gladly skipped all of this if he could have. When Sanballat finally got around to the purpose of his visit, he repeated the question he'd already asked, "What is this you are doing?" Then he added a more inflammatory one: "Are you rebelling against the king?"

Nehemiah barely kept his temper. "That's an extremely serious charge. Why would I rebel against King Artaxerxes? He's sponsoring this work."

"Ah, but does he know what you're really up to here in the backwaters of his empire?" Sanballat rose from his chair, causing the wood to groan with relief, then addressed the men on the council. "Nehemiah is new to our region and doesn't understand the dangerous political implications of fortifying this city. But I'm sure you gentlemen understand. And you also know that you'll be executed as traitors along with your leader when the king learns of your subversive activity."

Nehemiah's jaw ached from clenching it to avoid giving a heated reply. If any of his council members had doubts about his leadership, the portly Samaritan leader was reinforcing them. Nehemiah took a moment to calm himself before speaking, knowing two things with certainty: King Artaxerxes *was* on his side; and the ultimate authority for this project had come from God, not men. He didn't need to answer Sanballat's ridiculous charges. He simply said, "The God of heaven will give us success."

Sanballat smirked. "Let's say for a moment that Tobiah and Geshem and I believe you—and that King Artaxerxes also believes that your motives are honorable. How do you expect to accomplish such a monumental task?"

"One stone at a time."

Sanballat laughed out loud, creating a ripple of insulting laughter from among his entourage. Even stone-faced Geshem the Arab laughed derisively along with the others. Tobiah the Ammonite, who seemed to shift moods to match Sanballat's like a chameleon changing color, chuckled and rolled his eyes. Tobiah was the quietest of the three leaders, the least flamboyant. But Nehemiah knew from experience that sometimes the quiet ones were the most dangerous.

"Are we to believe," Sanballat asked, "that you're a professional architect and builder, Nehemiah? Do you have qualifications that you've kept hidden from us?"

"You'll see exactly how qualified I am when the wall is finished."

"Where do you expect to find a workforce of skilled laborers?" Geshem asked, his tone condescending, his expression skeptical.

"The men of Judah will do the rebuilding."

Nehemiah's comment caused more laughter, louder this time. "Your wall won't amount to much with farmers and tradesmen doing all the work," Tobiah the Ammonite said.

"He's right," Sanballat added. "If you expect your wall to offer any protection, it has to be built correctly, not cobbled together." He turned his back on Nehemiah and addressed the district leaders again. "Your governor is wasting your time. Your people's time. Their efforts would be better spent doing what they're qualified to do—growing wheat and barley and olives, herding sheep."

Nehemiah held up his hands to halt the twittering laughter and insults that followed Sanballat's remark. "Since you obviously don't believe we can accomplish this, what are you so worried about? Why make the long journey here? Why try to discourage us from doing something you believe is impossible?"

Sanballat finished his laughter with a cough and settled back

in his seat, his hands folded on his broad belly. "As governor of
The Land Beyond the River, it's my duty to warn you that the
Persians will most certainly interpret your actions as rebellious."

"Nonsense. You saw my letter of authorization from King
Artaxerxes. Or did you fail to read it carefully?" Nehemiah
looked directly at Geshem, who had barely given the document
a glance.

"My aides looked at it," Geshem said. "And they don't recall
reading anything about fortifying Jerusalem."

He was right. The letter didn't specifically say that. But in
his appeal to King Artaxerxes, Nehemiah had made his inten-
tions clear: *"If it pleases the king and if your servant has found
favor in his sight, let him send me to the city in Judah where
my fathers are buried so I can rebuild it."* King Artaxerxes had
granted all of Nehemiah's requests.

"Would you like to see the letter the king wrote to Asaph,
keeper of his forest?" he asked. "In it, the king commands Asaph
to give me timber to make beams for the gates and for the citadel
near the temple and for the city wall."

Sanballat didn't reply, turning to the council leaders again.
"Listen to me, gentlemen. Shallum . . . Rephaiah . . . Malkijah . . . we've worked together in the past, and I know that
you've also worked closely with Tobiah. None of you is a fool.
Surely, now that you've had time to think about it, you realize
the futility of this plan and the foolishness of the man who is
leading you into such dangerous folly. Attempting to rebuild
miles and miles of city wall is a tragic waste of time and manpower that could be put to better use during these difficult
economic times."

Nehemiah had heard enough. "If your delegation's purpose is
to mock and ridicule me and to undermine my work, then I think
your official visit has come to an end. Good day." He would
have walked out, but Sanballat rose from his seat to stop him.

"You forget that I ran the province of Judah before you arrived out of nowhere. I could be of assistance to you. So could Tobiah, who knows this land and its people much better than you do."

"I haven't forgotten. The province of Judah became impoverished under your rule and the enormous taxes you imposed."

"I didn't cause the drought, Governor Nehemiah. I care about these people and have their best interests in mind—and you obviously don't."

Tobiah rose to join the assault. "Your decision affects the entire Land Beyond the River, including the province that I govern. Sanballat, Geshem, and I all have a share in what happens in Judah. "

"We Judeans are *God's* servants," Nehemiah replied. "And we will continue rebuilding the wall. But the three of you have no share in Jerusalem or any claim or historic right to it."

"How dare you!" Sanballat shouted.

"I dare because King Artaxerxes appointed me governor of Judah. I'm doing the work that he and my God gave me to do. You and anyone else who oppose me are opposing God."

"Your God spoke to you and told you to build?" Tobiah mocked. "You have some nerve! Who do you think you are? Moses? The Messiah? Only they may claim to hear from our God." Tobiah turned to the high priest. "Eliashib, are you and your fellow priests going to allow such blasphemy? Your governor just claimed to have direct revelation from God!"

Nehemiah didn't wait for Eliashib's reply. He walked toward the door, turning back to say, "You are welcome to stay and enjoy the meal my servants have prepared for you. But I have no more time to spare for you and your taunts. I have a job to do. The God I serve will give us success."

He heard the anxious buzz of voices behind him as he strode from the room. His aide Jehohanan hurried out with him. "You've insulted Governor Sanballat and the others," he whispered on the way down the hall. "I've never seen him so angry."

"Well, I'm angry, as well. He took advantage of my hospitality to mock and ridicule me and my work."

"He's a very powerful man. I'd watch my back, if I were you."

Nehemiah knew the danger of what he had just done. But he would admit to no one, not even his aides or his brothers, that he was afraid. In Persia he'd kept careful watch over the king's safety—never his own. Whenever he drank from King Artaxerxes' cup or tasted his food, Nehemiah always knew that it might be poisoned, that he might die protecting the king. The need for constant vigilance had been nerve-wracking, at times. But now it was his life that might be threatened. The hatred he felt toward these three enemies was mutual. If they plotted to kill him, Nehemiah wondered if the work would proceed or if the people would be too fearful to continue.

"This visit won't be the end of their attempts to stop us," he told Jehohanan. "It's just the beginning. They won't give up until we stop building, and I have no intention of doing that."

Ephraim and Hanani caught up with him a few minutes later. "That was a masterful performance," Ephraim said. "You didn't back down one inch."

"It ended in a standoff," Nehemiah said. "They aren't going to back down, either."

"What's next?" Hanani asked. "What would you like us to do?"

Nehemiah halted in the hallway of their residence, very aware that from a safety standpoint, their home was not at all secure. "We need to pray—continually—that the Almighty One will help us. And that He will turn our enemies' insults back on their own heads."

"We are praying, Nehemiah. Morning and evening."

"Good. And we're probably going to need weapons. Look into that for me, Hanani. There may come a time when we'll need them. In the meantime, we'll need to remain alert day and night. Now let's get back to work. I've wasted enough time with these men."

JERUSALEM

Chana watched as the builders stretched a taut level line across the top of the stones to make sure the new construction was straight and level. "Using a plumb line is exactly the kind of precision work that I can do," she told her father. "And I know I can do it much better than your clumsy laborers can." Sorting stones had been interesting at first, but now Chana wanted a new challenge. She hounded Abba every chance she got, trailing behind him at the worksite with the cord in her hand and a clay weight dangling from it. "Just let me try it, Abba. I know I can do it."

When he finally gave in, he stood at the bottom of the scaffolding while Chana climbed up for the first time, prepared to catch her if she fell. The structure was shaky and the climb precarious, but she hid her unease as she made her way to the top. The wall perched on top of such a steep slope that the height made her dizzy, but she got the hang of the job in no time. By the end of the week, Abba realized what a good eye she had and stopped objecting as she climbed up and down the scaffolding and crawled around on top of the six-foot-wide wall to make sure the builders kept it straight and true. She loved standing on a level row of freshly laid blocks to gaze out at the view of the Mishneh and the Judean hills beyond.

Her sister Yudit was also adept at climbing up and down the scaffolding, proving to be an expert at choosing just the right stone to jam into the crevices between the larger ones to create a snug fit. The job that Sarah loved best was surveying the largest building blocks and finding ones that weren't too badly burned or crumbling, then showing the workers which edges needed to be chiseled off to make the stones fit tightly together. Chana now heard the constant sound of chipping and chiseling and grinding and pounding even in her sleep. And she slept better every night than she had in more than a year.

This morning Chana was halfway up the ladder of scaffolding with a plumb line in her hand when she heard shouting behind her. "Whoa! Whoa! Stop! Where are you going? Get down from there!"

She turned to see Governor Nehemiah standing below her and quickly made sure her skirt was modest. "Are you talking to me?" she asked.

"Of course I am! What do you think you're doing up there?"

"I'm checking this course of stones to make sure they're plumb."

"No, no, no! Get down from there and leave this area immediately! And you—you both need to leave, too!" he said, spotting Yudit and Sarah.

"Why?" Chana asked.

"Why!" Nehemiah was almost too outraged to speak. Chana didn't move from where she stood on the ladder. "Because this is dangerous work! Women don't belong anywhere near here!"

"We're very familiar with the dangers. We've been working here since the first day."

"Who's your site leader?" he asked, glancing all around.

"Our father, Shallum ben Hallohesh. I heard you say in your speech, Governor, that each section leader is responsible for

213

choosing his own volunteers, and our father chose us. We have his permission to be here."

"Where is Shallum? I need to speak with him. And in the meantime, *get down* from there!" Chana still didn't move. Nehemiah looked strong enough and angry enough to scoop her up in his brawny arms and carry her home once she did.

"Abba went to talk to Ephraim ben Hacaliah about getting more timber," Sarah told him. She looked suitably frightened of Nehemiah and so did Yudit, who had stopped gathering stones and had come to stand near the foot of the scaffolding.

"Somebody go find him," Nehemiah commanded. "Tell him I need to speak with him immediately. And the three of you—go home!" He planted his hand on Sarah's shoulder and gave her a little push. Chana scrambled down the ladder.

"Don't tell us what to do, Governor. This is our city, too. Our inheritance."

"I cannot allow this. What will people say when they come through the Valley Gate or visit me at my headquarters and see *women* working? I'm ordering you to go home where you belong."

"I don't suppose you know the story of Zelophehad's daughters?" Chana asked, hands on her hips. "It's in the Torah. The Almighty One said that daughters have a right to their father's inheritance if he has no sons."

"What are you talking about? You're not even making sense!" He stood as if bracing for a fistfight. Chana wrapped her arm around the leg of the scaffolding, certain that he would throw her over his shoulder any minute and carry her home. Yudit and Sarah—the cowards—slowly inched away from him, heading down the slope toward the gate.

"Why are you defying me, defying convention, and . . . and common sense? Is it sheer, muleheaded stubbornness or what? Why won't you leave like any normal woman would, and go home?"

His insults infuriated her, making her words spill out. "I was betrothed to a man, Yitzhak ben Rephaiah—"

"I know the story. He was murdered."

"Well, you obviously have no idea what it's like to lose someone you love. Or what it's like to know that if only there had been better protection—"

"You're wrong. I do know both of those things."

"Then you should also know how hard it is not to be angry with God. How impossible it is, at times, to continue to believe in His goodness." Chana knew she was spilling thoughts that she'd never shared with anyone, thoughts that she should keep to herself, but once she'd opened a tiny window to her heart, she couldn't stop. "I go to the temple and worship Him because it's expected of me, and sometimes I succeed in believing in a loving God, but just as often, I don't. This morning we sang the words, 'His love endures forever.' And I couldn't see it. There is so much rage still seething inside me that I could murder Yitzhak's killers with my own two hands and set their houses ablaze with their families and little ones inside. And I know that my hatred isn't pleasing to God and has no place in my heart when I stand in His house of worship. But what can I do with it? Where can it go?"

Nehemiah didn't reply. He stared at her as if stunned by her outburst. Chana unwound her arm from the scaffolding and took a step toward him. "The men who killed Yitzhak were never found, never brought to justice. And so I'm pouring all of my rage into building this wall. I know it won't bring Yitzhak back, but it might keep another killer out. It might spare another woman the grief of losing someone she loves."

He was quiet for a long moment before saying, "Even so, I can't allow it. You're a woman."

"Thank you for noticing. But you can't stop me."

They stood toe-to-toe, neither one of them backing down. She had to look up to see him, the top of her head level with his chin. All of the workers watched and listened. Nehemiah was the governor and she a mere woman—reasons enough for her to submit and obey him and go home. She wouldn't do it.

"This isn't the end of this discussion," he finally said. He turned his back and strode away, passing Yudit and Sarah on his way to the gate. Chana watched him go, her legs too shaky to climb the scaffolding again that day.

⋅⟫ ⟪⋅

Nehemiah still trembled with fury as he marched through the Valley Gate and back to his headquarters inside the city. He would find Shallum and tell him exactly what he thought of his impudent, disrespectful daughter. What kind of a father couldn't control his children? Shallum certainly didn't deserve to be the district leader of Jerusalem if he was too weak to stop his daughter from pushing him around. Nehemiah reached the shade of the rush-covered roof that served as his field headquarters, but the only person there was his brother Hanani.

"Where's Ephraim?" he asked. The girl said her father had gone to talk to him.

"I don't know. I haven't seen Ephraim since this morning."

"Shallum ben Hallohesh and his daughters—do you know them?" Nehemiah asked.

"I know Shallum, leader of the half-district of Jerusalem. And I'm aware that he has daughters, but I don't know them. Why?"

"There are three of them, and they're working on the wall. I saw them myself a few minutes ago. Women! Moving stones and climbing the scaffolding and using a plumb line!"

"Really?" The fact that Hanani was barely able to hide his amusement made Nehemiah angrier still.

"Our enemies are already mocking us. I'm just thankful they didn't see those three women when they made their state visit. Shallum's section is right beside the Valley Gate. It's outrageous!"

When Hanani took a step back, Nehemiah knew he had to

cool his temper. He grabbed the water dipper and plunged it into the jar. Gulped down a mouthful of water. Filled the dipper a second time and poured the water over his head. That woman had made him angrier than he'd been in a long time. *"You obviously have no idea what it's like to lose someone you love,"* she had accused. But Nehemiah knew exactly how she felt. Even though the men who'd killed his father had been brought to justice, Nehemiah's rage was still there, the same as hers. Yet it had never occurred to him that it might displease God to worship at the temple while hoarding that rage. And as much as he hated to admit it, he understood what motivated her to work on the wall. Hadn't he done the same thing, using his anger as fuel to rise to the position of cupbearer and ensure the king's safety? *"I'm pouring all of my rage into building this wall,"* she'd told him. Wasn't he doing the same thing? Letting anger drive him to rebuild Jerusalem's wall?

Nehemiah pushed a few drawings around on his worktable, remembering her confession that she was angry with God. Nehemiah was angry, too, if he was honest with himself. God hadn't protected his parents, and so he'd taken over for Him, trying to protect everyone he loved. Then another thought occurred to him. What if Sanballat and Tobiah were right and God hadn't ordered him to rebuild the walls? What if he had petitioned the king and obtained the decree by the sheer force of his own stubborn will? He quickly pushed that thought aside, just like the scrolls. Of course he had heard from God. The Almighty One's hand was upon him.

"You know what infuriated me the most?" Nehemiah asked his brother. "She refused to stop working and go home. Even when I commanded her to. It was as if she was taunting me."

Hanani covered his mouth to hide his smile, pretending to smooth his beard. "She must be quite a demon-woman if she made you lose your temper. You stayed so calm and serene when Sanballat, Tobiah, and Geshem taunted you."

"I'd sooner stand up to Sanballat any day. He's more rational than she is."

"What does this woman who dares to defy the governor of Judah look like?"

He didn't want to tell Hanani that she was annoyingly attractive, the kind of woman men wanted to shelter and protect. He had noticed how pretty she and her sisters were the night he'd eaten dinner at their home, but he'd forced himself to ignore them, aware that it was wrong to gaze at women that way. He hadn't wanted to stare today either, but he couldn't help noticing the way her clothing had clung to the curves of her body in the heat.

"And that's another thing, Hanani. These women are surely a distraction to the men who are trying to work."

"I see." Hanani was still trying to hide his smile. "I guess that answers my question."

"Since you think this is so funny, I'm going to leave it up to you to take care of this problem."

"Me? Why?"

"Because I have a wall to build. I can't waste any more time on this problem. Find Shallum and tell him to send his daughters home. They can't work on the wall ever again."

CHAPTER

25

JERUSALEM

All of her father's pleas and demands couldn't change Chana's mind. Tired as she was from her day's labors, she continued to argue with Abba as they sat eating their evening meal, determined to return to the wall tomorrow. "We're doing real work, Abba, you know we are. And we're good at what we do. The other laborers are used to having us work alongside them. They've accepted us and are grateful for our help. You can't tell us to stop now, just because Nehemiah has a problem with it."

"He's the governor, Chana. Our leader. We need to respect the leaders God has given us."

"Even when they're wrong? Where does it say in the Torah that women can't build a wall? Nowhere! This is just his own ridiculous bias. Why won't you explain to him that he's wrong?"

"Chana, I think we all need time for our tempers to cool. Tomorrow is preparation day for the Sabbath, and I think it would be better if you girls stayed home and cooked our meal. Work on the wall will stop early tomorrow to give the men time to return home to their families. And you'll need to prepare extra portions to feed any of our workers who live too far away to go home."

"And after the Sabbath ends? What then?" Chana asked.

"We'll talk about it when the time comes and not before."

She agreed to stay home and help prepare the Sabbath meal with her sisters and the new servants they'd hired. "But I'm going back after the Sabbath," she told Yudit and Sarah the next morning as she shoveled ash from the hearth to begin cooking. The fine dust turned her hands gray. "I'm not giving up my work on the wall!"

"I love working, too," Yudit said as she ground grain into flour with her hand mill. "But I don't want to make Abba angry. I don't like fighting with him."

"I don't either," Sarah said. She had already been to the King's Pool and back, carrying the heavy jar of water uphill so they could cook. "We can still help out by feeding Abba's workers. That's a huge contribution, isn't it?"

"Of course. But the new servants can easily do that. You loved building the wall as much as I did, didn't you? We shouldn't have to quit." Chana broke a handful of twigs into pieces and laid them on the warm coals, then blew on them to start the fire. "Nehemiah is a bully, throwing his weight around and coercing Abba to give in. The governor shouldn't have that much power. We're not breaking any laws by working. I'm not quitting until he shows me a law that says I have to."

Later that morning, Chana had just finished baking all the bread they would need for the Sabbath when a messenger arrived from Malkijah's house. "My lord asks that you please join him for Sabbath dinner this evening in his Jerusalem home," he told Chana.

"All four of us?" she asked. Their meal preparations were well underway, and she wondered what they would do with all the fish they had purchased in the marketplace.

"Master Malkijah very kindly asks that you come alone this time, miss."

Chana didn't know what to say. Sarah nudged her with her elbow. "Tell him of course you'll come, silly."

"Abba must have told Malkijah that you've agreed to a betrothal," Yudit added.

"Did I agree?" Chana asked. She was still so angry about being ordered around by the governor that she barely remembered.

"Yes, when you were trying to convince Abba to let us work on the wall," Yudit said. "How could you have forgotten?"

The messenger waited for her reply. Chana drew a steadying breath. "Please tell Malkijah that I will be happy to dine with him tonight."

"Very well. I will return before sundown to escort you to his house, miss."

The day's preparations helped Chana take her mind off the wall and the governor's unreasonable demands for a while, and she was in a good mood that evening when the servant arrived to escort her up the hill to Malkijah's Jerusalem home. But he lived close to the governor's residence, and Chana's anger boiled up all over again as she walked past it. Had the governor enlisted Malkijah's help in convincing her to give up her work? The thought infuriated her.

Just in time she remembered that she was Malkijah's guest. She needed to set aside her anger and be gracious to her host, who stood waiting at the door to greet her. "Chana! Welcome to my home away from home. I'm so pleased that you could join me tonight."

Most of the houses in Jerusalem had been rebuilt quickly by the returning exiles, with little thought to making them beautiful. But Malkijah's house was an exception, tastefully and expertly built. It might be small, but it was as luxurious as his country estate. The interior walls were paneled with cedar, not merely plastered. The stone floors had been laid in pleasing designs and covered with expensive imported rugs. Malkijah had a staff of servants to wait on him, and Chana recognized some of them from his estate in Beth Hakkerem, including the young girl named Nava.

"It's nearly sunset," Malkijah said, breaking into her thoughts. "Will you do me the honor, Chana, of lighting the Sabbath lights?" She did, reciting the blessing and thanking God for the command to rest on the Sabbath. When she and Malkijah sat down at his lavishly spread table, she was surprised to discover that she was his only guest. Malkijah held up the two loaves of bread and recited the blessing, then did the same for the wine. By the time he finished and they started eating the first course, Chana could no longer keep quiet.

"May I ask you a question, Malkijah?"

"Of course." His smile was so warm and genuine, she hated herself for suspecting him of conspiring with the governor. But she had to know.

"Are you aware that my sisters and I have been helping Abba rebuild his section of the wall?"

He grinned, his ebony eyes sparkling in the lamplight. "Yes, all of Jerusalem is talking about it."

"What are they saying?"

He took a sip of wine and set down his cup. "Opinions vary. Most people think it's outrageous. A few admire you for being so strong and patriotic, and they compare you to Queen Esther."

"Of which opinion are you?"

"Both. I agree that your actions are outrageous and probably very dangerous. I was so concerned for your safety when I first heard that you were scaling ladders and climbing scaffolding that I nearly went there myself to ask you to stop. Then I realized that your father would be just as concerned for your safety and would never put you or your sisters in danger. What bothers me the most is that people are gossiping about you, thinking ill of you, when they don't know you or your motives for helping."

"Our new governor is among them."

"So I've heard. On the other hand, you have spirit, Chana, and I like that. I would be bored with a wife who never tried anything new or was too frightened to leave the house or had no opinions of her own."

"Then you and Governor Nehemiah are certainly very different. I'm glad you don't feel threatened by my 'outrageous' actions and strong opinions. And thank you for having the courage to invite me here even though the entire city is gossiping about me."

"I didn't invite you here tonight to talk about your work on the wall, Chana." He looked away for a moment, as if suddenly shy, the bump on his crooked nose more noticeable in profile. "Your father told me that you have agreed to marry me."

Her sister Yudit had been right. Abba had kept his side of the bargain allowing her to work, and now she would have to keep hers. Chana suddenly felt shy, as well. "Yes. I have agreed."

"I'm very pleased to hear that," he said with a broad grin. "I promise to make your happiness among my highest goals in life."

"I hope I can make you happy, too."

"You already did by saying yes. Now, what I hoped we could settle tonight is a date when your father and I can sign a ketubah. And that we can also decide when the wedding will be. There's no point in a long waiting period between the two occasions, is there? I already have a home prepared for you."

A sudden memory brought a rush of grief: Yitzhak had been killed while preparing a home for her. She looked away from Malkijah, staring down at her hands, scratched and blistered from her work. "No, there's no point . . . But I would like to finish building the wall before we're married."

"If you would allow me to, I'll send a dozen servants to take your place and build it for you. But I have a feeling you wouldn't like that."

"You're right. I wouldn't."

He gave a crooked grin. "May I send just a few servants then, so you'll finish sooner?"

Chana felt a rising sense of panic at the thought of losing control over her life. She couldn't recall feeling like a fish snared in a net when she became engaged to Yitzhak. But she had been in love with him, and she didn't love Malkijah yet. She wondered if she ever would. "I enjoy the work very much," she said carefully. "I don't want to stop. And thank you for the offer, but I don't need help."

He leaned toward her, suddenly serious. "I know, but I need *your* help, Chana. I discovered that I did on the night you visited my home in Beth Hakkerem, the night that young man broke in. You took time to listen to him and figure out what happened. My wife used to do the same thing. Rebecca watched over our servants and listened to them, watched out for their needs and protected them. I fear no one is doing that, especially now that I'm away from home and working in Jerusalem. And I think you would do the job wonderfully well. You have a good heart and a feisty spirit. I know you would be a valuable asset to me and to our home. And that we would work very well together."

Was it mere flattery or did Malkijah really believe that? He looked sincere. Chana had seen how well-ordered his estate was, and she wondered if she really would find a purpose and a place in it.

"What I've been thinking," he continued, "is that we could sign the betrothal now, and the wedding would take place after the wall is finished. Our governor seems convinced that we can complete the work within a matter of months, not years."

Chana knew that a betrothal was just as binding as a marriage. She would be considered Malkijah's wife, and he would replace Abba as the one who made decisions for her. "Would you make me stop building if we become betrothed?"

Malkijah laughed. "I wouldn't know how to stop you, nor would I want to try." He smiled his crooked smile and reached across the table to take her hand. "Chana, I promise I'll never force you to do anything you don't want to do."

She had another thought and drew a steadying breath. "Will you stand up for me now, so I can continue working? Governor Nehemiah is pressuring Abba, trying to force him to send Yudit and Sarah and me back home. But working on the wall has lifted that horrible load of grief I've carried for the past year. I can't explain how free and how . . . how *happy* it has made me to work alongside my father and accomplish something as solid and enduring as that wall. Am I making any sense?"

"You want me to use my influence to convince Governor Nehemiah that he's wrong."

"Yes. Would you? You said that being married meant working together. And if we're betrothed, then you get to decide what I can and can't do, not the governor."

"If it would make you happy, Chana, then yes. I'll do what I can to convince him."

Her misgivings vanished as she twined her fingers in his. "Then I want to make you happy, too, Malkijah. We can become engaged as soon as you and Abba can arrange it."

⚜ ⚜

Their betrothal took place before a small gathering of family members, friends, and colleagues of Abba and Malkijah. Thankfully, the governor had not been invited but the high priest, Eliashib, had come. Malkijah insisted on holding the celebration in his Jerusalem house so his servants could prepare all the food. Chana wasn't sure how he had done it, but Malkijah had kept his promise and used his influence to make certain that she and her sisters could continue working on the wall.

She felt restless as she listened to one of the city elders read the ketubah that Abba and Malkijah had agreed upon. The two men had haggled good-naturedly over the dowry and the bride-price, making Chana feel like a melon in the marketplace.

The completed contract would be as binding as marriage vows. Only a divorce or a death could end it. When Chana and Yitzhak had celebrated their betrothal, she had been so overjoyed and excited she hadn't been able to hold back her tears. The jittery unease she felt about the ritual this time had no logical explanation, nothing she could name as a reason why. Malkijah was a good man who lived according to the Torah. He treated his servants well. He could amply provide for her. And he'd told Chana that he wouldn't try to change her or force her to do anything she didn't want to do. He said he liked her spirit. Her life had been suspended after Yitzhak died; maybe now she would begin living again.

She watched as Malkijah and Abba signed the ketubah before all the witnesses. Then Malkijah poured his finest wine into a cup and offered it to her. Chana accepted it from his hand and drank it. They were betrothed.

Shouts of joy and wishes for their happiness filled the room. Malkijah broke into a wide grin, and Chana smiled in return. Abba seemed as pleased as Malkijah. And yet . . . and yet Chana still wondered if she was doing the right thing. Was it guilt for trying to be happy again without Yitzhak? For being unfaithful to his memory and to the vows she made to him at their betrothal?

Malkijah lifted his cup of wine as he addressed all the people. "Please, help yourselves to the food that my servants have prepared—or I should say, *our* servants. They are yours, as well, Chana. We are so happy that you could celebrate this wonderful event with us. Enjoy!"

Nervous tension stole Chana's appetite. She couldn't eat. She stood aside to watch as their guests gathered around the platters of food and filled their cups with Malkijah's famous wine. When she felt a gentle tug on her sleeve, she turned to see Nava, the servant girl. "Congratulations, my lady," she said shyly. "I wish you many happy years with my master."

"Thank you, Nava. I hope . . ." But the girl scurried away as Malkijah approached.

"Can I take you away for just a moment, Chana?" he asked. "I believe our guests are all occupied at the moment." She followed Malkijah out to a small balcony with a view of the Mount of Olives across the valley and the star-filled sky above their heads. "How are you faring with all of this?" he asked.

"Everything is beautiful, Malkijah. Your servants did a wonderful job."

"May I share something personal with you?"

"Of course."

"Throughout this process, I have sometimes felt a little . . . guilty. There's no other way to describe it. I've felt as if I was being unfaithful to my wife's memory. You may have felt the same." He quickly went on before Chana could respond. "But tonight I realized something. If it had been the other way around, if I had died instead of Rebecca, I would have wanted nothing but happiness for her future. I wouldn't have wanted her to grieve for the rest of her life. And I realized that it doesn't tarnish her memory or my love for her in any way for me to marry you and be happy with you. Am I making sense?"

"Yes. And thank you for sharing that with me." The fact that he understood and had the same mixed feelings as she did somehow eased her mind.

"Come. We'd better go back," he said. He took her hand as they rejoined the party, and Chana found that her appetite had returned. She was able to enjoy the celebration and the blessings and congratulations everyone bestowed on her.

Later that evening as the party wound down, Chana went in search of her father and took a wrong turn, ending up in a passageway near the servants' quarters. As she retraced her steps, she overheard a conversation between the high priest and the city elder who had read the ketubah earlier this evening.

"What a shrewd move on Malkijah's part to marry Shallum's

227

daughter," Eliashib said. "This marriage will make him even more powerful than he already is."

"Yes, and he was wise to move as quickly as he did, before another suitor had a chance to marry the girl and claim Shallum's district."

"Malkijah is a very cunning politician. You can be sure that everything he does serves his own best interests."

Chana's knees went weak. She couldn't move. Was this why Malkijah had pushed so hard for a betrothal? Had he been charming and attentive simply as a means to marry her and inherit Abba's district? She felt duped. Manipulated. She'd made a terrible mistake in agreeing to marry Malkijah, and now it was too late to change her mind.

"Why are you hiding back here?" Abba asked when he found her. "You look tired, my angel. Come, let's find your sisters and go home." Chana followed them as if in a dream as they walked down the hill. Abba didn't notice her tears until they reached home. "What's wrong?" he asked. "I hope those are tears of joy and not regret."

"I've been so blind," Chana said, swiping them away. "I believed all the charming things Malkijah said about being well-suited for each other and finding contentment together. But I overheard the high priest talking tonight and realized how naïve I've been. Our betrothal was nothing more than a grab for power. Malkijah is marrying me so he can inherit your district. That's why he pushed so hard for a ketubah, isn't it?"

"Chana . . . Chana . . . calm down, my angel. Malkijah would never commit to a lifetime with you if he wasn't taken with your charms."

"But what if it was all an act? Eliashib said that marrying me was a shrewd political move on Malkijah's part."

"Of course it was. And a shrewd move on my part, as well. An alliance with Malkijah benefits us as much as it does him. He's one of the wealthiest men in the province. You will never need to work another day in your life with him as your husband. Think of your children, Chana, and what they'll stand to gain. And if this match happens to benefit Malkijah, increasing his land or his wealth—"

"Or his power?" she asked bitterly.

"Yes, or his power—then it's an excellent arrangement for all of us. Listen, you're a smart woman, Chana. You know how and why marriages are arranged. Every father in Judah tries to make the best possible match for his daughter, one that will benefit her and her family. Why are you so surprised by this?"

"I don't know . . . because . . . because my betrothal to Yitzhak was different. He didn't care about power; he loved me. I was foolish to believe that Malkijah was the same, that he was interested in me, not in what he stood to gain by marrying me."

"Listen, I believe that Yitzhak did love you, my angel. But he also knew very well that if he married you, he would become the leader of Jerusalem someday. He would inherit both halves of the district—my half and his father's. He talked about it all the time, remember? He used to brag that he would be king and your children would be little princes."

For a second time that evening, all of Chana's strength melted away. She had to sit down. "That . . . that was a joke . . ."

"Perhaps he treated it as a joke, but Yitzhak was very aware of the power and position he would gain by marrying you. He wanted those things just as much as Malkijah does. The two men are no different in that respect—except that Malkijah will only inherit half of the district of Jerusalem."

She covered her face and lowered her head to her lap. How could she have been so stupid, letting her love for Yitzhak blind her to his other motives? Chana remembered all the months she had wasted, grieving and mourning for him, how she had nearly stopped living, and she felt like a fool. And she was an even bigger fool for trusting Malkijah, falling for his charm and his sympathy, believing him when he'd insisted he understood how she felt.

Abba was still pleading with her to understand, but she didn't want to hear it. "I don't want to talk about it anymore, Abba. Please, I need to be alone."

She was betrothed to Malkijah. Their union was as binding as marriage. Chana couldn't dissolve the contract without forfeiting everything, including her father's good name and reputation. The scandal of a divorce would hurt Yudit and Sarah, too. And Chana would sacrifice any chance of getting married and having a family. She was going to become Malkijah ben Recab's wife, his pathway to more power. And she could do nothing to stop it.

CHAPTER

26

JERUSALEM
AUGUST

Nehemiah stood in the temple courtyard for the morning sacrifice, his prayers the same as he'd prayed since arriving in Jerusalem: for the Almighty One's help in quickly rebuilding the wall, for His wisdom in making the right decisions, and for His aid against their enemies. The temperature had fallen during the night, and the morning air felt cooler than it had in several weeks as a refreshing mountain breeze blew up from the Great Sea. He thanked the Almighty One that the long heat wave had finally broken. The work would proceed more quickly in cooler weather.

After whispering "Amen" and opening his eyes, Nehemiah immediately scanned the area all around him. His training had taught him to constantly assess his surroundings, to be aware of every detail, and quickly discern anything that looked different or out of place. It was second nature to him now. But this morning when he gazed around at the worshiping men, something was amiss. Nehemiah couldn't put his finger on it but the atmosphere seemed different. He sensed a charge in the air—as if a thunderstorm approached, even though the sky was a cloudless blue. The laborers gathered in the courtyard this morning looked restless, their attention distracted from the priestly ritual. Groups of men stood whispering together, their faces sullen and angry. None of them seemed focused on the temple service or on the priest who was about to pronounce the blessing to close the morning sacrifice. Was it Nehemiah's imagination, or were the men watching him?

He casually turned his head to look behind him and noticed something else that was different. Usually only a handful of women and children attended the morning sacrifice, but today they filled the outer courtyard. Hundreds of them. He leaned close to his brother Hanani and whispered, "Something's going on. Any idea what it is?"

"What do you mean?" His brother's senses weren't as well-honed as Nehemiah's.

"Look around, Hanani. The sacrifice is over, yet no one is leaving. And there are more people here than usual, certainly more women and children. I don't think I'm imagining that they're watching me."

Hanani gazed around and drew a quick breath. "You're right. What shall we do?"

"Stay calm."

For the first time since his escort of Persian soldiers returned to Susa, Nehemiah wished they hadn't. His brothers had worked behind the scenes to gather swords and spears and other weapons ever since the day Sanballat and the other provincial leaders left Jerusalem, and they'd unearthed a storehouse full of arms left over from the battles on the Thirteenth of Adar, nearly thirty years ago. Many of the weapons needed to be repaired, and all of them needed to be sharpened or the bows restrung. Nehemiah had commissioned every local blacksmith he could find to work on them and make them functional again, planning to arm his laymen workers in the event of an enemy threat. Now, seeing the restless mob that had gathered in the courtyard, he was glad that he hadn't.

He whispered a silent prayer, then turned to his brother. "Let's go. Start walking toward the stairs." Maybe the unrest he'd sensed was all in his mind. But as he started to leave, the mass of men, women, and children moved into the center of the courtyard, blocking his way.

"We would like a word with you, Governor Nehemiah." The spokesman had the sturdy build of a laborer, the tanned face and calloused hands of a man familiar with hard work.

"Certainly. What is it?" He kept his tone friendly and courteous, careful to show no fear or resistance.

"We have a grievance, Governor. And even though every one of us has worked willingly to help rebuild the wall, we refuse to work another day until you listen to us and help us."

This was bribery. Extortion. Nehemiah shouldn't surrender to their tactics. He should require them to go through the proper channels and present their petition without resorting to threats. But he also knew that if he refused to listen now, he might lose several valuable working days. Nehemiah needed all of these men on his side, even if their methods infuriated him. "What's your grievance?" He folded his arms across his chest, determined to show no emotion. *The hand of the Lord my God is upon me.*

"We need your help to correct a great injustice in our province—"

Before the man could finish, the courtyard erupted with everyone shouting at once, desperate to be heard.

"We're losing our homes, our livelihood!"

"We want our children back!"

"And our land!"

"We need food!"

"We're starving!"

Women wept as they held up raggedy, undernourished children for him to see. But Nehemiah found it hard to follow the thread of their protest in the thunder of so many angry voices. He looked at his brother, then back at the crowd, and all he could do was hold up his hands for silence. Tempers and emotions were so high that he whispered a prayer for Hanani's safety, afraid the crowd would trample him if it surged forward.

"I'm willing to listen," he shouted. "But you must speak one at a time. If this turns into a riot, then nothing will be accomplished." Even though Nehemiah pleaded for order, it took several minutes for the clamoring protests to die down. At last, the angry buzz of voices quieted. "Let one man speak for all of you." There was another mumble of conversation before the man who had first spoken stepped forward again.

"The drought has been severe. We and our sons and daughters are numerous. In order for us to eat and stay alive, we must get grain!" Again, everyone began shouting at once. As Nehemiah waited, a second man stepped forward.

"We're landowners, working to support our families on property that belonged to our ancestors before the exile. But we're forced to mortgage our fields, our vineyards, and our homes to get grain during the famine."

"On top of that," the first speaker added, "we had to borrow money to pay the tax the king imposed on our fields and vineyards."

During another loud protest against the king and his heavy taxation, Hanani leaned close to whisper to Nehemiah. "Our delegation to Susa learned that the Persian king collects twenty-million darics every year in taxes. None of it ever benefits the provinces."

When the mob finally calmed down, Nehemiah asked the men, "Who have you borrowed from? Who holds the mortgages on your land?" He expected to hear that it was Persian government officials like Sanballat and Tobiah. The people's answer shocked him.

"Our own brethren!"

"The wealthy few who have grown rich on our misfortune!"

"The rich nobles on your own council!"

"Is this true?" Nehemiah whispered to his brother as he waited for the shouting to stop.

"I don't know," Hanani said with a shrug.

"Although we're of the same flesh and blood as our countrymen," the man continued, "and though our children are as good at theirs, we have to subject our sons and daughters to slavery to the men who hold our mortgages."

"Some of our daughters have already been enslaved," the other speaker continued, "but we're powerless because our fields and our vineyards belong to others."

"This can't be happening," Nehemiah said, not because he doubted the protesters, but because he didn't want to believe that his fellow Jews would subject their own people to slavery.

"Ask them!" a young man shouted. "Ask men like Malkijah ben Recab how many of our children he enslaved!"

"At least in Babylon our families could stay together," a weeping woman shouted.

Nehemiah couldn't reply. The people's outcry and the charges they had brought forward infuriated him. He saw desperation in the eyes of the people in front of him and remembered the lavish meal he had eaten at Malkijah's home in Jerusalem. He had little doubt that what the protesters said was true. "I am very angry to learn about these abuses," he said when he finally could be heard. "I had no idea this was happening. Anyone who is starving may come to my residence this afternoon, and I'll give you and your family food. I'll order my servants to open my storehouses to you. From now on, you'll be under my protection. My table will be your table."

"That's just for today," someone shouted. "What about freeing our sons and daughters from slavery?"

"Give me time to find a solution. I'll meet with you again when I have answers for you."

"We're not working on your wall until you do something!"

Again, the outcry was so great that Nehemiah knew the crowd wouldn't be able to hear him even if he did try to plead with them to reconsider. He motioned to Hanani to follow him, then waded into the mob to return home. Nehemiah liked to keep a safe corridor of space around him at all times, and as he was forced to pass through the crush and press of the mob, he felt close to panic. Ever since the night he and his brothers crowded behind a piece of furniture to save their lives, Nehemiah hated tight spaces.

By the time he reached the bottom of the temple steps, he was breathing hard and drenched with sweat, but grateful to have open space around him again. "This is exactly what our enemies have been hoping for, Hanani. They want the work to halt. They want our people to be so deeply divided that they can no longer work together."

"What are you going to do?"

"I don't know yet. . . . Listen, I need you to open my storehouses like I just promised to do. In the meantime, if there is a solution to this problem it has to be in the Torah. I'm going to talk to Rebbe Ezra and see if he has any advice. I know the Almighty One commands us to help the poor."

But when he reached Ezra's home, he was distressed to learn that the rebbe hadn't returned from the morning sacrifice yet. Had there been a riot after he'd left? Had Ezra, the former governor, been caught up in it? Nehemiah waited, pacing in place, until Ezra finally arrived home. "Sorry," the rebbe said. "I decided to wait on the temple mount until the crowd dispersed."

"So, you heard what happened there this morning?"

"Yes, I heard."

"And is what they said true? Are the wealthy landowners really taking advantage of the famine to become even richer? Are they forcing their brethren to mortgage their land and enslave their children in order to put food on their tables?"

"I don't doubt that it's true. The drought has been very severe."

Nehemiah had to draw a deep breath and exhale slowly to remain calm. "And what does the Torah have to say about it? That's what I came to ask you, Rebbe. I want to demand that these outrageous practices stop immediately, but I need the law to back me up."

"Sit down, please," Ezra said. "I could use a seat myself." Nehemiah obeyed, but he perched at the very edge of the chair, waiting for Ezra's reply. "Concerning any impoverished men and women who don't own land and are without food," the rebbe began, "the Torah says we are not to be hard-hearted or tightfisted toward them but openhanded. We are to give generously and do so without a grudging heart. God says there will always be poor in the land, therefore He commands us to be merciful toward our needy brethren."

"So it's a command," Nehemiah said.

"Yes. Now, as for the men who do own land, the Torah allows for their property to be mortgaged in times of need. But at the end of seven years, the debt must be canceled."

"Even if it hasn't been repaid?"

"Yes. The Torah says that the man who made the loan shall not require payment from his fellow Israelite. He must cancel any debt his brother owes him, but only after seven years."

"That's a long time. Can we force these wealthy men to give back the people's land before then?"

"I'm afraid not. We can only appeal to them to show mercy. As for those who have been forced by circumstances to borrow money at exorbitant rates and sell their children into slavery, the Torah clearly says, 'Do not charge your brother interest, whether on money or food or anything else that may earn interest.' Any man who is currently exacting usury from his fellow Jews is breaking the law."

"I'll make sure that practice stops immediately."

"As for the sons and daughters of the poor who are being enslaved, the Torah forbids our people to hold a fellow Jew as a slave. I doubt that this has occurred. But the Law does allow us to sell our children or ourselves as bondservants if we become poor. Only for six years, mind you. In the seventh year they must go free."

"Six years?"

"Yes. And when they finally are set free, they are not to be sent away empty-handed. 'Supply him liberally from your flock, your threshing floor and your winepress,' the Torah says. 'Give to him as the Lord your God has blessed you.'"

"So no one is breaking the law if these children remain bond-servants for the next six years?"

"That's true. But I believe our compassionate God wants us to show compassion to one another."

"Yes, I do, too. That's exactly why I intend to tell all those men who are prospering during this famine and taking advantage of the poor that this has to stop."

"I would also remind them," Ezra said, stroking his white beard, "that the exile was caused by abuses such as these—injustice, the oppression of the weak by the strong, and failing to obey the Torah."

"I'll do that." Nehemiah stood, eager to begin. "Thank you for your help, Rebbe. I plan to call a meeting as quickly as I can arrange it and hold the guilty men accountable for these abuses. Will you stand with me and back up what I'm saying with God's Law?"

"Certainly. You'll be in my prayers, Nehemiah—as always."

JERUSALEM

Nava stood in the rear of the temple courtyard with all the other women, waiting in the place where she'd promised to meet Dan. She had been terrified for him when he walked up to the front of the mob to stand with the other men and confront Governor Nehemiah. Now he was safe. The governor had listened to their pleas. Nava stood on her tiptoes, trying to see above everyone's heads, watching for Dan. She finally spotted him pushing past the others to hurry back to her, and she laughed out loud with relief and joy.

"Dan, that was amazing! You were wonderful!" She grabbed his hands and squeezed them tightly, her heart aching for the day when they could finally hug each other at moments like this. His tanned face beamed with happiness.

"Did you hear what the governor said, Nava? He's angry about what rich nobles are doing, and he's going to find a solution."

"I hope he helps us."

"Me too. Maybe this nightmare will finally end. Maybe you can come home, and we can get married."

"I'm almost afraid to hope that anything will change."

"Wealthy men like Malkijah probably won't give up easily. But we've all agreed not to go back to work on the wall until we get relief. The governor will have to help us if he wants his wall finished."

"I'm late, Dan. I have to get back to the house. Walk with me." They hurried toward the stairs, still holding hands so they wouldn't become separated. The crowd moved slowly as they filed out, the men not in a rush since they weren't going back to work. Nava and Dan threaded their way around them.

"Malkijah and most of the other rich noblemen were probably here at the temple today," Dan said when they reached the bottom of the steps. "If they heard what the governor said, they're probably conspiring together, scrambling to find a way to keep all their money and servants."

"I'll try to hear what my master says when I serve his meals," Nava said. "And I have more good news to tell you since I saw you last. The other night, my master became engaged to that nice woman named Chana who defended you the night you came to the estate. She's very kind, so when I go back to Beth Hakkerem, I know I can ask her for help if Master—" Nava stopped, horrified. She had nearly blurted out the truth about Master Aaron.

"If what?" Dan asked.

"If . . . if Master Malkijah is unkind."

Dan pulled her to a stop in the middle of the street. "That wasn't what you were going to say, was it?"

"Please . . . I'm already late. I need to hurry."

"Nava, we've never lied to each other. Tell me the truth. What are you hiding?"

"Nothing." It was the truth because nothing had happened with Master Aaron—yet.

Dan held her shoulders and made her look at him. "We promised that we would always tell each other the truth—remember?"

She nodded. She also remembered that Dan had threatened

to kill Malkijah and his sons if they ever laid a hand on her. He would do it, too. She had to ease his fears. "Listen, ever since you told me that my master and his sons had a right to marry me, I've been terrified that it would happen, and that I would never be able to marry you."

"Even the thought of it makes me crazy."

"Well, my master's fiancée is very understanding. I told her that I loved you, and I believe she would help protect me from a forced marriage. My master listens to her. He listened the night you broke in, remember? That's all I was going to say."

"Then why did you stop in the middle of your sentence?"

Nava thought quickly. "Because I didn't want to remind you about my master's sons. I don't want you to worry. Please, Dan. I really need to get back to work. I haven't been set free yet, you know." She smiled, knowing he couldn't resist her smile, knowing he wanted her to be happy. When they were a dozen yards from Malkijah's house, she stopped again. "You'd better not come any closer in case someone sees you. I'll meet with you again tomorrow." She turned and sprinted the rest of the way to the rear door of her master's house.

The housekeeper's forehead was creased with anger as she met Nava at the door. "Where have you been?" She was older than the housekeeper on the estate, and hadn't approved of Ruth sending a servant as young and inexperienced as Nava to work in the master's Jerusalem house. Nava tried extra hard to please her, fearing she would send her back to Beth Hakkerem if she made a single mistake. Not only would Nava be unable to see Dan every day, but she would have to cope with Aaron's advances again. "I was about to send out a search party," the woman said. "I figured you had run away."

"I would never run away," Nava said. "I was late because there was a protest in the temple today and the crowds were so huge that they blocked my way. I had a hard time getting through. I'm so sorry."

"What kind of a protest?"

Nava hesitated, unsure how much to say. The housekeeper was a hired servant, not a bondservant. Her job of caring for this house and feeding all the laborers would be impossible if Malkijah set all his bondservants free. "Some of the area farmers asked the governor for help because of the drought. They said they're not going back to work on the wall until he does something about the famine." Nava picked up a broom as she talked, starting her usual morning chores of sweeping floors and cleaning the kitchen and washing the breakfast dishes. Maybe if she busied herself and worked hard, the housekeeper would forgive her for being late and not ask too many questions. Nava didn't want her to know that she'd taken part in the protest or that she was secretly meeting Dan. "I'll just gather the dishes from the dining room now—"

"Just a minute!"

Nava's heart beat faster, fearing she was in trouble. "Yes, ma'am?"

"You say the men aren't working on the wall today?"

"That's what they told the governor, ma'am."

"So we don't have to prepare a midday meal for them?"

"I-I don't know." Would Dan and all the other men have to go without food? Had they thought of that when they'd decided not to work? Then Nava remembered that the governor had promised to open his storehouses.

"Well, don't just stand there, get to work!" the housekeeper barked. Nava jumped to obey. But she was aware from snatches of overheard conversation that a servant had been sent to the Dung Gate to speak with Malkijah. And that her master confirmed that work on the wall and at his gate had come to a halt. He'd ordered not to feed any of his men until they returned.

Nava longed to tell her fellow bondservants about the protest at the temple, especially her friend Rachel. None of them had seen how angry the governor had been to hear about their plight or how he'd promised to help them. But as the day progressed, nothing changed except their workload. With no midday meal to prepare, most of the extra servants like Nava stood around with nothing to do. She and the others had come to Jerusalem in the first place to cook for the workers. Would she be sent back to Beth Hakkerem now that the work had stopped—back to Master Aaron?

The hope that Nava had felt this morning began draining away like water into sand.

JERUSALEM

Going to his field headquarters would be pointless for Nehemiah. Silence had settled over Jerusalem, replacing the constant background noise of shouts and grunts, sawing and chipping and chiseling. The laborers had carried through with their threat, bringing work on the wall to a standstill. Frustrated on several levels, Nehemiah returned to the governor's residence after his meeting with Rebbe Ezra and gathered his brothers and his three aides together in his private chambers.

"I've been pondering the people's accusations," he told them, "and after talking over the matter with Rebbe Ezra from a legal standpoint, I've decided on a course of action. The wealthy men who are taking advantage of their fellow Jews during the famine need to be confronted. How long do you think it would take to summon all the nobles and officials and district leaders here for a meeting?"

"Not long," Ephraim said. "Most of them are already in Jerusalem to supervise one of the sections of the wall or one of the gates."

"Good. Send out messengers right away," he told his aides.

LYNN AUSTIN

"Tell them I'm calling for a meeting tomorrow morning at the temple, immediately after the sacrifice."

"Do you think that's wise, Governor?" Jehohanan asked. "The wealthiest men are all on your council. Why not meet with them privately in your chambers? If the protesters overhear you at the temple they—"

"I want to be overheard. What I have to say should be said in public. The poor people need to know that I'm not hiding anything or working in secret."

"But to accuse Judah's nobles and officials of wrongdoing and shame them in public would—"

"Those who are doing wrong and violating the Torah should be ashamed. And those who have nothing to hide will be able to withstand public scrutiny." Nehemiah waited to see if anyone else had a comment, then sent his three aides away to relay his message. "Hanani, were our storehouses opened to the poor today?" he asked his brother. "Are they getting enough grain to feed their families?"

"Everything proceeded very smoothly. The people are grateful."

"You're a very cunning politician, Nehemiah," Ephraim said. "By giving to the poor, you've earned their undying loyalty and gratitude."

Nehemiah wanted to be angry with his brother for politicizing his motives, but his words had an element of truth. Nehemiah had wanted to please the masses so they would return to work on the wall. "I'm feeding them because the Torah commands me to," he replied with a sigh. "I hope the people's loyalty and gratitude go to God, not to me."

"Aren't you afraid that if you alienate the nobles and council members they'll turn against you?" Hanani asked. "Jehohanan might have a point about shaming them in public."

"I'm not here to win a popularity contest, I'm here to rebuild the wall," Nehemiah said. Although deep in his heart, he knew

245

he also wanted to be admired and applauded by the people he served, the noblemen as well as the commoners. "As for shaming the nobles, the reason I'm holding the meeting in the temple is so the Almighty One will have a chance to speak to them. As they stand in front of His sanctuary, they may be reminded that God sees their secret deeds and knows their motives."

"And what if things don't go the way you hope they will?" Ephraim asked. "What if a riot breaks out, poor against rich? Tempers are already near the breaking point."

"If our people are that deeply divided and the class hatred is that strong, then there's no hope at all for our survival as a people. Rebuilding the wall or anything else we try to do will be a waste of time."

Nehemiah didn't sleep well that night. He walked up to the temple early the next morning without waiting for his brothers and chose a place to stand alongside Rebbe Ezra as he worshiped. "I've called for a meeting with the leaders and nobles after the sacrifice to deal with the problems we talked about yesterday," he told him. "Will you say a few words to the men, too?"

"Of course. I've been looking into the matter more carefully since we talked."

More people than usual crowded into the temple courtyard for the morning sacrifice, and Nehemiah was pleased to see his council members there, along with the nobles and district leaders. As the incense ascended to heaven, he prayed that the men would listen to him, that their hearts would be moved with compassion, and that the Almighty One would heal the divisions among His people.

Nehemiah took his place in the outer courtyard when the service ended, in the same place he'd stood to announce his intention to rebuild the wall. He motioned for Rebbe Ezra to join him and waited for his officials to assemble in front of them. He wasted no time in making his accusations. "You are exacting usury from your own countrymen! As far as possible, we have brought back our Jewish brothers who were sold to the Gentiles. Now you are selling your brothers, only for them to be sold back to us!" His voice echoed off the temple walls as a shocked stillness settled over the courtyard. The men in front of him stood quietly, as if finding nothing to say.

"What you're doing isn't right. Shouldn't you walk in the fear of our God to avoid the reproach of our Gentile enemies? My brothers and I are giving the people grain to help them during this famine. You also should be giving charity. The Torah commands it. And it forbids the exacting of usury. It has to stop!"

He nodded to Ezra, letting the older man speak next. "I want to read you the word of warning that the Almighty One spoke to our ancestors before the exile," Ezra said, unrolling a small scroll. "He spoke through His prophet Ezekiel, saying:

"'You are a land that has had no rain or showers in the day of wrath. There is a conspiracy of her princes within her like a roaring lion tearing its prey; they devour people, take treasures and precious things and make many widows . . . the people of the land practice extortion and commit robbery; they oppress the poor and needy . . . I looked for a man among them who would build up the wall and stand before me in the gap on behalf of the land so I would not have to destroy it, but I found none. So I will pour out my wrath on them and consume them with my fiery anger, bringing down on their own heads all they have done, declares the Sovereign Lord.'"

The silence in the crowd was absolute. Ezra took his time rolling up the scroll, then faced the nobles standing in front of him. "We all know what happened to our fathers when they failed to heed the Almighty One's warning. When they continued to oppress the poor and needy. Will we now follow in their footsteps and do the same?"

Ezra stepped back, gesturing to Nehemiah to continue. "If you care about our nation and about our covenant with God," he said, "I challenge you to give back to the people their fields, vineyards, olive groves, and houses immediately, and also the usury you are charging them—the hundredth part of the money, grain, new wine, and oil. As Rebbe Ezra just reminded us, the destruction of Jerusalem and our exile were caused by our ancestors' refusal to live according to the Holy One's law. It was only God's undeserved grace and mercy that made it possible for us to return to our land. Will we now take advantage of that grace? God asks you to show mercy to the poor because He is merciful. Our ancestors owed Him their love and loyalty, their tithes, and their gratitude. Instead, they worshiped idols and forgot His covenant, amassing a huge debt of sin. The Almighty One didn't have to forgive that debt. He could have let us remain in exile. But He did forgive us—and here we are. If He can forgive our mountain of debt, can't we also forgive our brothers' debts?" Nehemiah paused to let his words settle over the silent people.

"Those of you who God raised up as leaders—you're supposed to be shepherds of His people. If they're suffering, it's your job to help them. Instead, you weren't even concerned enough about them to make this city safe. What kind of shepherds are you? You should help your brothers who are in need instead of charging them interest and forcing them to mortgage their land and sell their children as bondservants.

"I'm aware that the long drought led to this situation. But the Torah says the Almighty One will bless us with rain if we live right. Maybe He allowed this drought to show us the greed that's in our hearts. To change us into His servants. To give us an opportunity to show mercy. And we're failing the test. Please, I urge you to show compassion to those who are poor and starving and give them food, free of charge, as my brothers and I are doing. If men have borrowed money from you, stop charging interest and give back the usury you've illegally charged, or you'll be held accountable for breaking the law. If they've mortgaged their land to you and sold their sons and daughters as bondservants, I beg you to give back their land and their sons and daughters. You may be within the bounds of the law in taking them, but I appeal to you to show mercy—as God has shown us mercy."

A spontaneous cheer went up from the poor people at the rear of the assembly. But even before the sound died away, the district leader from Tekoa stepped forward to confront Nehemiah. "We have a legal right to expect payment for the loans we made. And we have a right to keep any mortgaged land and bondservants for six years."

"I know you do. But I'm asking you to show mercy and give up those rights."

"Why? I worked hard for what I have, and I managed my property well. Why should I bail out people who couldn't manage theirs? Should we all become poor together? That's nonsense!"

"Why are you siding with the poor, Governor Nehemiah," another nobleman asked, "and treating us like criminals when we're acting lawfully?" Their anger and lack of compassion didn't really surprise Nehemiah, but it saddened him.

"I care about the rich as much as I do the poor," he told them. "As your governor, I could impose a tax on all of you for my support, but I'm not going to do that. Neither I nor my brothers have demanded the food allotment that Governor Sanballat required before I came. I know what a heavy burden he placed on the people, taking forty shekels of silver from each of you in addition to a tax on your food and wine. His assistants lorded it over the people. But out of reverence for God, I didn't act like that. I never demanded the food allotted to me because I knew what a heavy load it placed on you. How can I live in luxury when there are people in this province who are in need? I have devoted myself to the work on the wall instead of acquiring land and servants and planting crops. Listen, if you won't give up your rights to repayment and help your brothers for the Almighty One's sake, then at least do it to avoid the scorn of the nations. The Gentiles know how our God set us free from slavery in Egypt. Is He now too weak to set His people free from slavery to their own brethren? And one more thing—if we free our brothers out of kindness and compassion, maybe one day the Holy One will free us from servitude to the Persians."

Most of the men standing in front of Nehemiah seemed chastened. It was time to ask them to act on what they'd heard. "Do you agree to do what I'm asking?" he challenged. "Will you find it in your hearts to show compassion?"

"We will give everything back," one of the leaders said.

"And we will not demand anything more from them," another added.

"We will do as you say."

The cheer that followed their promises was deafening. But just to make sure that these men wouldn't go back on their word, Nehemiah summoned the priests standing off to one side. "Have all these nobles and officials take an oath before God to do what they just promised," he told them. Then he got the crowd's attention again and made a dramatic show of shaking out the folds of his robe. "In this way," he shouted, "may God shake out of his house and possessions every man who does not keep this promise. So may such a man be shaken out and emptied!"

At this the whole assembly shouted, "Amen," and they praised the Lord in a loud voice.

Nehemiah stepped down from the platform as the priests took his place to administer the oath. "Let's get back to work on the wall," he told his brothers. They headed toward the central staircase leading down to the city, and once again hundreds of people crowded around Nehemiah to thank him, some reaching out to touch him or his robe. He fought to quell his rising panic as they closed in, knowing they meant him no harm.

At last he reached the city street below, and he could breathe again. He thought of the prophecy that Rebbe Ezra had read about God's condemnation of the leaders who hadn't sought justice for their people. That prophecy had been fulfilled in his ancestors' time, the leaders and kings contributing to their nation's destruction and exile. But Nehemiah was satisfied that this morning he had restored a measure of justice and righted a wrong.

Remember me with favor, O my God, he silently prayed, *for all I have done for these people.*

JERUSALEM

Nava stood in the tightly packed crowd at the temple, secretly holding Dan's hand as they listened to Nehemiah deliver his speech. *"Give back their land and their sons and daughters . . ."* the governor said. Dan joined the great cheer that erupted all around them but Nava couldn't utter a sound, her throat tight with emotion. When the noise died away she held her breath, waiting to hear how the rich men would respond. If only God would answer her prayers.

"Are they going to do it?" she whispered to Dan. Her hand ached from the strength of his grip.

"Maybe . . . I don't know . . . listen . . ."

"We will give everything back," one of the leaders said.

"And we will not demand anything more from them," another added.

"We will do as you say."

The cheer that followed their promises was deafening. Neither Nava nor Dan could resist the urge to hug each other with joyful abandon. Abba would get his land and vineyard back. Nava would go free. She could be with Dan for the rest of her life and never have to worry about Master Aaron again. "It's too wonderful to believe," she said as she clung to the man she loved.

When the governor made the men take an oath before God so they wouldn't go back on their word, Nava longed to watch Master Malkijah take the vow. But she was too far away to see who came forward to stand before the priests. As Governor Nehemiah plowed through the crowd to leave the temple mount, she and Dan rushed forward to thank him like so many others were doing. He had renewed her hope and given her a future.

"I need to return to work," she told Dan after the governor was gone.

"Why bother? You're going to be set free now. You can go home to your family."

"Maybe . . . but I'm not free yet. And now that the men will be returning to work on the wall, I need to help prepare food for them. The governor did his part, now we all need to do ours."

She and Dan made their way through the joyful chaos as poor families like theirs cheered and wept and celebrated the good news. The men who had left their farms to rebuild the wall hurried to their worksites. "Are you going back to help with the wall, too?" she asked Dan.

"Yes, but I want to go home first, and tell our families the good news. Just think! Our fathers' farms and crops will belong to them again. Their loans will be canceled. And best of all, you'll be coming home."

"Is it safe to walk there all alone?"

"I'll be fine in the daylight hours. Believe me, I'm so happy I could run all the way home and back again!"

"I'll see you tomorrow, then," she said as they neared Malkijah's house. He gave her hand a loving squeeze, and she ran the rest of the way to the courtyard door.

Nava couldn't disguise her joy as she hurried into the kitchen. "You're late again," the housekeeper said. "Where were you all this time? . . . And why are you grinning like you just found gold?"

"I have wonderful news! I went to the temple for the sacrifice and Governor Nehemiah held a meeting afterward. . . ." She looked around at the other servants, aware that everyone except the housekeeper was a bondservant like her. "He appealed to all the rich landowners to show mercy to families like ours who've become poor because of the drought. He asked them to cancel our debts and set all their bondservants *free*!"

Nava's friend Rachel covered her mouth as she gave a little cry. If it was true, she could go home to her husband and children. Nava saw the tangled mixture of hope and fear in everyone's eyes as they stared at her. She understood their reluctance to believe her.

"All the wealthy men agreed to do it," she told them. "I heard them! Governor Nehemiah made them come forward and take an oath before the priests promising to give everything back to us." She could barely stand still, wanting to jump up and down with joy.

"Did Master Malkijah take the oath, too?" Rachel asked. "Is he really going to give us our freedom?"

"I don't know for certain . . . it was too crowded to see. But surely he will. All the other leaders swore to do it."

"In the meantime, we have work to do," the housekeeper said, clapping her hands. "I assume this means that the work on the wall will continue?"

"I think so. I saw a lot of men hurrying to their worksites."

"In that case, we have a meal to prepare for a lot of hungry workers. Get busy."

Nava did her chores in a daze of joy, imagining all that awaited her in the next few days. She would return home and hug her mother and father and brothers for the first time in more than two months. She would work alongside them on Abba's land, knowing that it all belonged to him again. With their debts canceled, maybe she and Dan could be married at last. They would announce their betrothal, and Dan would begin digging the foundations for the home they would share.

Nava and the others finished preparing the midday meal, and a team of servants left to carry it to the workers at the Dung Gate. Master Malkijah was expecting dinner guests that evening, so Nava and the others had another huge meal to prepare that afternoon. But she took a moment to hug Rachel tightly when they were alone in the storage room. "We're going to be free! Can you believe it?" Nava whispered.

"No . . . I'm afraid to believe it. I want to hear it from Master Malkijah's own mouth."

When the master returned from his work at the Dung Gate late that afternoon, he went straight to his chambers to wash and change his clothes before his guests arrived. The servants watched his every move, holding their breath, waiting for the announcement that he would cancel their debts and set them free. But Malkijah never said a word about it.

Nava strained to overhear snatches of conversation as she served the evening meal, but the only thing the men talked about was the progress on the wall. She and the other servants were reluctant to go to bed, waiting for the announcement of their freedom. When Malkijah's last guest departed, he retired to his bedchamber. "Surely he hasn't forgotten, has he?" Rachel asked as they cleared the dinner table. "He must know we're all eager to hear him say it."

"Maybe he's going to make a grand announcement tomorrow," Nava said.

But Malkijah left the house early the next morning without eating breakfast. Nava and the other servants gathered in the kitchen to talk to the housekeeper. "Did our master say anything at all about giving us our freedom?" one of them asked.

The housekeeper shook her head. "Not a word. Nava must have been mistaken about what she heard at the temple. Now eat your breakfast and get to work. We have a lot to do today."

Instead of eating, Nava hurried up to the temple for the morning sacrifice. She found Dan waiting for her in their usual place, his eyes filled with hope. "Are you ready to go, Nava? I told your family that I would bring you home today, and they were overjoyed to hear the news. They can hardly wait to see you and—" He stopped when he saw her tears. "Nava, what's wrong?"

"I'm not free yet. Master Malkijah never said anything about it when he came home last night. And he left again this morning without saying anything."

"I don't understand. The men took an oath before God."

"I don't understand either. It was hard enough to have our dream snatched away the first time, but if it happens again . . ." She couldn't finish. Dan steered her out of the courtyard and down the stairs, neither of them in the mood to worship the Almighty One.

"Let's just go home to our families," Dan said. "Come on, what can Malkijah do to us?"

Nava longed to go, imagining herself at home again with the people she loved. But she knew she couldn't. "I can't leave yet, Dan. I promised Abba that I would work as a bondservant to help repay his debts, and I can't disappoint him. Besides, Malkijah could take away Abba's land if I don't work for him. That was the deal they made. I need to work until the debt is officially canceled and I'm set free."

"Then let's find him, either here at the temple or where he works at the Dung Gate. Let's demand to know why you aren't free." Dan's short temper fueled his impatience. He wanted to take action and do something, and his pent-up energy would be dangerous until his anger cooled.

"Dan, we can't confront my master. Our fathers are the ones who need to talk to him, not us."

"Nava, no! We need to—"

"We need to stay calm and wait to see what happens. Malkijah is a very powerful man. Please, Dan."

He gazed into the distance toward home, and Nava saw him

fighting for control as if trying to calm a whirlwind. "Fine. I won't confront him. I'll get my father and yours and all the other men who are in debt to him, and we'll confront him together. Do you know if he's going back to Beth Hakkerem soon or should we talk to him here?"

"He usually goes home for the Sabbath."

"If he doesn't set you free by then, we'll demand to know why not."

For the rest of the week, Nava and her fellow bondservants hung in suspense, waiting for their freedom. Nothing happened. Malkijah traveled home to Beth Hakkerem for Shabbat, and the day of rest seemed a month long as Nava waited for Dan to return from confronting him. When she finally saw Dan climbing the temple steps on the first day of the week, she guessed from his angry expression that the news wasn't good.

"What happened? What did he say?" Nava asked.

"Malkijah refuses to set anyone free. He's not canceling anyone's debts."

Nava's strength drained away, along with her hope. She needed to sit down. She stumbled forward and sank onto the top step, ignoring the flow of people coming up for the sacrifice. She listened to the Levites singing the liturgy in the distance, *"Give thanks to the Lord for he is good. His love endures forever,"* and wanted to scream at them to stop. Why praise a God who didn't answer her prayers, a cruel God who gave her hope and then snatched it away again?

"Did Malkijah give you a reason why?" she finally asked. Dan sat down on the step beside her.

"He said he can't afford to do it. He wouldn't even meet with us. He sent his manager out to tell us, instead."

She would confront Malkijah herself, Nava decided, as soon as he arrived home from the Dung Gate this afternoon, or maybe this evening when she waited on him at his table. She would demand to know why he was so greedy and cruel when all the other masters had freed their bondservants. But Nava's courage melted when she realized that he might send her back to his estate if she angered him. Back to Aaron.

"What about the woman he's betrothed to?" Dan said, breaking into her thoughts. "Didn't you say she was kind to you?"

"Yes. But what can she do?"

"Let's ask her to help us. Maybe she doesn't know that her future husband is the only man in the province who won't show compassion."

"I suppose it's worth a try. But how will we find her? I don't know where she lives."

"Does she come to the morning sacrifice? We could wait beside a different set of stairs every morning until we see her. I think I remember what she looks like—short and pretty, with dark, wavy hair and a narrow face?"

Nava nodded. "Let's do it."

Dan stood and offered his hand to help her to her feet. She couldn't risk hoping again, but it felt good to have a plan, to be taking action. They chose the western stairs first and stood at the top when the sacrifice ended, on opposite sides, facing the busy stream of exiting people. Nava scanned hundreds of faces, searching and searching, determined not to give up until . . . and there she was! Walking with an older man and two younger women. As soon as Nava spotted Chana, she forced her way into the crowd, swimming upstream through the powerful current, not caring who she elbowed and shoved aside.

"Miss! Miss, wait! Please!" she called, not daring to call Chana by name.

Chana halted and the people with her halted, too. "Nava? Is everything all right?"

"No, miss, it isn't. Please, I need your help."

Chana hesitated, then said, "Go ahead, Abba. I'll catch up." She took Nava's arm, and they stepped aside to avoid the buffeting crowd. "Tell me what's wrong."

Nava's words came out in a babbled rush along with her tears. "All of the rich leaders took an oath to free their bondservants. I heard them doing it, miss. But Master Malkijah refuses to set us free."

Chana's dark brows came together in an angry frown. "He *refuses?*"

"Yes, miss. He told my father and all the other men who've mortgaged their land to him that he won't do it. Other servants are going back to their families, and I want to go home so badly! I miss everyone so much and—" Nava saw Dan watching from the other side of the stairs and dropped to her knees. "Please, miss! Please! Can't you talk to our master and ask him to change his mind?"

"Stand up, Nava," Chana said, tugging her arm. "You don't need to beg. I'll talk to him."

Nava watched Chana rejoin her group and felt a sliver of hope, as slender as a thread.

CHAPTER
30

SAMARIA

We came *this* close!" Tobiah said. He held his thumb and forefinger an inch apart and waved them in Governor Sanballat's ruddy face. "*This* close to an uncontrollable riot breaking out in Jerusalem, the poor against the rich. *This* close to a work shutdown that would have halted construction on the wall for good!"

"What happened?" Sanballat asked.

Tobiah shook his head, his arms falling to his sides. The words tasted bitter in his mouth as he spoke them. "Nehemiah averted the crisis. He pacified the people. Work on the wall is continuing."

"I can't believe that man's luck!" Sanballat shouted.

Tobiah watched as the heavyset man struggled to stand, leaning on the arms of his shabby throne. The blustering Samaritan disgusted Tobiah, but he needed him as an ally. He needed Geshem, too, although he trusted the sinister Arab leader even less than he trusted Sanballat. Geshem rarely sat down during their meetings in Sanballat's private chambers, pacing like a lion, restless to pounce, his long robes trailing across the floor behind him. The three men were alone in the room after Tobiah

260

insisted that all the servants be kept away. He knew better than anyone how easy it was to spy on your enemies.

"How did Nehemiah do it?" Sanballat asked, finally managing to rise to his feet. "Is the man a sorcerer or a magician that he can mesmerize so many people? How does he get them to blindly follow him?"

Tobiah gave a short laugh, hating to admit the genius of Nehemiah's strategy. "He made himself their messiah. He fed them with food from his own storehouses and arranged for their freedom. He shamed the wealthy nobles into taking an oath, making them agree to give back the lands that were mortgaged during the drought and to set all their bondservants free."

"And the nobles agreed to this? That's impossible. I know how greedy some of those local leaders are. There have to be some who refused to do the governor's bidding. Find the disgruntled ones, Tobiah, and get them on our side."

"I'm already working on that. My son knows some of the men who didn't take the oath. As soon as I leave here I'm going to Jerusalem to attend a family event. Nehemiah won't even know I'm there. I'll seek out the disgruntled ones and make them our allies. My sources tell me that the peace between rich and poor is very fragile at the moment." He sank onto a cushion and helped himself to the dates and raisin cakes his host had provided.

"Your plan is good, Tobiah," Geshem admitted, "but there has to be more we can do. Nehemiah must be stopped. If we attack this problem on several fronts, we'll have a better chance of a victory on one of them."

"We'll have to hurry," Sanballat said. "You say they're making progress on the wall?"

Tobiah nodded. "I'll survey it myself when I go there, but my spies tell me that the gaps are being closed. They say the wall has been rebuilt to nearly half its height in some places."

Geshem groaned. "Once Nehemiah's fortress is complete,

he can keep everyone out—including my trade caravans and Sanballat's army. He can keep you out, too, Tobiah. We need to fight back before the wall is finished."

"Listen to me." Sanballat held up his hands as if commanding Geshem to stop pacing and Tobiah to pay attention. "We need to attack the workers themselves and make them too terrified to continue. Take them by surprise. Before they know it or see us, we will be right there among them, and we'll kill them and put an end to their work. Everyone will be too afraid to continue, imagining that they're next. I guarantee those cowardly Jews will quit and run home if their lives are threatened."

"Good. I like that," Tobiah said. "And we may only have to stage a few attacks if we do a good enough job of spreading rumors and terrorizing the people. We'll get all the neighboring Samaritan and Ammonite towns to whisper rumors that we're coming for the Jews. Let fear infect them. There's nothing like the dread of an unknown enemy who may attack at any moment to cause panic. The Jews will all quit and go home."

"My caravans go throughout the province," Geshem said. "They can help sow rumors and warnings under the guise of friendship."

"I don't think they should be groundless warnings," Sanballat said. "I have the means to send armed men right into Jerusalem. If there is even one attack, perhaps a few deaths, then rumors are no longer rumors and the work will halt. Agreed?"

Tobiah and Geshem spoke at the same time. "Agreed."

The decision seemed to diffuse much of the tension in the room. Sanballat returned to his seat, and even Geshem relaxed enough to scoop a handful of dates from the bowl. But Tobiah knew they still faced a formidable opponent in Nehemiah. The man had an uncanny ability to convince the people to follow him. Having several nobles on their side may not be enough.

"What about Nehemiah?" he finally asked, voicing his fear. "We need to take him seriously as our enemy. He's not only extremely popular with the people, but he's shown leadership genius."

"We must destroy him," Geshem said. The vehemence of his reply made the hair on Tobiah's arms stand on end.

"How?" he asked.

"By every means we can think of," Geshem said. "Discredit him in the eyes of the common people. Drive a wedge between him and the nobility so they'll turn against him. Get King Artaxerxes to see him as a dangerous rebel. Threaten Nehemiah's life so he's too afraid to continue. . . ." He paused. "Kill him ourselves if we have to."

"Tobiah, you know those Jews better than we do," Sanballat said. "Is there something in their religious beliefs that we can use to our advantage and accomplish what Geshem suggested?"

Tobiah sat up straight as an idea began forming in his mind. "I think I do know of a way. The Jews believe that God will send another deliverer like Moses one day, a messiah who will feed the poor and defeat all their enemies. I taunted Nehemiah with this idea when we met with him before—but what if we used the Jewish prophecies to make everyone believe he really is the messiah? He's already fulfilling some of those expectations such as helping the poor. We can plant the seeds of this idea in people's minds, just like we planted the seeds of rebellion. All we need to do is hire a credible prophet."

"I don't see the point in all that," Geshem said.

"Hear me out," Tobiah said, rising to his feet. "The promised messiah is supposedly a king who will restore David's throne. We'll use those prophecies to prey on Nehemiah's pride, and if he accepts the people's pleas for a king, the Persian emperor will destroy him. It shouldn't be hard for a false prophet to help frame Nehemiah as a traitor. I'm told that he hinted at winning freedom from Persia in one of his speeches. But even if Nehemiah doesn't take the bait, the people will be disappointed in him for not freeing them and they'll turn against him."

"Do you know any prophets you can hire?" Sanballat asked.

"I have a man in mind. Possibly a woman, too. But they'll expect to be paid. Are we all willing to contribute something to hire them?" Tobiah would need the money in hand before he left Samaria. He knew Sanballat's legendary stinginess from experience.

"Yes, yes, we'll contribute," Sanballat said. "It's a good plan. But I'm still going ahead with the attacks. As Geshem said, we need to fight this war on all fronts."

Tobiah hated to be the voice of pessimism, but he didn't want to underestimate their enemy. "And if none of these plans work?" he asked.

Geshem pierced him with his night-black eyes. "Simple. We'll lure Nehemiah out of the city and kill him ourselves."

JERUSALEM

Chana hurried downhill from the Valley Gate to Malkijah's assigned section at the Dung Gate, her anger growing with each step she took. Nava's news that Malkijah refused to set his bondservants free filled Chana with a determination to end their betrothal. How could she marry a man who disobeyed the Torah and refused to help the poor? A man who was only interested in wealth and power?

She hadn't visited the Dung Gate since the work began, and she was amazed by how much progress had been made. No longer a pile of burnt rubble, the gate was taking shape again with a chamber for the guards and a tower that rose above the opening where the doors would hang. The laborers were hard at work, using a crane and a team of oxen to hoist a huge stone into place. But instead of working alongside the men the way Chana and her sisters did, Malkijah stood off to one side supervising them, wearing an expensive linen tunic. He didn't notice her until she walked up beside him and said, "May I have a word with you, please?"

"Chana? Is something wrong? Is it your family?" The concerned expression he wore looked convincing, but she knew what an accomplished actor he'd been in winning her trust. She wasn't going to let him deceive her again.

"We're all fine. That's not what brought me here."

"Come, there's a little patch of shade beneath the gate but unfortunately no place to sit down." He led her beneath the roof and dipped a cup into a clay water jar. "Would you like some?" She shook her head and watched as he drank it himself. "What is it, Chana? You look upset."

"I am upset. I was worshiping at the temple on the morning the workers staged their protest, asking the governor to help them. Were you there, too?"

"Yes. I go to the sacrifice every day."

"I've followed this drama from the very beginning. I heard the governor's speech last week and the prophecy that Rebbe Ezra read. I watched the landowners come forward and vow to do the right thing and set their workers free. Yet I'm told that you haven't freed your bondservants. Or should I say *our* bondservants? You said they belonged to me, too, now that we're betrothed."

He met her gaze, unflinching as he replied. "I didn't take the oath to release them, Chana."

"Why not?"

"I couldn't vow before God to do something that I knew was impossible. I can't release all of my workers at once. Do you have any idea how many I have? You saw my vineyards and fields and olive groves. My entire estate would fall apart without their help."

"Can't you set them free and hire them back to work for you? Pay them wages?"

"Pay them with what?" he said, spreading his empty hands. "I already have paid them. That's what a loan is, Chana. It's an advance on their salaries. They've already agreed to work for me in return for the loan. I can't afford to pay them twice."

She was becoming more upset, more confused, as he calmly

replied to all of her questions. "All of the other wealthy land-owners are extending charity to the poor."

"All of them? You're certain of that? You've checked their records?"

"Of course not."

"And you've checked my records, too? You're certain that I'm not being charitable to those less fortunate than me?"

His serene response infuriated her. "The Torah clearly says that usury is wrong, Malkijah. We're forbidden to charge our fellow Jews interest."

"And do you know for a fact that I'm charging them interest?"

She couldn't reply. Was he being defensive by answering her questions with another question or was he telling the truth? She remembered Nava's pleas and tears and said, "To you they're just servants who are needed to run your grand estate, but they're real people, Malkijah, with hopes and dreams of their own. I had no idea when I agreed to marry you that you care more about your wealth than you do about them."

He exhaled, staring at his feet for a long moment before looking up at her again. "I'm disappointed in you, Chana. You asked people to believe the best about you when you defied convention and went to work on the wall, yet you're judging others based on outward appearances. Right now you're judging me."

"I'm not judging—"

"You're thoroughly convinced that what you believe about me is true, that I'm as stingy and greedy as you say I am. You came all the way down here to accuse me."

"I came to ask why you haven't set your bondservants free."

"Because my estate would collapse with no one to run it. I wouldn't be able to give to the poor or to provide for my sons or my future wife. The men who work for me here at the Dung Gate would have no one to support them while they labor. This wall would never get finished—which is what our enemies are hoping for, by the way."

"All the other landowners have freed their servants."

"Do you know that for a fact? And do you truly understand what the consequences would be if I freed all my servants?"

She shook her head, ashamed to answer out loud. Malkijah was being maddeningly patient with her.

"I know this sounds arrogant, Chana, but until the famine ends, my servants are better off living with me. At least they have food and a safe, warm bed to sleep in. If I set them free, they would return to homes that were hard-hit by the drought. How can I help the poor by sending them all home to empty storehouses?"

"You can give charity."

"I am giving charity. I not only feed and clothe the bond-servants who work for me, but I'm feeding their families back home, as well. Don't you think I have a right to expect work in return for feeding them? What would become of our province if all the poor people decided to stop working and simply lived off the generosity of the rich?"

"The Torah says we should be generous to the poor."

"I agree. And I believe I'm being very generous. Listen, I don't know how this hornets' nest of unrest became stirred up, but anytime the poor rise up against the rich without understanding the details or the consequences, it's a recipe for disaster. I wouldn't be at all surprised to learn that our enemies planted the seeds of this turmoil."

Chana thought his idea was absurd, a way to blame their nameless enemies for his refusal to help. "You could at least set some of your bondservants free," she said, thinking of Nava.

"How would I choose which ones? My estate could no longer function if I freed everyone, and it wouldn't be fair to let some go and make others stay. Besides, my household functions as a unit."

"Other men are setting their bondservants free." She was aware that she had run out of logical arguments and was repeating herself.

Malkijah exhaled again. "Have you visited their estates? Do you know for a fact that their situations are exactly like mine? Give me a little credit, Chana. And please get all the facts straight before accusing me."

Chana knew that the real root of her anger was the discovery that Malkijah was marrying her for her father's power. In her frustration, she decided to get him to at least admit to that greedy motive. "Why did you want to marry me, Malkijah?" she asked.

"I thought I explained my reasons, but I will repeat them, if you wish. I want to be happy again, the way I was with my first wife, Rebecca. I want companionship, a partner I can trust and work with. I thought you and I would understand each other because we both know what it's like to lose the person we loved. And as I got to know you, I discovered that you are a kind, intelligent woman who could help me manage my home and the abundant blessings that the Almighty One has given me. . . . Oh, and there's one more reason that I may not have mentioned. I also wanted to marry you because I think you are a very attractive woman."

"And it's not because I could offer you the power and prestige of my father's position as district leader of Jerusalem?" she demanded to know.

"Of course. His prestige is part of who you are, Chana. Growing up as Shallum's daughter has shaped you into the woman you've become. When people decide to marry, they're always marrying into an extended family with all of the benefits and advantages it brings."

Abba had said the same thing. Why had she not seen the truth before?

"Now let me ask you a question," he said quietly. "Can you honestly say you would have considered marrying me if I were poor? Or that your father would have considered it? He wanted something from me, too—and so did you, as I recall."

269

"I was never after your wealth—"

"No, but you wanted to continue working on the wall, re-member? And so you said you would agree to a ketubah if I used my influence to convince the governor to let you work. How was that bargain any different from all of the other ones your father and I made?"

She couldn't reply. She felt her cheeks flaming and was grate-ful that Malkijah had spoken in a low, calm voice the entire time, so that no one had heard her making a fool of herself.

"Marriage involves compromise, Chana. And yes, bargain-ing for the things you want—which is what we both did. And correct me if I'm wrong, but wasn't Yitzhak ben Rephaiah also aware of the power your father's position would give him?"

Her tears began to fall. Her throat was so tight she couldn't speak at the reminder of Yitzhak's true motives. Malkijah pulled out a square of clean linen from the folds of his tunic and handed it to her to wipe her eyes. "I'm sorry if I've disappointed you by not releasing my bondservants, but it's impossible for me to do so at the moment. My estate has also suffered from two years of drought. Without workers to help me, I wouldn't have any crops to harvest and nothing to give to the poor."

She felt like a fool.

"Do you have any more questions, Chana? Because I should get back to work."

When she shook her head Malkijah started to leave, then turned to her again. For the space of a heartbeat, his face re-vealed his vulnerability, and she saw that her accusations had hurt him.

"I have one more question for you, Chana," he said softly. "What is it going to take to get you to trust me?"

CHAPTER

32

JERUSALEM

Nehemiah was preparing for bed when someone banged on his door, startling him. "Nehemiah, it's me—Hanani."

He went to the door and opened it, his heart racing. "What's wrong?"

"You'd better get dressed. You just received an urgent message."

Nehemiah pulled his tunic on over his head and shoved his feet into his sandals without bothering to fasten them, then followed his brother down the passageway to his workroom. All of the lamps had been lit, and his three aides and his brother Ephraim were all waiting for him. "What is it? What happened?"

Ephraim's expression was grim as he held up the message. "A few hours ago at dusk, a group of our workers were attacked by a gang of armed men. The workers were returning to their home village a few miles away after building the wall all day. Two of our men were killed, three more were injured."

"Was it a robbery?"

"No. Nothing was taken. The murderers fled as quickly as

271

they had come but not before making it clear that they would kill again if we didn't stop rebuilding the wall."

Nehemiah's first instinct was to gather weapons and give chase, even now, in the dark of night. But it was much too late to defend his slaughtered men. He couldn't undo what his lack of precaution had already done. He sank down on the nearest seat, devastated and enraged by the news. "Two innocent men—murdered! My workers! I had a duty as governor to protect them . . . and I failed!"

"You couldn't have foreseen this," Ephraim began. "No one knew—"

"I should have foreseen it!" he said, raising his voice. "I'm a security expert! It's my livelihood! And I knew about the dangers, the attacks and murders that happened before I came. Yet I was too focused on rebuilding the wall to take precautions. I failed to keep my laborers safe!" None of the men tried to contradict him. The licking flames of the oil lamps danced in the silence as Nehemiah fought to control his fury. And to decide what to do next. "Rehum, find out if the men had families, and ask what I can do for them."

"Yes, my lord."

"Levi and Jehohanan, summon the nobles and officials to my council chamber for a meeting as soon as it's light."

Nehemiah took a long moment to gather his thoughts while his aides hurried out. "That arsenal we found that was left over from the Thirteenth of Adar—is it ready, Hanani?"

"Yes. The blacksmiths have nearly completed their work."

"Good. Ephraim, spread out the map of the city walls," he said, rising from his chair. "We need to come up with a plan to safeguard Jerusalem and our workers from now on until the wall is finished."

Nehemiah and his brothers stayed awake for the rest of the night, organizing a series of guard posts at each of the unfinished gates and at the most vulnerable breaches in the wall.

His lingering guilt and anger over the deaths of his two laborers kept him awake and drove him to find a solution. When it was time for his council meeting the next morning, Nehemiah walked into the chamber to pandemonium as his area leaders and officials shouted and argued with each other. He quickly took his place at the front and was attempting to restore order when the district leader of Beth Hakkerem approached him.

"There's something very important I need to tell you, Governor," he said in a low voice.

"Can it wait, Malkijah? Everyone seems to have something important to tell me."

"I think you'll want to hear what I have to say first—in private."

"Very well." Nehemiah sighed impatiently and followed him off to the side. Malkijah leaned close to his ear, speaking softly as the uproar continued in the hall. "Are you aware that one of your aides, the young man named Jehohanan, is the son of Tobiah the Ammonite?"

"What?" Nehemiah pulled back, staring at Malkijah in disbelief. "Is this a joke? You can't mean our enemy Tobiah?"

Malkijah nodded. "I do, Governor."

Nehemiah couldn't speak. He quickly scanned the room and spotted Jehohanan talking with Hanani. The young aide had always struck Nehemiah as exceptionally bright and ambitious—but he also recalled a few times when Jehohanan had seemed negative and discouraging. Nehemiah shook his head in disbelief. *Tobiah's son?* How could he not have known? He cursed himself for yet another security breach, for trusting others to choose his aides instead of checking their backgrounds himself. He knew better than anyone else the need for caution when deciding whom to trust. "How can this be, Malkijah? And why am I the last man in Jerusalem to find out? Why didn't you warn me sooner?"

"I didn't realize Jehohanan was your aide until this morning, when he came to my house to summon me to this meeting."

"And nobody except you thought to warn me about him? No wonder our enemies seem to know our every move. They've heard every word I've whispered in confidence these past few weeks." Nehemiah wanted to throw something or break something—preferably Jehohanan's neck or the neck of the man who'd recommended him. "This is unbelievable!" he said through gritted teeth.

"To be fair, Governor, I don't think too many people know about the connection between Jehohanan and Tobiah. Jehohanan married into a well-respected Jewish family and has studied and lived in Jerusalem all his adult life. I have no proof at all that he's a traitor. Tobiah has many allies and connections here in the city, including his father-in-law, Shecaniah ben Arah."

"Tobiah the Ammonite has a Jewish wife?"

"Yes, just like his son. But Tobiah has always kept his ties to these Jewish families out of the public eye. And the in-laws haven't broadcast the news either, since mixed marriages with Ammonites are forbidden. I learned about these connections quite by chance."

Nehemiah continued to survey the room, wishing he had a sword for protection, wondering who else among these men might be a traitor or a spy. "What about my other two aides, Rehum and Levi?"

"I don't know anything about them. I'm sorry."

"Thanks for the warning, Malkijah. I appreciate it. I'll have to send all three of them away so we can conduct this meeting in relative secrecy—and so Jehohanan doesn't suspect that I'm wise to him yet. If there's anyone else who you believe has mixed loyalties, please let me know at once."

"I will, Governor."

Nehemiah watched as Malkijah rejoined the other leaders. The noise in the room made his head hurt as he scrambled to think of a valid excuse to get Jehohanan out of the room. He came up blank. He motioned to Ephraim, who hurried over.

"What's wrong? You look worried—or should I say, even more worried than usual?"

"I just learned that Jehohanan is probably a spy."

"What?"

"Did you know he's the son of Tobiah the Ammonite?"

Ephraim stared at him, shaking his head. "No. . . . A wolf in the sheepfold?"

"Can you help me think of a way to get all three of my aides out of this meeting?"

"Go ahead and get started. I'll think of something."

Nehemiah took his place on the platform and began calling for silence again. He saw Ephraim off to one side, collecting the three aides, and a moment later they left. Nehemiah knew he had to get past his anger at himself for this second security failure and get on with the meeting—but how? All he could think of was how he'd been deceived. He tried to recall who had recommended Jehohanan in the first place, wondering if he was a traitor as well—and if he was in this room. The dawning sun hadn't made its way into the long, narrow council chamber yet, adding to the gloom. Why hadn't the builders had sense enough to add windows? And more doors? There were only two doors and they were at the far end of the room. Nehemiah felt trapped with no escape, and it fueled his anger and a nameless panic. Then he saw Malkijah standing in the audience and knew he had at least one friend.

"I need everyone to quiet down and listen!" Nehemiah said, pouring all of his frustration into restoring order. "I won't let this meeting get out of hand. We're wasting too much time as it is." When the men were reasonably quiet, he said, "In case you haven't heard the news by now, two of our workers were ambushed and killed on their way home to their village last night. The attackers made it clear that they'll kill again unless we halt construction on the wall." He had to pause to regain control over his rage and grief.

"We've heard," Rephaiah said. "The news is spreading all over Jerusalem. It means that the rumors we've heard, warning of an imminent attack, were true."

"What rumors? I heard nothing about them. Why wasn't I told? And now two of my men were killed last night!"

"I-I assumed your aides had informed you."

Nehemiah lowered his head. He had trusted the wrong men to keep him informed. "Where are these warnings coming from?" he asked when he could speak again.

"Some have filtered in from our Gentile neighbors and trading partners," Rephaiah said. "Reliable merchants whom we've partnered with for several years. Their caravans travel widely and often bring us news."

"I'm from the district of Mizpah," another man said. "We live side by side with our Gentile neighbors, and they've been coming and telling us ten times over, 'Wherever you turn, they will take you by surprise and attack you.' I thought you'd heard, too, Governor."

The leader from Gibeon added, "Our enemies are saying, 'Before they know it or see us, we'll be right there among them, and we'll kill them and put an end to their work.'"

Nehemiah's frustration boiled over. "Why didn't anyone take these threats seriously? I should have been told that our workers were in danger. We all know that our enemies don't want Jerusalem's walls to be rebuilt."

"Well, after what happened last night," Meshullam said, "my workers have decided to quit and go home before they're the next victims. They've heard that more attacks may come at dusk as they return from their various construction sites. Their families are begging them to stop working, saying it's too dangerous to continue."

"We're not quitting!" Nehemiah said. "That's exactly what our enemies want! Besides, we're nearly half finished. The walls have been restored to almost half their original height in most places."

"Then you'd better summon an army to protect us," Meshullam said.

Nehemiah shook his head. "If you mean the provincial army under Sanballat's command, they can't be trusted. The threats and attacks are likely coming from him."

Meshullam looked indignant. "That's slanderous. You have no proof of that claim."

Nehemiah suddenly made the connection. Meshullam was Jehohanan's father-in-law. He had borrowed Meshullam's mule that night last July when he'd surveyed the walls. Meshullam was the one who had endorsed Jehohanan as an aide. Another wolf in the sheepfold. Once again, Nehemiah's anger at himself for lowering his guard made him furious.

"Why don't you send to Susa for help?" someone shouted before Nehemiah could reply. "Ask them to send soldiers."

"Susa is a thousand miles away. It would take nearly two months for our swiftest messenger to get there, and another two months for help to arrive—if it arrived at all."

"Then the construction must stop until help comes," Meshullam said.

Once again, the room erupted into chaos with everyone talking at once. "Quiet down and listen to me!" Nehemiah shouted. "We're going to do two things—and neither one of them is to stop building. First, I'm going to make sure that every man who works on the wall is armed with a weapon. I've already been preparing an arsenal in the event that something like this happened. As soon as I dismiss this meeting, my brother and I will hand out swords, spears, and shields to all your laborers." Once again, guilt and rage choked off Nehemiah's words. If he had taken this step of arming his workers sooner, his two men might still be alive.

"From now on, I'm posting guards day and night to meet this threat," he said when he could continue. "I'm stationing men at the unfinished gates, and behind the lowest points in the wall, and at all the exposed places where the enemy might attack. The guards will go on duty immediately and remain there day and night until the danger is past or the wall is completed, whichever comes first. Every laborer and his helper will remain inside Jerusalem so they can serve as guards by night and workmen by day. Because the work is extensive and spread out, and we are widely separated from each other along the wall, I'll have a signal trumpet with me at all times. Wherever you hear the sound of the trumpet, join us there to fight." He hoped he could get his guards into place before Meshullam or Jehohanan or any other spies had time to tell his enemies his plan. Nehemiah calmed his anger at the possibility of these traitors in his midst by reminding himself that he had an even more powerful ally than his enemies did. "Arming ourselves and taking action is only the first thing," he said.

"What's the second?" someone asked.

"We're going to pray. All of our efforts will be worthless if God isn't on our side. But I have faith that He is on our side and that He will fight for us. Therefore we have nothing to fear. Our enemies will not prevail. If your workers are fearful and ready to quit, remind them of the God we serve, the God who forgave us and restored us and promised never to forsake us if we're faithful to Him. One of the reasons we're rebuilding this wall is to bring glory to the Almighty One and show our enemies that He's with us. The way to replace fear with faith is to pray."

As soon as he dismissed the meeting, Nehemiah and Hanani opened the armory and distributed weapons, appointing a leader over each guard post. Nehemiah chose a sword for himself, then went in search of Jehohanan and found him with his brother Ephraim at the field office near the Valley Gate. Nehemiah took a stance in front of the young man, his hand resting casually on the hilt of his sword.

"You didn't tell me that you're the son of Tobiah the Ammonite, Jehohanan."

"I didn't think it mattered. My father and I worship the same God you do."

"Of course it matters. And if you believe that it doesn't, you're either very naïve or a very clever imposter."

"You're being misled about Tobiah's loyalties, my lord. He isn't your enemy. He would gladly work by your side. He supports what you're doing."

"Then why did he come here with Sanballat and Geshem to mock us?"

"Things aren't always as they appear, Governor."

"That's true," Nehemiah replied. He was aware that Jehohanan's statement could be interpreted several ways. "That's why I'm sending you home. You no longer have a job in my administration."

He expected an angry response, an argument, but Jehohanan simply met his gaze and said, "It's been a pleasure to serve you, Governor." There was no sarcasm or bitterness in his tone. Then he walked away.

"What did you make of that?" Nehemiah asked his brother. "Am I wrong to be suspicious? Are Tobiah and his son our allies or our enemies?"

"I don't know," Ephraim replied, scratching his beard. "Tobiah came with Sanballat and Geshem as part of their delegation, remember? He mocked us just like they did."

"True. But is he in league with them? What motive would Tobiah have to want to halt our work?"

"I don't know. But we need to find out."

Later, Nehemiah told his other two aides that they were no longer needed, either. "Rehum, I know you're supervising construction on a section of the eastern wall. That work is important enough to give it your full attention from now on. Levi, you would be of more help to me by working on the wall, as well."

Nehemiah would need to post guards at all the entrances to

his residence. He would interview all of his servants himself, checking into the backgrounds of the people closest to him, people he had blindly trusted until now. He should have done it a long time ago. He watched Rehum and Levi walk away and realized that aside from Ephraim and Hanani, he no longer knew whom he could trust.

CHAPTER

33

Malkijah's parting question from the other day still haunted Chana. *"What is it going to take to get you to trust me?"* She didn't know the answer. She sighed as she bent to help Yudit fill the leather sling with fist-sized stones, then waited for the workmen to haul it to the top. The wall was slowly growing higher, but the rubble-strewn embankment where she and Yudit worked looked unchanged. Did these rocks multiply overnight?

"This stone is ready to go into place," Sarah called up to the foreman. She stood beside a huge building block, twice as big as she was, that the workers had shaped. Abba had been reluctant to send them to work alone while he rushed off to a meeting with the governor at dawn, but Chana had assured him they would be fine. Her work was what sustained her; at the end of each day she could stand back and see how much she had accomplished. But when the wall was finished, she would have to marry Malkijah.

Malkijah. How could she marry him when she still had so many doubts? Was he truly motivated by greed, or had he told the truth about why he hadn't freed his servants? *"What is it*

281

going to take to get you to trust me?" At least he'd admitted that he was marrying her for Abba's power, wanting to control Jerusalem as well as Beth Hakkerem. Unlike Yitzhak, he had been honest about that much. Chana's thoughts circled around and around in her head like carrion birds, her emotions changing from anger to sorrow to grief—the same heart-numbing grief she'd felt after Yitzhak had died—and then back to anger again.

"Why haven't you been singing these past few days, Chana?" Yudit asked as they waited for the sling to be emptied and tossed down to them again.

"I don't know . . . I just don't feel like it."

"Is something wrong?" Yudit asked. "When we first started building the wall you seemed so happy, but these past few days you've been sad again."

"Nothing's wrong." Chana turned and walked toward the scaffold, pretending she had work to do. She should apologize to Yudit, but she didn't feel like it. Her lingering doubts about Malkijah and even about Yitzhak made her feel angry at everyone. Yet she knew it was her own fault for being so blind and naïve.

Her only reason for getting up in the morning was to work on the wall. Each time she dropped her plumb line and strung her level line, she felt confident and self-assured. The massive wall rose from the ruins, solid and unmoving, one of the only things straight and true in her life. She knew she was doing a good job and thought she'd earned the other workers' respect. Now she wondered if it was only because she was Shallum's daughter.

Chana was halfway up the scaffolding when Abba returned from his meeting in the council chamber. She saw him emerge through the gate, walking briskly, and his usually jovial face looked worried. He beckoned for her to come down, calling to Sarah and Yudit, too. "Stop what you're doing, my angels. We're going home."

"Right now? It isn't even noon," Yudit said, stuffing strands of her wild hair beneath her scarf. "We have plenty more hours of daylight ahead of us."

Chana climbed down partway and stood on one of the wide boards, her arms folded. "Did the governor tell you to make us stop? Because we don't have to do what he says, Abba. You're in charge of this section, not—"

"Hush, Chana. We'll talk about it when we get home, not out here where everyone can hear us." He spoke softly, and his voice had an unaccustomed urgency to it. "Sarah, Yudit . . . let's go."

Chana had to scramble the rest of the way down, then hurry to catch up as her father strode toward the gate with her sisters in tow. The governor had interfered again, Chana was certain of it. She held her temper as they walked up the Street of the Bakers toward home, but the moment they reached the court-yard gate, her fury boiled over. "You don't have to listen to the governor, Abba. I'm betrothed to Malkijah, and he said—"

"Just be quiet and listen." It was so unlike him to bark orders that she suddenly felt afraid.

Sarah linked her arm through his, standing close. "What's wrong, Abba?"

His mouth was set in a firm, hard line that Chana recognized as determination, not anger. "A group of laborers were ambushed last night on their way home from working on the wall. Two of them were killed. Now rumors are circulating around the city and the province that our enemies are about to attack again in order to force us to stop building. That's why the governor called the meeting today. The other district leaders have heard the same warnings, coming from some of our trusted Gentile neighbors and trading partners."

The news sent a shiver of fear through Chana. "Is work on the wall going to stop?" she asked.

"No. That's exactly what our enemies want. But from now on, half of the men will work while the rest stand guard. Those who work will also be armed with swords. I'm going back to the armory in a few minutes to get weapons for all my workers."

"And then what?" Yudit asked.

"The governor is posting guards at the unfinished gates and all the exposed areas, but the workers are spread out along miles and miles of wall. An attack could come anywhere, anytime. If one does, Governor Nehemiah will signal with a trumpet, and we'll all rush there to help. Needless to say, the situation is much too dangerous for the three of you to continue working with me. I'm sorry."

"You're not going to fight, too, Abba, are you?" Sarah asked, still clinging to his arm.

"Of course I am. Why not?"

"Abba, I'm scared!" Sarah wrapped her arms around him and buried her face in his chest. He stroked her raven-black hair to soothe her.

"Our trust is in the Almighty One. We must all pray for His protection and help."

The threats unnerved Chana. But in spite of the danger, her only thought was that the one thing left to her—building the wall—was being taken away. She couldn't let that happen. "Abba, I know we can't work outside the wall anymore, but I could still measure and use a plumb line from the inside, couldn't I?"

"How would you climb up, Chana? We can't move the scaffolding to the inside."

Sarah's eyes went wide. "All that scaffolding! What if the enemy uses it to climb up and get inside?"

"There are easier ways for them to get inside," Chana said. "The gates aren't even finished yet. The enemy could walk right through the gaps."

"Why are you scaring her, Chana?" Yudit asked. "Don't be so mean."

"From now on," Abba said, "you will all stay inside the house where it's safe until the danger is past."

Chana knew she shouldn't have frightened Sarah. Why was she taking out her frustration on the people she loved? After Abba left, she stood at the gate that led from her courtyard to the street, feeling trapped. Her life was no longer under her own control—but had it ever been? And what about her future? Would she feel this endless cycle of anger and grief for the rest of her life?

She was still standing at the gate a while later, watching the carts and donkeys and foot traffic on the Street of the Bakers, when she realized that the man walking up the hill toward her was Malkijah. She recognized his brisk, confident stride, his dark, neatly-cut beard and scarlet-banded tunic. She wanted to run inside and hide and pretend she wasn't home after the way she had treated him the other day, but he smiled and lifted his hand to wave, and she knew he had seen her.

Malkijah was breathing hard from the uphill climb when he halted in front of her. She noticed the sword hanging from his belt. "I just talked to your father. He told me you were upset about not being able to help with the wall."

Chana blinked back sudden tears. "I enjoyed my work. And I was good at it."

"So I heard."

She nearly blurted out, *"That was the only thing that brought me joy!"* but realized how insulting that would sound to the man she was betrothed to. In that moment she also realized that Malkijah was her legal husband and could override her father's wishes if he chose to. "Will you let me work alongside you at the Dung Gate from now on?" she asked. "I promise I'll stay on the inside of the wall."

He took a moment to consider her request before replying, and his thoughtfulness impressed her. "I would like to say yes, Chana, I really would. But it's even more dangerous where I am than at your father's section. An unfinished gate is an easy target. And we're at the very southern tip of the city. It would take a long time for reinforcements to arrive if we were attacked."

"You said you wouldn't make me stop building after we were betrothed."

"I know. But the work has become much too dangerous. We'll be camping beside the wall day and night from now on and do our work with a sword in one hand." He pulled the one strapped to his side from its scabbard and handed it to her. It was so heavy she needed two hands to hang on to it. "Can you do your work with one of these?" he asked. Chastened, she passed it back to him without replying. "I agree with your father," Malkijah said. "The attacks could come at any moment, without warning. I lost my first wife, as you know, and there was nothing I could do to save her. If something happened to you, I would never forgive myself for putting you in danger. Please, Chana, you know what it's like to lose your fiancé so close to the wedding day."

She looked away, ashamed to realize that she'd shown no concern for his safety, even after he'd told her that the Dung Gate would make an obvious target. "Isn't it dangerous for you, too?" she finally asked.

"It's dangerous for all of us right now."

He could be killed, like Yitzhak had been. In spite of all her changing, conflicting, confusing feelings about Malkijah, Chana realized that she didn't want him to die. She was about to tell him so when he said, "Listen, I didn't come here to talk about all of this. I wanted to see you because I was upset about the way things ended the last time we talked. There were issues between us that weren't resolved. And I'm concerned that you may have second thoughts about marrying me." She stared at the ground without replying. "I came here to offer you an annulment. A way out of our betrothal."

"Is that what you want?" she asked. She was barely able to speak, her heart pounding at his offer. She remembered the terrible accusations she had made the other day, yet he was responding as a gentleman, not in anger.

"No, Chana," he said gently. "No. It isn't what I want at all. I want to marry you."

For a moment she saw herself as he must surely see her, and how Yudit and Sarah had seen her earlier today: ugly and deformed with self-pity and stubbornness, spewing her anger at the people who loved her. She had accused Malkijah of greed, of exacting usury, of having no compassion for the poor—and without any proof to back up those accusations. Even so, this was her chance to be free. He offered her a way out of their marriage contract. Did she want to take it?

Chana finally looked up at him, and his face blurred through her tears. He was a good man, and he'd been unfailingly patient with her even when her emotions and attitudes toward him had changed from day to day. She needed to find stability and peace in her own heart, acceptance and certainty about her future.

"Malkijah, I'm sorry I said all those things to you. Please forgive me." She paused, swallowing. "If you'll still have me . . . I still want to marry you."

He smiled his handsome, crooked smile. "I was hoping you would say that."

A few hours ago, Chana had felt panic and dread as she saw the day of her marriage approaching. Each stone that she'd set in place brought it one day closer. Now she could no longer rebuild the wall. But maybe there were other tasks she could do for the rest of her life, such as working alongside this man who said he needed and wanted her.

JERUSALEM

We're here to make preparations for a counterattack," Nehemiah told the handful of men gathered around the worktable in his private chambers. They were men he was certain were on his side, men who wouldn't betray his confidence. "I'm not satisfied to simply post guards and wait in fear behind miles of unfinished walls. Two of my workers were ruthlessly killed, and I won't allow any more of our people to become helpless victims. So along with stationary guards, I've decided to go on the offensive. If we can figure out the most likely places for the next attacks to occur, we can send armed volunteers outside the city wall to take our enemies by surprise and confront them head-on. I'll need men who are willing to fight for their brothers, their sons and daughters, their wives and homes."

He saw nods of agreement all around the table as he spread out his map, anchoring the corners of the scroll with clay weights. "I think most of you know Yehuda ben Aaron, the man who organized the defense of Jerusalem twenty-eight years ago on the Thirteenth of Adar. I've asked him to share his insights with us and the strategy he used to defend the city."

Yehuda rose to his feet. He was nearly seventy now, but still hearty and vigorous, with receding white hair and a sturdy build. He gazed at the men around the table with piercing gray eyes that seemed to miss nothing. "Back then, we knew we didn't stand a chance unless the Holy One helped us. The wall was in ruins and there were no gates, of course. We couldn't possibly defend all of the many breaches, so we decided to think like our enemies and figure out where they were most likely to attack."

"And we should do the same," Nehemiah said. "Let's put ourselves in their place and imagine which strategy they would use. Remember, their aim is to instill fear and halt construction, not to conquer the city and plunder it like on the Thirteenth of Adar." He saw nods of agreement from the men around the table.

"Back then," Yehuda continued, pointing to the parchment map, "we guessed that the enemy wouldn't approach the city from the east. The ridge is too steep on that side, and they would risk being seen as they crossed the Kidron Valley or marched up the steep slope."

"I agree," Nehemiah said. "I'm also posting fewer guards on that side. They're able to see for a considerable distance from that height and can sound the alarm if an attack does come."

"The northern approach by the temple has always been our most vulnerable one," Yehuda said. "We concentrated our forces there on the Thirteenth of Adar, knowing that our enemy was motivated by greed. They hoped for easy gain by plundering the temple treasuries."

"That's where this threat is different," Nehemiah said. "Sanballat and our other enemies want power, not gold. I doubt they would risk the Almighty One's wrath by attacking His temple. Besides, Sanballat has connections by marriage with the high priest and wouldn't want to jeopardize that. Even so, the Levite guards are preparing to defend the temple gates on the northern side. Our builders have made enough progress on one of the towers for it to serve as a useful lookout post."

Yehuda nodded and looked at the map again, tracing his finger down the long stretch of wall on the western side. "This approach was our secondary concern. The wall was so broken-down, with so many gaps, that we knew the enemy could easily slip through them. Not only that, but the ruined houses and buildings in the deserted Mishneh provided plenty of cover for a sneak attack. We were forced to spread out a good portion of our forces on that side of the city. On the Thirteenth of Adar we stationed the men by families, knowing they would fight harder to protect their flesh and blood."

"Good idea. I'll follow your example," Nehemiah said. He glanced at his brothers but already knew he had no intention of putting either of them in danger or allowing them to fight alongside him. "Fortunately for us, there are fewer gaps in the western wall now. But you're right, Yehuda—the Mishneh still provides plenty of cover for a sneak attack, especially at night. And that's what they're after—a surprise attack and a quick retreat. They hope to kill a few more of us and terrify everyone else into quitting. If they can distract us from building and force us to exhaust all our manpower defending the city, construction will stop. Let's prepare for an assault on the western side of the city and concentrate our forces at the Fish Gate, the Yeshana Gate, and the Valley Gate."

"Very wise," Yehuda said. "I agree with that decision. Now that still leaves the possibility of an approach from the south, at the Dung Gate. The land drops off steeply to the Hinnom Valley, but on the Thirteenth of Adar we decided to send some of our forces down there, just in case. We were glad we did."

"The Dung Gate is your territory, Malkijah," Nehemiah said. "I'll let you prepare however you think best for an enemy strike." He considered him a shrewd, trustworthy ally.

Malkijah nodded. "Thank you, Governor. My workers and I have already put a few measures into place."

Nehemiah stood and took a step back from the table, too

restless to remain seated like the other men. "I refuse to sit behind the wall and wait to be surprised. I intend to send small counterforces out at night along each of the main routes. We'll set up ambushes on high ground overlooking the paths that the enemy might use for a surprise attack."

"How long can you keep that up?" Ephraim asked. "Who knows when they'll come?"

"True," he told his brother. "But as it happens, two nights from now there won't be a moon. That's when I would attack if I were our enemies. I'm looking for volunteers from this group to command each of these counterforces."

The number of men who quickly volunteered buoyed Nehemiah's spirits. He appointed a commander to cover each possible attack route, then said, "I'll take charge of the approach to the Valley Gate myself. The rest of you, have your men find a high place where they can keep watch and stay undercover. When you see the enemy approaching, come out of hiding and fight. They're counting on the element of surprise, so let's surprise them instead. But don't give chase if they retreat unless you're certain you aren't outnumbered." He dismissed them to gather their men, adding, "Make sure you only recruit volunteers. Those who are too afraid to fight are better off standing guard behind the walls."

As soon as the men left, Ephraim grabbed Nehemiah's arm from behind and swung him around to face him. "Hey! Why didn't you appoint us to be your commanders?"

"You can't protect us all our lives," Hanani said, moving in from the other side. "We aren't children. We want to fight with you!"

The thought of his brothers facing a band of armed men in the dead of night turned Nehemiah's stomach. His instinct to protect them was still as strong as it had been on the night their parents had been murdered. "You're scribes, not soldiers, and—"

"Neither are any of these other men!" Ephraim shouted.

They were furious with him. Nehemiah needed to calm them down. "Listen, you're my two right-hand men. I need you to help me lead the people, and I won't put you in danger—"

Ephraim interrupted with a scornful huff. "And yet you're fighting—and you're the governor! That makes no sense! What if *you* die? Or are you somehow immortal now?"

Nehemiah couldn't explain his irrational need to confront his enemies head-on instead of cowering and hiding. He had to fight, even if it didn't make sense. "I have military training, and you don't. I was taught to use a sword in order to guard the Persian king, remember? I don't intend to die, Ephraim, but if I do, I'll need the two of you to take my place. You must finish rebuilding the wall for me. You know how to proceed with the work better than anyone else in this city."

"Our father didn't intend to die, either," Ephraim said, "but he did. I'm volunteering to fight, and you'd better not try to stop me." He strode toward the door and yanked it open.

"What about your family? Your children?"

"That's who I'm fighting for!"

A heavy stone sank to the bottom of Nehemiah's gut as he watched his brother storm from the room. Short of tying him up with ropes, he was powerless to stop him. The psalmist's words had run through Nehemiah's mind ever since the Levites sang them in the temple this morning and he thought of them now: *"Unless the Lord builds the house, its builders labor in vain. Unless the Lord watches over the city, the watchmen stand guard in vain."*

Were he and his men standing guard in vain? Was the Almighty One behind their plans to build and defend Jerusalem's wall, or wasn't He? Where was the balance between trusting God to defend his loved ones and taking the initiative himself? If he was honest, Nehemiah knew that his overpowering instinct to protect his brothers stemmed from the fact that God hadn't protected their parents on that long-ago night. And he was failing to trust God now, fearful of placing his brothers in His hands and allowing them to fight. Had Nehemiah saved his brothers that night—or had God?

"I'm worried that Ephraim will do something foolhardy just to prove he doesn't need my protection," he told Hanani.

His brother lifted the weights off the corners of the scroll and slowly rolled it up. "Let him alone, Nehemiah. He has a good instinct for self-preservation. All three of us do."

Nehemiah had tried all his life to be the strong, courageous older brother, to not let Ephraim and Hanani see his doubts and fears. But the flood of opposition that had come against him since he'd begun to build the wall—the ridicule of their enemies, the work stoppage, and now the deaths of two of his workers— slowly eroded his faith like the banks of a storm-swollen river. He needed to confide in someone. "Hanani . . . have you ever figured out why God sometimes allows evil to win?"

"Are you thinking of our parents?"

"I am."

"I've thought about that a lot over the years," Hanani said with a sigh, "and the only conclusion I've come to is that in some instances, we're incapable of understanding the Almighty One's reasons. We just have to trust that He has a plan, even if we can't see it."

"That's the difficult part—trusting."

"I've often wondered if Ephraim and I would be the men we are today if Mama and Abba had lived. If we would be living here in the land of our ancestors, raising our children here—and if you'd be here rebuilding the wall, for that matter. Or would we all be in Susa, serving a godless king instead of the Almighty One. We'll never know, of course. But here we are. And isn't that what faith is all about—believing in the Almighty One's goodness, believing that if He doesn't answer our immediate prayers, it's because He has larger, richer answers?"

Nehemiah remembered being filled with faith in the beginning, trusting that he'd heard from God and that His hand was upon him to accomplish His work. Now his enemies were doing their best to undermine his faith and keep him from his God-given task. Nehemiah made up his mind to persevere. To not allow his two workers' deaths to be in vain. He rested his hand on his brother's shoulder for a moment in silent thanks. "The wall is only half built, Hanani. Let's go finish it."

CHAPTER
35

J ERUSALEM

Relief washed over Nava when she finally spotted Dan climbing the stairs to the temple. He wore a sword strapped to his belt wherever he went, even when he came here to worship. He looked weary plodding up the steps, as if they were coated with honey and his sandals stuck to each one. The workmen now took turns building the wall and standing guard, and she could see that the heavy labor coupled with little sleep had drained Dan's strength. Nava ignored the flow of morning worshipers and hurried down the stairs in the opposite direction to meet him. "Dan! I've been so afraid for you. You look exhausted."

"I am, more than in our busiest harvest season. But it feels good to finally fight back against our enemies."

"Fight? You didn't tell me you had to fight."

"Well, I haven't fought yet, but . . ." He lowered his voice. "I may one of these nights." They reached the top of the steps, and he drew her aside. "I'm telling you this in confidence, Nava. The governor doesn't want the whole city to know about it. But he asked for volunteers to be part of a special force. We're going outside the walls every night to surprise the enemy before they have a chance to attack us."

"Don't volunteer, Dan. It's too dangerous."

"I have to fight. I need to protect you."

Nava wanted to plead with him not to go, to stay inside the walls where it was safe. But she'd seen how Dan's anger toward Malkijah grew and festered more and more each day. He needed an outlet for it before it destroyed him.

"I'm so tired of waiting," he had told her a few days ago. "Tired of being patient. I could kill Malkijah with my bare hands for keeping you his bondservant and refusing to cancel our debts."

Nava had tried to convince him that if Malkijah died, his son Aaron would inherit everything. "And believe me, everything would be much worse if that happened," she'd said.

Now they hurried across the courtyard to watch the sacrifice, which had already begun. Nava tried to pay attention, but her thoughts kept drifting back to what Dan had just told her and the danger he would be in. When it was time for prayer, Governor Nehemiah reminded the people of the need to ask the Almighty One for His help against their enemies. The people bowed their heads as the priest entered the sanctuary to light the incense, but Nava still couldn't pray. She didn't understand the Almighty One. Her family had prayed for rain for two long years, and it had never come. God could have set her free when the other wealthy landowners had shown mercy, but He hadn't softened her master's heart. She was still a bondservant. Was the Holy One angry with her? If so, she didn't understand why. Her faith had become as dry and lifeless as her father's drought-stricken land, her heart an empty well, where there was no more hope to draw from. The only comfort she found was in having Dan beside her every day, lanky and sun-browned and strong. At least they could be together for a few minutes each morning in the temple courtyard.

They said good-bye in their usual parting place, and that afternoon Nava helped prepare dinner for Malkijah and a guest. Her master had been on guard duty at the Dung Gate for two full days and hadn't returned home to eat or sleep during that time. She noticed dark hollows beneath his eyes as she carried platters of food and serving dishes in and out of the dining area and set them on the table in front of him. But she felt no pity for him, her anger seething like a brew of bitter herbs.

"Let's not waste time on small talk," Malkijah told his guest. "I need to return to my duties at the gate. Tell me why you asked to see me." His abrupt manner surprised Nava. Her master was usually a smiling, gracious host. The stranger seated across from him didn't seem perturbed by his rudeness.

"Very well. It has come to my attention that you didn't take the vow along with the other leaders to cancel your debtors' mortgages or free your bondservants."

Nava went still, a flush of anger rising to her face at his words. She was supposed to return to the kitchen after setting bowls of olives and figs on the table, but she lingered outside the doorway to listen.

"If you've come to accuse me of greed and coldheartedness, I've heard it all before," Malkijah said angrily. "From people I care about, no less. My current financial obligations make it impossible for me to give everything back."

"You've misjudged me, Malkijah," the man said calmly. "I didn't take Nehemiah's absurd oath, either."

Silence. Then Malkijah said, "My mistake. Please forgive me."

"You're not alone, you know. There are more of us than you think who refuse to be swayed by our governor's political maneuverings. And we've taken a different kind of oath."

"Go on . . ."

The man chuckled. "I need to know where your loyalties are,

first. I understand you not only serve on Nehemiah's council but you're part of his inner circle. One of his military commanders."

"That's true, I am. Which is why I need to cut this dinner short tonight and return to my post."

"Does the governor know you didn't take his oath to free your servants or cancel their debts?"

Nava strained to hear his reply. Maybe the governor would intervene if he learned the truth about Malkijah.

"I haven't told him," Malkijah replied. "If he heard it from someone else, he hasn't spoken to me about it. As far as I'm concerned, it's none of his business—and I would tell him that to his face. He has no idea what it takes to run an estate like mine."

"I'm not sure Nehemiah knows much at all about life here in our province."

"I follow the Torah to the letter of the law," Malkijah said heatedly. "I don't charge interest on my loans, and I give food and loans to all the farmers in my district who are in need. Nehemiah has no authority to compel me to cancel all the debts that are owed to me or to free my bondservants. It's impossible for me to do any of those things without putting my own interests at risk."

Nava's anger was building along with her master's. She risked a peek around the doorway and saw him leaning forward to face his guest, his face flushed. She quickly turned back and flattened herself against the wall where he couldn't see her. If he or the housekeeper caught her eavesdropping she would be in trouble, but Nava didn't care. She wanted to hear his stingy, coldhearted excuses for herself.

"Oh, I understand what you're saying, Malkijah," his guest replied. "I understand completely. I didn't take the governor's vow for the very same reasons. And I know several other men, members of the nobility, who are in the same situation we are. You aren't alone."

"That's good to know."

Nava heard the soft clinking of tableware as she waited. She was about to return to the kitchen when Malkijah's guest said, "There is a group of noblemen who have decided to band together to stop the governor and oppose his ridiculous demands. We thought you might be interested in joining us. And if there are other men you know of who feel the same as we do—perhaps such as your future father-in-law—we're hoping you'll use your influence to sway them to our side. Shallum is a powerful man here in Jerusalem and could be a great help to our cause."

"Who else is part of this group?"

"Ah," the man said. "That's where the oath I mentioned comes in. We need assurances that if we take you into our confidence we won't be betrayed."

"And I need to know who and what I'm swearing to before I'll give you my word."

The room was silent. Nava risked another peek. Both men sat forward in their seats, staring at each other. "I see," Malkijah's guest finally said. Nava watched as he leaned back and lifted his cup to take a drink of wine, then she turned away again. She shouldn't stay here and listen a moment longer. But the governor was a hero to her and to all the other poor people, and she was furious that these two men were conspiring against him.

"The quality of your wine is legendary, my friend," Malkijah's guest said. "It lives up to everything I've heard about it."

"Thank you."

"It would be a tragedy if it could no longer be produced. We've both seen how Governor Nehemiah craves the adulation of the masses. He has become a tyrant, willing to do anything to win their support. So let me ask you this: What would happen to you and to your vineyard if the governor turned his request into law? If he *demanded* that you free all your servants? Wouldn't you want a powerful group of nobles and fellow landowners on your side to fight his tyranny? Men who could successfully oppose him?"

"Do you think it will come to that? Could Nehemiah compel us to obey him?"

"Of course he could. He's the governor. He has the backing of a godless Persian king. He could compel us to do anything he wants." There was another long silence before the guest spoke again. "The men I represent have transferred our allegiance to a proven leader, a man who knows this province and our people and our financial obligations very well. We've been in constant communication with him ever since Nehemiah arrived. With backing from you and other influential men, we'll be in a position to get rid of the governor and replace him with a leader of our own choosing."

Again, there was a long silence. "I can't give you an answer tonight," Malkijah said. "I need time to decide. This isn't something to take lightly."

"I understand."

"You've trusted me this far—can you trust me with the name of at least one other member of this group besides you?"

There was another long pause. "Shecaniah ben Arah."

"I see. Powerful indeed. My estate is nothing compared to his."

Nava repeated the name over and over in her mind to memorize it as she hurried back to the kitchen. She had been gone much too long as it was. She still didn't know the guest's name, but she'd heard enough of the conversation to understand that Governor Nehemiah needed to be warned about what the men had discussed. She greatly admired the governor for helping the poor and she resented selfish, rich men like her master and his guest more than ever.

She waited for Dan at the temple the next morning, eager to tell him everything she'd heard, but he wasn't standing in their usual meeting place at the top of the stairs when she arrived.

Nava stayed there instead of moving into the courtyard with the other worshipers, and her fear for his safety began to flare and spread like a grassfire. If something happened to him, how would she ever know? They might tell his family in Beth Hak-kerem, but how would they get word to her? When the sacrifice ended and the flow of worshipers began streaming toward her, Nava was still waiting, staring down toward the Mishneh where Dan stood guard, heartsick with fear.

"Nava . . . do you have a moment to talk?"

She turned at the sound of her name. Her master's fiancée—her new mistress—stood beside her. "Yes, miss. Of course."

"I'll catch up with you," Chana told the other women who were with her. She and Nava stepped to one side. "I wanted to tell you that I spoke with Malkijah about not setting you and his other servants free. He explained to me that it was impossible to do right now—"

"And you believed him?" Anger and fear made Nava bold. She had nothing more to lose.

Chana blinked in surprise. "I . . . I have no choice but to believe him. I don't know how to run an estate as large as his. I'm so sorry I couldn't be more help to you—"

"He isn't the man you think he is."

"What do you mean?"

"Last night I served dinner to him and a guest. This guest said there is a group of rich men and nobles who haven't taken the governor's oath, and he asked Master Malkijah to join their conspiracy to oppose the governor. They called Nehemiah a tyrant and said they've chosen someone else to replace him as governor."

Chana looked taken aback. "Are you certain you heard correctly?"

"Yes. I'm waiting here for Dan so we can warn Governor Nehemiah and—" She stopped, realizing what she'd just done. In spewing out her bitterness toward Malkjah, she'd confessed to his fiancée that she'd been eavesdropping. Worse, if Chana was on Malkijah's side, she would probably warn him and the other men that their plot was no longer a secret. They would do everything they could to stop Nava from betraying them. As panic swelled, she wanted to run and disappear, but the stairs were jammed with people.

"Do you know who Malkijah's guest was?" Chana asked.

Nava shook her head. She wished she had never opened her mouth. "I need to go."

"No, wait." Chana stood in Nava's way, preventing her from leaving. "You must be wondering whether or not you can trust me. I understand. To be honest, I'm also having trouble deciding who I can trust. But I want to assure you that I won't take what you just told me lightly. And I won't betray your confidence while I search for the truth."

"Thank you, miss." Nava wasn't sure she believed her. She slipped away from Chana and melted into the crowd, crouching low, weaving between people. Why had she opened her mouth? If Malkijah fired her, Abba would lose his land. Her family would starve. Reporting what she'd heard to the governor was one thing, but why had she foolishly confided in Chana? Nava raced down the stairs and through the streets. As she neared Malkijah's house, there was Dan, standing in the place where they usually parted every morning. Relief flooded through her, bringing tears to her eyes. She ran the rest of the way and into his arms. "I was so worried about you!"

"I'm sorry. I didn't make it in time for the sacrifice, so I decided to wait here for you."

"When you weren't at the temple, I was afraid that you'd had to fight and that something had happened to you."

"We kept watch outside the city all night last night, waiting for an attack, but it never came."

She was relieved that Dan was unharmed but still panic-stricken about what she had just told Chana. Her words poured out in a jumbled rush. "I have something to tell you, Dan. I overheard something shocking, but I think I just made a terrible mistake by telling Chana when I should have told the governor instead, and—"

"Whoa. Slow down. I can't make sense of a word you're saying."

She drew a breath, forcing herself to speak calmly. "Last night I overheard my master talking at dinner—"

"Nava! . . . Nava!" Someone behind her was shouting her name. She freed herself from Dan's arms and turned, terrified that it was Chana. Instead, Malkijah's housekeeper marched up the street with a broom in her hand and a look of fury on her face. "So! This is what you've been up to, is it? Someone told me that you weren't really going to the temple every morning. They said you've been meeting a boyfriend, but I didn't want to believe it."

"But I do go to the temple—"

"So I decided to see with my own eyes—and here you are! Cozying up to him!" The housekeeper had seen Nava nestled in Dan's arms for comfort.

"You don't understand. Dan and I are going to be married—"

"Oh, I understand. You aren't religious at all . . . you're a loose woman!"

"Now, wait just a minute—" Dan said, but the housekeeper cut him off.

"No, you listen to me, young man! Nava belongs to our master. He could have you severely punished for interfering with one of his workers."

"Interfering . . . ?"

"You know what I mean! And if Nava has your child while she's still a bondservant, that child will belong to her master, not you!"

"What?" Dan looked stunned, as if the housekeeper had struck him in the head with her broom.

"There is no child," Nava protested. "We haven't—"

"Enough of your lies!" She gripped Nava's arm and dragged her toward the house.

"Let go of her," Dan shouted.

The housekeeper shook her broom at him like a weapon. "You stay away from her!" By the time they reached Malkijah's door, Nava's arm felt bruised from being yanked against her will. "It's my job to protect your virtue, Nava. That's why I'm sending you back to Beth Hakkerem."

"No! Please! I promise I won't see Dan anymore. I won't even leave the house. But please, please don't send me back there!"

"My mind's made up, so you can stop your blubbering. You betrayed my trust when you told me you were going to the sacrifices. You won't get a second chance from me."

Nava caught a final glimpse of Dan, still standing in the street, before the housekeeper pulled her through the door and slammed it behind them.

Chapter 36

OUTSIDE JERUSALEM

For a second night, Nehemiah and his men slipped through the Valley Gate and into the darkness to keep watch for an enemy attack. Last night the only thing his small band of volunteers had spotted were jackals hunting rodents and grasshoppers among the weed-filled ruins. He and his men had returned to the city as the sun began to lighten the eastern sky, exhausted from their long, worthless vigil. "Get some sleep," Nehemiah had told them. "We'll have to do this all over again tonight." But Nehemiah had dozed for only a short time, compelled by worry and nervous energy. He made the rounds of the city wall, making sure his workers were well guarded and that construction was progressing.

The fact that this crisis had slowed their work frustrated him. Only half of his men now rebuilt the wall, wearing swords at their sides while they labored. The other half stood guard, equipped with spears, wooden shields, bows, and armored breastplates. Those who carried materials did their work with one hand and held a weapon in the other, while his officers were posted in strategic places to respond quickly in case of an attack. Everyone worked from the first light of dawn until the stars came out at night. That's when Nehemiah and his men left the safety of the half-finished walls to watch the roadways for the approaching enemy.

Now, as they prepared for a possible assault on the second night, Nehemiah repeated his speech to the dozen men who had volunteered to watch with him. "If an attack does come, we'll very likely be outnumbered. Don't be afraid of them. Remember the Lord, who is great and awesome, and fight for your brothers, your sons and daughters, your wives and homes."

They took posts among the ruins of the Mishneh, positioning themselves behind deserted houses that offered a view of the main road leading to the Valley Gate. His men seemed tense and alert, wary of every little sound and movement. The sprawling area teemed with insects and was overgrown with weeds and briars. Dry grass prickled Nehemiah's skin as he crouched behind the ruins of a burned-out house. The only light on this moonless night came from millions of stars filling the cloudless summer sky.

After watching for more than an hour, Nehemiah heard a rustling noise behind him and whirled around. One of his volunteers, a lanky young man with sun-browned skin, came to crouch beside him armed with a bow and a quiver of arrows. He looked vaguely familiar to Nehemiah, and he tried to recall where he had seen him before tonight. "What's your name?" he whispered, still wary of whom to trust.

"Dan ben Yonah."

"You look very young to be a volunteer."

"I'm old enough. I know how to use a bow, and I'm not afraid to fight."

Nehemiah didn't respond, listening for sounds in the darkness—an owl hooting, the grinding of crickets, the quiet rustle of his men shifting positions.

"My family returned with Rebbe Ezra thirteen years ago," Dan whispered, "to the patch of land in the District of Beth

Hakkerem that belonged to our ancestors. But we were forced to mortgage it to a wealthy landowner named Malkijah ben Recab because of the drought."

Nehemiah suddenly remembered where he'd seen the young man before. "You came forward with the other men to protest at the temple, didn't you?"

"Yes, Governor. And we are very grateful for what you tried to do for us. But Malkijah didn't do what you asked him to. He didn't cancel our debts or give back any of our land. And he refuses to free his bondservants."

Before Nehemiah could reply, one of his other men whispered, "Over there!" Nehemiah looked where he pointed and saw movement, a darker shape against the shadows. His heart sped up. His men nudged each other into alertness, and they gazed into the darkness. Dan quietly pulled an arrow from his quiver and fitted it into his bow. As the shapes emerged from the ruins and scampered across the road to disappear again, Nehemiah saw that it was the same pack of jackals they'd seen last night, returning to rummage among the deserted houses.

He sat back again, his heart rate returning to normal. The young man still crouched beside him, waiting for his reply. If what Dan said was true and Malkijah hadn't helped the poor, then Nehemiah was very disappointed in him. He considered Malkijah an ally and supporter, relying on him to rebuild the Dung Gate. He'd already served as a valuable informant, exposing a potential enemy spy when he'd warned about Tobiah's son. Nehemiah had made Malkijah a commander, entrusting him with troops and weapons, putting him in charge of defending the southern approach to the city. In fact, his brother Ephraim had volunteered to fight alongside Malkijah because the gate was near his home at the southern tip of the city. A chill of dread shivered through Nehemiah when he remembered they were positioned there for a possible attack at this very moment.

Knowing whom to trust was an issue that continued to

plague Nehemiah. But at least Dan's accusation against Malkijah would be easy to verify. "I'll look into what you've told me," Nehemiah promised. He left Dan and silently moved away, climbing the remains of an outdoor staircase that led to the rooftop of one of the ruined houses. He wanted to be alone as doubt gnawed at him. The deep divide between rich and poor had begun to heal, but the wound might rupture all over again, halting the wall's progress if men like Malkijah refused to support Nehemiah's reforms.

His new lookout perch offered a clear view of the rubble-littered street and a large section of the deserted Mishneh. He crouched behind the remains of the parapet to wait. If the attack didn't come tonight, Nehemiah feared that his men would grow complacent and bored, letting down their guard instead of remaining alert and motivated. Or worse, that fear would creep in as stealthily as the jackals had, heightening the unnerving sense of being watched and preyed upon.

Midway through the night, Nehemiah spotted them. Not jackals this time but his enemies, advancing through the ruins like the flickering shadows of an oil lamp. He rubbed his eyes to make sure they weren't playing tricks on him. They weren't. More than two dozen figures, weapons drawn, crept along the margins of the road toward the Yeshana Gate. Nehemiah's men were outnumbered by more than two to one. Even so, he rose to his feet and whistled the signal to fight. His men let out a savage war whoop as he'd instructed them to do, so loud and bone-chilling that the enemy halted in their tracks. Nehemiah's archers, including Dan, unleashed a flurry of arrows as Nehemiah clambered down the stairs and ran forward with the rest of his men to stop the attackers. With his heart hammering harder than he could ever recall, he unleashed the protective fury that he'd long felt for his brothers in order to protect Jerusalem. It rendered him fearless.

It took only moments for the enemy to realize that they'd

lost the element of surprise. They scattered in a dozen different directions, zigzagging through the rubble, disappearing into the Mishneh's maze of winding, deserted streets. Nehemiah focused on one man and gave chase, sprinting to catch up. Now the moonless night worked against him, making it hard to follow his opponent and watch his footing at the same time. He saw Dan and the others also chasing the attackers, and he hoped they didn't attack one another by mistake.

After a few minutes of heart-pounding pursuit, Nehemiah gave up, furious that he hadn't caught up with his enemy, that he hadn't had a chance to fight him hand to hand. As his men slowly regrouped and gathered around him, he saw disappointment on their faces, as well. He beckoned to his swiftest runner. "Get a message out to all the other watch points throughout the city. Alert them of the aborted attack and warn them to remain vigilant." Then Nehemiah and his men returned to the shadows to hide once again and keep watch.

"Think they'll try again?" Dan asked.

"Possibly. But the element of surprise is gone. They know we're waiting for them."

"How many more nights do you think we'll have to do this?" another volunteer asked.

"Sanballat's spies may not have alerted him before now that we would be waiting, but he'll know after tonight. We'll do this every night, if we have to, until the threat eases. I'm not letting down my guard until the wall is finished and every gate is in place. But I have a feeling that once our enemies know we're aware of their plot and that the Almighty One has frustrated it, we can all return to the wall, each to his own work."

"They won't attack from the same direction the next time, will they?" someone asked.

"Probably not, but we'll keep guard over all of the western gates just to be sure."

As dawn finally lit up the Mishneh and the laborers and

guards returned to their work on the wall, Nehemiah gave his men permission to go home and get some rest. He had just reached his field office inside the Valley Gate when one of his messengers found him. "I have a report to deliver to you, my lord. In the last few hours before dawn, the enemy attacked your men outside the Dung Gate and—"

Nehemiah didn't wait to hear the rest. That's where his stubborn brother was fighting. Nehemiah sprinted down the hill to the gate, arriving in time to see his commander Malkijah and his brother Ephraim emerging with the other men through the gaping hole where the gate would be, looking weary yet jubilant. The relief Nehemiah felt was overwhelming. His brother appeared dusty but unharmed, with smudges of dirt on his clothes and bits of leaves sticking to his hair.

"The enemy crept up the Hinnom Valley," Malkijah told him, "taking cover along the base of the cliffs. But our scouts stayed alert and spotted them."

"Was there a battle?"

Malkijah nodded. "A brief one." Nehemiah noticed dark smears on Malkijah's tunic, a gory bandage wrapped around his left hand. "We bloodied a few of their men before they retreated, but we were outnumbered so we followed your advice and didn't pursue them. They were all Samaritans from the looks of them."

"You're injured," Nehemiah said.

"It's nothing, Governor. I'll be fine." Malkijah looked pleased with himself and his men. Ephraim also looked elated at having done battle.

"Our job is to guard the city, not get ourselves killed," Nehemiah said. "This may not be over yet, so go home and get some rest. All of you." He met Ephraim's gaze but didn't single him out, knowing his brother would resist being told what to do.

"My wound is minor," Malkijah protested, "and my work on the gate—"

"I insist you go home and have your hand looked after. You're a valuable member of my staff."

It wasn't until later that day that he remembered Dan's accusation against Malkijah. Nehemiah should have confronted him and asked if it was true, but lack of sleep and the long, tense night had dulled his thinking. He would wait for another time when they could talk in private. After all, hadn't Malkijah proven his courage and allegiance in battle last night?

CHAPTER
37

JERUSALEM

Chana's house was so close to the city wall that if she went up the outside stairs to the flat rooftop, she could watch the laborers setting building stones into place. Abba told her that half of the laborers now stood guard with spears and shields as the other half worked—and even those men wore swords. Chana longed to rejoin them and couldn't. So every afternoon after finishing in the kitchen, she climbed up to the rooftop where she could at least view the ongoing work. She squinted in the sunlight to watch the men check the plumb line and level lines and was annoyed to see that they weren't nearly as careful or accurate as she had been.

Fear had settled over the city. Chana felt the tension everywhere she went like a frayed rope about to snap. This morning at the well she'd heard the huddled women whispering their fears for their husbands and sons who stood guard during the night. When she and Yudit went to buy fish in the marketplace, the merchant had told them about their enemy's threats, relayed by an incoming caravan driver: *"Before the Jews know it or see us, we will be right there among them and will kill them and put an end to the work."*

Chana refused to cower at home, too frightened to go out. In fact, she would gladly continue building the wall if Abba would allow it. She watched with growing frustration as her father left home at dawn without her every morning and worked until the stars came out after sunset. "The sooner we finish the wall, the sooner we'll all be safe," he had told her this morning. "And don't bother to ask, Chana. The answer is still no."

She and her sisters helped the servants cook the noon meal for the workers, but Abba sent men to the house to fetch it, refusing to allow his daughters to venture outside the walls. Chana had a lot of time to think while she ground grain into flour, kneaded the dough, and baked the rounds of flatbread on the stone griddle. When she wasn't thinking about the wall, her thoughts continually returned to what Nava had told her when they'd talked at the temple. Was it really true that Malkijah and a group of men were conspiring against the governor? Chana didn't want to believe it. Malkijah worked so hard to rebuild the Dung Gate. He had volunteered to fight against the attackers himself. Surely he was loyal to the governor. Nava must have misunderstood.

But when Nava had relayed distressing news before, it had been true. Malkijah hadn't freed his bondservants. He didn't support the governor's social reforms. Chana still cringed when she recalled how she had confronted him. By the time he had explained his reasons, Chana felt foolish and petty for accusing him. Maybe there was a logical explanation for what Nava had overheard this time, too. *"What is it going to take to get you to trust me?"* Malkijah had asked. Should she trust him now? She had no choice. She'd told him she still wanted to marry him. Yet she couldn't forget Nava's accusation: *"He isn't the man you think he is."*

Chana had tried to raise the subject of a conspiracy with her father last night. He had returned from his work on the wall late in the evening, sweaty and exhausted. When she was alone with him after he'd finished his meal, she had probed for his opinion. "Abba, you're on the ruling council with some of the other nobles and officials. Are they all in agreement with Governor Nehemiah?"

"We haven't had a council meeting in a while. We're too busy working."

"But do you think they all support him?"

"From what I can see they do. Why?"

"I was thinking about how Nehemiah came out of nowhere and took over. And I know the council governed the province before he came. I wondered if any of them resented him for replacing their authority and ordering everyone around."

"If there's simmering resentment, I haven't heard it. Why are you asking about this, Chana?"

She had tried to seem nonchalant, knowing that if she aroused Abba's curiosity he might make her tell what she knew. "I'm just curious. I've been very surprised by what a strong, decisive leader Nehemiah is, and I just wondered if some people saw him differently."

Abba had slumped in his seat after dinner to sip the last of his wine, but he set down his cup and stirred as if preparing to rise. "Nehemiah united our people, eased a potential class war, and rebuilt our city wall from ruins—all in less than two months' time. I don't understand how anyone could resent him for accomplishing all of that."

"Me either, Abba—unless there are some wealthy nobles who resent being forced to take his oath and cancel the debts that the poorer people owe."

"I suppose. In that case, even a leader as strong as Governor Nehemiah will find it difficult to fight against basic human greed." Abba had retired to bed a few minutes later.

Now, by the time two laborers arrived to pick up the midday meal for all the workers, Chana was tired of doing battle with doubt and mistrust. She wanted to think about other things. "How is the work on the wall going?" she asked them.

"Just fine, miss."

"Although everyone is tense," the younger of the two men added. "We're still in great danger. There could be another attack at any moment."

"Did my father tell you to say that? I know he's trying to scare me to keep me away."

"No, miss. He never spoke to me about it."

"So we really are in great danger like everyone fears?" Chana asked. "Because I've only heard of one attack so far."

"No, just last night—" the younger man began, but the older one silenced him with a jab of his elbow.

"What are you hiding from me?" Chana asked. She moved the basket of bread she had just filled out of their reach. "Tell me or I won't send any bread with you. You'll have to scoop up your lunch with your hands."

The men exchanged a long look, then the elbow-jabber sighed and said, "You may as well tell her what you were going to say. I'm hungry."

"A group of our men prevented an attack last night, miss."

"Where? What happened? Was anyone hurt?"

"The enemy came sneaking through the Mishneh with swords and spears, right outside the Valley Gate." He seemed pleased to offer proof of the danger she would be in if she returned to work. "Our men were waiting for them, though, and fought them off."

"So no one was killed or wounded," she said. "Our guards did their job and kept everyone safe."

"Well, yes. But there was another attack outside the Dung Gate and the commander was injured—"

"The commander?" Chana felt the blood drain from her face. "Malkijah ben Recab?"

"Yes. How did you know—?" He was silenced again by a hard jab to his ribs.

"How badly injured was he?"

"I have no idea. Maybe it was just a rumor. . . . We should be going now, miss." He pulled the basket of bread within reach and slipped his arm through the handle.

Malkijah was injured? Memories of the night Yitzhak was attacked came flooding back, filling Chana with fear. Before the two workers were even out of her courtyard, she rushed into her room and pulled off her floury apron and the sweaty scarf that held back her hair.

"What are you doing? Where are you going?" Sarah asked when Chana came out a moment later with her clothes changed and her hair combed.

"I need to see if Malkijah is all right."

"Do you want us to come with you?" Yudit asked.

"No. I'd rather go alone."

She hurried up the Hill of Ophel to Malkijah's house, a knot of fear pulling tighter and tighter in her stomach.

The housekeeper who opened Malkijah's door looked surprised to see her. "Miss Chana, come in. What brings you here?"

Chana wondered if all of her whirling emotions were visible on her face. She forced herself to calm down, trying not to envision Malkijah lying pale and lifeless the way Yitzhak had, inching closer and closer to death. "I heard that Malkijah was wounded last night. Is he here? I came to find out how he is and if there's anything I can do."

The housekeeper smiled. "It's nothing to worry about, miss. Just a small wound to his hand."

"Are you sure?"

"Yes, miss. Quite sure. He's resting at the moment after being on guard duty all night, but would you like me to tell him you're here?"

"No, please don't disturb him. I'll see him another time." Chana turned toward the door, but the enormous relief she felt had turned her knees to water. She took a few wobbling steps and nearly fell over before the housekeeper took her arm and guided her to a bench.

"You sit here for a moment, miss. I'll fetch you a drink."

"Thank you." She felt ridiculous for being so weak. Malkijah wasn't seriously injured. He would be fine. So why were her eyes filling with tears?

She cared about him, she realized. She wanted him to be safe. She wanted a long, happy life with him. But she also knew that it might not happen if Malkijah joined a conspiracy against their governor.

Chana needed to speak with Nava again. Maybe if she had more information about this supposed conspiracy, she could finally put her worries about Malkijah to rest—or else try to convince him that it would be a mistake to join the rebels. But the servant who brought Chana a drink and a bowl of dates wasn't Nava. "Thank you so much," Chana said as she took the cup from her. "What's your name?"

"It's Rachel, miss."

"There's another servant who works here named Nava. Could you please ask her to come here for a moment?"

The woman swallowed and looked away. "Nava doesn't work here anymore, miss. She was sent back to our master's estate in Beth Hakkerem."

Her reply shocked Chana. "Do you know why?"

Rachel was about to reply when the housekeeper returned. She shook her head and quickly disappeared.

Nava had been sent away. Was it because of what she'd overheard about the conspiracy? Who else had Nava told about it? Then another thought chilled Chana when she remembered Nava's fear of Malkijah's son and the leering way he had stared at the girl. Nava had asked Chana for help, but what could she do now from so far away? Did she dare make accusations to Malkijah about his son's behavior?

"Chana, what a surprise to see you."

She looked up, startled, as Malkijah walked in. His lack of sleep for the past few nights showed on his tired face and red-rimmed eyes. He wore a linen bandage wrapped around his left hand. She sprang to her feet, relieved to see him, yet guilty for her lingering doubts about him. "I heard you'd been wounded. I came to see how you were."

"It's nothing. Only a flesh wound." He lifted his bandaged hand for a moment, then lowered it again. "I'm touched that you came, Chana. That you . . . care."

"I . . . I do," she said.

Malkijah smiled. "I need to return to my duties at the Dung Gate. Come, I'll walk you home if you'd like. It's on my way."

They walked through the streets together, side by side, the way she had promised to walk with him for the rest of her life. Chana had seen nothing at all of her surroundings as she'd raced up the hill to Malkijah's house earlier, blinded by fear. Now she noticed women sweeping their courtyards, white-haired men sitting on benches and stoops with their canes. She heard the singsong voices of children playing and the incessant sound of chisels against stone. There were no men in the streets except the elderly. Every able-bodied man in the province either stood guard or worked on the wall.

"I worry about you, Malkijah," Chana said when they reached her house. "I hate it that you could be in danger."

He looked down at her, his eyes soft. "It's times like these when the future is uncertain that we need to live our lives to the full. Don't waste time in useless worry, dear Chana, fretting over what might never happen. Worry doesn't change a single thing. Just live."

She watched until he was out of sight, then went to tell Sarah and Yudit the good news that Malkijah was unhurt. Afterward, with nothing else to do, she climbed the stairs to the rooftop to watch the construction on the wall. As Abba had said this morning, the sooner they finished, the sooner they would all be safe.

If only she could help.

CHAPTER

38

BETH HAKKEREM
SEPTEMBER

Nava walked back to Beth Hakkerem with a group of servants who were returning to harvest Master Malki-jah's early grapes. Her fear of his son Aaron multiplied with every step. She tried to huddle in the middle of the group as they climbed the last hill and entered the walled compound; when Aaron was nowhere in sight she nearly fainted with relief. She ran to the goat pen first and found her friend Shimon.

"I see you're back," he said. A faint smile flickered across his weathered face. But as happy as Nava was to see him, she didn't smile in return.

"Shimon, can you please help me hide from Master Aaron? I'll do any work you ask me to do if you'll please make sure he doesn't see me or know that I'm back."

Shimon frowned, then looked away. "It's not up to me where you work, girlie. Talk to Penina."

The kitchen seemed miles away from the goat pen. Nava peeked from behind the fence, careful to look in all directions before sprinting across the open space to the kitchen courtyard. Once there, she tried to crouch low and hide behind one of the chopping tables as she searched for the little cook. The other kitchen servants stopped what they were doing to stare as if Nava had lost her mind. A moment later Penina emerged from the storeroom, her face creased in an angry frown. "What in the world are you doing here?"

Nava was reluctant to admit the full truth. "I came back with the men who are going to work in the vineyard—"

"Why are you crouching beside my table like a beaten dog? Stand up."

"I don't want Master Aaron to see that I'm back."

Penina gave an irritated groan. "Not this again!"

"I'll do any work you ask me to do, but please help me hide from him."

"For the next *six years*? No. I won't do it," she said, shaking her head. "It's going to be impossible to stay hidden, and when he does see you, what then? He'll know what you've been doing and that I helped you. No. It'll be much worse for both of us if we try to deceive him."

Nava closed her eyes, unable to stop her tears. The hopelessness of her situation overwhelmed her, and she sank to the ground. With Aaron in charge of the estate, she knew with horrible certainty what would happen. Penina stood above her, her bony arms folded. "Listen to me. I won't hide you, but I'll do what I can to protect you. I'll talk to Ruth about it, too. That's the best I can do."

"Thank you," Nava mumbled.

"Now stand up and go make some goat cheese. We haven't had a decent batch of it since you went to Jerusalem."

Nava stayed out of Aaron's sight for nearly a week while he supervised the grape harvest. Then he happened to pass by the pen early one morning when Nava and Shimon were milking the goats. He had appeared out of nowhere, so suddenly that she didn't have time to duck out of sight. "Well, well, well," he said, leaning against the fence. "Look who's back. You know, it's a funny thing—I'm in charge of this estate, and I had no idea you had returned."

"I came back with the vineyard workers—"

"And here you are milking goats. Why haven't you been serving my meals? I thought I decided that's where you belonged. You're much too pretty to work with that old man and his smelly goats. Come with me."

Nava's knees had begun to tremble, and she wasn't sure she could stand. Shimon gestured for her to remain seated. "She has a way with the animals, Master Aaron," he said, hobbling toward the fence. "That other little oaf scares them. Curdles their milk."

"Then find someone else."

"Your father takes great pride in his herds. He'd want the best for them. And that girlie is the best. Let her finish, Master Aaron. It's hard for me to do the milking these days." He held up his wrinkled, twisted hands.

Aaron pushed away from the fence and stood up straight. "Don't tell me what to do, old man. If you can't do your work, then it's time to get rid of you."

Shimon lowered his head as he shuffled across the pen to take Nava's place on the milking stool. He nodded to her, telling her she should go.

"Come on, Nava, I don't have all day," Aaron called.

She let herself out of the pen and followed him across the yard to the house. When she didn't move quickly enough for him, Aaron grabbed her wrist and pulled her along. As they passed the kitchen area, she managed to catch Penina's eye and gave a silent plea for help. Nava was terrified of where Aaron might be taking her as he led her through the doorway into the house. She nearly collapsed with relief when Ruth, the formidable housekeeper, met them just inside the door. "Where are you going, Master Aaron? Did you forget something?"

Nava could tell that he wasn't expecting to meet Ruth. He released Nava's wrist. "No . . . I just . . ."

"And you stop right there, girl," Ruth said, looking Nava up and down. "Don't you dare come inside my nice, clean house before you've had a bath. You smell like the goat pen."

"That's where I found her," Aaron said. "She's supposed to be a household servant, remember? But I found her milking goats. I want her to serve all my meals."

Ruth shook her head. "She's no good in the dining room, Master Aaron. I gave her a chance before sending her off to Jerusalem but she was much too clumsy. Always breaking dishes, spilling perfectly good food onto the floor. You know how your father hates waste. He would have my head if he saw the damage that girl did."

"Besides," Penina said, coming up behind Nava, "I need her to help me in the kitchen. I'll have extra men to cook for until the grapes are harvested. And she makes the best goat cheese I ever tasted. Even your father praised it."

Aaron had the look of a man who knew he was beaten. But only for now. He lifted his chin, his lips pressed into a mean, hard line. "I don't have time to argue with a bunch of stubborn servants. We'll finish this discussion later."

"Thank you," Nava whispered as Aaron strode away. "I was so afraid!"

Penina waved away Nava's thanks, still frowning. "Don't think I didn't mean it when I said I needed your help. Come on." She marched Nava back to the kitchen. "Start making cheese. And it better be extra good so you don't make a liar out of me."

It took a long time for Nava's hands to stop shaking. Thankfully, she didn't see Aaron for the rest of the day. She returned to the goat pen that evening to help with the milking and to thank Shimon for trying to help.

"It was kind of you to stand up for me this morning."

Shimon gave his customary grunt. "Instead of running scared, you need to ask God for help. You know how to pray, girlie?"

Nava led the first goat to her stool and sat down, resting her forehead against the goat's side, reluctant to admit the truth. "I stopped praying months ago, Shimon."

He limped over, glaring down at her. "Now, why would you do a foolish thing like that?"

"Because God hasn't answered any of my other prayers. Nothing in my life has gone the way I wanted it to."

"You think I chose to spend my life in someone else's goat pen?"

She looked up at him. "Then how can you still pray?"

"How can I not?" he said gruffly. "The Lord is our shepherd, and we are His sheep. We need Him as much as these animals need us."

Nava sighed and bent her head to her task again. "Sometimes I wonder if God is angry with me. Why else would He put my family and me through all this hardship? He could send rain, make our crops grow—He can do anything. But He doesn't."

"So you do believe in Him. You just don't trust Him. And you want your own way."

She looked up again. Shimon was making her angry. "Isn't God supposed to answer our prayers?"

"Depends on what you're praying for." He walked away to lead another goat to his milking stool, and Nava thought the conversation was over. But when he sat down beside her again he said, "These goats sometimes kick and fight and want their own way. When we take them out to graze and make them walk through the hot, dry wilderness, they don't like it. But we know it's for their own good to go up into those hills. They'll find what they need there. You can either trust the Good Shepherd, girlie, or kick and fight. Seems to me you're kicking."

Nava was outraged. "I don't see how letting Master Aaron have his way could possibly be for my own good."

"That's because you don't see things the way God does. He may not have answered your prayers yet, but that doesn't mean He hasn't heard you." She watched as his gnarled hands pulled steady streams of milk into the bucket. He slowly stood when he was finished and said, "You shouldn't pray only when you want something from God."

"Then why else?"

"Did you only talk to your father when you wanted something from him? Or did you tell him you loved him once in a while? Did you ask him what job he wanted you to do? Or thank him for taking care of you?"

"You make it sound so simple."

"It is simple." He went off to fetch another goat while she was still milking her first one. "Tell me, did you ever want your own way and your father said no?" he asked when he returned.

She thought of how she and Dan had wanted to marry right away, but both of their fathers had said no. "Yes, sometimes."

"Did your father have a good reason for saying no?" Shimon asked.

"Yes." Neither family could afford to have them marry.

"Was his decision for your own good?"

She was reluctant to reply, seeing where Shimon was leading her. She untethered the goat when she was finished and led another one to the post. "Yes, it was for everyone's good," she said, sitting down again. "But how can any good come from what Master Aaron wants?"

"Maybe there's a reason you can't yet see."

"Even if he was the richest man in Judah I wouldn't want to marry him. I'm in love with Dan."

Shimon stopped working and looked over at her, his eyes glistening. "Then if you know what real love is, you should be praying for Aaron, not for yourself. Because he doesn't understand what love is all about."

Nava wanted to protest, but the soft look in Shimon's eyes silenced her. How could he feel sorry for someone as cruel as Master Aaron?

"That boy has everything in the world," Shimon continued, "yet he's cold and dead inside. Does he seem happy to you?"

"No." She thought of Dan, who had nothing, and remembered the joy on his face when he'd brought her the sack of quails that spring morning. She thought about her other unanswered prayer—to be free. Was there a reason why that one hadn't been answered yet? The ring shining in Shimon's ear reminded her that he could have had his freedom long ago. "Why did you choose to stay here, Shimon, when you could have been set free?"

For the first time he hesitated, as if reluctant to answer. When he did, his voice was surprisingly tender. "So I could pray for Master Malkijah and his sons. I pray for them every single day."

"Why? I've seen how mean Master Aaron is to you. Why would you stay here and pray for him?"

"I have my reasons." He closed down, like a door firmly shut and locked. When he rose to walk away, she knew their conversation was over. But then he glanced over his shoulder at her and added, "You need to pray for our masters, too."

Nava shook her head in silent reply as she squeezed milk into the bucket. When she'd first arrived at the estate she'd been determined not to allow the weeds of bitterness to grow. But the fear she felt toward Aaron had watered them. So had her anger and resentment toward Malkijah for not setting her free. Pray for them? They had everything, and she had so little. And now they wanted to take away the little that she did have—her future with Dan.

No, Nava thought as she untethered the goat. No, she couldn't pray for them.

JERUSALEM

Y ou're going up to the rooftop again?" Yudit asked when
the noon meal was finished. "Why do you torture yourself
by watching the men work, Chana? You know we can't
help Abba anymore."

"I know. But there's nothing else to do." She and her sisters
no longer prepared a huge evening meal since Abba worked on
the wall until it was almost too dark to see. He arrived home
exhausted every evening and ate a simple dinner by lamplight
before going to bed. "I like to watch the progress," she told
Yudit. "You should see how far they are—almost to the Tower
of the Ovens."

"We're still helping, you know," Sarah said. "We're doing
our part like all the other women by cooking for the men. They
would starve if it weren't for us."

"The servants Abba hired can cook just as well as I can,"
Chana said. "Probably better." She took off her work apron
and headed toward the outside steps.

"Watching is only going to frustrate you," Yudit called to
her. "And make you grouchy."

"I know. But I'm going up anyway." The view from the rooftop seemed to change a little more each day. Before Nehemiah came, Chana had been able to see over the broken-down wall and across the central valley into the deserted Mishneh. Now the wall blocked her view, towering higher than her rooftop. Abba's section from the Valley Gate to the Tower of the Ovens was three-quarters finished. He had described to Chana how his crew worked with the crew at the tower to make sure the wall joined tightly, just as they had worked with the crew at the Valley Gate. It was all so exciting. And now, in spite of their enemies' attempts to halt it, the wall was nearly finished.

She watched three men on top of the wall guide a large block into place from the swinging crane ropes. They suddenly stopped. The ropes went slack even though the block wasn't in position, and the men scrambled down the scaffolding and out of sight on the other side. Two more men who had been checking the level lines in another place also stopped and climbed down, followed by the two sentries who stood guard on top. The incessant pounding and chiseling ceased. Were they being attacked? Chana's heart sped up as she listened for the sound of the trumpet blast, ordering all of the workers to come to their neighbors' defense. But instead of the trumpet and the clash of swords, she heard a man screaming in agonizing pain on the other side of the wall.

She listened for sounds of fighting and didn't hear any. The cries continued. Had there been an accident? Was one of Abba's workmen injured? *Lord, help him, please! Help him!* She pictured a block of stone shifting, crushing someone's leg or arm beneath its weight. But the longer she listened, the more convinced she became that the voice she heard crying out in agony was her father's.

Chana ran down the stairs, through her courtyard, and out of her house without stopping. She raced down the Street of the Bakers to the Valley Gate, pushing past anyone who got in her way. The cries went on and on in the distance as she hurried through the gate along with a growing crowd of men. They had unsheathed their swords as if fearing, as she had, that they were under attack. The screaming would die away for only a few seconds at a time before continuing.

"Abba!" she shouted as she raced toward the knot of gathered men. Convinced more than ever that it was her father's voice, she elbowed her way through the bystanders and saw her father lying on the ground, writhing in pain. She didn't see any blood or wounds, no huge blocks of stone pinning his limbs, but two workers held his shoulders, another one his legs, trying to hold him still. Was something wrong with his heart?

"Abba! Abba, what happened?" She knelt beside him, her lungs heaving. "What's wrong? What happened?"

He looked up at her, but only heart-wrenching moans poured from his mouth. Tears filled his eyes as he tossed restlessly.

"What's wrong with him?" she asked the man holding his shoulders.

"He lifted a stone from that pile over there and uncovered a nest of scorpions. They were Death Stalkers."

This was much, much worse than she'd feared. She saw an angry red welt on Abba's hand, and all of his fingers and part of his forearm had swollen to twice their size. "No! No . . . !" she said as tears filled her eyes. The pain from the scorpion's venomous sting was said to be excruciating and, hearing Abba's pitiful cries, Chana believed it. She also knew why the scorpion was called the Death Stalker. She wanted to do something to help him, to save his life, but didn't know what. Work on the wall had stopped as the men gathered around, staring uselessly.

"Somebody fetch a litter," she yelled. "We need to carry him home. . . . And find someone who knows what to do for him, how to save him!" It seemed to take forever for the men to bring a blanket to use for a litter. Abba screamed again as the workers lifted him onto it. Chana went alongside, holding

Abba's other hand as the men carried him home. He was biting his lip to keep from crying out, his beloved face knotted in agony. "Go slowly!" she begged as they carried him through the Valley Gate and up the street. "Don't jostle him too much!"

They finally reached the house, and Chana ran ahead to open the gate. She directed them to her father's bed, shouting for Sarah and Yudit. Her sisters came running, but there was nothing any of them could do except hover over him, listening to his terrible moans and silently pleading with God to save him. It seemed like hours passed before a white-haired woman named Miryam arrived to help. She was a healer who had dealt with the Death Stalker scorpion before. She gave Chana and her sisters a list of ingredients she would need to make a poultice and the names of certain leaves that could be ground up and given to him to drink to ease his pain. They divided up the list and Chana ran to the marketplace, grateful for the chance to finally do something. Word of the accident had spread, and people kept stopping her to ask how Shallum was and how they could help. Chana answered abruptly, telling them she had no time to talk.

By the time Chana returned with the last of the ingredients, Miryam had begun brewing the poultice. Yudit piled pillows behind Abba's shoulders and spooned the elixir into his mouth to help ease his pain. Sarah fanned him with palm leaves to cool him in the heat. The poison had traveled all the way up Abba's arm, bloating his face. When Miryam laid the finished poultice in place, draping it all the way up Abba's arm, he cried out. Chana had to leave the room, the memory of watching Yitzhak die magnifying her fear.

An hour later, whether it was the poultice or the elixir or the Death Stalker claiming its prey, Abba finally closed his eyes and fell asleep. Chana drew Miryam aside where her sisters couldn't overhear. "Is it a good thing that he's finally resting or are we losing him?" she asked. "His breathing sounds so labored."

"The drink we gave him put him to sleep. But it's the Death Stalker's venom that's closing his airways."

"What else can I do? I need to do something."

"We've made him as comfortable as we can. Now we can only wait and pray."

"Is he going to die?" Sarah asked, coming over to where they whispered. "We can't let him die."

"Your father is a strong man. He stands a good chance of pulling through. The Death Stalker's sting does its worst on the very young and the very old."

"It could have been any of us," Yudit said, joining the huddle. "We all handled those stones every day." No one replied, knowing she spoke the truth.

As time passed, Chana grew restless again, driven by the urge to do something besides sit and wring her hands. When she heard a knock outside at their gate, she jumped to her feet and hurried out to answer it. To her surprise, Governor Nehemiah stood there, along with the man with the signal trumpet who followed the governor like a shadow everywhere he went, ready to sound the alarm. Nehemiah's exhaustion shocked Chana, his gestures and speech slowed as if he moved underwater. His clothes looked as though he had worked and slept in them for several days. They smelled like it, too.

"I heard what happened to your father," Nehemiah said. "How is he?"

"Abba's pain seems to have eased a bit. Now we can only wait and see."

"I'm so sorry this happened. We've all been braced for another enemy attack this past week, and I don't think any of us expected something like this. Tell Shallum I was asking about him, and let me know if there is anything I can do besides pray."

"I will. Thank you for your kindness, Governor."

After he was gone Chana could no longer fight the urge to do something. The activity on the wall alongside her house seemed unusually quiet, and she remembered how the construction had halted, the men standing around as if afraid to return to work. Would they have sense enough to continue without Abba there to direct them? Or were they all too afraid to lift another stone? A few hours still remained before the evening sacrifice and there would be an hour or two of daylight after that in which work could be done. The more Chana thought about the construction coming to a halt, the more convinced she became that she needed to take her father's place. The men needed a supervisor and no one knew the work better than she did. She motioned for her sisters to come out where they could talk and told them her plan.

"Chana, no! You can't! It's too dangerous!" Sarah said.

"I can't just sit here and watch Abba suffer. I can't bear it. I need to do something, so I'm going to take over for him. Send for me if there's any change."

When Chana arrived outside the wall, the men still milled around halfheartedly, just as she'd feared, even though at least three hours had passed since the accident. They quickly gathered around her to ask about her father. "He's resting. Time will tell." With anger fueling her courage, she faced the waiting men, all of them older, stronger, and more experienced than she was. "Listen, I'll be taking over for my father until he recovers. You may not like taking orders from a woman—believe me, I don't enjoy giving them. But Abba trusts me, and I know what has to be done here. My father made a commitment to rebuild the wall from the Valley Gate to the Tower of the Ovens, and as his firstborn heir, it's my job to help him keep that commitment."

The men seemed too subdued by her surprising announcement and their lingering horror from the accident to reply. Chana took advantage of their shock and surprise to start issuing orders. "Show me where you left off and what remains to be done. I see that stone block up there is still attached to the crane, but it isn't in the right place. And we can't let this mortar dry out and go to waste. Let's get busy."

The wall looked wonderfully familiar from this side even if the armed guards standing rigidly on duty were an uneasy reminder that an attack could come at any moment. Chana strode down the length of her section all the way to the Tower of the Ovens to talk to Hasshub ben Pahath, who was in charge of rebuilding that tower.

He stopped what he was doing when he saw her and hurried over. "How is Shallum? He was in such horrible pain."

"We're doing everything we can for him at home. But the work on his section mustn't stop. I just came to tell you that I'll be taking over for him until he's well." She turned away before he could sputter his protests. Hasshub had made it clear from the start that he disapproved of Shallum's daughters working beside him. He would think even less of her working alone.

Shortly before the evening sacrifice, Chana saw Governor Nehemiah making his usual rounds, inspecting the wall and his security forces. She could have hidden from him but decided not to. He would hear about what she was doing soon enough. She saw his surprise and concern when he spotted her. "Chana, what are you doing out here? You need to get back inside the walls at once!"

"I can't do that, Governor. I'm supervising the work for my father until he's well."

His concern quickly transformed into anger. "Oh no, you're not! It's much too dangerous, for a whole host of reasons. I came here to assign a new foreman—"

"You don't need to do that. I know the work better than anyone. My father gave his word that he would rebuild this section, and I'm going to help him keep it."

"I will not allow you to put yourself in danger." He reached for her shoulder as if to steer her back toward the gate, but she eluded his grasp.

"Why not? Because I'm a woman?"

"Yes, of course because you're a woman! If that scorpion had bitten you, you'd be dead! You can't carry a sword, you're barely half the size of these men, and we have unseen enemies out there who could attack any minute!"

"It may surprise you to know that women can be every bit as courageous as men."

"I'm not questioning your courage, I'm questioning your common sense!" Nehemiah glanced around as if aware they were attracting attention. He lowered his voice, speaking through his clenched jaw. "If you don't leave voluntarily, I'll order my men to carry you home."

"Don't waste their time—or mine. I'll simply come right back. I admire you a great deal, Governor. Now kindly return the favor and respect my right to help my father the best way I know how."

"You are the most frustrating . . . stubborn . . . exasperating woman I have ever met!" His shout drew attention, and he looked away from her for a moment, staring up at the temple mount as if trying to cool his temper. "Listen, I need to attend the sacrifice now and pray for your father. But this conversation isn't over."

Chana stayed until dusk, the work distracting her from her worry for short periods of time. As the first stars appeared, she returned home to see how Abba was doing. Yudit's distraught face told her he wasn't any better. "He's getting worse, Chana. He can hardly breathe."

She went into his bedroom and sat down beside him, listening to his labored breaths. It made her chest ache to hear him. "Please don't die, Abba," she whispered. "Dear Lord, please don't let him die."

The thread that tethered Chana to the Almighty One seemed gossamer thin. But she closed her eyes and prayed, determined to hang on to it tightly and not let go.

JERUSALEM

Nehemiah was relieved to see his youngest brother waiting for him in the temple courtyard for the evening sacrifice. "Did you hear what happened to Shallum a few hours ago?" he asked Hanani without a word of greeting. "What do you know about the scorpion's sting? Is it fatal?"

"It can be. And so can exhaustion. Look at you! Why don't you go home and rest? For weeks you've been staying up all night, running all over the city by day, walking around the wall countless times—you can't keep this up, you know."

"I manage to catch a few hours of sleep here and there. How are you and Ephraim holding up? And how is our workers' morale?"

"Everyone was shaken by what happened to Shallum today. It could have been any of us. We've all been digging through the rubble, handling stones, reaching into all the places where scorpions like to hide."

"We need to pray for him. And for the work. And for help against our enemies. If we don't take time to pray, we may as well not bother to do anything else."

They took their places in the men's courtyard and Nehemiah

closed his eyes, letting the music soothe him as the Levites sang the liturgy. *"Find rest, O my soul, in God alone; my hope comes from him."* He remembered how he used to rise early in the morning to pray when he lived in Susa, confessing his sins to the Almighty One, relying on Him for strength and discernment. And he also remembered how God had answered his prayers and brought him this far, helping him accomplish the work he had set out to do.

"He alone is my rock and my salvation; he is my fortress, I will not be shaken." Ever since facing opposition, Nehemiah had wrestled with the question of whether it was a warning from God that he was headed in the wrong direction, or whether the enemy's attacks were designed to keep him from his God-given task. When he prayed here at the temple, closing his eyes to everything else and silencing the turmoil inside, Nehemiah knew he was following God. He needed to persevere and not give up.

"Trust in him at all times, O people; pour out your hearts to him, for God is our refuge." He silently thanked the Almighty One for successful victories over their attackers. And as the priest entered the sanctuary to light the incense, Nehemiah prayed for strength to complete his work, for continued protection from his enemies, and for God's healing hand to be upon Shallum. *"One thing God has spoken, two things have I heard: that you, O God, are strong, and that you, O Lord, are loving."*

Nehemiah was still thinking about Shallum when the sacrifice ended, and he remembered Shallum's obstinate daughter. "She went back to work on the wall," he told Hanani as they walked back across the courtyard.

"Who did? What are you talking about now?"

"That muleheaded woman, Shallum's daughter. Remember how we tried to get her to stop working on the wall once before? Well, she was finally forced to stop when the threat of attacks made it too dangerous. But she's back again. She says she's taking her father's place as supervisor. Of all the ridiculous things to do! You need to stop her, Hanani."

"Me? I didn't get anywhere with her last time. And then her fiancé, Malkijah, came to her defense, too."

"I forgot that she was betrothed to Malkijah. . . . I heard that he didn't take the oath, Hanani. I don't know what to make of that."

Hanani shook his head in bewilderment. "You're rambling. For everyone's sake, get some rest."

Nehemiah saw his other brother heading toward the stairs and signaled to him to stop and wait. He was relieved to see that Ephraim, like Hanani, wore an armored breastplate and carried a sword. "You look like you've wrestled with a pack of lions and lost," Ephraim told him. "You're going to wear yourself out."

"I told him the same thing," Hanani said. "He doesn't listen."

"You may be right," Nehemiah said, "but before I do wear out, I'm going to finish this wall."

"Do you even bother to eat?"

"When necessary."

Ahead of them, a small crowd had gathered near the top of the stairs to hear a woman shouting in an age-wizened voice. "Now what?" Nehemiah murmured, remembering how the last protest had halted construction. He was tall enough to look over the people's heads and see a wrinkled, gray-haired woman who stood with upraised hands, gazing toward heaven in ecstasy.

"The Holy One of Israel is with His people," she said, "and His hand is on His servant Nehemiah. There is a king in Judah! Therefore rejoice and be glad in His chosen king who has brought us victory over our enemies, and rebuilt the ruins of Jerusalem. Rejoice and be glad, O people, for there is a king in Judah who feeds you as in days of old and who looks upon the needs of the poor. . . ."

Nehemiah turned and hurried down the stairs without waiting to hear more. He didn't know why, but her words made him uncomfortable. So did being in crowds, where the people often reached out to touch him and thank him. "What did you make of that?" he asked his brothers when they were out of earshot. "Who is she?"

"Her name is Noadiah, and this is the third or fourth time I've heard her," Hanani said. "She's been showing up all over the city, saying pretty much the same thing. This is the first time I heard her speak at the temple, though."

"I've heard her before, too," Ephraim said. "Her 'prophecies' rub me the wrong way."

"Why?" Hanani asked. "She's only trying to encourage the people."

"Nehemiah isn't our king. She shouldn't even imply such a thing. . . . I'll see you tomorrow." He continued down the street instead of turning toward their residence.

"Ephraim, wait." Nehemiah jogged to keep up with him. Hanani did, too. "Where are you going?"

"I'm on night duty at the Dung Gate."

"Would it do any good at all for me to ask you not to go?" Nehemiah said. "We have plenty of other volunteers now."

"Save your breath. I would never forgive myself if someone got killed guarding my home and my family while I stayed where it was safe. . . . There's Malkijah. I need to speak with him before he leaves."

"Wait," Nehemiah called again. His brother halted, looking impatient. "You've been working alongside Malkijah for a while now. Can I ask you a question about him?" Ephraim nodded. "Someone told me that he broke his oath and didn't free his bondservants or cancel their debts. Do you know if that's true?"

"I have no idea. Ask him yourself."

"And while you're at it," Hanani added, "you can talk to him about Shallum's daughter. Malkijah is betrothed to her."

Being reminded of Chana made Nehemiah angry all over

again. Didn't he have enough to worry about without adding her to his list? He pushed his anger aside for now as he approached Malkijah, determined not to confront him with everything at once. "I see you're making excellent progress," Nehemiah began. "You took on a very critical task with this gate because it's at the junction of the three valleys. And you've had the added responsibility of safeguarding the King's Pool. Great work!"

"Thank you, Governor."

"I suppose you heard what happened to Shallum today?"

Malkijah's smile faded to a look of concern. "Yes, he's my father-in-law. I'm going up to see him now that Ephraim is here to take over."

"I spoke with his daughter earlier. She has taken it upon herself to work in Shallum's place after he was injured."

"Chana? What do you mean—on the wall?"

"Yes. She says she's supervising the construction for him. I asked her to stop and warned her that she's in danger, but she wouldn't listen. I was hoping you could talk some sense into her."

"I'll try. . . . But I can't promise I'll succeed. One of the things that attracted me to Chana was her lively spirit. I gave her my word before we were betrothed that I wouldn't force her to do anything against her will. I don't think it's a husband's place to order his wife around."

"Even when she's in danger?"

"Knowing Chana, this is something she probably needs to do, especially after what happened to her father today. She wants to rebuild the wall in order to protect the people she loves."

The frustrating thing was that Nehemiah understood how Chana felt, what motivated her. If she weren't a woman, he would applaud her courage. "There's something else, Malkijah . . . I'm very reluctant to speak to you about this, but I don't like gossip and rumors. I always prefer to learn the truth myself, whenever possible. Is it true that you didn't cancel your debtors' loans or free your bondservants when all of the other nobles did?"

Malkijah lifted his chin. "Yes, it's true."

The young man named Dan had told the truth. It wasn't a rumor.

Malkijah's steady gaze never wavered. "I never took the oath at the temple, Governor, so I'm not guilty of breaking it."

"May I ask why you didn't?"

"Because my estate couldn't function if I had. I need workers, especially during this drought, so I can harvest enough food to survive and pay my taxes."

"But your workers are growing resentful, especially after watching their neighbors go free."

"I can't set them free right now. I'm sorry."

"Might you be willing to reconsider after the harvest? The peace between the rich and poor is very fragile right now."

"I will gladly open my books to you," Malkijah said, his tone growing heated. "I'll show you all the ways I'm helping the poor, the things I've done for the good of the people in my district. It's true that I still have bondservants, but I'm feeding them and their families. And I'm not charging interest on their loans as I continue to carry them. My workers have no cause to be resentful."

Nehemiah didn't know what to think. He paused for such a long time that Malkijah finally said, "I can see you're disappointed in me. If you'd like, I'll resign as commander and reassign the construction of this gate to whomever you choose. I'll return to my property in Beth Hakkerem."

Again, Nehemiah didn't reply, his sleep-deprived mind taking longer to think and to reach a decision. "That won't be necessary, Malkijah," he finally said. "Carry on." He walked away, wondering if he had just lost a trusted friend and supporter—or if Malkijah had only pretended to be one from the beginning.

CHAPTER

41

JERUSALEM

Time seemed to slow as Chana sat cross-legged on the floor at her father's bedside, listening to his tortured breathing, his weary moans. He awoke again as night fell and looked over at her, his pain-filled eyes swollen nearly shut. "I'll fetch some more elixir," she said, scrambling to her feet.

"Not yet, my angel. Sit by me." His voice sounded tight and hoarse, as if it pained him to speak. Chana sat down and took his uninjured hand in hers, kissing the back of it. "Chana, don't grieve again if I die."

"Abba—"

"Be happy with Malkijah. . . . I trust him with you and your sisters."

"Please don't talk this way. You'll live, I know you will."

"God willing, Chana . . . God willing . . . But don't stop singing, my little bird. Don't sink into that well of grief again. Promise me."

Chana met his gaze, her vision blurred by tears. "I promise," she whispered. She would keep her word. Abba nodded slightly and tried to smile.

"And if I die, Chana . . . don't ask God, 'Why?' Ask, 'How?' . . . How can I make the world a better place? How can I show His love?"

Tears rolled down her cheeks. "I will, Abba."

"I'm praying for my three girls . . . that He'll keep you strong." He smiled and closed his eyes again. "Sing for me now, my angel. . . ."

She choked back the knot in her throat and began to sing softly to him. *"As the deer pants for streams of water, so my soul pants for you, O God. . . ."*

In the past few months since work began on the wall, Chana knew she had finally grown up. She'd faced the truth about her betrothal to Yitzhak and seen the ugliness of her self-pitying grief for him. She'd learned what it meant to make a commitment and keep her word, deciding to trust Malkijah and not annul their betrothal. Abba also had given his word when he'd signed her ketubah and when he'd committed to rebuilding the wall. Chana would do everything in her power to help her father be a man of his word. So many decisions in her life weren't hers to make, but these were.

"By day the Lord directs his love, at night his song is with me—a prayer to the God of my life. . . ." She thought of Queen Esther as she watched Abba drift in and out of sleep. Esther's life had also been under others' control. She'd been orphaned, carried into exile, forced to join the king's beauty contest, chosen for his harem, then marked for execution. Yet Esther had shown courage and intelligence as she'd used the means available to her to bring about change. Chana wondered what means she had available to change things in her loved ones' lives.

"Put your hope in God, for I will yet praise him, my Savior and my God. . . ." In spite of her ongoing argument with Governor Nehemiah, she respected him and the work he was trying to accomplish. That's why worry over the conspiracy that Nava had overheard—and Malkijah's part in it—continued to plague

Chana. Her father was a district leader, loyal to Nehemiah; she should report what she knew for Abba's sake. But how could she do that without betraying Malkijah? *Lord, show me what to do*, she prayed.

Chana was deep in thought, asking the Almighty One for help, when her sister Yudit came to the bedroom door. "Malkijah is here. He wants to talk to you." Yudit took Chana's place at Abba's bedside while Chana rose and went out to where Malkijah stood waiting in the courtyard. A crescent moon hovered just above the wall and stars filled the sky above Jerusalem. They had no right to shine so brightly, so beautifully, with Abba so gravely ill.

"Was that you singing, just now?" he asked. "It sounded beautiful."

"Thank you."

"How is your father? And how are you?" Malkijah looked as weary as the governor had, his eyelids drooping when he blinked as if they wanted to remain closed. "Is there anything I can do?"

"Everyone keeps asking that. I don't think there's much anyone can do. We're trying to relieve his pain and the swelling with poultices. Now we just have to wait."

"I heard you're taking his place, supervising his section of the wall."

She exhaled. "News travels fast in Jerusalem. . . . Please don't ask me to stop, Malkijah."

He started to speak, then didn't. Chana waited. "At least let me send a bodyguard to protect you," he finally said.

"That's not necessary."

"Chana, remember your concern when I injured my hand?" He held it up for her to see, the linen bandage dazzlingly white in the moonlight. "Can you imagine how I must feel, knowing the danger you're in when you're outside the wall? Our enemies could shoot arrows from a distance without warning."

"How will a bodyguard help against arrows?"

"He'll give me peace of mind." She didn't reply, chafing at the idea of having a watchdog trailing behind her. "I have so many things on my mind right now, Chana, including my concern for your father and for you. Don't make me add one more to them by refusing to take a guard with you."

She nodded her agreement, sorry for her stubbornness. "If it would ease your mind."

"It would. I can imagine how worried you must be about your father. If you need to talk about it . . ."

Chana was about to say that she had Yudit and Sarah to talk to, then realized that maybe Malkijah needed someone to confide in. He had just told her he had many things on his mind right now, and she wondered if the conspiracy was one of them. Maybe Chana could work behind the scenes, like Queen Esther, and talk him out of joining it. If Malkijah trusted her, perhaps he would listen to her.

She surprised him by taking his hand and leading him up to her rooftop, where they could be alone. The shadow of the wall loomed above them in the darkness, blocking out the moon. "Maybe it would help if you talked to me about these things that occupy your mind," she said. "I can see that you need rest."

"Do I really look that bad?"

"Yes. How long has it been since you went home to eat and sleep and change your clothes?"

He smiled. "I can't remember."

"Tell me what's worrying you, Malkijah."

His smile faded. He stared into the distance, taking a long time to reply. "I think I've lost the governor's trust. He's disappointed in me for not taking his oath." He looked at her again and said, "I know you were disappointed in me, too. I tried to explain to him why I couldn't do it, but I'm not sure he understood. I even offered to resign."

"What did he say?"

"He wouldn't accept my resignation. But the loss of his

confidence worries me, especially now. I need him to trust me more than ever."

"Why?" she asked, dreading his reply.

Again, he hesitated as his mind seemed to wrestle with something. "Chana, I need your help. I need to tell you something that no one else knows. But first I have to be sure I have your complete trust."

Her heart raced as she paused to think. She had pledged her life to him, and their marriage had to be based on trust. Abba had just said that he entrusted all three of his daughters to Malkijah's care if he died. And now Malkijah needed her help. She took his hand again. "Yes. You have my trust."

He let out the breath he'd been holding. "I was asked to join a group of noblemen who are plotting against the governor. I pretended interest so I could find out who is behind it, and I got them to give me one more name—Shecaniah ben Arah. That means Tobiah the Ammonite is involved, because he's married to Shecaniah's daughter. Tobiah has been trying to gain power here in Judah for a long time. He probably wants to govern in Nehemiah's place. I've agreed to meet with the group again so I can find out what their plans are and who else is involved in the conspiracy. Then I can warn Governor Nehemiah—if he'll still listen to me."

"Why don't you tell him now?"

"He has too many men surrounding him. Until I learn who some of the other conspirators are, I can't trust anyone. Some of the men closest to Nehemiah might be involved. Even his brothers, for all I know."

"But if this goes too far and you get caught, everyone will think you're a traitor."

"I know, I know. That's why I'm telling you. I may need you to back up my story."

She felt frightened for him and very worried. He walked a dangerous path. Then an idea for how she could help began to form in her mind. "Nehemiah makes his rounds every day, inspecting the progress on the wall," she said. "When he comes to my father's section tomorrow, I'll talk to him in private and tell him everything you just told me about the conspiracy. I'll tell him you aren't a traitor but that you're trying to find out who the rebels really are."

"Make sure you're alone with him, Chana, and that no one else is listening—not even his brothers or the trumpeter he takes everywhere."

"Should I tell him about Shecaniah ben Arah?"

"Yes. And tell him that Meshullam is the man who asked me to join. Meshullam also has ties by marriage to Tobiah. I know Nehemiah has received letters from Tobiah, trying to intimidate him into forming an alliance, but tell the governor that neither Tobiah nor his father-in-law nor his son-in-law can be trusted. They're behind this conspiracy."

"I will."

"And, Chana, Nehemiah's life may be in danger. He shouldn't trust anyone until I find out who else is involved."

"Please be careful, Malkijah."

"I will." He patted the sword that hung from his belt. "I have to go. Thanks for your help."

Chana walked downstairs with him, knowing she wouldn't sleep, knowing she not only needed to pray for her father but also for Malkijah and the governor.

"And, Chana . . ." Malkijah said before closing her gate, "don't leave this house tomorrow without the guard I'm sending."

CHAPTER

42

BETH HAKKEREM

S weat dampened Nava's forehead as she stood over the fire, cooking onions and garlic and chunks of savory lamb. She and the small kitchen crew had worked since dawn to prepare the midday meal for the grape harvesters. She missed working in the Jerusalem house alongside her friend Rachel. "In the city, we had to cook for three times as many laborers as this every day," she told Penina. "And it was much hotter there than here."

"It's still early in the harvest season," Penina told her. "Things will get busier once all the laborers return and the full harvest begins." She walked to where Nava worked and sprinkled handfuls of cumin and coriander into the pot. The fragrant aroma filled Nava's nostrils, making her stomach rumble with hunger. She thought of her parents and older brothers, wondering if they were harvesting their grapes—and if they had enough food to eat.

"How is the progress on Jerusalem's wall coming along?" one of the other servants asked Nava. "Could you see it from our master's house?"

"Not from his house, but I had a good view from the top of the temple mount. The wall around the city looked nearly finished when I left."

"Already? That was fast."

"Yes. Hundreds of men all work on it at the same time. And they even built a fortress on the north side by the temple."

Mentioning the temple reminded Nava of Dan, and a knot of grief lumped in her throat. She had no idea when she would see him again. She missed being near him at the sacrifice every day, secretly holding his hand, being reassured of his love. They'd enjoyed more than a month together before she'd been sent back here to Beth Hakkerem, and now she worried that without her by his side, Dan's anger toward Malkijah would burn dangerously hot.

At last the lamb was cooked and the bread baked. But Nava had no time to sit down and rest and eat. "You need to help us carry the food out to the vineyard to the workmen," Penina told her. "We'll all eat outside with them."

"But isn't Master Aaron working in the vineyard, too?"

"He may be. It doesn't matter. I need your help. Stay close beside me if you're worried."

Nava was worried. Shimon had told her to pray, not for herself but for Aaron. She didn't understand how she could pray for a man she hated, nor did she really believe that prayer would do any good. She lifted a full water jug and balanced it on her head, remembering the countless jars she had carried to help water Abba's land. She slipped her arm through the handle of a basket of bread and followed the other women out of the compound, making sure to stay close to Penina. They climbed uphill to the vineyard, halting at the lowest terrace where they laid out the food. The workmen quickly gathered around, grateful for the refreshment.

Just as she'd feared, Master Aaron arrived to eat with his workers, and judging by the spotless linen robe he wore, he wasn't doing much work. He didn't even have a knife to cut the stems or a basket to collect the grape clusters like all the other men did. Nava turned away the moment she saw him and hurried over to stand beside Penina with her back to him. When she felt a hand on her shoulder, she knew it was his.

"Here you are, my beauty," he said. "What a nice surprise. And I see you walked all the way up here without dropping the water jug or spilling the bread. Who was it that said you were clumsy? They were wrong."

"Do you need something, Master Aaron?" she asked.

He leaned close to whisper, "You." He still had his hand on her shoulder and the hot weight of it seemed to burn all the way to her skin. Penina held out the basket of bread to him, and he finally pulled his hand away to take a piece. "Which dish did you cook?" he asked Nava as he bit into it.

"I helped Penina cook the lamb."

"It looks delicious—just like you." He grinned at her, but his smile didn't reach his eyes. Shimon was right, Aaron didn't look happy, even though he was the master of all these people, the heir to this prosperous estate. *"Pray for him,"* Shimon had said. But she couldn't do it.

"Come on, Nava," Aaron said. "I'm going to help myself to this food, and I want you to sit right beside me while I eat."

Her stomach turned at the thought. But she would be safe, she told herself, with so many other people around. The kitchen crew arranged the food in the middle of a rug and all the workers sat around it in a circle, dipping into the bowls with their bread. The men quickly moved aside to make room for Aaron and he sank down on the rug, propped on one elbow while he ate. Nava knelt beside him, keeping her eye on Penina and the other servers eating off to one side. Nava planned to jump up and go with her the moment Penina prepared to leave.

"What are you thinking about, my beauty?" Aaron asked as he chewed a mouthful of lamb.

She decided to tell him the truth. "I was thinking that you have so much. All of this will be yours someday. Yet you don't seem to care about any of it. And you don't respect your father."

An angry look replaced his smirk. "What are you talking about?"

"I've seen you stealing his wine. And when he asks you to work, you disobey him the moment his back is turned."

He glanced around as if to see if anyone had heard her. "That's none of your business," he said. "You never saw any of those things."

Nava drew courage from his anger. Maybe if she made him mad, he would leave her alone. "I'm working here because I want to help my father pay his debts. He didn't want me to become a bondservant, but I offered to do it because I love him. My love will cost me six years of my life. Would you do the same for your father?"

His nasty grin settled back into place. "I'll never have to. My father and I are noblemen, not common farmers." He made *farmer* sound like a curse, not the blessing she knew it was. She thought of how Dan loved growing wheat and olives and grapes and wanted nothing more than to marry her and work on his land.

"What do you really want, Master Aaron?" she asked.

He leaned close, his breath warm on her face. "You . . . I have a right to make you mine, you know."

Nava's heart raced. "You have a right to marry me, but that isn't what you'll do. You'll steal what you want like you stole the wine, then refuse to take the blame."

"And no one is going to stop me."

"What would your father say if he knew what you were doing behind his back?"

Aaron leaned close again. "He won't ever know because you're not going to tell, are you? Besides, he would believe me before he'd believe a lowly, disgruntled servant. And you know what? I always get what I want."

"And will that make you happy? You might take what isn't yours, but something important will still be missing."

"What could be missing?" he asked, spreading his hands. "Look around. All this is mine. Including you."

Nava did look around, and she saw that the servers had finished eating. They were starting to gather up the leftovers. She rose to her feet. "I have to go."

"No, you don't." He gripped her ankle. "I'm the boss, and I'll tell you when you can go."

"Your workers are watching you," she said, tilting her head toward the circle of men still seated around the rug.

She knew he couldn't do anything to harm her without making a scene. The moment he released his grip on her ankle, Nava hurried away to join Penina and the others. "Are you okay?" Penina asked.

Nava nodded. "I think I made him angry."

"Why did you do a foolish thing like that? You better hope he doesn't punish you for it."

Nava had all afternoon to worry about Penina's warning and wonder how Master Aaron might retaliate. When it was time to milk the goats at the end of the day, she told her friend Shimon what had happened as they sat side by side on their milking stools. "Master Aaron ordered me to sit with him at lunch, so I started talking to him. I asked why he was so disrespectful to his father, stealing his wine and disobeying him. I made him angry, Shimon."

"You're the first person in a long time to stand up to him."

"Penina said he would probably make me pay for being so outspoken, and now I'm more worried than ever."

Shimon stopped milking. He looked over at Nava with a wistful smile on his face. "You may be the answer to all of my prayers for that boy."

"Me? How? Aaron came right out and admitted what he wants from me, and it's exactly what I feared. What if it happens, Shimon?"

"I've witnessed a lot of terrible things in my lifetime. A lot of injustice. But the Almighty One always brings good from it."

"How dare you sit there and tell me that God wants me to get attacked! That He'll bring something good out of it!" She bolted to her feet, scaring both of their goats. "I thought you were my friend, but I don't want anything to do with you and your horrible prayers. You can finish milking by yourself."

Shimon grabbed her arm, stopping her. "If Aaron has his way with you, one of two things will happen. Malkijah will either set you free, or Aaron will have to marry you. Either way, our master will finally see what sort of a man his son is, and how his own greed has contributed to it."

"You're wrong! Neither of those things will happen because Master Malkijah will never believe me."

"I'll make sure he does this time. I've been praying for him to wake up and discipline his sons while there is still time. If the Almighty One answers my prayers, maybe Malkijah will set all of his other bondservants free, too. Rachel can go home to her husband and children. That young stable boy can go home to his family and grow up a free man."

"My virtue is too great of a price to pay. I want to marry Dan, not Aaron."

"If your young man refuses to marry you because of something that happened that was out of your control, then what kind of a man is he? What does that say about his love for you?"

"And what does it say about you that you would ask such a sacrifice from me? Why are you praying for all these things to happen? Why are you praying for our greedy masters at all?"

He finally released her arm. "I have my reasons."

"I think I have a right to know what those reasons are." Shimon didn't reply. "I thought you were my friend," she said again, then hurried back to the kitchen, leaving Shimon to finish milking the goats by himself.

That night, Nava moved her sleeping mat to the other side of the half-deserted dormitory, making sure she slept right beside Penina's bed.

JERUSALEM

Nehemiah looked around in frustration at the knot of men standing by his field headquarters, getting ready to follow him. His escort was turning into an entourage, slowing him down as he toured the wall each day, inspecting the progress. He hated being hemmed in by crowds. The guards with their swords and spears were probably necessary, especially if the enemy attacked. He needed the trumpeter to sound a warning. And his brothers served as his closest aides and confidantes. But the rest of the men—nobles from Beth Zur and Keilah and Mizpah along with their followers and servants—made Nehemiah uneasy. Were these men loyal to him, or were they gathering information for his enemies?

A growing posse of common people also trailed him on his rounds, people who reached out to touch him or thank him for the food he'd contributed from his storehouses or express their gratitude for freeing them from bond service. Many of them insisted they wanted to guard and protect him, in spite of his assurances that he already had capable guards. Their adoration had made Nehemiah uncomfortable at first, and he had tried to send them away. But he had slowly become accustomed to it, and now, as their adored leader, it seemed ungracious of him to reject their expressions of thanks or to shoo them away.

"Listen, all of you," he said as he pushed his way through the growing crowd, preparing to leave. "It isn't advisable for all of you to come. It's going to be a long, difficult walk on a very hot day. And I can already tell you about our progress—the wall is nearly finished. Only the gates and a few sections of wall still need to be rebuilt."

The district leader from Mizpah stepped forward. "I think I speak for all the others when I say that we want to see the work for ourselves. Please, lead the way."

Nehemiah gave up and headed toward the Valley Gate. On the night he'd first inspected that gate, the fallen stones that blocked the opening had forced him and his men to pass through in single file. Now the wide casemate gate had newly built chambers for guards and a lookout tower on top.

Nehemiah turned south, taking the road through the Central Valley, as he had on his nighttime inspection two months ago. The jumble of toppled stones that once formed a massive blockade had been cleared away, then recut and used to rebuild this long, five-hundred-yard stretch of wall to its original height. All the gaps had been closed. He stopped to speak with Hanun, the section supervisor, and congratulate him for a job well done.

"You and the residents of Zanoah volunteered for a very long section," Nehemiah said. "I've seen firsthand the monumental effort it took your building crew to move all this debris and reshape it into a wall. Thank you for working so hard."

Farther on he came to the King's Pool, now completely hidden behind the new wall. It was no longer possible to draw water from outside the city wall the way his escort of Persian troops had done when they'd camped in this valley. The fresh springwater that filled the pool could be safely accessed only from inside the city. "Once again, Jerusalem's water supply is secure in the event of a siege," he told the men looking on.

They came next to the Dung Gate, which occupied a strategic point of land at the junction of the Hinnom, Kidron, and Central Valleys. Malkijah and his men had worked hard—not only restoring the gate but also the tower above it, which provided an outstanding vantage point in all three directions. The doors weren't finished or hung in place, nor had the cobblestone street been restored. Nehemiah greeted Malkijah but didn't stay to talk with him, still wondering what to make of this leader who refused to support his social reforms.

He continued up the Kidron Valley, arriving at the Fountain Gate, which perched on a bare scarp of bedrock. It looked nearly complete except for the doors and bars. The stairs leading from the gate up to the city had also been restored. From here, Nehemiah's way had been blocked on that first night, and even after dismounting, he'd been unable to proceed very far. Debris from the deteriorated terraces still lay strewn across the hillside, but he could see that the new wall, built higher up on the edge of the cliff, neared completion.

From here the city's ridge sloped uphill, and the wall was too high above his head for Nehemiah to inspect properly. He retraced his steps, entering the city through the Fountain Gate, then climbed the steps and continued up the hill through the city. "Look at all the deserted homes in this part of Jerusalem," he told his brothers. "It seems a shame that no one ever rebuilt them or lived in them."

"The entire Mishneh is deserted, too," Hanani said. "Not enough people want to settle in Jerusalem."

"I can understand why people would want to return to their ancestral land, but can you think of any way we can eventually repopulate the city?" No one had an answer for him.

They continued walking on the inside of the wall, following the street up to the Water Gate where Nehemiah saw a gathering crowd. "The Almighty One hears our cries," a woman shouted. "He gives us victory over our enemies! They are afraid to attack!"

Nehemiah recognized the prophetess Noadiah's voice. "Let's go a different way," he said. He tried to turn around, but the people following him jammed the street.

"Governor Nehemiah!" the prophetess called out. The crowd surged and moved around him like water until he and Noadiah stood in the middle of it, surrounded. "Blessed are you, Nehemiah ben Hacaliah. You have been called by the Almighty One, anointed like Judah's kings for His purposes. Since the days of Moses, God has promised to send His appointed leader to shepherd His people, and the Almighty One has His hand upon you. There is a king in Judah!"

"Listen, I'm your governor, not your king."

But the people took up Noadiah's chant: "There is a king in Judah! A king in Judah!"

"I'm not a king!" he insisted. No one listened to him. Nehemiah managed to push his way forward again, but now the crowd that had stopped to hear the prophetess followed him, as well, pressing close. Two guards walked on either side of him, but Nehemiah knew that anyone in the mob could pull out a knife and stab him before his guards could react.

"Is it true that you're the Messiah?" someone shouted.

"No. I came to rebuild the wall."

"But all the people look to you!" someone else said. "You've saved us!"

Somehow, the prophetess had worked her way ahead of Nehemiah and now she stepped in front of him, forcing him to halt. "God has made it clear, Governor, that if we return to Him, He'll give us victory over our enemies and restore our nation. He promised to set us free from foreign oppression. And the Almighty One is with you, Nehemiah ben Hacaliah. He granted you favor with King Artaxerxes. Now He asks you to rule His people."

"King Artaxerxes made me governor of Judah for only a temporary term. I have no more authority than that."

Once again, he plowed through the people. "Her so-called prophecy has me worried," Nehemiah told his brothers, who managed to keep up with him. His voice was low. "If news of it gets back to Susa—"

"Our enemies will make sure that it does," Ephraim said.

"I know. I may have to send my own messenger to the Persian king to assure him of my loyalty."

"But that could backfire if our enemies don't send a report," Hanani said. "If you protest too much, won't it seem like you have a guilty conscience?"

Nehemiah continued walking, his mind in turmoil. He didn't dare ask the question out loud, but what if Noadiah was right and God truly had chosen him to be king? What if the Almighty One had sent her to proclaim His will? As a mere cupbearer to Artaxerxes, Nehemiah never would have dreamed he would be here in Jerusalem, rebuilding the city, governing God's people. But the Almighty One had proven to be the God of the impossible. Maybe He really was calling Nehemiah to reign on King David's throne. Think of what else he might accomplish after the wall was finished. Independence from Persia? Freedom from their heavy taxation? He had the support and trust of the people and the nobles. And even if the Persian army did seem invincible, hadn't the Almighty One helped Joshua conquer the Promised Land against enormous odds? Yet something about Noadiah's prophecy still didn't seem right to him. Should he trust her words or his own misgivings? She continued to follow him, encouraging the people to chant: "A king in Judah! A king in Judah!"

Nehemiah turned to her and to the chanting people. "Please stop. . . . I'm asking you to stop."

"How can we be silent?" Noadiah said. "The Almighty One has spoken! You'll see the truth when His words come to pass." The crowd responded with an enormous cheer.

He took the stairs to the temple, hoping to leave everyone behind as he continued his inspection of the walls on the north side of Jerusalem. The temple's citadel had always been one of his chief concerns, and he'd watched the priests, under the direction of Eliashib, labor to complete it. "We need more timber," the high priest told Nehemiah after greeting him.

"Talk to Ephraim," Nehemiah replied. "He can tell you when the next shipment is due to arrive." Nehemiah still questioned Eliashib's loyalty after Rebbe Ezra's warning that he had ties with Sanballat by marriage. How could the Almighty One's high priest allow his grandson to marry a Samaritan? The question remained unanswered.

The afternoon heat pressed down on Nehemiah like a weight by the time he reached the three western gates. The main roads from the Mediterranean Coast, Samaria, and Damascus all converged in this section of the city below the temple mount. The gates looked nearly finished, lacking only their doors. Surely Judah's enemies knew the wall was close to completion. What would they do next to try to stop him?

As he neared the Valley Gate where he had begun his tour, Nehemiah saw Shallum's daughter directing the final stages of work on her father's section of the wall. His temper threatened to race out of control, but he kept it in check by observing how solid and strong and high this section was. How it joined seamlessly with the Valley Gate and the Tower of the Ovens. In a few more days it would be finished, and Chana would be forced to go back inside where she belonged. She strode over to him when she saw him approaching, and he noticed that she had a guard with her, following her movements like a shadow.

"Good afternoon, Governor."

"Good afternoon. How is your father?"

Her chin quivered with emotion. "He's no better. He suffered terribly last night, barely able to breathe. Miryam says we'll know in a few more days if . . ."

"I'm sorry." He wouldn't make her say it. He pointed to the wall and said, "Your section looks solid. And nearly complete, I see."

"Yes. It is." She was being very gracious, not combative like yesterday. Yet something made her nervous. Was it concern for her father? "Governor, do you have a moment to talk?" she asked. She stared pointedly at his entourage and added, "In private?"

"Let's go over here." Nehemiah held up his hand to keep the others back, then walked a few yards away from everyone to stand with Chana in the shadow of the wall. He waited. When she finally spoke, her voice was so low he had to lean close to hear her above the tapping chisels and creaking crane ropes.

"Malkijah ben Recab asked me to relay a message to you. Meshullam ben Berekiah and a group of other nobles asked him to join a conspiracy against you. Several officials are involved, including Shecaniah ben Arah—which means that Tobiah the Ammonite is behind this."

Nehemiah fought the urge to groan out loud. Would the opposition and intrigue ever stop? He had feared from the very beginning that he couldn't trust some of men on his council, but to learn of an active conspiracy among his noblemen shook him. He glanced at his entourage, wondering if any of these men were involved.

"Malkijah wants you to know that he is loyal to you," Chana continued. "But he's allowing the conspirators to believe that he's on their side so he can find out who the others are and what they're planning."

"A spy?"

Chana nodded. "Yes."

"Why didn't he tell me himself?"

"Because he doesn't know if he can trust the men surrounding you. Any one of them might be a traitor in disguise. Malkijah asked me to relay the message to you, thinking they wouldn't suspect a woman to be involved."

"I see."

"He also wanted me to warn you to be on your guard. He

thinks the conspirators plan to assassinate you and replace you with Tobiah the Ammonite. You need to be very careful."

Would they kill his brothers, too? Nehemiah glanced over at Hanani and Ephraim and knew he needed to distance himself from them for their own good. "Please thank Malkijah for me."

"I will. He's meeting with the group again, and as soon as he has more information, he'll pass it on to you through me."

Nehemiah nodded. "I'm going to walk away now and pretend we were talking about the wall or your father or anything else but this."

"I understand."

But Nehemiah didn't move. There was something else he needed to say. "My opinion about you working on the wall hasn't changed," he said. "I still want you to go back inside and let someone else finish. But I do admire your courage, Chana."

He strode back to the others, trying to pretend that what Chana had just told him hadn't shaken him to his soul. Any of the men with him, even the young man who carried the signal trumpet, could be an enemy, not a friend. And the wall was so close to being finished.

"What did she want?" Hanani asked.

Nehemiah shook his head, waving his hand as if exasperated with her. "She's determined to defy me and continue building the wall. At least she has a bodyguard now."

Nehemiah returned to his headquarters then, but his mind could only focus on his brothers. He had kept them nearby, thinking they would be safe with him, but that was no longer true. There was a plot against his life, and he didn't want them to become innocent victims. "From now on we need to pour all of our effort in finishing the doors," he told them. "Ephraim, you need to concentrate on securing the timber we need. Hanani, I need you to work with Ephraim from now on.

Take guards with you wherever you go. Finishing the gates is our most important task."

"Are you all right?" Hanani asked.

For the space of a heartbeat, Nehemiah remembered huddling with Hanani and Ephraim behind the wooden chest as his parents were being slaughtered. He cleared his throat. "Of course I am. Go get started."

He couldn't deny that the day's events had shaken him. But he would finish building Jerusalem's walls, God helping him. And then he would try to figure out if it was the Almighty One's will for him to reign as Judah's king.

CHAPTER
44

SANBALLAT'S PALACE, SAMARIA

Tobiah tried to maintain a serene façade, masking his frustration and anger as he took his seat in Sanballat's private meeting room. His allies, Sanballat and Geshem, weren't as successful in hiding their anxiety. Sanballat fidgeted on his throne, his round face flushed and sweating. Geshem sat in a chair for once instead of pacing, perched straight-backed and rigid on his seat, his arms folded inside the sleeves of his robes. Nothing was going right for any of them.

By Tobiah's own calculations, he should be sitting in the governor's residence in Jerusalem at this moment, ruling in Nehemiah's place. The fact that he wasn't continued to astound and anger him. His network of faithful men reported Nehemiah's every move and worked to undermine him. He and Sanballat and Geshem had thrown numerous obstacles in Nehemiah's path, and had even attacked his workers. Yet nothing shook Nehemiah's firm resolve or halted the construction for very long.

"I heard that Jerusalem's wall has now been rebuilt," Sanballat said. "Is it true, Tobiah? Have you seen it?"

"It's true. The doors haven't been set in place yet, but no gaps remain in the wall." His allies murmured their unease and disbelief.

"How much longer will it take to complete the gates?" Geshem asked.

"Unless we stop them, they'll probably finish in time for the fall feasts."

"How is that possible?" Sanballat shouted. "The work began not even two months ago. I saw that crumbling, ruined wall myself and it's . . . it's just not possible to rebuild miles of walls in such a short time!"

"Especially with all the disruptions we've thrown at them," Geshem added.

"We greatly underestimated our enemy," Tobiah said, although it galled him to admit it. "Nehemiah not only refuses to quit, he shows no sign of fear. Somehow he has kept the people motivated and the work moving forward."

Sanballat shook his head in disbelief, his face turning redder still. "If he can accomplish this in a matter of months, who knows what he'll do next—and equally fast."

"That's what worries me," Geshem said. "How swiftly he moves! We never even heard of the man two months ago. He has become an extremely dangerous enemy."

"The way I see it, we have one last chance to halt the fortification of Jerusalem," Sanballat said. "Once he installs the doors of the gates, the city will be impregnable. It will take an army bigger than any of ours to defeat him."

"The only way to stop him is to kill him," Geshem said. His eyes bored into Tobiah.

"I've searched for opportunities to kill him," Tobiah said, "but Nehemiah is exceedingly cautious and always keenly aware of the security surrounding him. He has armed bodyguards. No one can get near him."

"We never should have let him get this far," Geshem said.

"He created a fortress for himself, and even if we do manage to kill him, any future Judean leader will also benefit from it."

Tobiah secretly hoped to be that next leader, governing behind Jerusalem's newly secure walls. "What concerns me," he said, "is that Nehemiah might grow even stronger and take over the entire region. And if the Persian king sees him as a threat, he will retaliate against all of us."

"What are we currently doing to stop him?" Geshem asked. "The sneak attacks backfired. Every Judean is now armed. Nehemiah has everything he needs to start a rebellion and assume control—the backing of the people, his own army, a fortified city . . ."

"Not everyone supports him," Tobiah said. "I've organized a group of Judean noblemen who are on our side, and they're conspiring against him behind the scenes. They'll never let Nehemiah grab total power. The prophets we hired have been at work, too, proclaiming Nehemiah as Judah's king and infuriating these leaders. They want control over their people again. He's a threat to them. They're working to undermine him from within and topple him." Tobiah didn't add that he was poised to take Nehemiah's place after that happened.

Sanballat shifted in his seat, tugging at the neck of his robe. "What about the common people, Tobiah? I hear they'll do anything for him. He's their Savior. Is there any way to discredit him in their eyes so they'll turn against him?"

Tobiah smiled to himself, noticing the subtle shift in this meeting. Sanballat and the other leaders asked him all these questions and looked to him for answers. They would be indebted to him once he solved the problem of Nehemiah, making it inevitable for him to take his place as Judah's governor. "I've been working on a plan that will reveal Nehemiah as a coward in front of all the people and even their religious leaders like Rebbe Ezra. All I have to do is get him to violate the Torah in a very public way."

Sanballat gave an uneasy shrug. "Anything is worth a try, I suppose. But is it enough?"

"We must do more," Geshem said. "I say we lure him out of the city so we can assassinate him along the way. He can't bring his entire civilian army with him if the gates are unfinished and the city is still vulnerable to attack. Nehemiah will have no choice but to leave most of his men behind. And as governor, he's obligated to meet with us if Sanballat, the regional governor, summons him."

"Yes. That's a very good plan," Sanballat said. "The people will lose heart if they lose their leader. They'll never complete all the gates."

Tobiah didn't say so out loud, but he wondered if Nehemiah might become an even more powerful figure as a martyr. "Let's do it," he agreed. "I'll keep working behind the scenes, conspiring with Judah's nobles and trying to turn the people and priests against him. You work on luring him out of Jerusalem and attacking him along the way. Nehemiah can't possibly survive all of these plans."

And then Tobiah's own plans would finally fall into place.

❧ ❦

From the top of the wall near the citadel, Nehemiah saw the official diplomatic messengers as they approached Jerusalem and arrived at the Yeshana Gate. But he returned to his work, unwilling to spare a moment of his time for them. Eliashib and the other priests who worked on the citadel seemed surprised that Nehemiah didn't immediately go down to meet the delegation.

"If you need to leave and respond to the messengers, Governor," Eliashib said, "we can finish this without you."

"The messengers can wait."

"But they're flying the banners of the Samaritan capitol."

"I don't care if they're flying Persian banners. Finishing this gate is much more important."

When Nehemiah finally did return to his residence later that afternoon, he found a group of Judean nobles waiting impatiently for him. "We're very concerned about this message from Samaria," they told him. "We've been waiting to see what it's about." Nehemiah had no idea if these noblemen supported him or were part of the conspiracy, but he took his personal bodyguards into the council chamber with him, just in case. He broke the clay seal bearing Governor Sanballat's official stamp and glanced over the document before speaking.

"It's a summons, signed by Sanballat, Tobiah the Ammonite, Geshem the Arab, and the Edomite leader—all of our neighbors. They're holding a conference to discuss matters of common interest among the provinces of The Land Beyond the River. The message says, 'Come, let us meet together in one of the villages on the plain of Ono.'"

"The plain of Ono?" one of the nobles asked. "That's northwest of here near the Great Sea. Why make it so far away?"

"They deliberately chose a remote area on the farthest limits of Judean territory," Nehemiah said.

"When will this conference take place?" another nobleman asked. "We must follow diplomatic protocol and attend. We've always tried to maintain good relations with the other provinces that make up The Land Beyond the River."

"Go if you'd like," Nehemiah said, rolling up the scroll, "but I won't be attending. They're scheming to harm me. This isn't an innocent invitation, it's a trap."

"How can you be so sure?"

"It reminds me of Cain's seemingly innocent invitation to Abel: 'Let's go out to the field'—away from witnesses, away from help."

"We could take soldiers with us," the leader of Mizpah said.

Nehemiah shook his head. "We don't have professional soldiers. If our enemies attacked us along the way, I would be putting innocent people at risk—fathers, husbands, sons. Besides, I won't leave Jerusalem undefended. I need every available man to stand guard until the gates are finished. Our enemies probably know that, which is why they're asking to meet now and not a few weeks from now when the gates are completed."

"If you're the only leader who refuses to come, Governor, they could accuse you of treason," a nobleman insisted. "The Persian government expects us to cooperate with area leaders. It will look like an act of rebellion if you refuse."

"Or an act of cowardice," another nobleman added.

"I don't care how it looks," Nehemiah said. "Let people think whatever they want to. I'm not foolish enough to walk into their trap. Nor will I halt construction to attend a phony conference."

"How would you like me to respond to the message?" his scribe asked.

"Send this reply back with the messenger: 'I am carrying on a great project and cannot go down. Why should the work stop while I leave it and go down to you?'"

"That's all?"

"That's more than sufficient."

CHAPTER
45

JERUSALEM

Chana returned home from working on the wall shortly before the evening sacrifice and went straight to her father's bedside. "Is he any better?" she asked her sisters. But even in the darkened room she could see Abba's pale, swollen face, hear his tortured breathing. Yudit led her out to the courtyard, with Sarah following.

"Miryam says his illness is at its worst. Abba can't swallow, he can't eat, can't talk. He can barely breathe."

"And one side of his body is becoming paralyzed," Sarah added. "Including the arm that the scorpion stung."

"We need to go up to the temple together and pray," Chana decided. "All three of us. Right now." Neither of her sisters had left Abba's side for days, and Chana knew they all needed to be reminded of God's power and sovereignty.

"But we can't leave Abba—" Sarah protested.

"Miryam will stay with him. Come on." Chana had spent hours praying for her father, believing that the Almighty One had the power to heal him—yet aware that He might not. When God hadn't healed Yitzhak, grief and anger had overwhelmed her, but she couldn't afford to let that happen this time. She had to be strong for Yudit's and Sarah's sakes. "We'd better hurry or we'll be late."

Chana practically dragged her sisters out of the house and up the hill to the temple. She hoped that as they stood listening to the Levite choir, inhaling the fragrant aroma of the sacrifice, and seeing the pillar of smoke ascending to heaven, they would find God's peace, His presence. Maybe their hope would be renewed, too.

They arrived just as the Levites began to sing the liturgy, and the words of the psalm led Chana into prayer. *"I cry aloud to the Lord; I lift up my voice to the Lord for mercy. I pour out my complaint before him; before him I tell my trouble."* When the song ended, one of the priests sacrificed the lamb, and the Levites helped prepare it for the altar. "We know the Almighty One is able to heal Abba," Chana whispered to her sisters, "but we have to accept His will no matter what happens."

"Not if He takes Abba!" Sarah said.

Chana thought of the moment when Yitzhak had died and said, "Yes. Even then. We have to trust God, even when we don't understand what He's doing."

"I don't think I can bear it," Yudit whispered.

"You know what Abba told me?" Chana asked. "He told me that he's praying for each of us while he lies there in bed. He's praying that we'll remain strong." She watched another priest enter the sanctuary to light the incense as the Levites sang, *"I cry to you, O Lord; I say, 'You are my refuge, my portion in the land of the living.'"*

"What if he dies?" Sarah asked in a tiny voice.

"We can't stop believing in God's goodness, even if Abba dies. He wouldn't want us to turn away from the Almighty One. He encouraged me to keep trusting after Yitzhak died, and he would tell us to do the same thing now."

"Why would God take Abba?" Yudit asked. "Everyone needs him. We need him."

Chana wrapped her arm around Yudit and pulled her close. "All our lives, we've believed that Abba's decisions were for our own good. We have to trust our heavenly Father the same way. Everything He does is for our good and for His purposes, even if we don't understand it."

By the time the service ended, Chana's faith did seem renewed. She hoped her sisters were encouraged, too. As they left the temple together, throngs of people gathered around them to ask about their father. These were people Abba had helped over the years, offering them advice, meting out justice, mourning with them when they grieved, praying for their needs, celebrating their joys. Many of them wept when Chana told them about his condition, and they promised to continue praying for him. "May we celebrate his recovery very soon," the last of the well-wishers said. Chana saw all the good her father had done, how both rich and poor held him in high regard. She remembered his words to her as she had sat by his bedside, and she shared them with her sisters.

"When Abba could still speak, he said that if he died, we shouldn't ask God 'Why?'—we should ask 'How?' How can we make the world a better place and show His love? And I just realized that Abba did that very thing after Mama died. He used his grief to become more compassionate, more giving. All these people who received Abba's care knew that God loved them because of him."

Sarah clung tighter to her, resting her head on Chana's shoulder as they walked. "Do you think Abba is going to die?"

"I honestly don't know." But either way, Chana knew that she wanted to follow her father's example, becoming a more compassionate person, no longer wrapped up in her own selfish interests but serving others the way he had.

Later that evening, Malkijah came to the house. Chana took him up to the rooftop to talk in private. Lamplight flickered in the windows of the houses below them, but it seemed a pale imitation of the vast expanse of twinkling stars above their heads revealing the greatness of God, the frailty of men. "I told Governor Nehemiah about the conspiracy," she said, "and how you only pretended to join it."

"Good. I have more names." Malkijah gave her a piece of parchment small enough to fit in the palm of her hand. The heading on top of the list said *Wedding Guests.* "I made it look like a list of people we're inviting to our wedding in case it falls into the wrong hands."

Chana barely glanced at the names, struck by the heading: *Wedding Guests.* She had promised to marry Malkijah when the wall was finished. And it was nearly finished. They would become man and wife soon. She prayed that her father would be there to celebrate with them. "I'll give this to the governor," she said.

"No, show it to him, but don't give it to him. It's too risky. Then burn it in the fire."

"I will."

"I assured the other conspirators that I would try to recruit your father when he recovers, so that gives me a good excuse to come here and pass new information on to you. We're meeting again at my estate in Beth Hakkerem. They're going to confide their plans to me then."

"At your home? Why are you inviting these evil men there?"

"It was their idea. They want me to prove my loyalty by agreeing to be seen with them, conspiring in my home. It's also evidence of my involvement if we're caught."

"Malkijah, please be careful. We have a wedding to plan, a real guest list to make." She didn't need to add that she had lost her fiancé once before, this close to their wedding. They were both well aware of it.

He lifted her hand and kissed it. "Don't worry. I'm always careful."

The next morning Chana went out through the Valley Gate to Abba's section of the wall for the last time. The work was finished. She merely had to supervise as the workmen dismantled the crane and took down the scaffolding and cleared away all the equipment. She watched for Governor Nehemiah while overseeing the work, anxious to show him Malkijah's list. When he finally arrived, it shocked her to see that two of the noblemen on Malkijah's list of conspirators accompanied him on his inspection tour.

"How is Shallum?" Nehemiah asked when he saw her.

"May I speak with you in private about him?" She drew him away from the others and stood with her back to them. But Nehemiah continued to survey his surroundings in his unusual, cautious way. She had once thought it strange that he always remained vigilant, unable to relax. Now she understood the very real dangers he faced. "My father is no better. He's at a critical stage, unable to eat, barely able to breathe."

"I'm very sorry to hear that."

Chana slid the parchment into his hand. "Here. This is for you to see. Malkijah asked me to show you this list of names and then destroy it." She watched his face as he read it and saw his jaw tighten.

"Please thank him for me."

"They're meeting again at his estate in Beth Hakkerem. He hopes to learn their plans. I'll let you know afterward." Nehemiah nodded and walked back to the waiting men. He took a few minutes to inspect the wall and compliment the workers on a job well done, then he and his entourage moved on toward the Valley Gate. Chana wondered how the governor coped with the knowledge that two traitors followed him wherever he went.

At the end of the day, Chana thanked all of her workers and returned home from the wall for the last time. She felt melancholy as she walked up the Street of the Bakers, sad to see the work she had enjoyed so much coming to an end. What could ever replace it? As she came through the gate, Yudit rushed out to meet her, smiling as she grabbed Chana's hands in hers.

"I have wonderful news! Abba is awake and talking again. He even ate a little soup."

Chana fell into Yudit's arms, hugging her tightly. "Oh, thank God! Thank God!" Then they hurried into his room to join him and Sarah. Chana sank down beside him, overjoyed to see him alert and no longer in pain, although he was still far from well. "I have good news for you, Abba. Your section of the wall is done. It's finished! We removed the scaffolding today and dismantled the crane. When you're back on your feet, we'll go out together to see it."

"My angels!" He managed to smile, despite his badly swollen face. "What would I do without my angels?"

"We were afraid you'd be seeing real angels, Abba," Sarah told him. "We were so worried about you."

"Paradise would have been a great disappointment to me," he said. "There couldn't possibly be any angels up there as beautiful as you three."

Chana rose to her feet again. "Come on. We need to go up to the temple for the evening sacrifice and thank the Almighty One for answering our prayers. We'll be back soon, Abba."

"Yes, go. Go. And thank Him for me, too."

Tears of joy and thanksgiving streamed down Chana's face throughout the service. Nearly losing her father had tested her faith, and she knew the ordeal had changed her. She would never take the people she loved for granted again. And like her father, she was determined to reach out to others from now on, to help them any way she could. As she left the temple again, Chana remembered her promise to help Nava, remembering how the servant girl had been sent back to Beth Hakkerem—back to Malkijah's son. Chana was trying to decide how to help when she spotted Malkijah in the crowd. "I'll catch up with you," she told her sisters. "I want to tell Malkijah the good news."

"Chana, you're smiling," he said when he saw her. "Can I assume your father is better?"

"Yes! He's awake and alert and asking for food."

"That's wonderful news."

Chana thought of Nava and said, "May I go with you to your estate for the meeting, Malkijah? I want to be there to support you."

"I don't want to involve you in this conspiracy."

"I'm going to be your wife soon. I already am involved. Please, I would like to get to know my new home and our servants." She could see his reluctance, but he finally agreed.

"I should warn you that the other men will probably exclude you from the meeting."

"That doesn't matter," she said. "Come home with me now, Malkijah, and say hello to my father. He'll be so happy to see you."

"Not nearly as happy as I am to see him."

Chana felt like singing as they descended the temple stairs together and walked down the hill to her home. The Almighty One had answered her prayers. Abba would live. Her section of the wall was finished. And now she would begin a new chapter in her life. She would become Malkijah's wife, walking beside him this way for the rest of her life. The idea still frightened her, but shouldn't life be an adventure?

CHAPTER
46

BETH HAKKEREM

Sweat dampened Nava's hair and the back of her tunic as she added more fuel to the cooking fire. She had spent the long, hot day standing over the hearth cooking lentils and chickpeas, stirring Penina's savory lamb stew, keeping the hearth fire going and the baking oven hot. Her master would return home from Jerusalem today, bringing guests, so the kitchen staff had to prepare an elaborate evening meal for them. Penina bustled around the courtyard shouting, "Watch what you're doing! . . . Be careful! Don't let that burn!" Everything had to be perfect.

Nava was drawing water from the well for her goats late in the afternoon when Master Malkijah and his guests arrived. She stood with her water jar, peering at the group as they dismounted near the stables, and it shocked her to see that one of the guests was the man who had conspired at dinner in Jerusalem. Her master had invited him to his estate—which meant that Malkijah was a traitor. Then Nava saw him help his fiancée, Chana, down from the saddle, and her remaining shards of hope vanished like snow in the sunshine. She couldn't expect any help from Chana if she was a traitor like the others. Nava

374

didn't understand how Chana could marry Malkijah knowing how greedy he was, how he refused to free his bondservants and cancel their debts. And that he was conspiring against Governor Nehemiah. As Malkijah's new wife, Chana would be on his side—and on Aaron's side—not Nava's. And she would be forced to continue working here for six long years.

She finished filling the water jar and finally let her bitter tears fall as she joined Shimon in the goat pen for the evening milking. "What's wrong, girlie?" he asked.

"I hate them! I hate them all!"

He sat down on his milking stool beside her with a sigh. "The Torah tells us not to seek revenge or bear a grudge. It says we must love our neighbor as we love ourselves."

"You should hate them, too. Our masters are liars and traitors."

"You have proof of that?"

"Yes. When I was in Jerusalem, I overheard Master Malkijah and another man conspiring against Governor Nehemiah—and now that man is one of Master's guests tonight."

"Conspiring? What do you mean? What did they say?"

"There's a group of noblemen who think the governor has too much power, and they want to stop him. They don't want him to help all the poor people like us."

Shimon stopped milking. He appeared shaken as he sat slump-shouldered on the stool. "I don't believe it of him. Malkijah wouldn't do something like that."

"Well, he is doing it. Now do you see what kind of man he is? He's not only selfish and greedy, he wants power!"

Shimon still hadn't moved. "It isn't right," he murmured. "What he's doing isn't right. And he knows better. . . ."

"Don't pray for him anymore, Shimon. He's a traitor. I wish I could think of a way to report him to the governor. I know Nehemiah is on our side. He tried to help us, and so now we should help him."

"We're not going to say anything, girlie."

"Why not? Why won't you speak up?"

"I don't want to see Malkijah ruined."

"Well, I do. He deserves it."

"Believe me, I want our master and his sons to see the greed in their hearts more than you'll ever know. I pray every day for them to change. But you and I can't change them. Even the governor wasn't able to make Malkijah be kind to the poor. Only God can change his heart."

Shimon's attitude toward their master baffled Nava. "Why do you even care? Why not just walk away from here and be free? You would never have to see any of them again."

He shook his head, his craggy face quivering as he battled his emotions. "I'll never leave here. I'll keep praying for Malkijah and his sons until the day I die." He turned to face Nava and their eyes met. "And I'm praying for you, too."

"That he'll set me free?"

"Yes. Free from the bitterness that's destroying you."

She looked away and finished the evening milking without speaking to Shimon again. He was right. In spite of all her efforts, Nava had allowed the poisonous vine of bitterness to grow and flourish and strangle her heart. But didn't she have a right to be angry? Her master was a greedy man who cared nothing about her or his other servants. He'd raised his sons to be even greedier than he was. They'd taken Abba's land, his flock of goats, and his crops. And they had taken Nava away from the man she loved. Yes, she had a right to hate them.

She was still upset after she'd finished all her work and retired for the night. Penina was already asleep after a long day of cooking, but Nava tossed for what seemed like hours, growing angrier and angrier at the traitors who dined in splendor instead of helping the poor. She climbed out of bed again. Across the courtyard, Malkijah and his guests still sat in the dining area even though it was late in the evening. Nava decided to eavesdrop and find out what they were discussing. Maybe then she could figure out a way to report them to Governor Nehemiah before it was too late.

She left her sleeping quarters and crept through the kitchen area in the dark. Watchmen patrolled the gates and the perimeter of the walled compound at night, so she took the long way around to the open-air dining room, sneaking past the main house and beneath the bedchamber windows. She hid behind a pomegranate tree next to the house, crouching in the shadows, away from the light that spilled from the lampstands in the dining area. She waited for her breathing to slow and her heart to stop pounding, listening to the occasional laughter, the sound of tableware clinking. One of the guests loudly praised Master Malkijah's wine. But most of the time they talked in low, mumbling voices that she couldn't quite hear. She needed to inch closer.

Nava was searching the shadows for a hiding place closer to the dining room when she heard rustling footsteps behind her. But she'd heard them a moment too late. Before she could turn all the way around, someone grabbed her from behind, clamping his hand over her mouth. "Don't make a sound or I'll kill you right here," he whispered. She recognized Aaron's voice, the scent of his clothes. Fear and panic squeezed her heart and stole her breath. She struggled and kicked and fought with all her strength, but he was much bigger and stronger than she was. He pinned her arms to her sides, his grip so tight she thought all her bones would break. His other hand pressed against her mouth, stifling her screams.

He lifted her up as if she weighed nothing at all and dragged her away from the dining room and into the darkness, heading toward the black void between the house and the wall of the compound. Nava was running out of air, out of strength. She couldn't keep fighting and struggling much longer. Aaron was going to have his way with her.

Lord, help me! Help me, please! she prayed. She was sorry for turning away from God, sorry for refusing to pray all these months—but she would do everything right from now on. She would serve Master Malkijah willingly and without bitterness for the next six years if only God would hear her prayer and save her. *Please, please help me!*

Aaron pulled her to the ground and pinned her beneath his weight, knocking the air from her lungs. He tore her clothing with one hand while the other hand remained over her mouth. "Stop fighting me, or this will be even worse for you," he said, his voice calm and cold. Nava kept fighting, knowing she would rather die than submit to him.

Suddenly the light of the stars above them disappeared behind a shadow. The dark shape of a man loomed above them. *Shimon.* He yanked Aaron from behind, lifting him and pulling him off Nava. As soon as Aaron's hand came away from her mouth, Nava began screaming for help. Shimon must have been watching over her all this time, and now he had come to rescue her. Aaron was so enraged that as soon as he rose to his feet and regained his balance, he punched the old man in the gut. Nava heard the sickening thuds as Aaron punched him again and again before shoving him roughly to the ground and kicking him.

But Nava's screams had brought help. She clutched her torn clothes around her as servants came running from every direction, including Penina and Ruth. Master Malkijah and Chana came, too. Aaron didn't have time to run away. Now they would all see what kind of man he was, what he had tried to do.

Chana quickly knelt beside Nava. "You poor girl. Are you hurt?"

"He came after me and . . . and threw me on the ground," Nava sobbed. She looked around for Shimon to confirm her story, but he was still lying on the ground, moaning in pain from Aaron's blows.

"Please, everyone return to the table," Malkijah told his guests. "This is nothing to worry about. Just a dispute between my servants. Pour everyone some more wine," he told his house servants. He waited until the guests and most of his servants had gone away, then said, "Tell me what happened, Aaron."

"I came outside for a walk, and I caught the old man attacking her. I stepped in to save her."

"Liar!" Nava shouted. "He's lying! Aaron would have had his way with me if Shimon hadn't stopped him."

"How dare you accuse my son of such a thing?"

"It's the truth! He's been following me for weeks, trying to get me alone. He even taunted me, saying he could do whatever he wanted to me and get away with it because no one would ever believe me."

"She's making it all up, Father," Aaron said calmly. "She thinks I'll have to marry her if she accuses me. The old man is probably in on it with her. I'll bet they staged this entire thing so they could trap me and accuse me. You know I wouldn't lower myself to be with a common servant."

"What do you have to say, Shimon? Somebody help him up."

One of the servants bent to help him, but Shimon cried out in pain. "No, don't! . . . I-I can't move . . . I think my hip is broken."

This was the nightmare Nava had feared. Malkijah would believe his son, not her, not Shimon. She looked up at Penina and Ruth and the other remaining servants and pleaded with them in desperation. "We need to tell our master the truth. Penina, tell him what's been going on. Please! You've seen everything. You know! . . . Ruth, you know the truth, too. Somebody tell him!"

They all looked down at Shimon, still lying on the ground, his lip bleeding from being punched. "Yes," he said with another groan. "Yes, it's time for the truth." And as if in answer to Nava's prayers, one by one the other servants spoke up.

"I'm sorry to say it, my lord," Ruth said, "but Master Aaron has been chasing after the girl for some time."

"I've seen him with her, too," Penina said. "She's terrified of him."

"You've known Shimon since you were a boy, my lord," Ruth added. "Do you honestly believe him capable of this?"

"Well, I certainly don't believe my son is capable of it." Malkijah crouched beside Shimon and said, "Tell me the truth, old friend. What really happened?"

"The girl is telling the truth. Aaron tried to rape her. I've been following her, keeping an eye on her because I was afraid something like this might happen. When I tried to stop Aaron, he punched me and pushed me down."

Malkijah rose to his feet again. Nava held her breath, waiting, wondering what he would do. "I don't know who to believe," he finally said. "No son of mine would be capable of such a thing." But the anger and certainty had gone out of his voice, replaced by shock and numbed disbelief. "Tell me the truth, Aaron."

"I already did tell you, Father." He was such an accomplished liar that he could look his father in the eye without flinching, remaining calm and cool. "I don't know why these servants have a grudge against me, but you can't possibly believe them. Maybe they're trying to get even with you for not setting them free. That girl is behind it all. She's a troublemaker."

Malkijah spread his hands. "Who am I supposed to believe?" He turned to Chana, who hadn't said a word since kneeling beside Nava. She looked up at Malkijah now and said softly, "I think you do know the truth in your heart."

Malkijah's expression hardened in anger. Nava couldn't guess who it was directed at. "I need to return to my guests," he said. "Go inside, Aaron. Someone get a litter and help Shimon to his bed. I'll deal with this tomorrow, after my guests leave."

Chana rose to her feet. "Leave the servants to me, Malkijah, and go back to the table."

"Are you certain?"

"Yes. It will be my job to oversee them after we're married, won't it? Please make my excuses to our guests."

Nava knelt beside Shimon while she waited for the men to fetch a litter, holding his hand tightly in hers, weeping at the sight of his bruised, bleeding body. "I'll never be able to thank you enough. You saved me, Shimon, you saved me! And now look at you. What can I do? How can I help you?"

"I'm just glad you're not hurt, girlie." She could tell by the way he breathed that he was in pain.

"I'm so sorry," she wept. "I never should have gone out alone. I should have known this would happen. I should have known!"

"Maybe this will finally open our master's eyes . . . show him what his sons are like . . . show him his own soul and the lies he's been telling himself."

"But I don't think he believes us, Shimon. I think he believes Aaron."

Before Shimon could reply, Chana returned with a blanket for a stretcher and four servants to carry it. Shimon cried out in pain when they lifted him onto the litter, then moaned again when they laid him on his pallet in his room near the goat pen. Nava felt helpless as Chana and Penina hovered over him. "Please take care of him," Nava begged. "He has to be all right again, he has to! It's my fault he got hurt. He was trying to save me."

"I'll do what I can," Chana said. "My father has been ill, so I know some herbs and leaves we can mix to help with the pain." She told Penina what she needed and the little cook hurried off to prepare them.

"Master Malkijah will never believe me," Nava told Chana while they waited. "Now everything will be worse because Aaron will try to get even with me for accusing him. And you're on their side, too, aren't you?"

"No, Nava," Chana said. "I believe you. And I'll try to convince Malkijah to believe you as soon as his guests leave. But he's a very proud man. And he loves his sons. It's going to be very difficult for him to accept the truth."

Nava was reluctant to trust her. Chana had failed once before when she hadn't convinced Malkijah to set his servants free. She would probably fail again. "Are you part of the conspiracy, too?" Nava asked her. "One of tonight's guests is the man I heard talking with Master Malkijah in Jerusalem."

Chana pulled Nava aside, away from the others. "Please don't tell anyone, but Malkijah is secretly on the governor's side. He's trying to find who the other conspirators are and what they're planning. That's why he had to return to the table tonight."

"And you believe him?" Nava asked. "How do you know he isn't lying to you? Maybe he doesn't want you to know he's really a traitor." For the space of a heartbeat, Nava saw a flicker of doubt in Chana's eyes.

Then she shook her head. "No, I know he isn't. I helped him pass the traitors' names to Governor Nehemiah."

"Are you sure the names were real?"

Chana looked away. "I have to trust him, Nava. He's going to be my husband." She returned to Shimon's bedside, and they waited in silence for Penina to return.

After feeding him the brew and doing everything she could to make him comfortable, Penina beckoned to Nava. "Come on. That's all we can do for now. We need to go back to bed."

"I want to stay with Shimon."

"I'll stay with him," Chana said. "You can go. He'll be asleep soon."

But nothing could make Nava move from her friend's side. "Do whatever you want," she told the others. "But I'm staying."

47

BETH HAKKEREM

Chana awoke early the next morning and quickly dressed so she could go out to Shimon's room near the goat pen to see how he was. He was still asleep, and Nava sat close by his side, where she had obviously spent the night. She wore the clothes that Aaron had torn last night, the edges held closed with a piece of twine. At first Chana wondered why Nava hadn't changed out of them, then realized the girl probably didn't have anything else to wear. She rose to her feet when Chana entered. "Will you stay with him, miss, while I take care of the goats?"

"Of course. Take your time." She settled into Nava's place, looking down in pity at the poor man. Purple bruises marred Shimon's craggy face. His bottom lip was puffy and split. Chana had seen the marks from Aaron's blows on his stomach and ribs last night and couldn't imagine the coldhearted cruelty it took to strike an elderly man. His midsection resembled a pregnant woman's, swollen beneath his thin undergarment. After a few minutes Shimon stirred and opened his eyes. "How are you feeling?" she asked. "Are you in pain?"

"It's not so bad. . . . Where's Nava?"

"She went to feed and milk the goats. She stayed with you all night."

"She's special. Like a daughter to me . . . She thinks last night was her fault, but it wasn't. God is at work in this. Will you help me convince her?"

"I'll do my best."

He tried to move, then stopped and groaned in pain. Chana dipped the rag in the bowl of water Nava had been using and let Shimon suck on it for a moment. "I know I won't survive this," he said afterward. "I've been around a long time and seen enough to know that my hip is broken. Old bones don't heal. Nava needs to be prepared for it."

Chana wanted to contradict him, to urge him to be strong and believe that the Almighty One would heal him, but she could see the calm acceptance on his pallid face and knew better than to offer words of false hope. "I don't know what to say, Shimon. I'm so sorry this happened."

"I've lived a long, full life. But if you could help Nava accept that it wasn't her fault and that God is at work, I'd be obliged."

It was the second time he'd said that God was at work. Chana didn't understand. "How do you see the Almighty One working, Shimon? What Aaron tried to do to Nava—what he did to you . . . was so horrible, so cruel."

"You believe we're telling the truth and that Aaron is lying?"

"I do."

He studied her for a long moment. "Are you going to marry Master Malkijah?"

She was surprised by the change in topic. "Yes. In a few weeks."

"Is it true what Nava overheard? That he's a traitor? That he's plotting against the governor?"

For the space of a heartbeat Chana felt a flicker of doubt as she remembered Nava's question: *"How do you know Malkijah isn't lying to you? Maybe he doesn't want you to know he's really a traitor."* It vanished just as quickly. "I know he isn't a traitor,

Shimon. I helped him pass information about the conspiracy to Governor Nehemiah. He's only pretending to join them so he can learn their plans and expose them."

Shimon's entire body seemed to relax. He smiled faintly. "I knew he wasn't capable of such a thing."

Chana remembered Malkijah's disbelief that his son might be guilty and saw the same love and devotion in the elderly servant. "You seem very fond of Malkijah. I guess you've known him for a long time."

"I was already working here when he was born. He loved the outdoors when he was a boy, and his father used to let me take him up into the grazing lands with the herds. Malkijah enjoyed the adventure of being out in the open, away from his mother's coddling. He was their only child."

Chana had noticed the ring in Shimon's ear last night and knew what it meant. "You were a bondservant, yet you chose to stay and work here?"

"I could have been free many years ago."

"I suppose that says something about Malkijah's kindness to his servants. But I'll be honest—I was disappointed when he didn't set them free a few months ago like so many of the other men did. He explained that he couldn't run his estate without workers, but I feel so sorry for young people like Nava who face six years of bondage. That's such a long time for someone so young."

Once again, Shimon studied her carefully. "You are a very compassionate woman, miss. Not many rich ladies would come down to a shepherd's shack to help a crippled old servant. I'm glad you'll be part of Malkijah's life."

"I only wish I could do something more for you."

He stared up at the rafters for a long time before saying, "Maybe there is something. Can I trust you with a secret?"

"A . . . a secret? About you?" She wondered if he'd committed a terrible crime in the past. He seemed like such a kind, gentle man.

"I've carried it all these years, and I need to get it off my chest before I die."

Chana leaned closer, not sure she wanted the burden of Shimon's secret. But she remembered how Abba had helped people by listening to them and becoming involved in their lives. And she also knew that Shimon was right about dying—few elderly people survived a broken hip, and if they did, their final years were pain-filled and difficult. She took his hand, giving him permission to confide in her.

"Of course you can trust me."

He sighed and stared up at the rafters again, as if searching for a place to begin. "I became a bondservant to Malkijah's father when I was a young man, newly married. I worked as a shepherd in charge of his herds. My master wanted a son more than anything else in the world, but his children kept dying— three of them before they were born, two of them surviving for only a few days. It grieved him and his wife no end. About a year after my wife and I married, we had a son. We named him Matthias, God's gift. It was one of the happiest days of my life. That boy was the world to me from the moment I laid eyes on him. I held Matthias in my arms and promised him that when my bond service ended, I would build up the finest herd of sheep and goats in all of Judah—just for him. I would do it all for him.

"But something went wrong, and my wife couldn't stop bleeding after Matthias was born. There was nothing the midwife or I could do except watch the life drain out of her. And the night she died, my master's wife went into labor for the sixth time."

Chana covered her mouth, afraid of what he was about to say. He saw her and nodded. "You know what happened, don't you? When my wife died, I wanted to die with her. My newborn son was crying to be fed—and his mother was gone. Who was going to feed him, take care of him?

"The midwife was running back and forth between this room and the big house, looking after both women. And when the master's newborn son died like all the others had, she convinced me to give my son Matthias to them. Neither the master nor his wife would ever know, she said. My son would grow up to be a nobleman instead of a shepherd. He would inherit everything—land, riches, a title. . . . So I agreed." Shimon paused, his voice choked with grief, as if his loss had occurred yesterday, not thirty-seven years ago. "I gave away my son and buried my master's son with my wife.

"I made a terrible mistake that night, and I've been paying the price ever since. I should have raised my boy myself. We would have been poor, but maybe then my grandson wouldn't be . . ." He couldn't finish. Chana squeezed his hand, remembering last night. Shimon would likely die from his own grandson's brutality. Chana wished she could ease his terrible grief.

"Does Malkijah know you're his father?" she finally asked.

Shimon shook his head. "He almost found out, once. My brother's sons thought they'd figured it out after hearing rumors and gossip over the years and seeing the family resemblance. They were jealous of their rich cousin who had everything when they had so little. They picked a fight with him when we were all together one night up in the pasturelands. I wasn't there to witness it, but they accused him of looking down on them, thinking he was better than they were because they were poor shepherds and he was a nobleman. They weren't entirely wrong—Malkijah did act superior sometimes and liked to throw his weight around. But when they accused him of being nothing but a dirty shepherd like them, he went after them. Got into a brawl and got his nose broken. It's still crooked to this day."

"Did he believe what they said?"

"No. Because even his parents didn't know the truth of what I'd done." Shimon paused and sighed again. "I stayed here all these years so I could watch my son grow up. And I kept my promise to build up the finest herd of sheep and goats in Judah for him. I'm proud of him in so many ways. He's a wise and wealthy man, a well-respected leader. But he's far from perfect. My unanswered prayer after all this time is that God will change Malkijah's heart. My son is blind to the greed that's hidden there. He doesn't fully trust God and would be angry with Him if he lost his wealth. He's afraid to set his servants free or cancel their debts because he doesn't believe that it all came from God to begin with. He thinks he earned it with his hard work and that he has to keep on earning it, keep hanging on to it for security. God should be his security.

"It's the same with God's grace," Shimon continued. "Malkijah believes that if he follows all the rules in the Torah, God has to bless him. He doesn't see that the Almighty One's blessings are a gift that none of us deserves. Blessings aren't earned. And his cousins were right—Malkijah still believes that his noble birth puts him above the common people and gives him the right to rule over them. And so every day I pray that God will give him compassion for people like his lowly shepherd father. That He'll open Malkijah's eyes to what his sons—my grandsons—are really like. You and I can't change him, miss. Only God can do that. But I see Him at work in what happened last night to Nava and me. And He brought you into his life. I trust that God is finally going to answer my prayers."

By the time he finished, Chana's heart felt as if it was breaking along with his. "What can I do, Shimon?" she asked softly.

"Pray for him after I'm gone. The way I've been doing."

"Should I tell him the truth about you? About his birth?"

"That's up to you. Maybe someday, if God shows you that the time is right. The right time never came for me. Malkijah is . . ." He was about to say more when Nava returned.

"I finished the milking, Shimon. And Penina gave me permission to stay with you today. You can leave, miss," she told Chana.

Chana saw the mistrust in Nava's eyes and wondered how

she could earn it back. "Come to Jerusalem with me, Nava. We're leaving this morning. I think you should get away from here for a while."

She shook her head, her chin lifted. "I won't leave Shimon until he's well again. He saved me."

"But you'll be alone with Aaron."

Nava's expression turned hard and cold. Chana could tell that it was anger, not fear. "Master Malkijah still doesn't believe the truth about Aaron, does he?"

"Not yet. But I pray that he will."

"What about justice for Shimon? And for me? Why won't he do the right thing?"

"I don't know the answer to that," Chana replied. "I promise that I'll do whatever I can on your behalf, but I'm not Malkijah's wife yet." She gave Shimon's hand a comforting squeeze and quietly left. She didn't know if the weight of his secret had lifted from his shoulders, but it certainly felt very heavy on her own.

JERUSALEM

Nehemiah rose at dawn and walked across the Hill of Ophel and down the Street of the Bakers to his head-quarters inside the Valley Gate. With the wall completed, the craftsmen now used the space to create the massive doors of Jerusalem's gates. Today they would hang the Yeshana Gate in place. Shipments of timber for the doors arrived by oxcart caravans from the king's forest and lay piled in rows, ready for the carpenters to saw them into planks. As Nehemiah surveyed the work in progress, he felt the same excitement and elation he'd felt two months ago when he'd first entered Judean territory and had approached his destination after a long, weary journey. He had accomplished his goal and completed the wall in nearly the same amount of time it had taken him to travel from Susa. He marveled at how drastically his life had changed in only a few short months. And now with his work all but done, he wondered what the Almighty One would ask him to accomplish next. The more he'd thought about Noadiah's prophecy and listened to the people's praises these past few weeks, the more he wondered if he truly was destined to be Judah's king.

He heard footsteps, saw men approaching, and watched as

the guards on night duty at the open gate transferred their watch to a new shift of men, exchanging swords and shields. The unfinished gates were the only places where soldiers still stood watch, and most of the men who'd labored on the wall and guarded the workers had returned to their own villages and farms.

By the time the sun crested the eastern ridge, Nehemiah's carpenters arrived and the sound of sawing and hammering filled the morning air. Outside the gate, blacksmiths fanned the coals until their makeshift furnace blazed. They would spend the day forging bars and hinges and nails for the new gates. The sound would soon echo off the new walls.

Later that morning, the chief carpenter informed Nehemiah that the pair of doors for the Yeshana Gate was ready. "Would you like to watch us hang them, Governor?"

"Lead the way."

Workers used a crane to maneuver the first door, twelve feet tall and over three inches thick, onto a sledge. It took three teams of oxen yoked together to drag it uphill to the gate. Nehemiah silently praised God as he stood in the opening that had been nothing but a rubble-strewn hole when he arrived. Now the broad walls and high watchtower extended well above his head. He put his hands over his ears to muffle the deafening sound of hammering as workers fastened supports into the new wall to hold the bars that would seal the doors shut at night. With the Almighty One's hand upon them, their months of hard labor now neared completion.

But Nehemiah's joy quickly faded when Ephraim and Hanani arrived at the site and came to stand beside him. "What's wrong? What are you doing here?" he asked. He'd been careful to avoid being with his brothers, even avoiding the daily sacrifices if he knew they would be there. Fear for their safety worried him far more than fear for himself. He had to lean close to hear their reply above the nearby pounding.

"We're here for the same reason you are," Hanani said. "We heard that the doors to the Yeshana Gate were being hung in place, and we came to watch."

"But don't you need to be—?"

"We know what you're doing," Ephraim interrupted. "We aren't stupid."

"What are you talking about?"

"We know you've been pushing us away, keeping your distance."

"And we know why," Hanani added when the pounding ceased for a moment. "Your life is in danger, and you think you're protecting us."

Nehemiah moved out from beneath the gate tower and into the open area just inside the wall, his brothers following. "We can't let down our guard," Nehemiah told them. "Especially now." He didn't need to remind them that their parents had done that very thing, thinking the threat was over once the Thirteenth of Adar ended. They surely remembered.

"We aren't relaxing our guard," Ephraim told him, gripping the hilt of his sword. "But we're not going to keep our distance from you, either."

"We're brothers," Hanani added.

They weren't backing down. Nehemiah had to admit that he enjoyed having them by his side again. He stood with his brothers, well out of the way, as workers fastened the massive new door to a crane with ropes and slowly hauled it upright. The three of them watched in amazement as the door dangled, suspended in the air. Then, with workers guiding it, the crane lowered it into place on its huge hinges. It was dangerous work for all of the laborers. If the oxen that powered the crane balked or bolted, or if the ropes snapped, the door would crush dozens of workers.

At last the door hung in position and the ropes could be removed. Nehemiah wanted to shout at the men to hurry, feeling a powerful urgency to finish before their enemies finally succeeded in stopping them. He was so close to being able to close the gates and keep their enemies out. But according to the list of names from Malkijah, some of Nehemiah's enemies were already inside Jerusalem's walls.

"Governor Nehemiah!" One of the workers on top of the watchtower shouted down to him. "It looks like another delegation of Samaritan messengers is coming."

Ephraim and Hanani followed Nehemiah as he climbed the steps to the top of the tower and gazed down the road into the distance. "You're right. Those are the uniforms and banners of Sanballat's messengers. It's probably another official summons from the governor and his friends. They've sent me the same message four times now, and each time I've given them the same reply. This will be the fifth one."

"It shows their desperation," Ephraim said. "And how threatened they are by God's work."

"Let's not read it out here. Come with me to my chambers." He descended the stairs and walked the short distance across the Hill of Ophel to his residence. When the message arrived, he sent everyone except his brothers out of the small room he used as a private office. "I'll let you read it when I'm finished," he told the noblemen and their aides who continually hovered around him. If being shut out angered some of them, so be it. Nehemiah had missed sharing the exclusive counsel of his brothers these past weeks, freely speaking his mind and heart. They sat down around the worktable in the middle of the room.

"This letter is already open," Hanani said in surprise. "There's no seal. Why would Sanballat send his aide with an unsealed letter in his hand?"

"Maybe they've been sharing the contents with the public all along the way," Ephraim said.

"Or else he's implying that the public already knows the

contents," Nehemiah said. "That it's common knowledge. Go ahead and read it, Hanani."

He unfurled the loosely rolled scroll and looked it over. "This letter is different from the others. Sanballat is the only leader who signed it this time. It says: 'It is reported among the nations—and Geshem says it is true—that you and the Jews are plotting to revolt, and therefore you are building the wall . . .'"

"I wonder how many spies are working to spread that lie for Sanballat and Geshem," Nehemiah said.

"'Moreover,'" Hanani continued reading, "'according to these reports, you are about to become their king and have even appointed prophets to make the proclamation about you in Jerusalem: There is a king in Judah!'"

"*I've* appointed them?" Nehemiah asked. "That's absurd!" He still wondered whether the prophets' messages were from the Holy One or his enemies—but he knew he hadn't hired them.

"This is serious," Ephraim said. "These rumors Sanballat refers to amount to treason on your part. And he said our neighboring nations have heard about them, too."

"'Now this report will get back to King Artaxerxes,'" Hanani continued reading, "'so come, let us confer together.'"

"Isn't that nice?" Ephraim asked, his tone biting. "Your friend Sanballat is offering to help you get out of this trouble you're in. He couldn't intimidate you into quitting, so now he's claiming friendship."

"The truth is, my 'friend' Sanballat is plotting to murder me," Nehemiah said.

"You seem convinced of that. How do you know?"

"My instincts tell me it's true. He has tried everything else to stop me, so killing me is the only choice he has left."

"Does it worry you that King Artaxerxes might hear a rumor that you're planning a rebellion?" Hanani asked.

"Of course it does. For all I know, my enemies have already sent letters to Artaxerxes accusing me of rebellion and saying

I rebuilt Jerusalem to use as my fortress. Persian troops might be marching here this very moment."

"I hope they don't get here before the doors are hung," Hanani said.

Nehemiah appreciated his brother's attempt at humor, but Sanballat's accusations were too serious to ignore. "I should have sent my own messengers to the Persian king when these rumors first surfaced, assuring him of my loyalty."

"Why didn't you?"

Nehemiah didn't reply. He hadn't because there was a chance that God really was asking him to rebel and become Judah's king. Why else would the Holy One help him win Artaxerxes' favor and clear the way for him to come here and fortify the city? "It doesn't matter now," Nehemiah finally replied. "It's much too late to send a message to Persia."

"How do you want me to respond to Governor Sanballat's letter?" Hanani asked.

Nehemiah exhaled. "Tell him, 'Nothing like what you're saying is happening; you're just making it up in your head.'"

"Anything else?"

"Well, I would love to add that we know what he's up to— that he's trying to frighten us, thinking our hands and spirit will get too weak for the work before us. I would like to tell him that his letters only hardened my resolve and encouraged me to pray for God to strengthen me. But let's not bother adding all those things." He rose from his chair, eager to return to the Yeshana Gate, having wasted too much time already on this letter. "The only way this intimidation will end is if I finish the wall, so that's what I'm going to do."

Ephraim stopped him before he reached the door. Nehemiah saw his deep concern. "Are you really as brave and fearless as you claim to be? Don't you ever have doubts or feel afraid?"

Nehemiah knew that of all the many people in his life, he could be honest and vulnerable with these two men. "I'd be lying if I said I wasn't afraid," he said quietly. "I don't want to die, but I know it's a very real possibility. Day and night, wherever I go, the thought of a sudden attack is always in the back of my mind. Yes, I wish I could find someplace safe to hide, but I don't know where that place would be. We know that it's possible to be assassinated by someone you believe you can trust."

He took a few steps toward the door, then turned back and gestured to the letter still in Hanani's hand. "That message from Sanballat was unsealed. It's common knowledge that he summoned me to a meeting and I didn't go. People probably think I'm a coward, afraid to leave Jerusalem. . . . Sometimes I wonder if I am a coward."

Ephraim shook his head. "Hanani and I know better."

"Trust God," Hanani said.

"I do trust Him. But there's no guarantee that I'll be safe just because I'm doing God's work." He thought of their parents again. "Send my reply, Hanani. Seal it, and send it back to Sanballat. I have more gates to finish."

Chapter
49

BETH HAKKEREM

Chana couldn't stop thinking about Shimon as she ate breakfast with Malkijah later that morning beneath the dining trellis. Everything about this estate seemed perfect with attentive servants, pristine courtyards, and magnificent views of vineyards and olive groves. Yet Chana also saw the ugliness that marred her future husband's home—not only in the brutal events of last night, but in the underlying attitude of greed that fostered it. She watched Malkijah, seated across the table from her as he spoke to the servants about their breakfast, and couldn't help noticing that his crooked nose marred the perfection of his handsome face.

Shimon knew Malkijah better than anyone else did, and Chana suspected that he was right about Malkijah's love of wealth. Shimon was certainly right about his blindness toward his son. But what could Chana do about it? How could she make sure that Shimon and Nava received justice for what Aaron had done? She wasn't Malkijah's wife yet. Shimon's words kept coming back to her: *"Only God can change his heart."*

"Where are Meshullam and your other guests this morning?" she asked when the servants left. "Aren't they eating with us?"

"Most of them went home last night. Meshullam wanted to get an early start this morning. And I need to return to Jerusalem as soon as possible. The doors to the Dung Gate are nearly complete and ready to be hung. It will be a huge job. I need to be there."

She leaned closer to him, lowering her voice. "Did the conspirators tell you their plans last night?"

"Not everything." He glanced around and leaned toward Chana. "They want to get as many council members and priests on their side as possible. Once they have a majority, they'll call for a meeting. They'll tell the governor he's outnumbered and demand that he hand back the governing power they had before he arrived. They'll keep him on as a figurehead, at best."

"When will this council meeting take place?"

"As soon as they have a majority behind them. There's a great deal of fear and speculation at the moment that the common people are going to crown Nehemiah as their king. The nobles want to prevent that from happening. Otherwise, once Nehemiah becomes the king, the nobles will have lost everything."

"What if Nehemiah doesn't give in to the council?"

She saw his jaw tighten before he spoke. "Some of the men favor assassination."

A shiver of fear washed through Chana. Might these cold-blooded conspirators kill Malkijah, too—especially if they discovered that he was deceiving them and spying on them? The servants brought the food, and she waited until they laid platters and bowls on the table and returned to the kitchen before speaking. She had no appetite but knew she should eat before their journey. "I don't understand how these noblemen can simply take over," she said, pulling a warm flatbread from the basket. "Wasn't Nehemiah appointed governor by King Artaxerxes?"

"Yes, but Persia is a thousand miles away. Artaxerxes doesn't know what's going on in this far-flung province beyond the river.

The conspirators have the support of Sanballat and Tobiah and Judah's other neighbors, who are threatening to report him as a traitor. They'll use fear as a lever to convince Nehemiah that he's outmaneuvered."

She thought about Nehemiah's tenacity and said, "I don't think he'll back down."

"I don't either, in spite of the danger he's in." Malkijah piled bread and cheese and olives onto his plate and began to eat.

Chana's stomach churned from all of the unsettling events. "How will we get a message to the governor now that my section of the wall is finished?" she asked.

"I don't know. I've been trying to think of a way."

Chana suddenly thought of one. "When Nehemiah comes to the Dung Gate, tell him my father is recovering and would like to see him. I can pass the information to him when he comes to our home."

Malkijah looked up at her and nodded. "It's a good plan. Thank you. This whole dangerous business of the conspiracy has occupied too much of my mind and my time. I hated leaving you with that mess last night involving the servants. I'm sorry. Could you make any sense of it? How is Shimon?"

"Not good. His hip is broken." She paused. "His injuries will probably kill him."

Malkijah stopped eating. He looked stunned. "I didn't think he was that badly injured. He's been a loyal servant for many years." Chana waited for him to comment on his son's part in Shimon's injuries, but he didn't. "I wish it hadn't happened right now, with this conspiracy to worry about and the façade I'm forced to keep up when I'm with the other nobles. Then there's the Dung Gate that needs to be finished—that's still my primary responsibility."

It worried Chana that he had changed the subject, avoiding the need to address what had happened. "About last night . . ." she said. "Is it possible that the servants are telling the truth? And that your son is lying to you?"

Malkijah's dark eyes flashed. "Why would Aaron lie to me?"

"Why would the servants lie?" she asked, determined not to back down.

"I suppose they're angry because I didn't give them their freedom. They're getting even by accusing Aaron."

"But Shimon could have been free years ago, and he chose to stay here. Do you think he would lie to you? Or that he would hatch a plot to deceive you?"

Malkijah exhaled, massaging the worry lines in his forehead. "I don't know, Chana. I don't know who or what to believe. Someone isn't telling the truth, but I can't believe that it's Aaron. People resent us because of our wealth and noble birth, and jealousy can lead them to make up all sorts of lies." Chana remembered the story of how Malkijah's nose had gotten broken and wondered if he was recalling the same incident. "Will you be ready to leave within the hour, Chana?" he asked, changing the subject again.

"Of course. But I think you should go see Shimon before we do."

Malkijah set down his cup and pushed his chair back, preparing to leave. "I will. But it will have to be quick."

Chana had to force back sudden tears at his abruptness. Malkijah's brief, distracted visit might be the last time Shimon would ever see his beloved son. "One more thing," she said, stopping him again. "I don't think it would be wise for us to go back to Jerusalem as if nothing ever happened with your servants last night. If it can't be resolved, we should at least separate the antagonists until we can learn the truth."

"Do you want to take the servant girl with you?"

"That would be the easiest solution, but she is taking care of Shimon and won't leave his side. We may have to take Aaron with us, instead."

"He can't leave. He's overseeing the estate for me."

Chana prayed for wisdom as she carefully chose her words.

She knew she could be outspokenly blunt at times, but she needed to tread carefully as she reasoned with this man who wasn't her husband yet. "Maybe you don't remember how many of your other servants also accused Aaron last night. For whatever reason, they don't seem to like him. Is it wise to leave him here in such an atmosphere of mistrust? It might be better for both sides if they had some time apart."

"That means I'll have to assign a new overseer. That's going to take time, and I wanted to leave right away."

"I can make sure Aaron is awake and ready to go if that will save you some time. We can still arrive in Jerusalem well before noon." Chana waited. She had no right to push him or to expect him to listen to her.

"Very well. We'll take Josef with us, as well. Maybe they would enjoy watching the Dung Gate being hung in place. Would you mind asking the servants to awaken my sons and help them pack? I'll go talk to my manager."

"And you'll talk to Shimon, too?" Chana asked before he could leave.

"I will." Malkijah would see that Shimon was dying. She prayed it would shock him into confronting Aaron for his brutal attack.

Within the hour they were on the road, the four of them traveling together along with a few servants. Aaron looked disgruntled, and Chana caught him shooting angry looks at her like arrows, as if it were her fault that he'd been yanked from his bed and forced to come. They were within sight of Jerusalem when Aaron seemed unable to hold his tongue a moment longer.

"Am I being punished for something, Father, that you assigned another overseer in my place and made me come with you? Haven't I done a good enough job while you were away?"

"You've done a fine job, Aaron. But some of the servants seemed angry with you. I wanted to give them time to cool down. Besides, I thought you and Josef might like to see the progress we've made on the wall. The gate I'm responsible for should be finished in the next day or so."

It upset Chana as she listened to them talk that Aaron didn't acknowledge his actions or ask about Shimon. And it worried her that Malkijah was such a poor judge of his son's character and seemingly blind to his faults. As a father, it was his job to discipline him and teach him right from wrong, molding his character. Malkijah admitted that he'd indulged his sons after their mother died—but Chana had lost her mother at a young age, too. She thought of all the ways Abba had gently yet firmly shaped her and her sisters. How he'd guided Chana out of her grief and self-pity after Yitzhak died. Abba never would have tolerated lying, and Aaron's violence would have appalled him.

A wave of unease washed over her as she considered her upcoming marriage to Malkijah and his family's many problems. Shimon was right; she couldn't change Malkijah or his sons. Only God could change their hearts. But she could try to be an influence in their home, offering advice and praying that Malkijah would see the truth about his sons for himself. He wasn't facing the evidence of what Aaron had tried to do to Nava last night or that his actions would probably cause the death of a trusted servant—a servant who was Malkijah's own father.

If this was the work that the Almighty One wanted Chana to do now that the wall was finished, she felt inadequate for the task. Making a difference in this family's life, bringing them into alignment with the plumb line of God's truth and justice, would be immensely challenging. Should she share Shimon's secret with Malkijah? If so, when? And how? The truth about Malkijah's birth still astounded her. His father wasn't a wealthy nobleman named Recab, ruler of the District of Beth Hakkerem, but a humble, God-fearing shepherd named Shimon.

CHAPTER

50

BETH HAKKEREM

Nava watched from the doorway of the shepherd's hut until Aaron was out of sight before returning to her place at Shimon's bedside. She soaked up more water on the twisted rag and gave it to him to drink, then took his icy hand in hers again. It worried her that his face had turned the pale, bluish-white color of milk. "What were you watching over there?" Shimon asked her.

"I was just making sure that Aaron really did go to Jerusalem with the others." Nava offered him more water, but he shook his head. "What did Master Malkijah say to you before he left?" she asked him. Shimon had sent her away so they could speak in private. It was just as well. She was still much too angry to face her master. Anything she said to him might only make matters worse.

"Malkijah told me how sorry he was that this happened. . . . And that he hoped to see me well again when he returned."

Nava turned her face away so Shimon wouldn't see her tears. He was gravely ill and getting worse, not better, with each hour that passed. Along with his broken hip, something else must have broken inside when Aaron had punched him repeatedly.

Shimon's belly was tender and painful, swelling like a pregnant woman's. "Did our master promise to get justice for you?" she asked. "Doesn't the Torah say that wrongdoers must pay for injuring other people?"

"He'll search for the truth and do what's right. Malkijah is a good man."

"You mean *Matthias*?" she asked quietly.

Shimon sucked in his breath at her words, then moaned at the pain it caused. When he could speak again he said, "You were listening to a private conversation. Hasn't eavesdropping caused enough trouble for you, girlie?"

"I'm sorry. I didn't mean to listen, but the other servants helped me with the goats so I could finish sooner. I hurried back to you, and—" She halted, lowering her head in shame for what she had done. "You aren't mad at me, are you, Shimon? I'm really sorry."

"No . . . I don't suppose it matters much."

But Nava knew that it did matter. Shimon was Malkijah's father—and Malkijah didn't even care enough about him to make Aaron pay for what he had done. She was going to say as much, but Penina arrived with some of Chana's brew to help ease Shimon's pain. He couldn't sit up to drink it so Nava soaked a cloth in the concoction and had him suck on it.

"Shimon," she said after Penina left, "why didn't you tell me the truth about our master? Why did you confide in Chana, of all people?"

"I wanted to tell you. But I was afraid you'd use the truth as a weapon to hurt my son. If I thought you could forgive Malkijah for keeping you his bondservant, I would have told you."

"*Forgive* him? That's impossible. Do *you* forgive him for treating you this way?"

"Of course I do. And I forgive Aaron for what he did, too."

"How can you? It isn't fair!"

"No, it isn't. But is it fair that the Almighty One has to

forgive us again and again? He expects us to be like Him and forgive each other."

Nava stared down at Shimon's hand, still held between her own. She could never forgive either one of her masters, especially if Shimon died.

"Now that you know the truth about my son," Shimon said after a moment, "what are you going to do with it?"

She didn't reply right away as she made up her mind. "Nothing," she finally said. "I don't want him to know you're his father. He doesn't deserve a father as wonderful as you." She choked back her tears and added, "Besides, he wouldn't believe me anyway."

Shimon smiled and gestured for more medicine. After Nava had given it to him, she saw him summoning his strength. She leaned closer. "Listen, Nava. I know I don't have much time, and I need you to really hear what I have to say. . . . If you hold on to bitterness and anger toward our masters, you'll end up in the same mess as Aaron. He pretends to respect his father, but there is rebellion and anger in his heart. Don't be like him. You agreed to be a bondservant to help your family. Can you do it with a grateful attitude, without bitterness? Remember, our master isn't obligated by law to set you free."

"But I want to marry Dan. I love him, and six years is a long time to wait."

"I know, girlie, I know. But maybe the Almighty One has you here to teach you to trust Him, to get closer to Him. . . . Tell me, when you knew Aaron was watching you, did you pray and ask God to protect you? Or weren't you on speaking terms with God?"

"You're saying that what happened was my fault for not praying?"

"Not at all. I'm saying that God used even this evil deed for His purposes. He wants you to trust Him again. And he wants Malkijah to wake up to what his sons—"

"But he didn't wake up! He doesn't believe us."

"We haven't seen the end of the story yet. But I hope you'll see that God was at work, watching out for you, even though you were angry with Him. I couldn't sleep last night, so as I was laying here praying I heard Him urging me to get up and find you."

Nava covered her mouth to hold back a cry. She had blocked out all memories of last night because they were too horrifying to relive, but she suddenly remembered that after Aaron had grabbed her she had prayed, *Lord save me!* And Shimon had come out of nowhere. She remembered telling God she was sorry for turning away from Him, sorry for refusing to pray all these months, and she had promised to serve Master Malkijah willingly and without bitterness for the next six years if only God would hear her prayer and save her. And He had.

"Sometimes the Almighty One answers our prayers by using other people," Shimon said. "Your family prayed for rain during the drought because they didn't want to starve. God answered their prayer—not by sending rain, but by sending Malkijah, who obeyed the Torah and loaned your family money for food. God does answer prayer. You can trust Him for your future with Dan. But you need to pray for Malkijah and for Aaron, like I told you to do."

Nava closed her eyes. "I made such a mess of things."

"It isn't your fault that Aaron was attracted to you and tried to assault you, any more than it was your fault that it didn't rain for two years. God is at work. We can't understand how He chooses to answer our prayers, but He will answer them, one way or another."

"And if I pray and ask Him to make you better, will He answer that prayer?"

"Probably not the way you're hoping. But He can still bring good out of whatever happens to me. Don't ask God what He's doing. That's the wrong thing to ask. Ask Him what *you* should be doing."

Nava realized that if she hadn't turned bitter toward her master, she never would have left her bed to eavesdrop on him. And Aaron wouldn't have caught her alone. And Shimon wouldn't be lying here bruised and broken. She couldn't undo all those mistakes and make Shimon well again. Life and death weren't under her control. But she could choose to let go of her anger and bitterness. She could choose to trust God the way Shimon did. And she could choose to serve her master cheerfully and faithfully.

"I'm going to pray anyway and ask God to heal you," she told Shimon.

"Go ahead, girlie. You do that. God always answers our prayers. But just remember that sometimes His answer is no."

CHAPTER

51

JERUSALEM

Nehemiah paused outside the gate to Shallum's house and turned to the entourage of men who still insisted on following him everywhere he went. "You need to wait out here," he told them. "Shallum has been very ill. He deserves his privacy." His bodyguards started to follow him as Chana opened the gate, but Nehemiah made them stay outside, too. He suspected that she might have more news about the conspiracy. "I won't be long," he told them.

He found Shallum sitting up in bed. He still looked haggard after wrestling with the Death Stalker, and one side of his face seemed paralyzed, making his words sound slurred. But Shallum was alert and clearly on the mend. "I heard you were recovering, Shallum. I'm glad," Nehemiah said.

He sat down and spoke with him for a few minutes before Chana returned to the room. "I have a message for you from Malkijah," she said. Nehemiah stood, guessing she would take him someplace private. But she shook her head. "Abba knows all about the conspiracy, Governor. I told him what's been going on."

"And I'll help you and Malkijah any way that I can once I'm on my feet again," Shallum said. "I still wield a lot of influence in the council chamber. Go ahead, Chana. Tell the governor what you know."

She spoke in a soft, urgent voice as if afraid someone might be listening. "Their plan is to get as many nobles as they can on their side, then call for a council meeting. They're going to try to force you to give up control so they can govern the way they did before you came."

The plan made Nehemiah angry, not afraid. "And if I don't concede?"

"They'll threaten to expose you to King Artaxerxes as a traitor and intimidate you into cooperating." She wasn't meeting his gaze. Nehemiah suspected there was more.

"They're plotting to assassinate me, aren't they," he said.

"I'm afraid so."

Shallum shook his head, his voice quivering with outrage. "I've worked alongside these men nearly all my life, and I'm shocked by their actions. Shocked! You can bet Tobiah is behind this."

"How many council members have joined the conspiracy so far?" Nehemiah asked.

"Malkijah doesn't know. Everyone is working independently behind the scenes, trying to recruit sympathizers. Malkijah is supposed to recruit Abba. They're approaching these men one at a time the way they approached Malkijah, trying to win them over."

"Thank you," Nehemiah said. With anger coursing through him, he didn't trust himself to say more. He pretended to be calm as he rejoined the other men, as if he had no idea there were traitors among them. "Good news. Shallum should make a full recovery," he said.

"That is good news," the men agreed.

But Malkijah's information had fueled Nehemiah's growing sense of urgency. "The closer we are to finishing," he told his brothers over dinner that evening, "the harder my enemies will work to eliminate me."

"Maybe you should hire more bodyguards," Ephraim told him.

"I refuse to give in to fear."

His brothers both began pleading with him at the same time, trying to convince him that sensible caution and faith-filled courage weren't contradictory. One of Nehemiah's servants interrupted them.

"There is a priest at the door who would like to speak with you, Governor."

Nehemiah rose to go and both of his brothers rose with him. He wanted to command them to stay at the table with their wives and finish their dinner, but he already knew they wouldn't listen to him. The young priest who waited just inside his door was a stranger. "I come only as a messenger, Governor Nehemiah. One of the chief priests, Shemaiah ben Delaiah, would like to speak with you. He has received a word for you from God."

"A word from God?" It sounded ominous. Yet maybe this was the answer he'd been praying for. Nehemiah had asked the Almighty One to make it clear whether or not he was being called to serve as Judah's king, as the people were begging him to do. Ever since the prophetess had first planted the idea in his mind, it had continued to grow and fill his thoughts, especially as the wall neared completion and his current leadership role came to an end. "Why didn't Shemaiah come to speak to me himself?" he asked.

"He is shut in at his home."

"Shut in? What do you mean?"

"He is a devout man of God and has given up worldly interests to remain in his house and devote himself to spiritual pursuits. He is one of the Holy One's prophets," the priest added with a touch of awe in his voice.

A few minutes later, after successfully talking his brothers out of joining him, Nehemiah left with the young priest and two guards to walk to Shemaiah's house. It was only a short distance

410

up the Hill of Ophel from his governor's residence in an area where many of the temple priests had their homes, adjacent to the wall they had helped build. Nehemiah's curiosity grew with each step he took, wondering what the chief priest would say. But at the same time he remained alert, half-expecting to be ambushed. If he were honest, he had to admit that he coveted the role of Judah's next king. It would be a fitting reward for accomplishing his God-given task of rebuilding the wall. He found himself hoping that it would turn out to be Shemaiah's message to him from the Holy One.

He knocked on the door of the priest's modest home. "Governor Nehemiah. You came," Shemaiah said after opening it. Then he surprised Nehemiah by stepping outside and closing the door behind him instead of inviting him inside. "Quickly now—we must leave here. You are in great danger." He walked further up the hill, his steps brisk as he headed toward the main stairway to the temple mount. Nehemiah and his two guards had to hurry to keep up.

"Where are we going?" Nehemiah asked.

"We can't meet in my home. It's much too dangerous." Shemaiah appeared very dignified and prosperous—wearing a robe of fine linen, his graying hair and beard neatly trimmed—for a man who was shut away and devoted to spiritual pursuits. He wasn't at all the wild-eyed, fanatical prophet Nehemiah had expected to meet. But why was he leading him through the dark streets? And where were they going? His actions seemed very odd.

They reached the temple stairway, and Nehemiah had to watch his step as they climbed by the light of a pale crescent moon. His guards also had difficulty seeing their way, but Shemaiah flew up the steps as if torches lit his way. He crossed the temple's outer courtyard, where the worshipers gathered each morning and evening, and Nehemiah guessed that Shemaiah would take him to one of the many side chambers beyond the public courtyards. The priests and Levites had robing rooms back there, storerooms for the tithes, and kitchens to prepare the meal offerings. But Shemaiah led them straight through the gate from the outer court, across the court of men, and up to the entrance to the inner court, where the priests ministered at the altar of sacrifice. The coals on the huge altar glowed red in the darkness and Nehemiah smelled the aroma of roasting meat. He halted.

"Wait. Where are we going?" He had the unsettling feeling that if he went any farther he would be trespassing on sacred ground.

"Tell your men to wait out here," Shemaiah said. "You and I need to meet in the house of God, inside the temple. We need to close the temple doors because men are coming to kill you. By night they are coming to kill you."

Nehemiah's heart raced out of control. "You want me to seek refuge in the temple courtyard, at the altar of asylum?"

"No. Even that's too dangerous. You need to seek refuge inside the sanctuary. It's the only safe place for you until the city gates are finished."

"*Inside* the holy sanctuary?" Nehemiah wondered if he was dreaming, if this was a nightmare.

"Yes! You must! Your assassins are already in this city, and you don't know who they are."

Nehemiah was well aware of the conspiracy of nobles from Malkijah's reports. He was about to tell Shemaiah that he did know who some of his enemies were, but he hesitated, wondering if he could trust the priest. "My guards will protect me."

"They won't be able to stop your assassins. Come." Shemaiah stepped into the priests' courtyard, beckoning him to follow.

Fear pounded through Nehemiah and quickened his breath. He fought the urge to duck low, to find a place to hide, to save himself. Yet he couldn't bring himself to follow Shemaiah. Only the anointed priests could enter God's holy sanctuary.

"Hurry!" the priest urged.

Nehemiah shook his head. "Should a man like me run away? Should one like me go into the temple to save his life? I won't go! I'm not a coward who runs away or hides when there's danger."

"But I have a word from God for you. This is what you must do. You're His chosen leader. Your life must be spared at all costs."

"The Torah forbids laymen like me to enter the temple. I won't transgress the law, even to save my life."

"It's permissible to violate the Torah in order to save a life. Please, Governor. I urge you to hurry! Do you want to die?"

Nehemiah couldn't deny the panic he felt. His heart pounded wildly and fear tightened his chest. But Shemaiah's plan seemed wrong. "Wouldn't you also be violating the Torah if you went inside with me? Your life isn't in danger."

"No . . . but . . ." He didn't have an answer to that.

He was a false prophet, Nehemiah realized. No true prophet would ever urge someone to disobey the law. A true prophet would encourage him to place his life in God's hands and have faith in His power. Nehemiah stepped back from the gate. "God didn't send you. You're prophesying against me because Tobiah and Sanballat hired you."

Shemaiah had trouble meeting his gaze. "I don't know what you're talking about. God warned me that you're in danger. His sanctuary is the only safe place for you."

"No," Nehemiah said, growing more certain now. "No, you were hired to intimidate me so I'd commit a sin by doing this. You want to discredit me by enticing me to violate the Torah."

"You're making a big mistake, Governor Nehemiah. God did tell me to warn you. Don't ignore His message. Your life is in danger."

"It's probably true that my life is in danger. But God speaks to us through His Torah, and He doesn't contradict Himself. He is able to rescue me from my enemies, if He chooses, and I won't have to violate the Torah to do it."

"Listen to me, I beg you." Shemaiah's voice became more high-pitched as he grew frantic. Perhaps Tobiah and the others would pay him only if he succeeded. "The people need you to lead them, Governor. They're hoping you'll restore David's throne and the kingdom of Judah."

"If God truly intends for me to be king, He'll protect me the way He protected David from King Saul. David never disobeyed the Torah to save his life. And he refused to murder Saul, even when he had two chances to do it, because the Torah forbade it. I'm not going to do this cowardly thing, Shemaiah. I'm going to trust God."

He turned and walked home without looking back. Even with guards by his side, Nehemiah felt afraid and badly shaken—whether from the temptation he had narrowly avoided or from the raw fear Shemaiah had instilled in him, he didn't know. Perhaps both. He strode through the dark streets with heightened senses, alert to every sound, scanning the shadows for movement.

When he reached home, Nehemiah and his guards carefully inspected each room and hallway and courtyard before entering them. His brothers were still awake and wanted to hear what Shemaiah had to say. "He was a false prophet, probably hired by Sanballat and Tobiah to scare me into violating the Torah," he told them. "If I had entered the holy sanctuary as he was urging me to do, I would have forfeited my right to govern. When Judah's kings disobeyed the Torah, their sin led the entire nation into exile."

"Why did he want you to enter the sanctuary?" Ephraim asked.

"He said my life was in danger and that my enemies were coming to kill me tonight."

"Do you believe that's true?" Hanani asked.

"Even if it is, I'm not going to hide inside the temple."

"We'll stay awake with you and stand guard," Ephraim offered.

"Thank you, but no. You should guard your families. I'm choosing to trust God." Nehemiah went into his bedchamber alone and closed the door. The room felt stuffy with all the window shutters bolted, but he felt safer that way. Should he remain awake all night? Would he even be able to sleep if he did lie down? The only way to dispel his terrible fear, Nehemiah realized, was to pray.

Whether he lived or died, his life was in God's hands as it had been ever since he was a child. Yes, evil existed, but God was in control. Nehemiah stood in front of his window, facing the temple, and closed his eyes as he lifted his hands in prayer. *Remember Tobiah and Sanballat, O my God, because of what they have done; remember Shemaiah, and the rest of the people who have been trying to intimidate me. Strengthen my hands, O Lord, so I can complete the work you've given me to do.*

When he finished praying, Nehemiah felt at peace. God had brought him here to build the wall, and He would keep him safe until it was finished. Nehemiah lay down in his bed and slept through the night.

He woke up rested the next morning and went up to the temple with his brothers for the morning sacrifice. Afterward, as they were getting ready to descend the stairs, Hanani stopped him and pointed to the western horizon. "Nehemiah, look!"

A jolt of alarm quickened his heart. Was it enemy soldiers? Should he find a trumpeter and sound the alarm?

"Clouds, Nehemiah!" Hanani said, nudging him. "Those are storm clouds on the horizon, coming from the Great Sea. This is the season for the early rains—and they're coming!"

Nehemiah was speechless. He gazed at the distant splotch of gray that marred the vast expanse of blue sky, unable to move until Ephraim nudged him again. "We'd better finish that last gate before we all get soaked."

They hurried down through the city to the very bottom of the ridge, to the Dung Gate, Malkijah's gate, the last one to be completed. It took all morning for the first door to be lifted and maneuvered into place. Nehemiah stood inside the wall with his brothers and Malkijah, watching as the workers hung it on its hinges. The workers swung it open and closed a few times, testing the massive iron hinges, then prepared to repeat the process with the second door. By noon, clouds covered the entire sky, lowering over Jerusalem like a gray blanket. A damp wind had begun to blow, and Nehemiah saw rain slanting from the clouds on the distant hills.

By the time the second door was hung, the rain fell steadily. No one bothered to take shelter. Nehemiah heard children laughing nearby as they splashed in the puddles and lifted their faces to catch raindrops on their tongues. He felt like laughing with them. The wall was finished and the workmen could return home to plow their fields, the earth now softened by the rain. He watched as the second door swung slowly closed to meet the first one. A great cheer went up as the iron bars lowered into place as they would every night from now on. After standing in ruins for nearly a century and a half, Jerusalem's wall and gates were finished.

All around him, people were cheering—and getting soaked. Rain plastered Nehemiah's hair to his head and rolled down his face. His clothes were as wet as if he had jumped into a river. He didn't care. The ruined city was no longer a disgrace. The God of Israel was glorified.

"What day is it today?" he asked Hanani.

His brother thought for a moment. "The twenty-fifth day of Elul."

They had completed the wall in fifty-two days. A miracle! Less than six months had passed since King Artaxerxes had granted Nehemiah's request. Only two months had passed since he'd arrived in Jerusalem. And in five more days it would be Rosh Hashanah, the start of a new year.

"When our enemies hear about this," Nehemiah said, "all the

surrounding nations will be afraid and lose their self-confidence. They'll know that this work was accomplished with the help of our powerful God."

"And the nobles' conspiracy?" Malkijah asked him quietly.

"They can no longer deny that the hand of God is upon me. Perhaps once they realize that, they'll fear Him, as well."

Nehemiah resolved to no longer live in fear. His guards could return to their homes. It didn't matter if he died now that his work was done. And clearly, the Almighty One was with him. It was time to go home and get out of the rain. Dry off. Change his clothes.

"Governor Nehemiah," a voice called to him as he started walking up the hill toward his residence. "What's next?" The question had come from the crowd of people who continued to follow him nearly everywhere he went.

"Rosh Hashanah is next," he replied. "The beginning of a new year. We'll celebrate the fall feasts, and after that we'll dedicate the new wall." He wished he knew for certain what would come after that.

"Are the prophets right? Are you going to be our king?"

It was a question he continued to wrestle with. After working day and night these past few months, it was only natural to feel at a loss now that his all-consuming task of building the wall was complete. Would God give him another job to do to make use of his energy and leadership skills?

"A king in Judah . . . A king in Judah," the crowd began to chant.

Nehemiah didn't reply as he continued up the hill. Maybe his work wasn't finished after all. He knew he would have the full support of the people as their king and could continue to defeat Judah's enemies with the Almighty One's help. After organizing the work on the wall, it would be a simple matter to organize and train an army. He could start with the brave volunteers who'd waited in ambush with him to surprise their attackers. With an army and a walled city and a crown, he might be able to win his nation's freedom from the Persians.

The chanting crowd followed him all the way to his residence. "A king in Judah . . . A king in Judah!"

And Nehemiah realized how badly he wanted it to be true.

Part III

Extol the LORD, *O Jerusalem;*

praise your God, O Zion,

for he strengthens the bars of your gates

and blesses your people within you.

PSALM 147:12–13

CHAPTER
52

JERUSALEM

Chana thought of Yitzhak as Sarah and Yudit helped her dress for her wedding. She could barely picture Yitzhak's face anymore or recall the sound of his voice or his laughter, the memories eroded by time. She had prepared the garment she now wore for a marriage that had never taken place. Chana had been blindly, joyously in love with Yitzhak, and she knew she didn't feel that same love for Malkijah. *"Would you be willing to settle for contentment? For companionship?"* Malkijah had once asked her. She had replied, *"Yes, I believe I could find contentment here with you."* And as she'd gotten to know him these past months, she had even more reason now to believe they would be happy together.

"You look beautiful," Sarah told her. Chana gazed at her reflection in the bronze mirror and saw a woman whose happiness on her wedding day had indeed made her beautiful.

"It's a pity we have to cover you up with this veil," Yudit teased as she placed it on Chana's head.

"Wait! Don't cover her up yet," Abba said, hobbling into the room with his cane. "I want to see my beautiful daughter one last time before she leaves our nest to become Malkijah's

421

wife." He kissed both of her cheeks, and they hugged each other tightly. Chana didn't want to cry, but she remembered how she'd wondered if Abba would live to see this day. She saw tears in his eyes, too. "I know Malkijah isn't your first choice for a husband—" he began.

"But he'll be a very good one," she quickly finished, not wanting to be reminded of Yitzhak again. "I'm happy with your choice, Abba."

"There's just one thing," he said, lowering his voice. "I wish your mother were here to talk to you about . . . about what to expect . . ."

Chana laughed and laid her palms on his pale, round cheeks, now flushed with embarrassment. "Don't worry, Abba. The women in your district have filled in for Mama with all the advice I'll ever need."

"Good. Good . . . Shall we go out to the courtyard? Are you ready?"

Chana nodded, and they walked outside together to the vine-covered chair where she would wait for her bridegroom. Friends and relatives filled their courtyard, waiting with her for Malkijah's procession to arrive.

"The rain stopped just in time," Yudit said, lifting her palms to the sky. "I didn't want to pray for it to clear up since we need rain so badly, but the Holy One is smiling down on you, Chana."

She gazed at the western sky above the wall she had helped rebuild and saw the clouds slowly parting around the setting sun. The evening promised to be clear and dry. "Maybe our wedding feast will be lit with moonlight," she said.

They had decided to get married in Malkijah's Jerusalem home instead of his estate in Beth Hakkerem out of consideration for her father, who still tired easily. And perhaps it was better to be married in a different home than the one where Malkijah had wed his first wife. Chana also thought it best to keep Aaron away from the estate for a while longer. She wondered how he and Josef felt about their father's marriage, how they would adjust to having her in their home. These thoughts weren't supposed to occupy her on her wedding day, but they did.

Before long, Chana heard the joyful music of Malkijah's procession as it made its way down the Street of the Bakers, growing louder, closer. Her heart raced in time to the music as the people around her clapped and sang with the musicians. Malkijah arrived dressed like a prince, smiling and handsome as he came through the gate. She wondered for a moment if he was thinking about his first wife, Rebecca—remembering her the way Chana had thought of Yitzhak. It didn't matter if he did. It was good to recall the people they'd loved. But as Abba once said, she needed to live in the present—and trust the Holy One for her future.

Malkijah stopped in front of her and lifted her veil, making Chana smile at this traditional reminder of their ancestor Jacob. He hadn't taken a close look at his bride and had been deceived into marrying Leah instead of his beloved Rachel. Malkijah took Chana's hands and helped her to her feet. The music became even livelier and more joyful as they paraded up the hill together to his home. It seemed as though everyone in Jerusalem had come out to watch the procession, clapping and singing with the musicians, small children skipping ahead of them along the path.

The courtyard of Malkijah's home had been transformed. "It's so beautiful," she murmured. "Like *Gan* Eden." A canopy stood in the middle of it, decorated with vines and palm branches. Linen cloths covered the tables, spread with a banquet of food prepared for their wedding feast. Malkijah opened jars of his famous wine so guests could toast the new bride and groom. Chana stood with Malkijah beneath the canopy and vowed to be his wife for as long as they both lived.

Afterward, the feast began, with music and laughter and plentiful food beneath the starlit sky. Chana couldn't imagine a more perfect celebration or a more perfect evening shared with her family and friends. Even Governor Nehemiah had come at their request, looking content and relaxed for once. The only shadow on the festivities came when Chana glimpsed Aaron watching from the doorway. She'd face challenges in the months and years to come. But she and Malkijah would get through the hard times together, God helping them.

Very late in the evening, Malkijah took Chana's hand and led her into the bridal chamber. He took her into his arms and pulled her close, looking into her eyes for a long moment before bending to kiss her. As his lips met hers for the first time, Chana felt the strangest, most wonderful sensation—as if her insides were melting. "What are you thinking about, my beautiful bride?" he asked when their lips parted again.

She smiled up at him. "I was thinking how wonderful that kiss felt. . . . And how much I wished you would kiss me again."

Malkijah granted her wish.

CHAPTER

53

JERUSALEM

Nehemiah rarely left his residence on Shabbat to go anywhere except the temple. But now that the wall and gates were finished, his brother Ephraim had moved his family back to their modest home at the southern end of the city. He'd invited Nehemiah to share the noon meal with him, and they were walking down the Street of the Bakers together after the Sabbath morning sacrifice when they were halted by a caravan of merchants entering through the Valley Gate. A string of donkeys blocked the road, swaying beneath huge loads, carrying jars of wine and baskets of grapes and figs. Unbelievably, a second caravan followed right behind it, the pungent odor betraying its cargo of fresh fish.

"What's going on?" Nehemiah asked in astonishment. "They're bringing all this into Jerusalem on the Sabbath?"

"They're heathens," Ephraim said with a shrug. "They don't observe a day of rest."

"I need to do something about this." Nehemiah spotted the lead driver, more nicely dressed than the others, and called, "Stop! You, there—stop right where you are!" The ponderous caravan drew to a halt in the middle of the street. "I'm Nehemiah ben Hacaliah, governor of the province of Judah. Who are you? Where are you coming from?"

"These goods are from Tyre, but the merchants who sell them to the people of Judah live here in Jerusalem."

"If your merchants live here, they should know that every seventh day is a Sabbath day of rest when all work must stop. You cannot bring your goods into Jerusalem or sell them on the Sabbath."

The man took a stubborn stance, arms crossed. "This is news to me. The officials who governed this province before you never stopped us. In fact, Judah's nobility has a vested interest in our trade being successful."

"Not anymore. This practice must stop. There will be no more buying or selling on the Sabbath day—starting today."

"That's absurd! Even your fellow Jews don't follow such a law. Go out to some of their villages and see for yourself. The men of Judah tread their winepresses seven days a week and harvest their grain and olive crops, too. They'll be clamoring to buy my fish today as soon as we set up our booths in the marketplace."

"No, they won't. Not today. Turn your animals around and go right back out through that gate." Nehemiah planted himself squarely in front of the lead pack animal, blocking the way into the city.

"What are we supposed to do outside the gate? We have fresh fish to sell."

"You'll have to wait until the sun sets and the Sabbath day ends. And if your cargo spoils, you'll learn a valuable lesson for next time." When the driver glared at him, not moving, Nehemiah grabbed the donkey's bridle and started turning the animal himself.

"Wait! Don't pull on her. I'll do it." He shouted orders to the rest of his men and the caravan slowly turned around in the street, the donkeys braying loudly. The commotion drew people out of their homes, and Nehemiah saw men and women peering from their windows and rooftops to see what was going on.

"The Holy One has commanded us to remember the Sabbath day by keeping it holy," Nehemiah said, shouting so all the people could hear him. "You have six days to do all your work, but the seventh is a Sabbath to the Lord your God. On it you shall not do any work, neither you nor your servants nor your animals, nor the strangers within your gates. . . . That includes you and your caravan," he told the lead driver. "If you ever do this again I will lay hands on you."

Nehemiah's fury smoldered as he continued down the hill to Ephraim's house. "I've always stayed home on the Sabbath, so I didn't know this was going on," he said. "But trust me, it isn't going to happen in the future."

"Don't be surprised if those merchants set up their market outside the gates," Ephraim told him. "Or if our fellow Jews go out there to buy from them."

"Even on the Sabbath?"

Ephraim nodded. "This has gone on since Ezra retired as governor, but no one has tried to stop them before. Everyone reasoned that the merchants were foreigners who didn't have to keep the Law."

"If they're in my province, they have to obey our laws."

Nehemiah laid aside his anger for the sake of his family and enjoyed the day of rest. But as soon as the sun set, he finished making plans to hold a council meeting with all of his nobles and officials and district leaders. Part of the reason was to claim his authority before the conspirators gathered enough support to call their own meeting and challenge him. But the main purpose was to explain his future plans now that the wall was finished.

As he stood on the dais in his council chamber the next day, Nehemiah could guess by the expressions on the men's faces—either anger or curiosity—which ones were on his side and which ones supported the conspiracy. Maybe they would all desert him by the time the meeting ended.

He began without preamble. "Now that the wall is done and all the gates have been set in place, I'm putting my brother Hananiah ben Hacaliah in charge of supervising Jerusalem's defenses. He knows their strengths and weaknesses better than anyone. The temple citadel will be under the command of Hananiah. He's a man of integrity who fears God more than most men do." Nehemiah also knew that he wouldn't be intimidated by the noblemen behind the conspiracy.

"From now on," he continued, "the gates of Jerusalem will remain closed until the sun is hot, rather than opening at dawn. This delay will prevent any surprise attacks by our enemies before our citizens are fully awake. In the evening, the gatekeepers on duty will shut and bar the doors for the night before it gets dark. Hanani will also appoint residents of Jerusalem as guards, some at their posts and some near their own homes."

"I thought the threat of an enemy attack was no longer an issue now that the wall is finished," Meshullam said. Nehemiah knew him to be one of the traitors.

"The worst possible time to lower our guard is when we believe the crisis has passed," he said, remembering the Thirteenth of Adar. He paused, wondering if he should say more about having enemies in their midst, then decided to continue. "My next announcement concerns the Sabbath. Yesterday I encountered some merchants from Tyre who were bringing fish and other merchandise into Jerusalem to sell to the people of Judah on the day of rest. These merchants assured me that this is a common practice, allowed by the nobles of Judah before I arrived."

He paused again, waiting for their response. When no one spoke he said, "I rebuked them and sent them outside the city to wait. But now I'm rebuking you. What is this wicked thing you're doing—desecrating the Sabbath day? Didn't your forefathers do the same thing so that our God brought all this calamity upon us and upon this city? Now you're stirring up more wrath against Israel by desecrating the Sabbath. Is it any wonder that our province has been without rain for two years?"

He stepped down from the dais as his anger stirred him into action, walking between the rows of men and looking many of them in the eye. Some wouldn't meet his gaze. "These foreign merchants who don't know our God or His law assured me that Jews all over the province tread their winepresses and do other work on the Sabbath. These are *Jews*, people in *your* districts who are doing this, people who are supposed to know our God. Do you understand what the word *desecrate* means? It means turning what is sacred into common use and profaning it. Making the seventh day just like any other day by doing work or buying and selling instead of keeping the day holy and set apart as God commanded.

"Each of you is responsible for setting an example in your district. Our role as leaders is a sacred trust from God, not something we deserve or covet or strive for. We must govern with justice and integrity as God's representatives and follow His law, not our own. Here in Jerusalem, when evening shadows fall on the city gates before the Sabbath, the doors will be shut, and they won't reopen until the day ends. A temple priest will sound three blasts on his trumpet to announce the precise moment of sunset when the people must cease their labor. Three more blasts will follow to mark the division between the common day and the sacred one. The trumpet will be sounded again when the Sabbath day comes to an end. I've commanded the Levites to purify themselves and guard all the gates from now on to help keep the Sabbath holy."

If some of these leaders were disgruntled, their faces didn't reveal it. No one spoke or argued with him. All of the men on Malkijah's list were in this room, and Nehemiah knew they would report everything he said to Tobiah at the first opportunity. Let them. With God on Nehemiah's side, Tobiah would be no match for him. He no longer feared a coup by disgruntled members of Judah's nobility. His life was held firmly in His hands.

Nehemiah had one more announcement to make, but the room felt too dark and confining to him. "Follow me," he said as he strode toward the door. "There's something I want to show you." Outside, the rain continued to fall intermittently, but Nehemiah didn't care if he got wet. He led the men down the hill along the city's eastern wall, halting at the southern tip near the Fountain Gate. The misty rain beaded on the men's clothing and hair like tiny jewels. For their nation, the rain was every bit as precious as jewels.

"After surveying this city countless times while constructing the wall, I believe I know every square inch of it," Nehemiah said. "And it has bothered me for some time that although the city is large and spacious, comparatively few people live in it. Take this entire neighborhood, for instance. None of these houses have been rebuilt."

"What can we do about it?" Rephaiah said, lifting his palms. "Most of the men who returned with Zerubbabel or with Rebbe Ezra chose to return to their ancestral estates."

"I understand. But even with new walls and gates, this city and the Almighty One's temple will be difficult to defend if we don't have enough men living here. So here's my plan. More than thirteen years have passed since Rebbe Ezra arrived, and nearly one hundred years since the first families returned with Zerubbabel. During that time, no one has recorded our people's births and deaths. God has put it in my heart to assemble the nobles, officials, and common people and register all of them by families."

"You're taking a census?"

"Yes." It had occurred to Nehemiah that if the Almighty One did make him king, he would need to know how many fighting men he could recruit. "Yes, and once we have an accurate figure of Judah's population, I plan to cast lots and bring one out of every ten men here to live in Jerusalem."

Nehemiah could tell that his announcement surprised every man on his council. They began talking and arguing amongst themselves, and as he listened, Nehemiah was encouraged to see that more of them seemed in favor of the idea than opposed to it. He wiped the rain from his face and raised his voice to be heard above the noise. "I'm guessing that some men may decide to move here voluntarily, especially second- or third-born sons who won't inherit their fathers' ancestral land. And especially when they learn that I'll be rebuilding houses for them to live in at my own expense." The discussion rose in volume following his remarks. Nehemiah let it continue for a few minutes, then called for silence.

"I expect each of you to return to your own districts and begin the census registration as soon as possible. You're also responsible for holding the lottery to select one out of every ten men in your district to move here. If you have any questions, you're welcome to bring them to me in my audience hall. That's all, gentlemen. You are dismissed."

He strode up the hill without waiting to hear their comments or arguments. The rain was coming down harder now and he silently thanked God for it. *Remember me for this also, O my God, and show mercy to me according to your great love.*

CHAPTER
54

BETH HAKKEREM

Nava pulled her shawl over her head to shield it from the gently falling rain as she walked out of the gate of her master's estate, alone. Her only thought was to go home. Months had passed since she'd made this journey in the opposite direction, following Aaron's donkey, but her heart remembered the way. When she reached the small rise on the edge of Abba's property, she spotted her father out in his barley field, pushing his plow through the rain-softened earth. Her brothers worked behind him breaking up clumps of dirt and sifting out stones. Nava broke into a run.

"Abba!" she shouted. "Abba, Mama, I'm home!" Her father looked up and abandoned his plow in the middle of a furrow to hurry across the field to her. Mama must have heard her shouts, too, because she ran from the house to sweep Nava into her arms.

"Oh, my daughter! My sweet Nava! Are you home for good?"

"No, only for the day, Mama. . . . A friend of mine died this morning. The chief shepherd, Shimon." She cleared the lump of grief from her throat. "I . . . I needed to get away for a while."

Abba drew her into his arms next. "You walked here all alone?"

"Yes . . . I had to. I missed you so much!" She didn't tell them that she had simply left the estate without permission, without telling Penina or anyone else where she was going. She had been by Shimon's side when he had drawn his last, painful breath, and she knew she couldn't bear to watch them put his cold, pale body into the ground. Needing the balm of loving arms around her, she had walked out through the gate of the estate to come home.

"How long can you stay?" Mama asked.

"I need to be back before dark to take care of the goats." She didn't want to imagine returning to see Shimon's empty bed or his empty milking stool beside her own.

"Want me to run next door and tell Dan you're home?" her brother offered.

"Would you? I've missed him, too."

"Let's go inside out of the rain so we can visit," Mama said. They ducked through the door into the low-ceilinged room, and Mama stoked the hearth fire to help everyone dry off.

"The rain is wonderful, isn't it?" Nava asked as she wiped her face with the corner of her shawl.

"It's a blessing from God," Abba agreed.

"How are they treating you? Are you well? Tell us everything," Mama said.

"My master is good to me. I have new sandals, see? And they just gave me this new tunic to wear." She didn't mention that it replaced the one Aaron had torn. Her family leaned closer, listening eagerly as Nava described Malkijah's estate and the work she did for him each day. She didn't tell them what Master Aaron had tried to do or describe the details of how Shimon had died. She had promised Shimon she would forgive her masters and put away her bitterness, and the only way to do that was to dwell on the good things about living at the estate—the plentiful food, the friends she had made—and refuse to think about the bad.

"Master Malkijah just got married in Jerusalem, so I'll have a new mistress when he returns," Nava continued. "I've already met her, and she's very kind." Aaron would return from Jerusalem with them, but Shimon had assured Nava that she could trust the Almighty One to protect her.

"I've regretted sending you away every single day since you left," Abba said. "I even went with Dan's father and some of the others to talk to Malkijah, asking him to consider cancelling our debts like so many other nobles have done, but he refused."

"No, please don't worry about me, Abba. It's truly all right. And now with this rain, I'm sure your land will prosper again. I'm praying for the Almighty One to bless your crops this year."

She heard running footsteps outside. Dan rushed through the door, soaking wet and smiling as if he might burst from joy. Nava wanted to hold him in her arms so badly. "It's wonderful to see you, Nava. I think about you every day."

"I know. I think of you, too." Her brother must have told Dan that she was home for only one day, because he didn't ask how long she could stay or if she'd been set free.

Nava soaked in all the sights of home and her family's beloved faces as they talked, as thirsty for them as the ground was for rain. She was relieved to see that her family wasn't starving. Mama had grain to make bread, jars of oil, and lentils and chickpeas in the storeroom. Malkijah was feeding them until the famine ended as he'd promised, in return for Nava's service. She was thankful for that.

They ate a simple noon meal together as rain pattered on the roof, and it tasted better than any feast. Late that afternoon when it was time to return to the estate, Dan and one of her brothers walked there with her. Her brother lagged a few steps behind to give them privacy as they talked. "You don't have to wait for me," she told Dan. "Six years is a long time, and I want you to be happy."

"It's less than six years now. You've been there more than four months already."

Was that all? Nava didn't say so, but it felt like a lifetime to her. "Let's hope the time passes quickly."

He took her hand in his. "Remember the story of Jacob's love for Rachel?" he asked. "The Torah says he agreed to serve Laban for seven years so he could marry her, but to him they seemed like only a few days because of his love for her. That's what it will be like for me."

"I love you so much," she told him. But in her heart, Nava doubted that she and Dan would ever marry. Too many unforeseen things could happen in the next few years, and people's lives seldom worked out the way they expected them to. Shimon's life hadn't. Abba's hadn't. Hers certainly hadn't. Nava was afraid to hope that she and Dan would have a happy ending to their story. She wanted to have faith like Shimon. The Almighty One was her master from now on, not Malkijah, and she would yield to His will, whether that meant marrying Dan or not.

"I'd better say good-bye to you now," she said when they reached the edge of her master's property. Dan hugged her tightly. He didn't seem to want to let go, and neither did she. "It's been wonderful to see you, Dan."

"Good-bye, Nava . . . but only for now."

She released him from her arms and hurried up the hill and through the gate and into the compound so he wouldn't see her tears. She went straight to the goat pen to begin milking, filling the bin with a little grain for the animals to eat while she worked. She was leading the first goat to the stool when Penina came out to the pen.

"Where have you been? I've been searching all over for you."

"I'm sorry." Nava sat down, leaning her forehead against the goat's side as she worked. "I couldn't watch them bury Shimon. I . . . I had to get away." She wondered if she would be in trouble, if Penina would shout at her or punish her. But when Penina replied, her voice was gentle.

"Master Malkijah is coming home with his new wife tomorrow. When you finish milking, come to the kitchen. We have work to do to get ready."

Chapter

55

BETH HAKKEREM

When Chana arrived at Malkijah's estate, the atmosphere seemed different to her, the servants unusually quiet and subdued. The housekeeper came out with two maids to help with their bags, and tears filled the housekeeper's eyes when Chana asked about Shimon. "I'm sorry, ma'am, but he died from his injuries yesterday."

Malkijah reacted before Chana did. "What? Shimon is dead?"

"Yes, my lord."

"Where did you bury him? Show me." He left all of their things for the servants to unload, refusing the water and refreshments Penina had brought, and followed one of his servants out through the gate. Chana hurried along behind him but not before noticing that Aaron had disappeared.

The new grave was on a quiet hillside beneath an oak tree, where Shimon's sheep and goats sometimes grazed. Chana stood beside her husband as he stared down at the scarred earth, shaking his head as if unable to believe his friend was truly gone. "I've known Shimon all my life," Malkijah said, his voice rough with emotion. "He used to take me up into the pasturelands with him when I was a boy. Those times together are some of my happiest memories."

"Shimon told me those were his fondest memories, too."

Malkijah looked at her in surprise. "He did?"

"Yes, when I sat with him after he was injured."

"I loved sitting around the campfire with him at night and listening to his stories. He told me that David learned how to be Israel's king and to lead God's people by first being a shepherd. He said that tending my father's sheep would help me learn to be a good leader, too. . . . I can't imagine this estate without Shimon."

Chana reached for his hand. She would tell him the truth about his father someday, but this wasn't the right time.

Malkijah exhaled. "I guess I didn't realize that he was dying the last time we spoke."

"He was very badly injured on the night of the dinner. Aaron struck him very hard. I saw the bruises on Shimon's stomach from being punched."

Malkijah seemed shocked by her words, as if realizing for the first time that his son had caused Shimon's death. "Was that why he died? It wasn't from falling down?"

"I'm sure his broken hip contributed to his death. But he had been badly beaten, first. I don't understand why Aaron didn't simply subdue him or call for help. Shimon would have been no match for him."

"Excuse me, Chana. I need to be alone." He freed his hand from hers and strode across the field, climbing the upper hill to his terraced vineyard. Chana walked back to the house with the servant. The housekeeper led her to the room she and Malkijah would now share, and Chana helped the maids unpack her things. She remembered chatting and laughing with Yudit and Sarah as they'd helped her get ready to move, and she already missed having her sisters to talk with. She and Malkijah weren't quite used to each other yet.

Chana didn't see her husband again until that evening when she sat down to eat dinner with him and his sons. A drizzling rain fell, and the servants had moved the table inside the house. Malkijah was subdued as he talked quietly about the estate, telling Aaron and Josef what had been done in their absence and what remained to be done before the heavy winter rains began. Chana couldn't read Aaron's expression at all, but he seemed in a hurry to leave. "May I be excused from the table?" he asked the moment the meal ended.

"No, Aaron. There's something we need to talk about. But you may be excused, Josef." Malkijah waited until his younger son left, then said, "My chief shepherd, Shimon, died of his injuries yesterday."

"So I heard." Aaron looked nervous to Chana. He stared down at the table instead of his father, pinching the tablecloth into pleats with his thumb and forefinger.

"Tell me again what happened that night, Aaron."

He slouched back into his chair with a sigh. "I looked out my window and saw him following that servant girl. When he started attacking her, I ran out to stop him."

"Wait. You told me before that you were walking outside when you saw them."

Aaron shrugged. "What's the difference?"

"There's a big difference. One of those versions is the truth and the other isn't. I want the truth, Aaron. I'm trying to understand why my chief shepherd is dead. I'm told you hit him pretty hard."

"All I did was shove him away from the girl, and he fell down."

Malkijah rested his forearms on the table and leaned toward Aaron. "But the girl was lying on the ground when I arrived. How could Shimon attack her if he was standing up and she wasn't?"

Aaron shrugged. "I don't know. Maybe he pushed her down . . . or she fell."

"I thought you saw the whole thing."

"I can't remember. It happened days ago."

Chana could see that they were both growing angry, but Malkijah didn't let up. "The servants said Shimon had bruises on his stomach from being beaten."

"You believe *them*?" Aaron asked with a huff.

"Chana saw the bruises, too."

"I took care of him that first night," Chana said when they both turned to her. "He was in terrible pain and was bleeding on the inside from being punched so hard."

"Maybe I did hit him. I don't know—it all happened so fast. And that old man was a lot stronger than he looked."

"You do understand that your actions caused Shimon's death, don't you?" Malkijah asked.

"I needed to stop him. I thought he was going to hurt the girl. . . . It was his own fault, Father. If he and the other servants hadn't dreamed up that plot to frame me and accuse me, he would still be alive."

"I've been talking with the other servants, and they told me they saw you trying to flirt with the girl in the vineyard a few days before. They said you made her sit beside you while you ate, and she wasn't very happy about it."

"That's when I found out she's not an innocent young girl. She told me she knew that I would have to marry her if I was with her . . . that way."

Chana could no longer keep quiet. "Her name is Nava," she said. "I've spoken with her, too, and she has no interest in marrying you. She's in love with a young man named Dan. They hope to marry when her six years of service here have ended."

"Then she probably thought you would have to set her free if she staged this whole thing to make me look guilty."

Malkijah was quiet for a long moment before saying, "Your story keeps changing, Aaron."

"I don't know why the servants did this to me or what they were after!" he said, gesturing wildly. "You need to question them, not me."

"I already did. But right now I want to know if you're sorry at all for what happened to Shimon."

"It wasn't my fault."

"Yes, Aaron, it *was* your fault for being so rough on an elderly man. For letting your temper get the best of you. As the proverb says, a man who lacks self-control is like a city whose walls are broken down."

"It happened so fast."

"So you said. And now Shimon is dead." Malkijah's voice broke on the last word.

Aaron looked away. "You believe the servants instead of me, don't you?" he said sullenly. "Your own son!"

"I don't know whom to believe, but one of my most trusted servants is dead—a man I admired a great deal."

"You admired a *servant*? We're noblemen, Father. We're better than they are."

"You're wrong, Aaron. And if I've planted that prejudice in you, or nurtured your attitude of arrogant superiority, I'm deeply sorry because I know very few men who are better than Shimon. Godliness is no respecter of social class or wealth, and neither is evil. I used to be proud of my noble birth and my position as district leader, but in the past few months I've seen deceit and vileness among Judah's so-called noblemen, and they disgust me. Shimon, on the other hand, was a decent, God-fearing man."

"You can't be serious. He dreamed up this plot to frame me."

"The so-called *noblemen* who were at dinner with me that night are plotting against the governor. They want to have him killed. I know very well that men of noble birth are capable of lying and murdering. And I also know that humble shepherds like David are capable of ruling as kings." He took a moment to calm himself and said in a softer voice, "I only wish I could apologize to Shimon, and tell him how sorry I am."

"Shimon wasn't bitter about what happened," Chana said. "And he told me he forgave you, Aaron." He looked away.

"That sounds like Shimon," Malkijah said. "He was more of a father to me than my own father was. Abba was too busy working when I was young and never had much time for me. I tried not to make the same mistake with you and Josef. That's why I took you around with me and tried to teach you to take pride in your work so you could run this estate yourselves someday." He paused, clearing his throat, and waited until Aaron met his gaze. "And now, after spending the afternoon talking with each one of my servants, I've learned what has been going on here in my absence. I'm disappointed in you and Josef and the kind of men you have become."

For the first time, Aaron appeared frightened. He didn't have a reply for his father. But he still wouldn't admit that he had lied about Nava and Shimon. His stubbornness surprised Chana. Malkijah seemed to be waiting to hear the truth, as well, and when it didn't come, he ended the uncomfortable silence with a sigh. "We'll be celebrating Rosh Hashanah in a few days. Every seventh year, the priests read the Law out loud to all the people—and this is the seventh year. I believe it would be good for all of us to go to the temple and hear what the Holy One has to say."

"We just got home from Jerusalem," Aaron said. "Do we really have to go back?"

"Rosh Hashanah begins the new year, and I would like it to be a new beginning for our family, as well. We need to listen to the Law and prepare our hearts for Yom Kippur, the day we stand before God and confess our sins and seek forgiveness."

"Do I have to go?"

"Of course, Aaron. Of course you do. Regardless of how it happened, Shimon is dead because of you." He waited a long moment as Aaron continued to pinch pleats in the tablecloth. "If you have nothing more to say about what you've done, you're excused from the table."

Chana tried to read Malkijah's expression as he watched Aaron push back his chair with a noisy scrape and leave the room. She wished she knew her husband well enough to read his thoughts. She had no idea what to say to him about what had just happened, so she remained quiet, praying for wisdom. The servants had lit all the lampstands in the room, but the atmosphere still seemed dark and oppressive to her as she waited for Malkijah to speak. He stared down at his hands, folded on the table in front of him, his knuckles white with tension.

"As ruler of this district," he finally said, "I also serve as a judge. A death has occurred, so it's up to me to seek justice." He looked up at Chana and said, "You spoke with the servants that night, and with Shimon. Who do you think is telling the truth?"

Chana took her time, choosing her words carefully. "The first time I visited your estate, I spoke with Nava. She seemed frightened and sad, so I asked if she was being mistreated. She told me she was afraid of Aaron. That he watched her all the time. I paid closer attention after that, and I saw what she meant. Aaron did seem to be attracted to her in a frightening way."

"You believe the servants' version of the story? That it was Aaron who attacked the girl?"

She drew a calming breath, finding it harder than she'd imagined to tell Malkijah that she thought his son was a liar and a would-be rapist. "Yes, I do. I believe Aaron is the guilty one, and Shimon came to her rescue, like he said."

Malkijah propped his elbow on the table, resting his forehead in his hand. "I'm so ashamed of my son. Not only for what he did but for lying to me about it. I don't want to believe that he's guilty of attacking that girl or that he struck Shimon so hard when he didn't get his way that he killed him. But it's looking more and more like that's the truth. I spoke with each of my servants today, and the picture they drew for me of my sons' behavior shocked me." He massaged his eyes and added, "I'm also ashamed that you have to witness my family's sins and failures."

"Don't be ashamed. Neither of us is perfect. When I remember how I wallowed in self-pity and was angry at God, I'm ashamed of myself, as well. We're two imperfect people, Malkijah, doing the best we can to follow God. We should have nothing to hide from each other."

"I don't know what to do about this situation, Chana."

"Neither do I, but we'll figure it out together. You won't have to deal with this alone."

"I can't help thinking that it's my fault. I know I indulged my sons after their mother died—and I'm reaping the results of that now."

"Even if you did indulge them, the choices Aaron made aren't your fault."

"This is the part that's hardest of all to admit, Chana. . . . I made some bad choices, too. I became greedy these last few years, wanting more and more, wanting the security of full barns and storehouses when I already had more than enough. I told myself I was being kind to the poor when they had to mortgage their land to me, but the more land and servants I acquired, the more I wanted. I convinced myself that it was for my sons, for their future. But then when the other men obeyed Governor Nehemiah and canceled their loans and mortgages, I was afraid to do it, afraid to trust God and believe that I would have enough if I obeyed. You were right to condemn me, Chana. My greed set a terrible example for my sons, teaching them that they were entitled to take whatever they wanted—and now I'm paying the price."

"It's never too late to start over. Shouldn't our marriage prove that's true?"

"You're right, you're right. . . . But in the meantime, I have a storehouse full of regrets."

They finally rose from the table and retired to their bedroom for the night. But even after putting out the lamps, Chana knew her husband was still thinking about Aaron and Shimon, wondering what to do. "Would Aaron have turned out this way if we had been poor?" he asked aloud in the darkness. "If we weren't noblemen at all, and we owned nothing but a small patch of land? I would rather lose everything I have than lose my sons."

"Then why not try it?" she asked softly. "Give everything away, Malkijah. . . . Rich or poor, I'll always stand by you."

JERUSALEM

The eastern sky was just turning light as Chana walked with Malkijah and his sons from their Jerusalem home to the square in front of the Water Gate. From the corner parapet on top of the temple mount, the sound of shofars shattered the early morning stillness as the priests announced the Feast of Trumpets. It wasn't yet dawn on the first day of the New Year, but hundreds of people filled the streets, streaming from all parts of the city to hear the reading of the Law on Rosh Hashanah. The closer Chana got to the square, the more crowded the streets became, and Malkijah rested his hand on her shoulder so they wouldn't lose each other.

Workers had cleared away the construction debris, leaving a broad, open space for the people to assemble. A dozen priests and Levites took their places where everyone could see them on a high wooden platform built for the occasion. As the new day broke, Rebbe Ezra also climbed the platform, carrying the Book of the Law of Moses. The scroll's elaborate silver finials sparkled in the early light as he unrolled it. The people who had been seated stood up to listen.

"Praise the Lord your God," Ezra called out, "the great God who is from everlasting to everlasting!"

Chana joined the others, lifting her hands and saying, "Amen! Amen!" Then all the people bowed down and worshiped the Lord with their faces to the ground.

"You alone are the Lord," Ezra continued. "You made the heavens and all their starry host, the earth and all that is on it, the seas and all that is in them. You give life to everything, and the multitudes of heaven worship you. Give us understanding now, we pray, as you speak to us from your holy Torah."

Chana lost track of the passing of time as Ezra read aloud from daybreak until noon, facing the square before the Water Gate. Everyone listened attentively to the Law, and to the Levites who instructed them, making the Law clear and translating the Hebrew into Aramaic for those who didn't understand. The Levites also explained the meaning of the passages for the people's daily lives, so that everyone could understand what they heard. Many began to weep as they listened. Tears rolled down Chana's face, too, as the depth of God's love and grace became clearer and clearer to her.

Standing beside her, Malkijah seemed deeply moved as well. He lifted his hand to his face, pressing his eyes with his fingers as Ezra read the commandment, "'You shall not covet your neighbor's house. You shall not covet your neighbor's wife, or his manservant or maidservant, his ox or donkey or anything that belongs to your neighbor.'" She knew his heart was breaking from the mistakes he'd made in raising his sons. His shoulders shook with his grief when Ezra read the words, "'If a man beats his male or female slave and the slave dies as a direct result, he must be punished.'"

Chana resisted the temptation to glance at Aaron and see his response to the voice of the Almighty One in His Torah. Was he listening and joining in worship with everyone else? But she also knew that this day and the days of soul-searching and repentance leading up to Yom Kippur were meant for her every bit as much as for Aaron. She also had sinned against the Almighty One in her attitudes and deeds and neglectfulness, and she needed forgiveness as much as Aaron did.

By the time Ezra finished, the sun was high in the sky and the sound of weeping could be heard all over the square. Governor Nehemiah mounted the platform. "This day is sacred to the Lord your God," he said. "Do not mourn or weep. It's commendable that you feel sorrow for your sin, but it's also important to express your joy in our God and in the covenant He has made with us. Stop weeping, and celebrate with joy because now you understand the words He has spoken to you. Go and enjoy choice food and sweet drinks, remembering God's many gifts. Send some to those who have nothing prepared, thanking God for the privilege of sharing with others. This day is sacred to our Lord. Do not grieve, for the joy of the Lord is your strength."

As the people slowly left the square to return home, the Levites emphasized Nehemiah's words, calming the people and saying, "Be still, for this is a sacred day. Do not grieve."

"We need to go to Beth Hakkerem tonight," Malkijah told his family. "We must do as the governor said and send gifts to the people in our district."

"I'll be happy to help," Chana said.

Every day in that week leading up to Yom Kippur, Rebbe Ezra read from the Book of the Law, and Chana listened with all the people. On the evening before the Day of Atonement, she shared a meal with Malkijah and his sons in their home in Beth Hakkerem. Malkijah grew somber after they'd eaten as he addressed Aaron and Josef.

"Tomorrow, when the high priest carries the blood of the sacrifice before the Holy One's mercy seat, we will confess our sins and ask Him to forgive us and cleanse our souls. According to tradition, that includes asking forgiveness from one another.

God can't forgive us if we haven't asked the people we've hurt for forgiveness. His forgiveness mirrors our own."

He paused, waiting quietly for his sons' responses. Malkijah had told Chana that he wanted to be at the estate in case Aaron repented and decided to ask Nava for forgiveness. But Aaron remained stubbornly silent, staring out into the cloud-filled night as if thoroughly bored. It was his younger brother, Josef, who finally spoke in a halting voice.

"Father . . . I need to tell you something. The wine that went missing from your storeroom . . . ?" He gave his brother a frightened glance. "Aaron and I stole it. . . . I'm sorry, Father."

"Thank you for your honesty, son. Anything else?"

"Well . . . sometimes when you gave us a job to do . . . we made the servants do the work so we could go off and drink wine instead." He glanced at his brother again, but Aaron sat with his arms folded, his face as cold and hard as stone.

Chana knew her husband had spoken with all of his servants and was already aware of his sons' behavior. But he had wanted to give them a chance to confess voluntarily rather than accuse them, fearing they would add the sin of lying to all the others.

"I forgive you, Josef, and so will the Almighty One," Malkijah said. "But remember, a sign of true repentance is that we make a commitment to change. We turn from our sin and walk in a new direction."

Josef nodded. He seemed too distraught to say more. Again Malkijah waited, as if giving Aaron a chance to speak, but his elder son stared down at the table in sullen silence until his father finally excused everyone from the table. "I don't know what else to do, Chana," he said when they were alone.

"I think you're wise to wait. Doesn't the Holy One wait patiently for us to repent?"

They returned to Jerusalem for the Day of Atonement, but even after participating in the temple sacrifices on this holiest day of the year, Aaron remained unmoved. On the fifteenth day of the month, the Festival of Sukkot began, and Malkijah constructed a booth for them to live in during the days of the feast. Chana had never celebrated Sukkot this way before and neither had anyone else in Jerusalem. But when Rebbe Ezra read the words of the Law they'd found the command to go out into the hill country and bring back branches from wild olive trees and myrtles, palms and shade trees to make booths to live in to remember their years of wandering in the wilderness. The people obeyed, building huts on their rooftops and in their courtyards and in the courts of the temple and the square by Water Gate.

"We haven't celebrated Sukkot with such great joy in a long, long time," Shallum said when Chana and Malkijah shared a meal with him and her sisters. "Everyone's joy is so very great!" Including her own, Chana thought. Abba was well again, and she had found true contentment with Malkijah.

The weeklong Festival of Booths ended with a sacred assembly on the temple mount. In a spontaneous show of repentance, the people fasted and wore sackcloth and dust on their heads as they prepared to renew their commitment to God's law. Again, Chana stood in the courtyard with the others for three hours as Ezra read from the Book of the Law. Three more hours flew past as they stood confessing their unfaithfulness and the wickedness of their fathers. Then the Levites called out, "Stand up and praise the Lord your God who is from everlasting to everlasting."

What followed was one of the most beautiful prayers Chana had ever heard, recalling God's grace and power in creation, His covenant with Abraham, His deliverance from Egypt, and the parting of the Red Sea. The prayer spoke of God's faithfulness in the wilderness, even when His people were unfaithful, and the covenant He made with them at Mount Sinai. Throughout the recitation of her people's history, Chana recognized God's great compassion, how He saved her people time after time.

In all that had taken place, God had been just and had acted faithfully, while her people and nation had done wrong.

When the prayer ended, Governor Nehemiah stood in front and said, "In view of all this, we are making a binding agreement, putting it in writing, and are affixing the seals of the Levites and priests to it. We're promising to follow the Law of God given through Moses and to obey carefully all His commands, regulations, and decrees. With His help, we have finished Jerusalem's wall. And we learned in the process of rebuilding it to work together and to take care of one another, the rich helping the poor. Now we need to renew our commitment to God. I believe that He has withheld the rain and sent enemies among us so that we would return to Him. And so we're taking this oath today, promising not to intermarry with the peoples around us. We will no longer buy or sell on the Sabbath or any holy day. Every seventh year we will allow the land to rest, and cancel all debts. We'll give the required one-third shekel every year for God's temple, along with the first fruits of our herds and flocks, our meal, grain, fruit, wine, and oil. A tithe of our crops will go to the Levites, so that the house of our God will not be neglected."

When Nehemiah finished, Chana watched her husband go forward with the rest of the men to take the oath and affix his seal to it.

Later that evening she found Malkijah alone on the roof of their Jerusalem home and went to sit beside him. "What's wrong?" she asked. "I can tell that something is still bothering you, even after all of the sacrifices today at the temple."

"I didn't do right by Shimon. Even if it was an accident, justice must be done and his family must be recompensed for his loss. But I don't know where to find any of his family members. Years ago, when I went with Shimon to graze Abba's sheep, I met his brothers and several nephews who were about my age. They were all shepherds, and I believe they live somewhere in the district of Beth Hakkerem, but I don't know where." He stood as if too restless to remain seated and began pacing in front of her. "As far as I know, they are his only family. Shimon's wife died years ago, and he never had any children. But I need to find his next of kin, Chana. Will you help me?"

Her heart started beating faster. The time had come to tell him the truth. Her eyes filled with tears as she remembered Shimon's great love for Malkijah, and for a moment she couldn't speak around the lump in her throat. He saw her tears and said, "What is it, Chana? What's wrong?"

She motioned for him to sit beside her again as she searched for a place to begin. "Before Shimon died, he told me how you used to go into the fields with him when you were a boy. And he told me a story about a fight you had with his nephews . . . and how your nose got broken. Do you remember that fight, Malkijah?"

He reached up and absently pinched the bridge of his nose as if trying to make it straight again. "Yes, of course I remember."

"Do you remember what the fight was about?"

He hesitated then said, "Yes. The other boys said I wasn't really a nobleman but a common shepherd like them and—" He halted, frowning as he stared at Chana. "What are you trying to tell me?"

"They were telling the truth, Malkijah," she said. A tear escaped and rolled down her cheek. "Shimon is your real father. I'm weeping because I know how very much he loved you. How proud he was of you."

Malkijah shook his head as if stunned. "How . . . how can that be?"

"Shimon's wife died after giving birth to you. He was heartbroken and had no idea how he would ever take care of you. When his master's newborn son died a day later, the midwife convinced Shimon to trade babies and let Recab raise you as his son. Recab and his wife never knew the truth."

"So . . . *I'm* Shimon's next of kin?"

"Yes."

Malkijah covered his face with both hands. She could tell he needed time to absorb the truth. When he finally looked up again, he had tears in his eyes. "I wish I had known. . . . All these years . . ."

"Was I wrong to tell you now?" Chana asked, touching his arm.

"No," he replied, still shaking his head. "No. . . . But this changes everything."

Chapter 57

BETH HAKKEREM

Nava squeezed the curd-filled cloth with both hands, letting the whey drip into a pottery bowl. The process was messy, but along with caring for her goats, making cheese was one of her favorite tasks. Intent on her work, she was only vaguely aware of the whispered voices and halted activity in the kitchen until Penina hurried over to her worktable. "Leave that for now. Master Malkijah is asking all of his servants to come out to the main courtyard this morning. He has an announcement to make."

"Do you know what it's about?"

"No. No one does. Come." Penina bustled off again to gather the rest of her kitchen crew while Nava rinsed the milky whey off her hands and dried them with a towel.

Her master and mistress had done several surprising things this month, including opening their storerooms and providing a feast for their workers during the holidays. They had also built booths outdoors during Sukkot where they and all their servants ate and slept. Chana said it was to remember how their ancestors had lived in tents in the wilderness. "We live in a *sukkah*," she had explained, "to remind ourselves that we're under the Holy One's protection and care, just as our ancestors were in the desert."

Nava closed the kitchen gate behind her and followed the other servants into the main courtyard. Malkijah and Chana stood beneath the dining trellis facing them. So did Aaron and Josef. The family had returned from Jerusalem earlier today after attending the convocation at the temple. Nava found a place to stand beside her friend Rachel and whispered, "What now?"

"I hope it's good news," she whispered back, "and that it doesn't mean more work for all of us."

Malkijah lifted his hand, and the whispering stopped. "I'll make this brief," he said. "Those of you who are bondservants and are not paid wages . . . I'm setting you all free."

Nava inhaled a gasp of air. *What?* The world seemed to stand still for a moment as her mind whirled in stunned surprise.

"The family debts that brought you here are all canceled as of today. All of them. You're free to go home."

Nava gave a cry of joy. She and Rachel fell into each other's arms, laughing and weeping at the same time. "Is it true? Is it really true?" Rachel cried. "Oh, Nava, can you believe it?"

"No . . . No, I can't!" Nava was oblivious to everything else in the courtyard as she let the amazing news sink in. *I'm free! Free! Not six years from now, but today!* She heard shushing sounds as the others called for quiet again.

"What about your olive harvest, Master Malkijah?" the manager asked. He and Penina and Ruth were among the few who weren't bondservants but received wages for their work. "And the winter plowing? The trees and vines will all need to be trimmed, too. How will we do all that work without laborers?" Malkijah shook his head without replying. Nava was surprised to see that he was too overcome with emotion to speak.

"When can we leave?" one of the bondservants shouted out.

Malkijah cleared his throat. "You're free to leave anytime. Now, if you'd like."

An enormous cheer went up from the servants. "Let's go!" Nava said. She grabbed Rachel's arm, and they ran to their sleeping quarters to gather their meager belongings.

"This doesn't seem real," Rachel murmured. "I feel like I'm dreaming."

"I know . . . I know! It's a miracle!" Nava thought of the unfinished goat cheese she had left laying out and wondered if she should go back and help Penina clean up everything. But in the next moment she was picturing Dan and her family, and the joy they would all share at her wonderful news. She was going home—for good! "Let's walk together until the road forks," she told Rachel.

"I want to run all the way home!" Rachel replied. But when they finished packing and came out of their sleeping quarters, Master Malkijah was waiting near the door with Chana by his side.

"May I have a word with you, Nava?" he asked.

"Yes, my lord." Her heart felt sick with dread. It wasn't true after all. He was going to force her to stay. But his next words surprised her.

"I need to apologize for not believing you. For believing my son. I now know that he lied to me. I'm very sorry for what he tried to do to you. And while I can't undo his crime, I would like to give you this." He pushed a small leather pouch into her hand. It clinked with the sound of coins. "Consider it a wedding present. Chana tells me there's a young man you'd like to marry."

Nava's mind and tongue could barely form words. "Yes, my lord . . . Thank you, my lord."

"I would also like to return your father's flock of goats to him, along with some grain to feed them." Nava covered her mouth to hold back her tears as he gestured to a donkey that was loaded with grain sacks. "Will your goats follow you, or would you like some help herding them home?"

The courtyard whirled. "Th-they'll follow me."

"Again, my sincerest apologies. Can you forgive me?"

Nava remembered thinking she would never be able to forgive her masters. But she found herself saying, "Yes. Of course I forgive you. Shimon taught me that I should forgive others because God forgives me."

"Nava, it's my deepest wish that my son would also ask you for forgiveness, but he hasn't confessed or repented. Chana and I are praying about how to deal with him in the days to come."

"I'll pray for him, too."

He looked surprised. "Thank you. I know he must be punished for his actions, I just haven't figured out exactly how to do that."

Chana surprised Nava by pulling her into her arms for a hug. "God be with you, Nava," she said. "I wish you and Dan many years of happiness."

Nava's family looked stunned later that afternoon when they saw her coming up the road toward home leading the loaded donkey and her little flock of goats. "Nava . . . what is all this?" Abba asked. "What are you doing?"

"Master Malkijah freed all his bondservants and canceled all of our debts," she replied, laughing and crying at the same time. "Your land belongs to you again, Abba. And I'm free! I don't have to work another day for him."

"That's . . . that's unbelievable!"

Nava waited until Dan had raced over the hill from his farm to tell them the best news of all. "Master Malkijah canceled your father's debts, too, Dan. And he gave us this bag of silver so we can be married."

"Praise God . . ." Dan sank to his knees, his eyes closed as tears rolled down his face.

"What does he want in return for all this?" Abba asked. "It seems a little too good to be true."

"He doesn't want anything. But there's something I think

we should do to show our gratitude. Malkijah no longer has enough workers to finish the olive harvest or do the plowing, since he set everyone free. I think we should gather everyone in the district and volunteer to help him."

"Why should we do that?" one of her brothers asked.

"Because when God forgives our sin, we're so overjoyed that we serve Him willingly in return, don't we? I think we should show our gratitude to Malkijah the same way for forgiving our debts. He didn't have to do it. And it's costing him a lot."

"My little Nava," Abba said, pulling her into his arms. "I've been so worried about you, and all this time you've been growing wiser and kinder than all of us. Of course we'll help Malkijah with his harvest. I think it's a wonderful idea."

That night, Nava was much too excited to fall asleep. She rose from her pallet while everyone else slept and went outside to gaze at the familiar contours of Abba's land in the moonlight. She was home. The land and crops were Abba's again. Everything was back the way it should be, and the past few months might have been nothing but a bad dream.

Next spring, when the rain ended and the ground settled, Dan would build a room onto his father's house for her. They would live there together for the rest of their lives. Nava lifted her face to the heavens and silently praised God.

CHAPTER

58

JERUSALEM

Rebbe Ezra looked up from his work when Nehemiah entered his study, his pen still poised in his hand. The surface of his worktable lay buried beneath piles of scrolls and clay tablets. "Good afternoon, Governor."

"Good afternoon. Thank you for agreeing to see me, Rebbe."

"I'm very happy to. Please, have a seat."

Nehemiah glanced around the cluttered room for a place to sit and finally removed a pile of scrolls from a chair as he'd done the first time he'd visited, holding them on his lap while he and Ezra talked. Nehemiah hadn't wanted to take the rebbe away from his work by inviting him to the governor's residence, so instead he walked up here to the temple's archives. He also hoped for a chance to talk in confidence with this great man of God about the one question that still occupied his mind and heart.

"So, tomorrow you dedicate the wall," Rebbe Ezra said. "I assume all the arrangements are in place?"

"Yes. I sent word to all the Levites and singers to come to Jerusalem. They've been rehearsing the songs of thanksgiving and are ready to help us celebrate the dedication with cymbals, harps, lyres, and trumpets. I'm glad you agreed to lead one of the processions for me."

"I'm looking forward to it." Ezra laid down his pen and leaned back in his seat. "I understand you've been busy with a few more building projects. I'd thought we'd heard the last of the chisels and hammers for a while, but evidently we haven't."

"We're building new homes now, Rebbe. The census has proceeded smoothly, and the first settlers are already moving to Jerusalem. I commended the volunteers for their willingness to help repopulate the city."

"Excellent. Your term as governor has been a very busy one. Didn't you arrive here from Susa only a few months ago?"

Nehemiah smiled faintly. "It seems much longer than that. And when I think about all the events that took place in just this past month—setting the last gate in place; celebrating Rosh Hashanah, Yom Kippur, and Sukkot; the covenant renewal ceremony—I can barely take it all in. The Almighty One's hand has surely been upon us."

Ezra appeared thoughtful as he stroked his white beard. "And after tomorrow's dedication, what then? Jerusalem's wall is finished, the city is growing and becoming settled, the people have rededicated themselves to the Holy One. What's next for you, Nehemiah?"

He sat forward on the edge of his seat. "That's what I was hoping to talk to you about. I've been praying and asking God for an answer to a question I have—but the Holy One has been strangely silent."

"What's the question?"

Nehemiah hesitated, aware of how brazen the idea of becoming king might seem to this man of God. "Ever since the prophets first spoke of it, the people have been chanting for me to be Judah's king."

"Yes, I've heard Noadiah saying, 'There is a king in Judah.' And I've heard the people echoing her. You enjoy great popularity, especially with the poor."

Nehemiah sat back again, grateful that Ezra hadn't seemed

outraged by the idea. "But I need to know if it's just the people who think I should be king or if the Almighty One is truly calling me." He admitted only to himself how badly he wanted it to be true.

Ezra folded his hands on the scroll lying open in front of him. "Tell me—how did you know the Almighty One was calling you to rebuild Jerusalem's wall?"

Nehemiah thought back to that time. "God laid the city on my heart like a heavy weight. From the moment my brother Hanani described the broken-down walls and how disgraced Jerusalem was in the eyes of our enemies, I couldn't stop thinking about it. I fasted and prayed and asked Him to show me what I could do."

"Why did you want to rebuild God's city?"

"To bring glory to Him so His name wouldn't suffer the reproach and mockery of our enemies. With the city in ruins it made the God of Abraham seem powerless to help His people, but I wanted to show His power and might to the nations. I wanted the glory to go to God—"

He halted. His motivation had been to glorify God, not himself. Yet Noadiah's prophecies had done the opposite, glorifying Nehemiah in the eyes of the people—and in his own eyes, as well. He'd enjoyed hearing them praise his good deeds as they'd followed after him. Deep down, he'd wanted to reign as Judah's next king for the fame and honor it promised.

"O God, forgive me," Nehemiah said, clutching his head with both hands. "The prophets have spoken falsely! A true prophet of God would glorify *Him* as king, not me. Not a mere man." For years he had guarded the emperor against usurpers who would try to claim his authority and power—and now Nehemiah had foolishly tried to usurp the one true King's power and authority, claiming the glory for himself.

"I think you know what you need to do," Ezra said quietly.

"Yes." Nehemiah left the rebbe's study and went out to the temple courtyard to pray, standing to face His holy sanctuary and the great altar of sacrifice. He bowed his head, asking

the Almighty One for forgiveness. For humility. Ever since his
father had opened the door to someone he'd trusted and was
murdered, Nehemiah had worried about who to trust. Now he
realized that he could trust himself least of all.

"'Hear O Israel:'" he recited to himself. "'The Lord is our
God, the Lord alone.'" Nehemiah was merely God's servant,
not a king. Not the promised Messiah. The people should be
following God, thanking and praising the Almighty One—not
him. The new wall he had labored so hard to build couldn't
save the people. Only God could.

❧ ☙

The next day as all of Judah gathered for the dedication of
the wall, Nehemiah was certain that the sound of rejoicing in
Jerusalem could be heard far away. The priests and Levites had
purified themselves, and now they would purify the people, the
gates, and the wall. He assigned two great choirs to lead the
people in praise, giving thanks to the Almighty One, accompanied by two groups of priests with trumpets, harps, cymbals,
and lyres. He asked the leaders of Judah to go up on top of
the wall, as well. The two great processions started near the
Valley Gate in the center of the western wall. The one led by
Rebbe Ezra moved on top of the wall to the right, toward the
Dung Gate, while Nehemiah followed the second choir, moving
in the opposite direction. From the top of the wall he saw the
distant valleys and hillsides turning green from the recent rains.

"You turned my wailing into dancing;" they sang, *"you removed my sackcloth and clothed me with joy, that my heart may
sing to you and not be silent. O Lord my God, I will give you
thanks forever."* The glorious music took Nehemiah's breath
away. "I wish I could sing God's praises like these musicians,"
he told Hanani, walking beside him.

"Then who would lead the people?" Hanani replied with
a smile.

They marched on toward the temple mount, past the Tower of the Ovens, over the Yeshana Gate and the Fish Gate as far as the Sheep Gate on the north side of the city, while Ezra's procession circled in the opposite direction. When the two processions met again, everyone took their places inside the temple area. The priests offered great sacrifices, exalting and praising God because He had given them great joy.

"Arise, O Lord! Deliver me, O my God! Strike all my enemies on the jaw; break the teeth of the wicked. From the Lord comes deliverance." Nehemiah remembered all of his enemies' threats and plots, how they had tried to destroy him and stop God's work, and he praised the Almighty One for His salvation and deliverance.

At last a hush fell over the gathered people as Nehemiah mounted the platform to speak. "Would any of you have believed that in spite of all the opposition we've faced, we could rebuild this wall in fifty-two days?" A deafening cheer followed his words. He heard some of the people chanting, "A king in Judah! A king in Judah!" He waited for the shouting to die away again and said, "Something miraculous has been at work here. God has been at work. But these walls won't protect us if we're unfaithful to Him. As the psalmist wrote, 'Unless the Lord builds the house, its builders labor in vain. Unless the Lord watches over the city, the watchmen stand guard in vain.' Just as we built this wall on a firm foundation, we need to build our lives and our nation on a firm foundation of faith and trust in the Almighty One. Faith in what we can't always see. Trust that God is at work in every circumstance we face."

He squinted in the light as the sun emerged from behind the gray rain clouds for a moment. "Everything I've done since I arrived here a few months ago has been with the Almighty One's help. I would have been powerless to accomplish anything without Him. Now my job is finished." He paused to gaze down at the people who looked up to him so expectantly. "Sons and daughters of Abraham, I am not your king. You don't need a king. Our forefathers had kings, and they led us astray. We trusted in men instead of trusting the Almighty One, our true King. God will send the Messiah when the time is right. But in the meantime, perhaps there are lessons for us to learn by being in submission to the Persians. That's why, when my term as governor here is finished, I will return to Susa as I promised King Artaxerxes I would do."

Murmurs of surprise rustled through the crowd. Nehemiah raised his voice and said, "People of God, continue working together as you did while building this wall. Continue helping one another. Continue trusting the Almighty One. He alone is trustworthy. May He prosper and bless you all."

Nehemiah turned away from the cheering crowd and walked down the hill to his home, alone. *Remember me with favor, O my God*, he silently prayed.

⟢ ⟣

"See, I will send my messenger, who will prepare the

way before me. Then suddenly the Lord you are seeking

will come to his temple; the messenger of the covenant,

whom you desire, will come," says the Lord Almighty.

MALACHI 3:1

Glossary

Abba—Father, Daddy.

Apadna—A huge, open-air terrace used by Persian kings for formal ceremonies.

Beth Hakkerem—House of the vineyard.

Gan Eden—The Garden of Eden.

Hinnon Valley—The valley southwest of Jerusalem where child sacrifice took place.

Keffiah—A flowing head covering that reached to the shoulders.

Ketubah—The marriage contract that made a betrothal official.

Kidron Valley—The valley outside Jerusalem between the city and the Mount of Olives to the east.

Kippah—A small head covering worn by Jewish men.

Levite—A descendant of the tribe of Levi, one of Jacob's twelve sons, who later became temple assistants.

Purim—The plural of *Pur*, meaning to cast lots. The festival that celebrated the Jewish deliverance under Queen Esther.

Rebbe—Rabbi, teacher.

Rhyton—A cone-shaped drinking vessel used by Persian kings.

Shabbat—The Sabbath, a Jewish day of rest. It begins at sundown on Friday and lasts until sundown on Saturday.

Shema—Hebrew for "hear." The *shema* is the Jewish confession of faith found in Deuteronomy 6:4. It begins "Hear, O Israel . . ."

Torah—The first five books of the Bible, which contain God's Law.

A Note to the Reader

Careful study of Scripture and commentaries support the fictionalization of this story. To create authentic speech, the author has paraphrased the words of biblical figures such as Ezra. However, the New International Version has been directly quoted when characters are reading, singing, or reciting Scripture passages.

Interested readers are encouraged to research the full accounts of these events in the Bible as they enjoy THE RESTORATION CHRONICLES.

Scripture references for *On This Foundation*:

Esther 2:21–23; 6:1–3; 9:1–17
Nehemiah 1–13 (*Note especially 3:12—"Shallum son of Hallohesh, ruler of a half-district of Jerusalem, repaired the next section with the help of his daughters.")
Exodus 20:8–11; 21:1–11; 21:20; 22:25; 31:12–17
Deuteronomy 5:12–15; 15:7–18; 23:19–20; 31:11–13
Leviticus 25:39–46
Numbers 27:1–12
Joshua 1:1–9
Ezekiel 22:24–25, 29–31
Genesis 29:14–20

Bestselling author **Lynn Austin** has sold more than one million copies of her books worldwide. She is an eight-time Christy Award winner for her historical novels, as well as a popular speaker at retreats and conventions. Lynn and her husband have raised three children and live in Michigan. Learn more at www.lynnaustin.org.

More From Lynn Austin

To learn more about Lynn and her books, visit lynnaustin.org.

After years of exile in Babylon, faithful Jews Iddo and Zechariah are among the first to return to Jerusalem. After the arduous journey, they—and the women they love—struggle to rebuild their lives in obedience to the God who beckons them home.

Return to Me
THE RESTORATION CHRONICLES #1

The lives of the exiles left in Babylon are thrown into despair when a new decree calls for the annihilation of all Jews throughout the empire. In this moment, Ezra, a brilliant Jewish scholar, is called upon to deliver his people to Jerusalem, but the fight to keep God's law is never easy.

Keepers of the Covenant
THE RESTORATION CHRONICLES #2

Beloved author Lynn Austin offers a glimpse into her private life as she shares the inspiring, deeply personal story of her search for spiritual renewal in the Holy Land. With gripping honesty, Lynn seamlessly weaves personal events with insights from Scripture as she finds hope, renewed faith, and a new sense of direction in her journey throughout Israel.

Pilgrimage

More Fiction From Bethany House

Josephine vowed to rebuild her family's plantation after the Civil War. But in Reconstruction-era Virginia, life has become a matter of daily survival. When faced with the destruction of her entire world, can she find the strength to carry on?

All Things New by Lynn Austin
lynnaustin.org

Only two men were brave enough to tell the truth about what awaited the Hebrews in Canaan: Caleb and Joshua. This is their thrilling story, from the pits of slavery in Egypt, through the terrifying supernatural experience of the plagues, and finally, to the Hebrews' dramatic escape in the Exodus.

Shadow of the Mountain: Exodus by Cliff Graham
SHADOW OF THE MOUNTAIN #1
cliffgraham.com

After she is forcibly taken to the palace of the king, a beautiful young Jewish woman, known to the Persians as Esther, wins a queen's crown and then must risk everything in order to save her people . . . and bind her husband's heart.

Esther by Angela Hunt
A DANGEROUS BEAUTY NOVEL
angelahuntbooks.com